E

Escape to Nowhere

Amar Bhushan

KONARK PUBLISHERS PVT LTD
New Delhi • Seattle

KONARK PUBLISHERS PVT LTD
206, First Floor, Peacock Lane,
Shahpur Jat,
New Delhi-110 049.
Phone: +91-11-41055065, 65254972
e-mail: india@konarkpublishers.com
Website: www.konarkpublishers.com

Konark Publishers International
1507 Western Avenue, #605,
Seattle, WA 98101
Phone: (415) 409-9988
e-mail: us@konarkpublishers.com

Copyright © Amar Bhushan, 2012

Third impression 2012

ISBN 978-93-220-0810-9

All rights reserved. No part of this book may be reproduced or utilised in any form or by any means, electronic or mechanical, including photocopying, recording, or by any information storage and retrieval system, without prior permission in writing from the publishers.

This is a work of fiction. All characters in this book are fictitious and bear no resemblance to any person living or dead.

Editor: Anna Chandy
Typeset by The Laser Printers, New Delhi.
Printed and bound at Thomson Press (India) Ltd.

For my mother, whose interest in me begins and ends with my well-being.

Preface

For seven years, I deliberated whether to write this story. The worry was that it might appear to be a flashback to an incident of spying that was, not too long ago, passionately commented upon by pundits on security matters and extensively glamourized by the media. There was also a concern whether the story could be told without violating the provisions of the Secrets Act. Though the account was going to be drawn from a receding memory that had already begun to blur facts, there were a lurking suspicion that secrets could still sneak in unknowingly, complicating a laidback, peaceful life. Another misgiving was whether the narrative would interest readers other than those from the intelligence agencies. There was also a lingering doubt if this rendering of events would read as self-adulatory.

Then one day my dithering was put to a severe test. An officer asked me to look back at my experience of handling espionage cases and reflect whether there was any reward for pursuing them doggedly. He insisted that I was not in tune with times and had been wrong in putting undue faith in keeping conscience. He faulted my judgement in investigating one's own officer so aggressively when sober avenues of redressing the *lapses* were available. He said that he would rather have arranged for *counselling* for suspects to stop them from committing *irregularities* that hurt the reputation of the Agency than follow my prescription. He wondered why it did not occur to me that airing the dirty linen in the balcony only made one's house look ugly.

It was frightening to hear the officer. Was he suggesting that subversion of officers would be tolerated and contained as a matter of policy, while a country's secrets made their way to unauthorized hands? It was at this point that this story began its journey: a story for young intelligence officers, to show them the joy of pursuing truth and standing up to falsehood, illegalities and opportunism while undertaking operations. And, for others, to acquaint them with the travails of following a spy, expose them to the problems bedeviling the intelligence agencies and enlighten them about the fallacy of applying set notions and conventional wisdom in assessing success or failure of Intelligence operations.

My decision to write would have remained stuck to the drawing board but for the support given by my wife. She would frequently remind me that the only thing I was good at was writing. My endearing younger daughter kept encouraging me as the story developed but it was my eldest daughter who literally bullied me into completing the book. Whenever I sulked and slowed down snared by disbelief, she lectured, cajoled, and even got her kids to plead with me. She also read the draft many times over, suggested numerous changes in the arrangement of events and ruthlessly pruned passages that impeded the flow of the narrative.

It is impossible not to acknowledge the role of my maternal uncle, a discerning reader with no particular feelings for spy stories and a very tough customer to please. He not only went through the manuscript and suggested valuable changes but even offered to find a publisher. I am also greatly indebted to Anna, the editor who did so much to improve the text and whose pithy comments helped in straightening facts and filling in critical gaps. However, my special gratitude is reserved for Konark Publishers, who readily agreed to have a look at the script written by a fresher and take the risk of printing it. But for their decision to invest the necessary resources, the book would not have found an expression in its present shape.

Day 1

"It's a call from Zaki-ur. Would you like to take it?" Manini asked, keeping the caller on hold.

"Tell him, I will speak to him later," Jeevnathan said. He was the Head of the Security Division of the Agency, India's External Intelligence Service.

"Jeev, this is the fifth time he is calling. You can't be so rude. After all, he has been an old friend," his wife reprimanded. Before Jeev could react, she handed him the phone.

"Hello!"

"Jeev, I am Zak here. Are you feeling any better today? You sound very hoarse and weak. Mani mentioned that you were down with viral."

"I was in a terrible shape on Friday night. The throat still hurts but it's not so bad. I will take a couple of days to recover fully," Jeev said. "What's the news in Dhaka?" he asked.

"I have been in Delhi for the last five days, meeting my political contacts," Zak informed him.

"No one in the Agency told me about your visit. But I am not surprised," said Jeev.

"Actually it was a sudden decision. I didn't inform anyone," Zak clarified. "Will it be possible for us to meet before I return home tonight?" he asked.

"Come and have breakfast with me. I am not going to office today. You will, of course, run the risk of contracting the viral," Jeev warned in a lighter vein.

"Don't worry. I will take that chance," Zak said and hung up.

Jeevnathan often wondered if it was right to remain in contact with Zaki-ur. Was he not being a hypocrite in evading a rule that he wanted his colleagues to strictly adhere to? During his three and half decades of working in the Agency, he had come in contact with numerous sources, informers and

Intelligence crossovers both in India and abroad, but never allowed his professional relationship to become personal or permanent. If sources ceased to deliver, he dumped them and, if he stopped handling them because of a change in his assignment, he quietly retreated into oblivion, where no one could reach him. Sources knew him by different nom-de-plumes. A few enterprising assets, or those badly in need of financial assistance, tried to dig him out but in vain.

Only once did Jeev feel bad over abandoning a subconscious agent. He was a Pakistani economist and a fierce India-baiter. He had lost two of his elder brothers and an uncle in the India-Pakistan wars of 1947, 1965, and 1971. Somehow, the economist came to admire Jeev's forthright views on contentious bilateral issues including Jammu and Kashmir and nuclear weapons programme. But what finally broke the ice was Jeev's offer to issue his visa in a day for his family to visit Delhi and Jaipur, which for security reasons, was kept on hold for over a year. In due course, the thaw developed into mutual respect. While the economist would respond to queries out of trust, Jeev, in keeping with his mean priorities, operated his friend as a sub-conscious source. He kept copious notes of their deliberations and forwarded these regularly to the Headquarters. After Jeev returned to India at the end of his assignment, the economist tried to contact him several times on telephone numbers and addresses that did not exist. He must have felt cheated by yet another Indian for the rest of his life.

Jeev favoured rigid adherence to rules that forbade officers to maintain contact with their erstwhile assets. No wonder, he upbraided colleagues who continued to deal with their former sources despite ceasing to be their direct operational responsibility. They in turn, argued that since they had raised and built a personal rapport with a particular source over a period of time, it made sense that they continued to brief and debrief him to extract that extra mileage. They also claimed that their successors could not run the asset as productively as they would, just because he was paid by the new operative and therefore, had an obligation to maintain the same level of intensity in his work. In their opinion, successors were universally conceited and jealous of their predecessors and tended to run down the carry-over sources, denting their confidence and ability to deliver.

Jeev dismissed these arguments as self-serving. He maintained that it would not only make a mockery of the officer's cover who usually identified himself to the source in a false name and as someone who came from a different professional background but also compromise his new working environment. Moreover, it would render the successor ineffective in handling the source as the latter would have the benefit of running to the raising officer for support, whenever there was a conflict of interest between him and his current operative. It was also the surest recipe for courting disaster of a more serious kind, Jeev explained. With foreign assets being allowed to meet their previous handlers on a regular basis, the field would be left wide open for gullible officers to make indiscriminate contacts and run the inevitable risk of getting both the source and the handler exposed to predators among the foreign intelligence agencies.

But Zaki-ur was an exception. He was never a source in the classical sense. He was an intellectual with strong leftist leanings and a political activist with all his scruples intact. He was widely known in political, military, financial and official circles in Dhaka, but he spared no one in his weekly columns. Occasionally, he was misunderstood but in the end, everyone respected his views. He was one man you could not label. Jeev admired Zak's incisive reading of political developments and his passion for democratic values. He would spend hours discussing issues of mutual concern with Zak that helped to fill in the critical gaps in his information. But Jeev could never have the heart to recruit his friend as a source. That explained why Zak's particulars never found their way to the Agency's dossiers and he remained an unpaid source with no 'number'. However, his assessments and inputs kept reaching the Agency's

Headquarters in Delhi under different nom-de-plumes. Jeev knew that this practice was morally indefensible but his friend's inputs were too valuable to be held back. He did not mind living with this sin so long as he enjoyed listening to Zak, sharing his vision, anguish, and concern for Bangladesh.

Jeevnathan got ready and came down to the living room. He called Wasan, the Agency's Chief, also an old friend and requested for a day's leave. "I am down with viral," he informed the Chief.

"I can make out. The familiar roar is missing. But you don't have to be so formal. Just relax. If you need any help, let me know," Wasan sounded patronizing.

"Thanks," said Jeev and hung up. He was feeling too weak to carry on a polite conversation. He tried to read the morning newspapers but could not go beyond the first page. His watery eyes and persisting headache made reading irksome. Feeling out of sorts, he stretched on the recliner, closed his eyes and waited for Zak.

Zaki-ur came with a bouquet of flowers. The years did not seem to have worn down his charm, affable smile, and youthful appearance. The sheen of his intellect was intact and his memory was as sharp as ever. Manini, one of his many admirers, appeared briefly in the living room to greet Zak and left reminding that breakfast would be served as soon as they ran out of gossip and calumny.

"This policy of supporting both the ruling and the opposition parties by the Agency is not taking you anywhere. It is only dragging the bilateral relationship and making it difficult for the current leadership in Dhaka to trust you in breaking the stalemate either over water sharing, building an East-West transit corridor or conducting joint operations against terrorists and insurgents," Zaki-ur pointed out as he saw Manini leave. "You can choose only one of the two mainstream political parties for your investment and support. The talk of not putting all eggs in one basket is humbug. You should know that your traditional friends are losing faith in you. You have already forced a huge chunk of fence sitters, who believed in freedom, democracy and nationalism, to become opportunists and are willing to join any party that can fund their political interests. How can you finance a fundamentalist party that shelters your insurgents and provides operational support to radical groups like Jamat-e-Islami? Does the Agency really believe that Islamic fundamentalist outfits will ever give you preference over the strategic and economic interests of Pakistan? I was worried that this shift in support could have been dictated by your political leadership. That is why I am here. I have tried to put my views across to everyone who has a say in these matters but they seem to suffer from amnesia. You must tell your Chief to stop this operational distortion from eroding the enormous goodwill that you have built over the years with support from liberal democratic forces."

Jeev was taken aback by the intensity of Zaki-ur's outburst. "I appreciate your concern," he said in apparent discomfort, "but I no longer deal with Bangladesh. It may not be appropriate for me to take it up with Wasan. I am also not fully conversant with what has shaped a reversal in our policy," he added.

"I don't believe that such major decisions on Bangladesh can be taken without keeping you on board," Zaki-ur insisted.

"But that is precisely what has happened. I am not even sure if the Chief is a direct party to this decision. Actually, many such policies are now being framed by amateurs who have a romantic notion of Intelligence operations," Jeev lamented.

"I never heard you react with such resignation. Maybe it's time I should also shed my liberationist baggage and start reaping dividends of real politic," Zaki-ur remarked in apparent disgust.

"But Zak, if you look at it objectively it may not be a bad idea to have your contacts in all groups and parties," Jeev argued. "You never know whom you would need and when. But yes, friends and foes cannot be equated," he said.

"I still believe you should not ride too many tigers at the same time," Zak contended. "And, in case you have to pursue this ruinous course of action, you must make sure that your funding remains a watertight secret. No leader in Bangladesh would like to be known as an Indian agent or relish the idea of dealing with a fair weather friend," he stressed.

"I agree."

"Your Agency's funding is a widely known secret in Dhaka," Zak remarked. "If you want to know the names of recipients and the amount, go to the fish market near Baitul Mukarram. What is, however, hurting your friends most, is that you have chosen to finance leaders who are corrupt and political liabilities."

"I don't know what to say. You only make me feel worse," Jeev remarked.

"Do you know, Jeev? Our intelligence services disburse funds far more discretely to Indian insurgent groups and you are, of course, no match to the ISI. Have you ever been able to pinpoint their delivery mechanism and volume of assistance?" he asked with a wry smile.

"I will convey your views to the Chief but I don't think he can correct this aberration. He generally believes in swimming with the tide," Jeev observed. He then went on to enquire about Tapas in an attempt to change the topic of discussion.

"Don't ask me," Zak reacted sharply.

"What happened?" Jeev asked.

"Tapas became a financial wreck. Since he was not submitting reports, he was discarded by your officers and his payments were stopped. You know that he was never a source who would feed information on military or political matters. He was a foot soldier who sacrificed the most productive years of his life for the cause of freedom and secular values. Since the Agency started writing a stereotyped script to appraise the performance of its assets during the post-Ershad era, Tapas became a marginal player. Your successors forgot that you were paying him as a token of your gratitude. The poor fellow should have realized that he was a pawn in the hands of mercenaries. It is good for him that he is dying of poverty." The disgust was writ large on Zak's face.

"The pressure to drop Tapas from our rolls was there even in my time," Jeev recalled. "But I managed to sustain him, mostly by lying to the Headquarters. The Agency, as a matter of policy, pays you so long as you are useful and the utility is defined in statistical terms. Your emoluments are fixed by how many reports you provide and not by what you could possibly do when battle lines are drawn. But that's the way the system works," he elaborated.

"Don't worry. I have managed to find a job for him. I could not let him down when I knew how much he had suffered," Zak said.

"You make me feel so guilty," Jeev sighed. "How is Asad-ul-Zama doing? But for him the siege of Dhaka on the 3rd of December in 1991 would not have been possible," he said.

Zak took a few minutes to respond. "Asad died six months ago of pancreatic cancer. He did seek help from your officers for his treatment at the Tata Cancer Hospital in Mumbai as a matter of right. But your records wouldn't show that he ever worked for you. I never knew you had such a poor sense of history," Zak taunted. They did not discuss the issue further. Instead, they talked about their families and their latest interest in poetry and painting.

After Zaki-ur left, Jeev slumped on the sofa and dozed off. An hour later, his wife woke him up. She casually mentioned that Nathani, the telecommunication officer, had rung twice on the RIT (Restricted Internal Telephone).

"Did you not tell him that I was unwell?"

"He was not enquiring about your health and I didn't think it necessary to advertise it. It was about some meeting. He sounded desperate," she said.

Jeev went to the study to call Nathani. "Is there a problem?" he asked feebly.

"I am sorry to disturb you, sir, but it is rather urgent. We can come over to your residence to show you the draft before submitting it for discussion by the CCS (Cabinet Committee on Security) at 5 pm. It is after a very long wait that we have got this slot," Nathani informed.

"Keep the meeting tentatively for 3.30 pm in the office. I will try to make it," Jeev said.

Manini, who was standing nearby overheard.

"I knew you would go. You won't miss a chance to prove to your officers that you are such an indispensable national asset," she said sarcastically.

Jeev did not react to it and went back to the sofa to sleep again.

*

Exactly at 3.30 pm, Jeevnathan entered his room in the office. Nathani and two other technical officers were already waiting to obtain his approval on a draft proposal for mounting a sensitive mission to monitor hostile radar locations along the western border. During the two-hour meeting, Jeev examined the document meticulously to ensure that issues raised earlier by him had been comprehensively addressed.

Suddenly, the RIT rang. He ignored the call and kept reading the last three pages where precise parameters of the targets had been written out. However, the caller was persistent. Visibly annoyed with the ring byte, he looked at the RIT monitor to identify the caller but found no caller ID that he usually spoke to.

"Who is this?" Jeev snapped, as he picked up the phone.

"Sir, I am Venkatpathy, Desk Officer in charge of Cyber Operations. I need to see you urgently in connection with a sensitive piece of information."

"Don't disturb me. I am busy in a meeting," Jeev admonished and disconnected, taking no cognizance of Venkat's fervent plea.

It was audacious that a junior officer, not assigned to the Security Division, would directly call to seek an urgent appointment. He never encouraged his colleagues to socialize in the office and met them only if he needed them for compelling operational or administrative reasons. His meetings were mostly on a one-to-one basis and he seldom discussed matters with anyone, unless he was fully prepared to address all aspects of the case.

The RIT rang again.

"I am sorry, sir, but it is rather important. I can explain everything when I meet you in person," Venkat insisted.

"Come after half an hour," Jeev said curtly and disconnected up.

Venkat turned up five minutes before the appointed time. He waited nervously till he was summoned from the ante-room. He had met Jeev once at an official function but that was more of an encounter in a melee. The second time he met Jeev was in connection with obtaining sanction for additional men and equipment for launching an operation to intercept exchange of communication among terrorists on the web. The meeting lasted precisely two minutes. Jeev told him to leave the papers behind and dismissed him. Yet, Venkat felt that if anyone would act on his information it would only be Jeev. He was afraid of the man but was willing to take a chance in view of the gravity of the matter.

Venkat entered the room, pulled a chair, and sat down. He could see that Jeev was not well, his face was red and he was coughing.

"Sir, I didn't realize you were so unwell. I can come some other day," Venkat suggested. Ignoring the officer's concern Jeev came straight to the point. "You wanted to share some information. What is it about?" he asked.

"Sir, the behaviour of Mr Ravi Mohan, senior analyst of the Far East Asia Branch, has been very suspicious of late," Venkat pointed out.

"Why do you presume that?" Jeev probed.

"He keeps pestering me to brief him about my operational projects, how I crack passwords, hack secure e-mails, and what tools I use to break coded messages. He tries to be overly friendly despite being 3-levels senior to me and that too when he has no jurisdictional responsibility over my work. I am not the only one he approaches for information. Unlike other senior officers in the department, he spends a lot of time with junior colleagues from other branches. I am positive he must also be probing them for inputs," Venkat averred.

"Isn't it normal in the Agency for senior officers to interact with junior colleagues, working in different branches?" Jeev asked.

"Sir, what worries me is his undue interest in my operational tools and his repeated attempts to obtain information that is based on encrypted intercepts," Venkat elaborated.

"What are you actually trying to get at?" Jeev pressed for more clarity.

"Sir, I suspect Mr Mohan is working for a foreign Intelligence agency," Venkat said cautiously.

Jeev pushed his chair back to stretch his legs, admiring the young officer's courage and acute sense of observation. "Why didn't you report this matter to your immediate supervisory officer," he asked.

"Sir, I thought for several weeks over this dilemma. Today when Ravi Mohan called me for the twelfth time, I panicked. I was afraid that at some point you would come to know about my meetings and haul me up for passing unauthorized information to him," Venkat clarified.

"What has been your response to Ravi's soliciting?" Jeev enquired.

"So far I have given him misleading inputs on operational techniques employed by my unit in breaking codes and hacking email accounts."

"Keep this meeting of ours a secret," Jeev advised. "You have a long career ahead. In case your suspicions do not stick and words go around that you rumour monger against senior officers, you could be hounded for the rest of your life. At this stage, your inputs appear to be largely delusionary but I will certainly initiate inquiries to verify your claims," he assured Venkat.

"Sir, if you give me two minutes, I have something more relevant to share," Venkat was not willing to give up so easily.

"Go ahead."

"Four years ago, when I was posted at Bangkok, Mr Ravi Mohan, who was then my controlling officer at the Headquarters, insisted that I continue to operate Kenneth Mills, a resident journalist who reported on developments in South East Asia for the *International Herald Tribune*. I believed all along that this source was double crossing us and I wrote several letters to Mr Mohan to this effect but he refused to allow me to drop the source," Venkat recalled.

"Is it possible that you were over riding your suspicion?" Jeev probed.

"Sir, what triggered my suspicion was Mills' unfettered access to the diplomats of the US, UK, Canada, South Africa, and Australia and the uncanny similarity between reports that he submitted to us and the articles that he wrote for *IHT*. But instead of discarding Mills, Mr Mohan increased his salary without assigning any reason. I had to grudgingly accept his directions. Later on, I took up the matter with Mr Harjeet Singh, Head of the Far East Asia Division and Ravi Mohan's boss, who happened to stay overnight at my station on his way to Fiji. I mentioned to him that Mr Mohan's motive in retaining Mills on the roll was dubious. Mr Singh was furious and warned me not to indulge in calumny against senior officers. I never heard from him after that."

"But isn't it a normal practice for journalists to meet diplomats of other countries to obtain information?" Jeev interrupted. Venkat ignored to respond directly and went on to elaborate.

"Sir, every three, four months, Mills visited Delhi where he was hosted lavishly by Mr Mohan. Neither the source nor Mr Mohan ever briefed me about what transpired between them. Out of disgust, I once suggested that the Agency should run Mills directly as its source and I could be used only as a forwarding post of his dispatches. But my plea was summarily rejected." A call on the RIT interrupted their discussion.

"Are you coming home or do I send your medicines and food over?" Manini enquired.

"That will not be necessary. I will be there in ten minutes," Jeev replied coolly. Then he told Venkat that "it has been a very stressful day."

"Sir, are there any instructions for me?" Venkat asked.

"You can continue to meet Ravi but make sure that you keep me informed of all your interactions."

On his way back, Jeev thought about what Venkat had told him. He had a gut feeling that something was amiss and deserved a closer scrutiny. In truth, he never fancied Ravi's persona and found him fishy, mediocre, and suspiciously withdrawn—qualities that make an officer an ideal pick for talent spotters. Still, he could not quite figure out why a foreign Intelligence outfit would recruit a dumb-witted officer and why a man of Ravi's affluent background would incur the huge risk of selling national secrets for money?

It was 11 pm when Jeev retired to bed. Unable to sleep, he tossed around, feeling restless and weak. He wondered whether the Chief would agree to an investigation into the allegations of espionage against a Senior Analyst of the Department. He was also not sure if the surveillance could be kept a secret in an office, where almost everyone was obligated to Ravi Mohan for gifts, personal favours, and financial support. The biggest worry, however, was whether the CEU (Counter Espionage Unit) had necessary resources to collect clinching evidences to prosecute Ravi in a court of law.

"What's the matter with you?" Manini asked. "Is the headache still there?" She ran her hand across his forehead. It was warm and wet.

"I am okay, just feeling drained out," Jeev said.

"You are no longer young and I cannot understand your obsession with self-importance. I don't know when you will realize that there is also a life beyond the four walls of the Agency," she said.

"This time it is more serious," Jeev responded. Desperately trying to sleep, he turned over and closed his eyes. But his mind was wide awake. Was Ravi Mohan Agency's Aldrich Hazen Ames, the CIA's notorious double agent, he wondered.

The last time the Agency had caught an espionage agent from its ranks was in late eighties, when V.R. Shetty, a smart and bright senior officer posted in Srinagar, came to notice for passing information on J&K operations to a local lady doctor, who was actually an ISI operative. Following a preliminary suspicion that specific inputs appearing in intercepts about movement of security forces, infiltration of terrorists from POK and conversation between HuM, LeT commanders and their volunteers relating to their operational plans were being routinely leaked, Shetty was placed under surveillance by a joint team of the Agency and the Bureau. He made a clean confession of his crime after he was confronted with the incriminating video footages and subjected to intensive questioning. He was tried in camera, remained in prison for a few years and now leads a reclusive life.

The other case was of Vijay Shekhar, who was hounded out of the Bureau in the late nineties following his alleged involvement in espionage activities. Vijay was an extremely bright officer holding a senior position in the Bureau and certain to head the outfit two years later. By nature he was gregarious and an outrageous extrovert, which his senior colleagues, wearing long and jaded faces for having worked for the best part of their lives in suffocating ambience, found preposterous. Professionally, he was head and shoulders above his colleagues and had the rare gift of talking his way through to the sources, extracting relevant inputs and harnessing those tellingly in his intelligence reports. No wonder successive Bureau Directors could not afford to dispense with his services. A few of them hated his guts but stuck with him for his amazing reach to contacts and sheer brilliance.

Then one day, Vijay came to the notice of his own surveillance team for frequently meeting Miss June, a CIA lady officer of the US Embassy in Delhi. His detractors in the Bureau saw in this lapse a god sent opportunity to clip his wings fatally. They attributed unprofessional motives to the photographs showing his proximity to Miss June and made a naive government believe that he was an espionage agent. They also provided deliberate leaks to the media, prompting it to bay for his blood for his alleged involvement in a sex-driven espionage network. However, when it could not be conclusively proved that he peddled Intelligence, Shekhar was forced to seek voluntary retirement. The charge against him was that he did not keep his seniors informed of the nature of gifts that he received from the CIA operative and kept the Bureau in the dark about his indiscrete escapades. A bright career was thus cut short for spurious reasons.

Actually, Vijay was too smart to be trapped by a low-witted, unattractive operative. He could talk endlessly and spin yarns of believable inputs without conceding an iota of worthwhile intelligence. He always held important positions both in the Bureau and the Foreign Office and ran some of the most historic secret operations. If he had the temptation of selling intelligence he could have done so in abundance long before Bureau's surveillance cameras trapped him. If he went overboard, it was typical of his gung-ho style. Like several leaders of outstanding repute, he was uncomfortably liberated in personal life but quintessentially professional. Jeev had also dealt with Miss June for a long time and found her average both in looks and work. Long after she had left India, he thought someday, she might be willing to say whether Vijay was her agent or a part time boyfriend. A year later, an opportunity came when Jeev saw her travelling on the same cruise in Sydney. Her face fell when she saw him and she ran to the upper deck for cover. Before Jeev could catch up with her, she was lost among the tourists on board.

After his forced retirement, Vijay continued to be vilified and demeaned. He became the favourite punching bag of his friends and foes alike. His mentors did nothing to redeem his reputation. A colleague, known for his venomous writings and congenitally conspiratorial traits, remarked with conspicuous relief that if not detected, the Bureau might have been headed by a CIA mole. A few of his friends outside the Intelligence community including couple of foreign secretaries, strongly believed that Vijay could be anything but a spy but kept their views private for fear of being labelled as his collaborator. The media and security analysts of dubious denominations continued to accuse Vijay of infidelity to the Bureau and speak about him in the same breath as Shetty.

That night, Jeevnathan's dilemma was how to proceed in Ravi Mohan's case. If the suspect was working as a conscious espionage agent like Shetty, the task would be easier. An intrusive audio and video surveillance could be mounted to track Ravi's modus operandi, his contacts, his handler, and the spread of his network. The rest would be extracted during his coercive grilling in the interrogation centre. But what if he was acting indiscreetly like Vijay? He might simply be over inquisitive to know more about subjects that he was not dealing with and splurging money on friends and colleagues out of a compulsive habit rather than a choice. There could still be a third possibility. Ravi Mohan might be operating completely unlike any one of the two.

Day 2

Jeev woke up late to a cold winter morning. He felt slight breathlessness and a splitting headache. As he struggled to get out of the bed, he realized that he had been covered with an extra blanket, possibly by Mani in one of her rare, loving moments. After a leisurely wash, he went down to the living room where Mani was giving instructions to the cook. Feeling better after a light breakfast and medicine, he rang up his deputies, Ajay Varma and Kamath, Director of the CEU, and asked them to meet him in the office at 11.45 am.

"Don't go to the office," Mani said sternly. "Last night you were shivering and sweating. If you don't rest, the viral will fester. You know that your immunity level is very low. Even baby doses of antibiotics lay you down badly," she reminded.

"I will be there only for an hour," Jeev replied.

"I am worried what would happen to the country's security when you retire after six months," came her sardonic repartee. Jeev refused to pick up the gauntlet.

Jeevnathan was an hour late when he reached office. Ajay and Kamath were already waiting for him in his room. He took a few minutes to recover from a bout of intermittent coughing and then instructed his PS not to re-direct any call unless it was from Manini.

"You seem to have a very bad cough and cold. We would have come to your residence if the matter was so urgent," Ajay said.

Jeev ignored the deputy's concern and came straight to the point. "An anonymous caller told me last night that Ravi Mohan persistently elicited classified information from officers not assigned to him. He also claimed that Ravi might be working for a foreign Intelligence agency. The caller wouldn't identify himself nor had any specific inputs to support his allegations," Jeev said pausing for breath. "I think, since suspicions have been raised about involvement of a Senior Analyst in espionage, we should make some inquiries to be reasonably sure that the caller's fears are either motivated or unfounded." He started coughing again. KM went out and brought him a cup of black coffee from the vending machine which provided instant relief.

"I suggest you discreetly conduct a preliminary inquiry. Select the junior officers carefully for this task for, they are likely to go overboard," Jeev pointed to his deputy.

"Sir, I think the caller definitely has an axe to grind. If he is so concerned about our security, why doesn't he identify himself? Moreover, Mr Mohan is not the only senior officer who interacts with colleagues working in other units," Ajay argued.

Kamath, however, was more positive in his reaction. "I can quickly assemble a team of watchers to monitor the suspect's activities," he said. Jeev noted that Director CEU, Agency's most vocal vigilante, had already started treating Ravi as a suspect. But Ajay felt that KM's initiative was driven by misplaced enthusiasm. "Even if we assume for a moment that Mr Ravi Mohan is an espionage agent, being a trained operative he will expose our watchers in no time and raise hell, putting all of us on the mat," he cautioned. Jeev was not surprised at his deputy's weak-kneed reaction.

"So, basically what you are implying is that we trash the caller's information because we are afraid of its adverse fall out," Jeev remarked.

Ajay realized that he had probably put a false foot forward and decided not to comment further. Kamath, however, sought some clarity before he harnessed watchers in action.

"Sir, who do you think Mr Ravi Mohan is working for?" he asked.

"It is too early to even speculate," Jeev said.

No further discussion took place.

KM had barely stepped out of the room when Jeev called him on his mobile phone. "I would like watchers to be put on Ravi's trail latest by tomorrow," he emphasized. "For the time being avoid telling them why we are investigating the suspect," he cautioned.

Jeev returned home around 4 pm. Manini was waiting for lunch. "You are only three hours behind the schedule," she taunted him. "Wasan rang twice to check how you were doing today," she mentioned.

"And, what did you say?" Jeev asked.

"I told him the Agency's building was on fire and you had rushed to collect the debris."

"There must be more charitable ways of showing concern," Jeev retorted, taking a deep breath.

Day 3

Ravi Mohan was placed under surveillance. The watchers' brief was to follow him discretely whenever he stepped out of the Agency's building and keep a visual record of his contact with colleagues and others in the office or en-route. The watch was to be of low intensity and mounted from a safe distance. It was to terminate once the target entered his apartment complex.

At 10.30 am, Jeev walked into the Chief's room without any prior notice. He looked at Jeev summarily and continued reading a note. He said that he had to leave for a meeting after ten minutes.

"Mani was saying that a fire in the building pulled you out of your sick bed yesterday," Wasan remarked in good humour as he put the paper in his briefcase.

"You know her eternal cynicism about our work," Jeev replied. "Jokes apart, I have run into a serious situation. I thought I should inform you before it spun out of control." Then he gave a tailored version of his meeting with Venkat, but held back the latter's identity.

"Are you sure the caller is not a prankster or someone who has scores to settle with Ravi?" Wasan inquired.

"It's possible, but how would you react to Ravi's persistent interaction with junior colleagues of other branches, particularly with those who handle operational desks?" Jeev asked.

"It is inappropriate but as you know, most of us regularly interact with officers from other branches," Wasan said.

"I have already mounted a limited surveillance," Jeev dropped the bombshell, finding Wasan in a hurry to depart. The latter was taken aback but quickly composed himself.

"You never surprise me. Anyway, you are the security czar. Do what you deem is necessary." Wasan was curt in his response this time. Then he asked his aide to line up the escort and left to attend the meeting in South Block. Jeev followed him up to the elevator then turned left to take the staircase to go up to his room.

Day 6

The watchers produced 139 visuals and 14 spot reports at the end of three days' of surveillance. Jeev cursorily glanced through the reports. KM had noted in the margin that Ravi Mohan was either in contact with known relatives or officers from the Agency. He often took his colleagues out for lunch or tea to expensive restaurants and interacted mostly with those who had nothing to do with the Far East Asia Division that he supervised. He was meeting no one while travelling between his residence and the office and seldom went out for late night parties.

Jeev found it odd that Ravi should splurge money on entertaining his colleagues in five-star hotels. "Normally you extend this favour to high grade sources," he remarked.

"Sir, he is known to be a good host unlike his other affluent but miserly colleagues. I am told he is very generous to his personal staff and helpful to anyone who approaches him for financial and administrative assistance," KM said.

"I am not so sure about his wealth. I was told that during his posting at Nairobi in 1992, he suffered from coronary heart disease but he had no money to undergo a bypass surgery. It was only after contributions arrived from his US and Canadian relatives and friends that he could be operated at the AKH hospital in Vienna," Jeev mentioned.

"I didn't know that," KM seemed surprised.

"In hindsight, I can now see more clearly why he chose AKH for his surgery when he had cheaper options available in India and the US. I won't be surprised if a foreign Intelligence service arranged for his treatment. Maybe, you should access the list of his sources and contacts in Nairobi and see if anything strikes you as unusual," Jeev suggested.

"Sir."

"You should also expand the arc of surveillance a little wider to cover the activities of his wife," Jeev proposed. "Ravi may be using her as a courier to transfer documents to the handler, while he sits in the office to ambush any scrutiny of his suspicious activities," he said.

KM pursed his lips thoughtfully. He was not sure whether such overgrown ideas would yield any useful results.

As he got up to leave, Jeev mentioned that he would be leaving for Moscow later that night to cap two years' of hard bargaining over the price of critical components of a reconnaissance platform. "I didn't want to be away from Delhi at this juncture for a week but it is rather urgent," he said.

KM did not react. He collected the papers and left quietly.

Day 7

It was five in the morning when Ravi's residence in Defence Colony was placed under static and mobile surveillance. KM was there to ensure that watchers reported on time and took up positions 80 meters away from the suspect's apartment at the corner of a Mother Dairy kiosk. The watchers were divided in three teams of four men each. The first team was to be committed during 6 to 12 am, the second from 12 to 6 pm, and the third from 6 to 10 pm. The teams were also to act as mobile units whenever Vijita, Ravi's wife, stepped out of the house. These were in addition to a team of six watchers that was already covering the target's movements during the day.

For the whole of next week, KM compiled reports submitted daily by watchers, briefed and debriefed team leaders, went through their dispatches and visuals and recorded his comments. He expected that once Jeev returned from Moscow, he would ask for an update, followed by a brainstorming session.

Day 14

Kamath's apprehension was on the dot. As soon as Jeev emerged out of the immigration, he called KM and instructed him to meet in the office at 2.30 pm along with Ajay. The meeting began with KM submitting 162 observation reports from the surveillance teams and his analysis of the available evidence.

Jeev read KM's note first. It underlined that neither the suspect nor his wife met any foreigner and that the suspects followed a normal daily routine. While Vijita occasionally went out to socialize and shop, the suspect played an indulgent host to the Agency's officers in his room or in hotels. However, there was one event that struck as odd. The suspect went daily from the office to the Zair Club, an exclusive gym in the Defence Colony. Around the time when he reached the club, a diplomatic car invariably pulled in and a tall, white man came out and went inside.

"Develop the lead about this car," Jeev said, returning the papers to Kamath. "It is too much of a coincidence to be taken lightly. For all you know, Ravi may be using the time he spends inside the gym to hand over documents and obtain briefing from his handler," he pointed out.

"Sir, I have since obtained a few details of the car. It belongs to the Polish Consul General," KM informed.

"It doesn't make sense for a Polish CG to be Ravi's courier," Jeev said. "Agencja Wywiadu cannot be the final destination of Agency's reports. It is currently in a mess and caught in serious accountability issues. Moreover, it has hardly anything to gain from subverting one of our officers. I would have been worried if the car belonged to a British, Canadian, or Australian diplomat because they do front for the CIA," he clarified.

"Why are we ruling out ISI's hand in it?" Ajay interrupted, trying to make his presence felt.

"We are not ruling out anything," KM reacted in disbelief. "ISI doesn't need to subvert the suspect. It has already got numerous Indian collaborators in its kitty, spread across all sections of our society and disciplines," he stated emphatically.

"That's precisely the point that I am trying to make," Ajay said. "ISI remains the biggest threat to our security. For years, it has been using angry and disconnected Muslims for their terrorist operations and others for spying. Ravi Mohan could just be one more in their long list of espionage agents," he argued.

"I don't think ISI is relevant in this case," Jeev intervened to endorse KM's views. "It would rather invest in recruiting suicide bombers and equipping them with explosives and weapons. It won't run such a high-risk operation based out of Delhi to procure stale analytical reports and trite position papers. It is certainly not in their grain to waste resources on agents of information unless they can also be employed for executing 'action' on the field," he pointed out.

"Sir, ISI could still be interested in trapping a big fish just to prove that it can hit us anywhere and in any manner that it chooses," Ajay insisted.

"It has nothing more to prove about its lethal capabilities. You just have to look around to see their footprints everywhere. If we are unable to hit back, it is our problem and not theirs. Anyway, our immediate priority is to find out what Ravi is doing inside the club, particularly when the Polish CG is there," Jeev said, bringing the discussion to an end.

Day 15

For KM, placing a watcher inside the Zair Club turned out to be a nightmare. Only permanent members had the first right of entry in the club. Those who wanted to join it temporarily had to deposit Rs 45,000 as entry fee. The management also insisted on two credible references and admitted only residents of the colony or officers from the diplomatic community. For the CEU officers on the surveillance duties, their demeanour was a serious handicap. They could not pass as diplomats or residents of an upscale locality because of their burly look, awkward manners, and poor diction.

But KM was not the one to give up so easily. Pulling out the usual dirty trick from his sleeve, he tried to plant watchers surreptitiously by forging their status but did not succeed. They failed miserably to pull of their lies during their personal interview with the management. Then he offered money to an office clerk, who made tall claims but could not deliver the duplicate card. He also threatened the management with his non-existent CBI connections but that did not work. In despair, he promised an unrealistic sum to one of the security guards but the latter needed time to work his way through. Frustration led KM to seriously doubt the very usefulness of the exercise. Nothing, he estimated, had emerged from the field surveillance to indicate that the club could be the meeting point of the suspect with his handler. Besides, it hardly made any sense that the handler would choose a place so close to the suspect's residence for regular meetings. Finally, KM knocked at Jeev's door.

"Hang on. I am going out of Delhi for a day. Check with Ajay if he knows anyone who can help," Jeev said.

"Sir, I did raise this issue and he tried as well. He is afraid that if he pursues it further, the suspect may smell something foul and report the matter to the Chief," said KM.

"Fine, then let me come back."

Day 16

On his return from a rushed visit to the North East, Jeev was caught in a series of meetings and could be free to meet KM and Ajay only around 6 pm. Finding Jeev tired and eager to leave early for home, KM gave him a bunch of the latest observation reports and photographs and requested him to take them home and read at leisure.

"Give me a quick rundown on the day's developments," Jeev suggested.

"Sir, there is nothing new. The entire exercise is increasingly becoming repetitive," KM remarked.

"I still feel there is something wrong with the suspect's conduct. His persistence in reaching out to junior officers cannot be an innocuous exercise," Jeev pointed out. "We also have to ascertain whether there is a method in the selection of his prey or he is merely killing time. In any case, he is handling a very light desk and is also known to lack the aptitude to generate extra work," he said.

Ajay had a different perspective. "Sir, the suspect may be interacting with his colleagues simply to remain posted on the latest developments so that he comes across as knowledgeable to the visiting analysts from foreign Intelligence services," he argued cautiously.

"I am not ruling out anything at this stage. I would, in fact, feel relieved if Ravi was found compromising only principles of restrictive security for enhancing his awareness," Jeev said.

"Sir, I don't want to sound like a devil's advocate," Ajay clarified, "but like Ravi, most of us also want to remain updated on subjects that are not our direct responsibility. Before we go abroad for discussion with our liaison counterparts, we are briefed and provided reading material by area specialists on subjects that we do not deal with. But a one-time reading does not make our task easier. Mr Mohan is only one step ahead. He wants to remain in contact with the specialists on an ongoing basis," he explained.

"What have we come to? First, we violate rules of engagement. Then we find justifications to perpetuate it," Jeev countered in apparent disgust.

Ajay realized that he had probably gone beyond his brief.

"You do have a point," Jeev said after a few moments of uneasy calm. "Ravi may only be following a practice in vogue. But let's get a few gaps filled before we start questioning the merit in sustaining this operation. For example, we don't know yet what is happening inside Zair Club or what is the nature of Ravi's solicitations from officers, or whether he sounds too eager or too desperate while seeking reports. I suggest we monitor Ravi's internal and MTNL numbers in his office for a few weeks, just in case he is contacting his running officer."

"Sir," KM responded dutifully. Both officers came out and began walking back to their rooms.

"I don't know what you think about monitoring Ravi Mohan's internal calls but to me it appears to be a wishful move," Ajay opined. KM was equally peeved with Jeev's latest directive but opted out of endorsing views of his senior colleague for fear of being misreported.

Jeev stretched his legs, leaned back on the sofa and closed his eyes. The day had been very hectic. There was still a meeting to come up after half an hour to discuss the repositioning of communication interception devices along the north-eastern border. His thoughts raced back to the days when restrictive security was practiced rigidly in the Agency. Only a select few knew what liaison relationship was all about and barely a dozen desk officers were allowed to interact with their counterparts in the foreign intelligence services. Painfully, over the years, the norms governing liaison work were disfigured beyond recognition and as a consequence, the Agency's operations and reach of its technical and human assets became topics of common gossip.

This downslide owed its origin to a weird phenomenon. Since Pakistan, China, and international terrorism figured prominently in discussions with foreign Intelligence services, experts attached to these desks trotted around the globe exchanging information with their counterparts, while their colleagues sulked at Headquarters churning out reports on the peripheral regions. The fact that only a chosen few cornered the foreign trips festered a feeling of deprivation among majority of officers. Added to this was an underlying grudge that they were being deprived of lucrative benefits that were built into foreign tours enabling officers to bring home little extra money, appliances, liquor, and cheese through honest means.

A few populist chiefs of the Agency also felt seriously handicapped by the rigid application of rules governing selection of officers on liaison duties. It thwarted them from obliging their courtiers by sending them on, what was derisively described as, *foreign jaunts*. They argued, albeit spuriously, that all area specialists were not necessarily good interlocutors and that experienced officers were far more suited to discuss joint operations and raise the Agency's security concerns. Initially, the chiefs allowed only exceptions to crawl in but later on that turned into a deluge. The spoils of foreign trips began getting distributed recklessly. Officers not even remotely connected to subjects went abroad to talk about them on the basis of briefs prepared by area analysts. It was comical that a quintessential sycophant of successive chiefs would frequently go to brief foreign sleuths when he was not even working in the Agency. One just had to be the cat's whisker to board a flight. Naturally, presentations became sketchy and officers fielded queries like babes lost in the woods.

Milan Behal, a senior China analyst, would often complain that half his office time was wasted in preparing briefs and notes for officers who knew nothing about China but were assigned to take on Beijing's double-speak on whole range of security and strategic issues. Similar was the angst of Arun Roy, a senior Pakistan analyst, who knew every bit of that country. His depth of knowledge was such that Islamabad would probably have found his inputs more comprehensive than those from its indigenous sources for picking up the right man for its various constitutional appointments.

Over the years, the situation became worse. A couple of expatriate chiefs with no experience of growing with the ethos of external Intelligence and oblivious of constraints of liaison relationships turned the security environment within the Agency upside down by expanding the liaison network indiscriminately. The trend became infectious as more and more exotic locations were added to the list of liaison contacts. It was a different matter that most Foreign Intelligence services had hardly anything relevant to offer. But the purpose had been served. The scope for foreign travel by officers and their spouses was increased manifold. In the process, a large number of officers were exposed to the suborning overtures of Foreign Intelligence operatives, for whom it became much easier to identify Agency's officers and track down footprints of their sensitive operations. It also opened up an expanded pool of officers, riddled with weaknesses for money, gifts, scholarship for wards and good time, to be recruited as agents.

Inevitably, the glamour around the Agency's liaison exploits became a matter of envy. Soon the Bureau, Ministry of Home Affairs, CBI, Directorate of Enforcement, Ministry of External Affairs, National Security Council, and Defence Intelligence Agency embarked on making indiscriminate contacts with Foreign Intelligence services in the name of cooperation in various shades of strategic areas. The Agency opposed doggedly for years FBI's attempts to set up its units in India, contested rationale of the Bureau and others organizations to open new bases abroad and questioned the wisdom in sending officers to attend sub-standard courses and seminars offered by Foreign Intelligence services. However, these arguments rang hollow because the Agency itself had vandalized the essence of liaison contacts.

The officers were now up for grabs. If they were not picked up, it was because of their limited utility. Home ministers and national security advisors could also not resist the lure of meeting visiting intelligence chiefs, giving latter a larger than life role in defining the mutual security relationship. The new arrangement substantially reduced the effectiveness of the Agency chiefs in talking tough on bartering of Intelligence inputs and bargaining hard for strict reciprocity in joint operations. Sadly, the diktat crafted by the few wise men of late seventies that the Agency alone would be responsible for chartering the raft of liaison in the treacherous waters of security, was lost forever in the scramble for extra dime.

A buzz finally broke Jeev's reverie. "Sir, the tea must have gone cold. Can I send for another cup?" His PS was on the line. Jeev didn't know when the first cup of tea had been served.

"That will be wonderful. Have the officers come in for the meeting?" Jeev asked.

"Sir, they are on the way and should be in your room any moment," he said.

Day 17

Tapping the internal telephone inside the Agency was a task cut out for desperadoes. The telephone exchange functioned under the 'WEE' unit, which ensured that the Exchange was neither infiltrated nor misused through a rigid system of checks, enforced by four levels of supervisory officers. During office hours, it was manned by twelve operators and at 7 pm, it was shut down and locked after switching over a few *essential* lines onto the automatic mode. Even in most demanding situations, where time was of essence, it was impossible to make the WEE in-charge agree to allow monitoring of a call without written approval of the Chief.

For KM that was not the problem. Jeev could always obtain the sanction from the Chief. The main worry was how to keep the monitoring under wraps. He, therefore, needed someone who could take risk and was reliable. He went through dossiers of the employees of the telecommunication division and zeroed in on Kak, a desk officer.

Kak was a lone ranger in the hostile terrains of his division. He ran into frequent problems with his seniors over procurement of equipment, which he found wasteful, over-priced, and greed-driven. He was extremely vocal in his criticism and never hesitated to put his career on the line by stressing his dissent. No wonder, he was regularly superseded despite his technical abilities and fierce honesty. He continued to rot at the level of a desk officer because his supervisors assessed him as arrogant and insubordinate, year after year. KM estimated that since Kak was disgruntled, yet intensely loyal to the department and adventurous in spirit, he could fill the bill perfectly. It came as no surprise to him that Kak readily agreed to collaborate when KM approached him.

Displaying a rare ingenuity, Kak proposed to create a leak in the Exchange without the knowledge of line operators and bring all internal calls of Ravi Mohan to the Nerve Centre (NC) that KM had set up as a mini-control room to handle the operation. It took the wily telecommunication officer just two hours to plan the operation and execute the breach and, one and half days to test its workability.

Day 19

The NC monitored the first call at 10.20 am. Ravi was calling someone but there was no response. Five minutes later, he again called the same number but no one answered. Twenty minute later, he dialled again. This time a lady picked up the call but did not readily announce her name.

"Is that Usha Pandey?" Ravi asked.

"No, I am her PA. May I know who is speaking?"

"I am Ravi Mohan."

"Good morning, sir."

"Has she not come to the office?" Ravi inquired.

"Sir, she is not likely to be here before noon."

"Did Mr Rajan come to see her?"

"No, sir."

"If he drops in, please remind him that the lunch is at 1 pm at the Imperial."

Everyone present in the NC smiled at each other with a sense of relief. Kak's monitoring efforts had come off without glitches.

The first day's harvest was quite impressive. At 6.30 pm, KM grabbed a bunch of tapes and walked down to inform Jeev that interception of Ravi's internal calls had commenced.

"That's a great start," Jeev commended. "And, don't forget to reward Kak when this whole thing is over. Let no one know that he has made it happen. By the way, did you have a chance to go through the monitored calls?" he asked.

"Sir, the tapes are yet to be transcribed. A detailed analysis of calls and surveillance reports will only be possible after a week. However, I have cursorily checked a few recorded calls. Ravi contacted fourteen officers today, all from other units, but did not probe them about their work nor sought any reports.

He, however, insisted that they drop in for *a good cup of tea, a hot cup of coffee or fresh lime water*. Today, he is taking Rajan, head of our Western Bureau, out for lunch to the Imperial," KM reported.

"Any progress in placing your man inside the club," Jeev inquired.

"Not so far, sir."

"Let me see if I can do something. Meanwhile, if you are sanguine about keeping the interception of internal calls a secret, then try to explore the possibility of monitoring Ravi's MTNL numbers, to identify callers from outside and to figure out who amongst them sounds suspicious," Jeev suggested.

"I will discuss this with Kak and see if he can do it," KM assured.

Day 20

Kak reacted enthusiastically to the proposal. He said it was a challenge worth accepting but insisted on involving three of his favourite technical hands. KM initially opposed the idea for fear of exposure but gave in, following an assurance that they were best in the business and discreet.

Around 8.30 pm, Kak and his team set out to work on the new task. KM was in the office, catching up with pending papers. In between, he checked with Kak once, who confided that he was deliberately proceeding slowly to avoid undue curiosity from squatters in the area. At 10 pm, KM left for home. After an unusually quiet dinner, he went out with his wife for a stroll in the park in their locality but kept thinking about Kak and wondering if he was able to accomplish the job without any hiccups. In between, his wife attempted to speak to him about their son's wayward habits and the need to start looking for a groom for their daughter. When she failed to draw him out, she inquired if everything was alright in the office. KM still did not respond. Once the park was deserted and the lights were switched off, they headed home. He saw his wife off at the main entrance and told her to lock the door from inside since he couldn't say what time he would return. When he left, his daughter was fast asleep. His son, who studied at the Institute of Mass Communication, had still not come back home. It had lately become his habit to spend his nights with friends in the campus. KM often scolded him for being irresponsible, but he knew it was also his fault. He hardly spent any time with his family and lived only for his work.

KM reached office at 2.30 am and went straight to the NC where Kak and his colleagues were having tea. He did not like the presence of junior linesmen in the NC and made his annoyance profusely visible by refusing to acknowledge their greetings. He remained frosty till Kak and his colleagues got up to leave.

"You stay behind," KM pointed to Kak. After the linesmen left he chided Kak for bringing them to the recording room that no one, not even the Chief, knew about.

"The tapping would not have been possible without these two boys. Trust me, they are very reliable." Kak tried to calm him down.

"Anyway, how did it go?" inquired KM.

"The good news is that we have successfully breached the junction box that feeds lines to Ravi Mohan's direct numbers and the one that comes to his room from outside through the Exchange. You can now listen to all his incoming and outgoing calls in the NC. The bad news is that six more lines have been inadvertently breached, giving you an access to their calls as well," Kak explained with a measure of satisfaction.

"Don't mention this to anyone," KM said.

"I won't. The NC will record only Mr Ravi Mohan's calls, unless you want me to tap the other lines." Kak then spent some time explaining how the calls would be monitored and recorded.

At 3.30 am, KM locked the NC and took the staircase to come down to the hallway. He walked past the half-sleepy sentries to emerge onto the sprawling lawn and ambled around the building for some time to make sure that no one was watching. He soon caught up with Kak who had walked out of the building separately and was waiting outside the main entrance. On his way home, KM dropped Kak in Lodhi colony. It was 4.45 am when KM had parked his car in the garage and switched off the porch light. After that he left for an early morning walk.

Day 21

The Chief and Jeev emerged from the executive lounge after lunch and walked together. "It's more than three weeks since you mentioned about Ravi's inappropriate conduct. Has anything come out of the inquiry?" Wasan asked, as they approached the lift area from where they were to branch off for their respective rooms.

"Watchers have so far drawn blank," Jeev said. "They have not seen Ravi contacting any unknown person but spotted him visiting an exclusive club in his neighbourhood where a number of diplomats go for work outs. We are trying to ascertain if Ravi meets any diplomat there," he explained.

"I hope you are not shadow boxing. In fact, if anyone needs to be kept on a tight leash, it's your director. He has a tendency to overreach himself and hound employees unnecessarily," Wasan remarked.

"Do you want me to shift the focus of inquiry from Ravi to Kamath?" Jeev retorted sharply.

"I guess I hit a raw nerve. I should have realized that you blindly support your subordinates," Wasan said.

"It's no time to win brownie points by debating peripheral issues. For your information, we have also started monitoring Ravi's internal and external calls. It confirms that he regularly calls officers from other branches to his room. Beyond that, there is no indication of his likely involvement in espionage. Anyway, it's just the beginning," Jeev said. By now they had entered the Chief's room.

"Why can't we tell Ravi to stop eliciting information and warn others of punitive action if they don't adhere to sharing their reports on a need-to-know basis?" Wasan asked.

"We don't know as yet whether he is eliciting unauthorized information from his colleagues. Moreover, since the allegations are of a serious nature, it would be premature to simply wish them away by admonishing Ravi and his collaborators," Jeev pointed out. "What actually intrigues me is why Ravi does not meet anyone other than known faces. Either he is innocent or working as an espionage operative for a very smart Intelligence agent," he said.

"I doubt if any Intelligence service will recruit this fool." Wasan was dismissive.

"You never know," Jeev said.

"To be honest with you, I am getting worried about its adverse effect on the Agency's image," Wasan confided.

"On the other hand, I believe, the nation will be proud that under your leadership, we busted an espionage network operating in our midst, and admire our objectivity for not even sparing a senior officer," Jeev teased.

"I don't know about the nation but I am certain about one thing," Wasan said brushing aside his friend's jibe, "the Bureau, security experts, and the media will use this opportunity to slit the Agency's reputation. I get a feeling that we are inadvertently providing fodder for their cannon," he said.

"We don't need to sweat over what others think as long as we are doing the right thing. As for the fodder, we are still a long way off from harvesting any incriminating stuff," Jeev remarked.

They stopped talking when a waiter brought in coffee. Jeev gulped down his coffee and left. On the way back to his room, Jeev peeped inside Vinod Doshi's room. Doshi was Director in-charge of Insurgency Operations. Finding him closeted in a meeting, he met his gaze, quickly retraced his steps, closed the door and left. While he was waiting for the lift to come up, he saw Doshi hurrying towards him.

"Is your meeting over?" Jeev asked as Doshi approached him.

"Sir, is there anything that you want me to do?" Doshi enquired.

"Drop in whenever you are free," Jeev said, as he entered the cabin.

Jeev liked Doshi immensely for his dynamism, positive approach and knack for getting things organized. Doshi would never offer a no for an answer and was always ready to help. His experience of working in Delhi Police came very handy whenever Jeev needed any logistic support. Doshi, however, had a compulsive habit of laughing loudly at trivial issues, which sometimes irritated his seniors. But he never meant to offend anyone. KM found him too gregarious for comfort in an Intelligence setup and could never quite understand how Jeev, so discreet and withdrawn, was fond of Doshi.

Taking a break from clearing files, Jeev rang up Prashant Vaish, one of the five Directors of Special Operations, to check if he could come over at 8 pm. Vaish responded positively. Jeev's next call was to KM who said that he was in the midst of listening to an important intercept. He told Vaish that he would come over as soon as the transcript was ready.

Doshi came in at 6.30 pm, looking relaxed and eager. As he settled down, Jeev said that he needed help in planting a man inside a gym.

"No problem, sir," Came Doshi's prompt reply.

"It has come to our notice that Ravi Mohan goes to Zair Club in Defence Colony for his daily work-out." Jeev chose to be more specific. "The Club," he said, "is frequented by diplomats mostly from western countries. Ravi has been seen meeting a Consul General and two other whites there but he has so far not reported to the top brass about the nature of his interactions. We had approached the club management but they have not been too helpful. It is really important for us to place a watcher inside the Club to find out whom he meets and why," he explained.

"Sir, I will arrange entry of your officer," Doshi responded without batting an eyelid.

Jeev wondered whether Doshi made commitments as a matter of habit or he genuinely believed in his capacity to deliver at all times.

Kamath dropped in within minutes of Doshi's departure. He reported that NC was flooded with intercepted calls but these were largely of no consequence. Ravi continued to call the same officers and avoided discussing any operational subject on telephone. "This exercise is not worth the effort we are putting in," he claimed.

Jeev was in no haste. "Let us listen to Ravi's calls for a few weeks more and see if any clue pops up," he said. "I was also thinking that since Ravi has been very careful in his telephonic chit chats, it is crucial that we know what transpires between Ravi and the officers in his room. That alone can clarify whether he is consciously eliciting inputs to serve the interest of a foreign Intelligence service or merely encouraging junior officers to speak out of turn on their subjects to satiate his thirst for information," he contended.

KM did not react.

"How quickly can you start monitoring the conversation inside his room?" Jeev asked.

"Sir, I will have to discuss its feasibility with experts," KM said reluctantly.

"Let me know if you run into problems," Jeev said.

KM collected his papers and left, alarmed at the ever growing wish list of Jeev.

The last to come in was Prashant Vaish. He was the only junior officer who had the license to take liberties with Jeev but he was also aware of the hazards in dealing with the mercurial security head of the Agency. Vaish never joked, laughed loudly, or spun juicy tales about officers' personal lives, but he had the right to disagree and refuse to comply with instructions which he considered were not in conformity with rules. Jeev respected his astounding grip on rules, his judgement, and clarity of mind. Vaish was probably the last of the dwindling tribe of officers whose noting on files never reflected bias of regionalism, friendship, caste, or service affiliation.

Jeev told Vaish that he required details of Ravi Mohan's foreign and internal postings in connection with an inquiry and his leave from Headquarters during the last ten years. He further said that since the matter was sensitive, he couldn't entrust it to anyone else.

"Sir, I will try. If I know the exact purpose, my task will be easier," Vaish hinted.

Jeev smiled but said nothing.

"Sir, it may be difficult to tackle Vipul, Desk Officer, Special Operations. He is usually very possessive about information regarding foreign postings and tours. But I will definitely make an effort to get around him," said Vaish.

"I leave it to you how you pilot the inquiry. I am in no hurry," Jeev said.

For the next half an hour, Vaish discussed a couple of contentious issues which he felt might irreparably harm the operational interests of the Agency. He said that a devious proposal was on the anvil to reach out to insurgents groups in Myanmar to take on ULFA and NSCN, ignoring how adversely this would impact the bilateral liaison relationship that had been assiduously built over the years with great care and caution. He also referred to the attempts being made by a section of officers to pitch for continued funding of Huriyat leaders in Kashmir under a misguided belief that they would covertly strengthen the government's peace initiatives and neutralize the local terrorist outfits. He said that he failed to comprehend how the Agency could trust those ISI clones and congenital mischief makers. He then showed two files, in which he believed the Chief had grievously erred in approving proposals on his Deputy's suggestions. These related to floating of NGOs to influence and instigate political and economic processes in Nepal and Pakistan. He requested Jeev to get these wasteful investments immediately aborted.

"Even if these cases merit a relook, it wouldn't be proper for me to take them up with the Chief since I don't deal with the subject," Jeev said. "The Chief could also take an adverse view of your showing these files to me," he cautioned.

"I know," Vaish relented.

"Okay, leave these files with me," Jeev agreed on second thoughts. "I will record my views on a separate sheet of paper which you can subsequently incorporate in the files and send these under your signature," Jeev smiled. He was happy that the Agency was not yet bereft of conscience keepers.

For Vaish, seeing Jeev smile was a rare sight.

Day 22

Bugging Ravi's room turned out to be unexpectedly smooth. P. Murthy, Director of the Bugging Unit and one of the few friends of Kamath in the Agency, offered the latest devices and best technicians for the job. But he also warned that customizing the room for picking up sound bytes entailed a very high risk of exposure. He pointed out that it was easier to bug rooms of targets in hotels and guesthouses where the management provided full support but bugging your own house was a tricky affair.

"Are you suggesting that we drop the idea of bugging his room?" KM asked in dismay.

"No. But you should be aware of the risks so that you are not caught napping when it hits you," Murthy said.

"You can count on my support. I won't let you down if anything goes wrong," KM assured him.

"That's alright but there is another problem. After Waghle's case, we have been forbidden by WEE to bug our officers unless there is a written authorization from the Chief," Murthy said.

Waghle, a former Chief's principal staff officer, was an outlaw. He exercised power much beyond his brief, revelled in flouting rules and issuing unauthorized operational and administrative whips in the name of the Chief. He patronized lackeys and unleashed misplaced aspirations among them. The nemesis finally caught up with him when he organized bugging of rooms of two senior officers without proper authorization. A subsequent inquiry found him guilty and he was removed from service. The Director and two others junior employees of the Bugging Unit who had provided and planted the devices were punished with substantial reduction in their salary.

"I can request Jeev to talk to you if you think that I am acting like Waghle," Kamath said.

"No, that's fine. But we need to be careful."

Murthy devised an ingenious plan to deploy the bugs. Since it was not considered safe to steal the duplicate key from the CCF(Central Control Facility) with so many officers manning the area round the clock, he took the Agency's senior locksmith into confidence to do the job. Once the security staff inspected the room and was gone, the locksmith successfully disengaged the security latch of Ravi's room by repeatedly manipulating its lever, making way for the technicians to enter the room at 9 pm. It took the technicians nearly seven hours to conceal the devices at places where Ravi usually sat to engage his colleagues in conversation. Three more bugs were pasted at vantage points in the ceiling to pick up the conversation from anywhere in the room. Subsequently, all bugs were connected through a complicated circuitry to the lines going to the Nerve Centre.

That night Kamath stayed behind in the office. He was apprehensive that guards who moved around the floors of the building could intercept the technicians and raise hell for tampering with the suspect's room. Since Murthy's boys were essentially academicians by temperament, they might fumble to come up with believable alibis at the right moment, he assessed. Therefore, he decided to be available at short notice. He went out of the building, brifly, at 11 pm and returned after having food at a nearby roadside restaurant. At twenty minutes past 4 am, his mobile shrieked, pulling him out of deep slumber.

"The mission is over. We will take another ten minutes to wind up and leave," Murthy said.

"Was it a smooth ride?" asked KM, feeling rather groggy.

"Absolutely. No one at any of the three exit doors checked why we were leaving so early in the morning, what we were doing inside the building, and whether we had any specific permission to stay overnight," Murthy reported.

"I am not surprised. If officers cannot secure their information, why blame poor guards for not securing the building," KM said.

Day 23

In the morning, the floor security assistant unlocked Ravi's room and switched on the lights. Fifteen minutes later, sweepers came to clean the floor and dust the furniture, phones, photocopier, and the television. At 10 am, Ravi walked in followed by his PA and driver.

"The bugs are working fine. We can hear what is being spoken in the room," Murthy reported to KM from the NC. Within minutes, KM rushed to the NC, put on the audio gears and started listening to the conversation. He heard Ravi asking Miss Mukta Sethi, his desk officer, to show him the fortnightly report before it went for printing. Next, he dictated a note to his PA, requesting for Chief's approval to visit the US for three weeks to attend his daughter's engagement ceremony. Later on, he asked his peon, Inder, to get the passbook updated and spoke to a clerk to find out the status of his pending tour bills.

"Sir, the bugs have become operational. If you have time please come to the NC to hear the suspect talk," he requested Jeev in excitement.

"I am in a meeting. Convey my appreciation to Murthy for doing a good job," Jeev said.

Day 24–26

In two days, Ravi's conversation filled fourteen tapes. His approach to extracting information was simple. He would vaguely raise the topic and leave it to the desk officers concerned to respond. Since his queries were not specific, the desk officers would rattle off everything that they knew. In between, Ravi interjected with expressions like, *is it so or that's a good point.*

The bugs near the television and the coffee table recorded Ravi's interactions most prolifically. It was easier now to identify officers inside the room and make out the subjects that were being discussed. But there was still no clue whether the suspect noted down the points that he gathered from officers or simply chatted. To KM's bitter disappointment, the taped deliberations frequently sounded disjointed and subdued by a chorus of jarring voices. He had to strain to hear the conversation due to persisting interference of the TV's sound with the transmission of audio signals. Being a trained operator, Ravi always chose to sit closer to the TV and routinely increased the volume before initiating a conversation. Consequently, queries and responses emanating from this area lost clarity. KM brought this snag to Jeev's notice when he went to brief the latter on the result of the listening devices.

"Then how do you plan to deal with it?" Jeev lobbed the problem back in KM's court.

"Sir, I have spoken to Murthy. He says he can handle it."

"That's reassuring," Jeev said and called PS to come in to take dictation.

KM ignored the hint to leave and continued to sit.

"Sir, I have to show you a paper that I came across in one of the old files," he said.

"What is it about?" Jeev asked.

"Sir, Mr Karthik Pillai had e-mailed his assessment on the notorious Aldrich Ames case of 1994 to the then Chief, in which he suggested to put in place a mechanism for watching employees, who had traits and potentials of Ames to double cross the Agency. It is a very illustrative read. I thought you might be interested in glancing through it," said KM.

"What was our reaction?" Jeev inquired.

"The office note is silent on what action was taken. The Chief merely signed and sent it through his deputy to my predecessor where it was lying in layers of dust. No one seems to have read it or even acknowledged it," KM said.

"Mr Pillai should have realized that he was entering into a dialogue with a Chief who was known for his addiction to superficialities. Someone should have told him that his righteous sense of security had no takers in the Agency. But the least that the Chief could have done was to acknowledge. Mr Pillai certainly didn't deserve a contemptuous silence for his labour," Jeev reacted in disgust. Then he put the paper in his briefcase.

"I will read it before I sleep. That's generally the time when I absorb the essence of writings most," he added in a lighter vein.

The opening page of Pillai's mail had a summary of the case. Ames, a 52-year-old operative of the CIA, was arrested by the FBI on 21 February 1994 on charges of conspiracy to commit espionage on behalf of Russia. He had been a CIA employee for 31 years and mostly served in directorate of operations. His espionage activities began in April 1985 and he was believed to have received substantial payments in lieu of passing information. His wife, Maria del Rosario Casas Ames, was also arrested for the same offence. A CIA team that was sent to Moscow to speak with the Russian Intelligence Services, returned empty handed.

In two subsequent pages, Pillai highlighted the conspicuous traits of Ames. In his concluding remarks, he suggested that the CEU must always keep employees of the Agency under their observation to find out whether they suffer from the following behavioural oddities of Ames. He also wanted the CEU to be engaged in prior consultations before assigning officers to sensitive jobs. Dwelling on the flaws in Ames' persona, he wrote:

(a) Ames and his wife had expensive living habits and lived well beyond their means. For years, CIA took no notice of large expenditures incurred by an employee making annually less than $70,000.
(b) Ames entertained his colleagues and friends in a style that was beyond the means of an employee at the level of his seniority.
(c) He had willingly let himself be used by Moscow.
(d) He exposed the identities of many CIA moles.
(e) He was an alcoholic.
(f) He used to take details of sensitive CIA moles in Moscow, out of his office on his laptop.
(g) Over a dozen middle and senior level officers of the CIA knew all this for years but did not alert the Director, CIA.

Jeev smiled as he finished reading Pillai's mail.

"What is it that you are smiling at? I thought official papers made for very drab reading," Mani remarked as Jeev put the paper inside an envelope and switched off the light.

"You know Mr Pillai and his incorrigible sense of dark humour," Jeev said, trying hard to avoid telling her the real reason.

"I know but that cannot be the reason," Mani reacted, turning over to her side to sleep.

Day 27

"I read Mr Pillai's mail last night and felt as if he was writing about Ravi Mohan," Jeev said as he returned the mail folder to KM. "Look at the uncanny similarities. Ravi also has expensive living habits and entertains friends and colleagues in style. He enjoys his drinks and I won't be surprised if he is an alcoholic. At least one senior officer, who was apprised of Ravi's double crossing, kept quiet. Several middle- and junior-level officers who have known for years about his unusual interest in their information have opted out of reporting the matter either to the Chief or to their respective supervisors. The only real difference between the two is that our Ames is not computer savvy nor does he have a laptop to work on," he added.

"Sir, do you think the CIA could be replicating its bitter experience with Ames on the suspect?" KM asked.

"You never know. We will soon find that out. Anyway, when is Murthy going to remove the glitches in the bugs?" Jeev inquired.

"He has kept his team ready and may try to do the job tonight," KM said.

Murthy did not anticipate that his task would run into complications from unexpected quarters. The key to the main door provided by KM turned out to be the wrong one at the last moment. The right key could be accessed from the CCF only around midnight by one of KM's contacts. As part of a routine drill, the security latch that Murthy had opened in the earlier break-in was also changed by the security staff a day earlier. With no options left, Murthy plucked out the lock assembly and finally entered the room at 1.30 am. After the job was done, he placed the lock back in the slot under controlled light, restored the door key to the CCF and walked out of the building without any fuss.

Day 28

The floor security assistant opened the suspect's room in the morning with some difficulty. He had to rotate the key four to five times in the latch hole. Later on when Ravi tried to open the door, the latch got stuck. He rang up the maintenance office to send someone to rectify the problem urgently. While he was sitting with Miss Sethi, a technician came to set the latch right.

Meanwhile, KM joined Murthy in the NC to check the efficacy of the new set of listening devices pasted during the previous night. To their relief the bugs were transmitting conversations flawlessly after cancelling outside noises. Of the several calls made by the suspect during the day, the one in which Ravi was heard talking to a representative of Xerox India Co. put KM on alert. The suspect inquired if someone could come over to his residence to repair a shredder with cross cutting blades. He mentioned that he had been using the machine for the last one and half years and that it was covered under an international warranty. The company representative explained that the warranty was not applicable to India and gave a rough estimate of Rs 3000 as the repair cost. Ravi casually said that money was not an issue so long as the shredder was repaired at the earliest.

The call raised a number of questions. What was the suspect doing with a cross-cutting shredder in his house and why was he so desperate to get it fixed as soon as possible and at any price? Later in the day, KM shared his misgivings with Jeev.

"You are missing out two more needles in the haystack," Jeev pointed out. "First, the suspect has been using the shredder for the past eighteen months—a period that roughly coincides with his presence at the Headquarters. It implies that he has been shredding documents ever since he returned from his last assignment in Belgium. Second, the machine has an international warranty. So, either it was handed over to Ravi in Belgium or it was made available to him in Delhi by someone who has a stake in his dubious dealings. But let us first find out what is it that he needs to regularly destroy," Jeev said.

"Sir," KM reacted involuntarily. He collected the papers and left. "Jeev is beating around the bush," he thought. "Every time you go to him, he has one more task ready for you to pursue. Ravi may be destroying classified papers at home but is it not true that most of us regularly shred photocopies and draft notes of classified nature at home," he wondered.

Day 29

KM spent the whole day in the NC reading and listening to transcripts of the suspect's calls in the hope of stumbling over one piece of evidence that would conclusively implicate the suspect in espionage. Later in the evening, he picked up a few interesting transcripts and barged into Jeev's room unannounced.

"What's the matter?" Jeev enquired, miffed at KM's sudden appearance.

"Sir, you must read these transcripts. I have suitably edited them and given my comments, wherever necessary," he said.

Jeev opened the folder and cursorily glanced through the transcripts. Before he began to read, he wanted to know the significance of the numbers marked against each passage. KM explained that it was the combination of letter and a number, for easy retrieval of the tape and the starting point of the conversation, should there be a need to verify the accuracy of contents.

The first transcript was marked T24.

[The suspect inquires innocuously from General Hari Vaishnav, Head of the Military Division (HMD), about the latter's Paris visit. In doing so, he appears to have touched a sensitive chord with the General.]

Gen. Hari: I was not allowed to go to Paris. Actually, my visit was for UK. But on the way back, I wanted to meet an arms dealer, based in Paris. I had cultivated him when I was posted in France as Defence Attaché. He had contacts who dabbled in clandestine arms shipment to rogue elements in Pakistan, Afghanistan, Bangladesh, Sri Lanka, Philippines, and Thailand. He also regularly fed information on illegal arms shopping from European and Chinese arms markets by subversive groups. I had, therefore, requested the Chief to let me meet the source, primarily to revive the contact and ascertain if he could still be useful.

Ravi: I don't think the Agency ever had such a critical source.

HV: That's the reason the Chief approved my proposal and personally gave me a brief. Subsequently, the office booked my tickets and made hotel reservations in Paris. But just when I was to board the flight at Heathrow for Paris, Bipul Prasad, the deputy chief, called and instructed me to return to Delhi on the first flight. When I came here I found that Prasad was upset that my Paris tour had been approved by the Chief without his knowledge. So he decided to cut the trip short on his own.

R: I know Prasad. He expects obedience of a slave from his officers.

HV: You know, this is the third time I have been treated so shabbily by this man and I feel like going back to the Army.

R: Did you discuss this with the Chief?

HV: I did but he only said that he would look into it.

R: Please don't lose your cool. This department has many things to offer. You have to be little patient. You will regret it if you take any decision in anger. In the Gita it is written that anger demonizes a man and forces him to choose irrational options.

HV: I know. And, thanks for coffee.

"I think I underestimated Ravi's talent for exploiting his colleagues' disappointment," Jeev remarked. "But what amazes me is how the General could fall into the trap so easily to reveal sensitive information about the source," he said.

"If you peruse the other transcripts, you will notice that the suspect also knows how to be persuasive or demanding and how to beat a hasty retreat in case officers refuse to oblige," KM pointed out.

Jeev picked up other transcripts and began to read.

T26
[The suspect asks a desk officer of the Special Cell, why copies of the Bureau's reports on activities of diplomats are not being routinely marked to him. The officer apologizes and promises to put him on the mail list from next week.

Suddenly, without any provocation, the desk officer goes overboard and inquires whether Ravi would also have interest in other reports of the Bureau.

Ravi: If it is not too much of a hassle please show me the list of reports that the Bureau sends. I will mark the ones that I need. Actually, only a few Bureau reports interest me.

Desk officer: Sir, for the list I shall require a written authorization from the deputy chief.

[Ravi immediately scales down his request and reverts to his original demand.]

T29
[The suspect is at his persuasive best while speaking to Praveen Shah, a desk officer and custodian of personal particulars of the Agency's operatives abroad.]

Ravi: I don't know whether I should ask you for this favour but I am under tremendous pressure from my family members.

Praveen Shah: What is it, sir?

Ravi: My niece, Archana, is working in Kabul for USAID and we haven't heard anything from her lately. You must be aware of last week's bomb attack near the UN office. Her parents are worried about her welfare since she hasn't called them till now. If you can give me the telephone number of Saket Athawle of our Kabul unit, I can request him to find out whether she is safe.

Shah: It's a genuine request. Please note down the number.

[Shah reads out the numbers.]

"Everyone seems so eager to impress Ravi with his share of information," Jeev sighed, handing the papers back to KM and complimented him for his pithy comments and concise editing of the transcripts.

"Sir, I didn't want you to waste your valuable time in the suspect's inane chit-chats," KM said.

"That's very thoughtful of you. Editing is never easy," Jeev contended. "The danger of not sticking to the original always lurks behind and there are more chances of getting swayed by temptation to interpolate your own version. In fact, your edited stuff is so neat that I got suspicious about its authenticity," he said.

"Sir, I have not added or deleted one word from my side," KM asserted.

"You don't have to defend yourself," Jeev said.

Day 31

Two days later, Kamath put up tapes and original transcripts for Jeev's perusal but held back the folder containing his comments and notes. He was still upset with Jeev's comments on the accuracy of his edited version of intercepts. Jeev had a quick look at the material and returned. "From the next time onwards, mark the transcripts that you think are important and bring the tapes only if I ask for it," he said.

KM realized that Jeev had seen through his petty display of ego and promptly made amends. He pulled out a folder from the briefcase and handed it to Jeev. "It has a set of edited transcripts which I thought might interest you. I have also tried to summarize the contents of a few tapes and offered my comments as objectively as I could," he said.

What Jeev subsequently read was deeply disturbing.

T47
In calls to different desk officers, the suspect would ask for copies of the note sent to the government on latest developments in Kashmir, Pakistan-North Korea nuclear nexus, South Block's latest position on boundary dispute with China, Dalai Lama's views on the return of Tibetan refugees to Lhasa, CBMs proposed by India to improve relations with Beijing and common areas of cooperation on security issues identified by India, China and Russia.

In Ashish, the desk officer for Europe, the suspect found an eager collaborator. In one call, he confided to Ashish that because of his advancing age, he experienced difficulty in remembering details and that's the reason why he was in the habit of noting down what he discussed with his colleagues and requested for copies of their reports.

T54
Seven calls later, the suspect fanned Ashish's ego, "I hear that you have devised an excellent system of cataloguing the source particulars for quick access and updating the data on a regular basis," he said and asked if Ashish could show him the format on his desktop.

T61
The suspect thanked Ashish for "letting him copy it". Encouraged by the officer's unfettered responsiveness, the suspect employed a different ploy to extract information about the Agency's assets in Europe.

"Your format was of great help," he threw the bait, "but my officers were unable to feed the data. I don't know if you can bring along the source particulars of one of the European stations and show me how to do it," he said.

"I have no problem, sir. To you, I can make available the source profile of all European stations." Ashish promised.

Spot Report 439
The same day, watchers reported that Ashish went with the suspect for lunch at Hotel Oberoi.

U6
The suspect lured an officer from the scientific division to brief him on nuclear developments in Pakistan. "It's too technical for me to fully comprehend," he said and requested the officer to send the talking points so that he could properly brief his North Korean source.

P14

To a desk officer dealing with Sri Lanka, who initially expressed reluctance to share inputs, the suspect used a mild threat. "The Chief has asked for an inclusive report on LTTE's terrorist network in South East Asia and suggested that I also incorporate your inputs," he said. The officer promptly acquiesced.

Jeev took his eyes off from the note and leaned back on the chair. He told KM that he would go through the remaining transcripts the next day since he had an official dinner to attend at 8 pm and it was already 7.45 pm.

"Sir, you must listen to this," KM pointed to a particular tape. "It's about his impending visit to Patiala," he said and played that tape.

[After an initial exchange of pleasantries with Naheed Khan, Patiala Police Chief, the suspect came to the point.]

Ravi: I plan to visit Patiala on Thursday and return to Delhi the next day.

Khan: You are most welcome, sir.

Ravi: I have to meet someone there in the afternoon. I will reach Ambala by Shatabdi Express in executive class and from there, go to Patiala by road. I don't know if you can arrange a vehicle for this part of the journey.

Khan: Please don't worry. I will depute an officer with a vehicle to receive you at the railway station. He will escort you wherever you want to go in the city. His name is Inspector Amarjeet and he will be in uniform. Do you want me to reserve a room for you in the police officers mess?

Ravi: That's not necessary. I have already booked a suite in Hotel Narain Continental.

Khan: Sir, please dine with me at my residence on Thursday. If it is fine with you, I would like to invite a few local district officials, prominent politicians, and businessmen to join the party.

Ravi: I will, of course, have dinner but keep it private.
Khan: I understand.
Ravi: Thanks.

"Why do you think Ravi is going to Patiala and who could be this *someone*," Jeev asked as KM was taking the tape out from the recorder.

"Sir, I know what you are hinting at but I doubt if the suspect would go all the way to Patiala to meet his handler, unless it is part of a very intricate plan to obtain briefs at places outside Delhi?" KM argued.

"Has he applied for leave?" Jeev inquired.

"He doesn't generally."

"Please cover the visit," Jeev said.

However, KM had reservations. He insisted that being total strangers to Patiala, his watchers would get unnecessarily exposed.

"I will take that risk. When Ravi says that he has some work in the city, he may actually be referring to his proposed meeting with his running officer. If he had to travel for personal reasons, there was no need for him to duck his seniors. It is obvious he has something to hide during the visit," Jeev averred.

"Sir, it's not unusual for our officers to bunk work," said KM. "In the past I reported numerous instances of officers' absence without leave to your predecessors but they took no notice of these lapses. They probably believed that the Agency's interests would be served better in the absence of its freeloaders. Trust me, Ravi is not going to apply for leave," he said.

"Do you suggest that Bhan, his supervisor, won't notice the absence of his senior analyst for two days from the office?" Jeev asked.

"Precisely. The suspect, in any case, is not holding an operational desk that would require Mr Bhan to check on him frequently. If somehow, his absence gets noticed, his PA Sharma will instantly cook up an alibi. And, if the matter is urgent, Mr Bhan can always ask for Miss Sethi who is more pleasant and articulate to interact with," KM explained.

"You sometimes carry your cynicism to an extreme," Jeev remarked. "You think you can bunk and I won't know?" he asked.

KM did not react. Instead, he reminded Jeev that he was running late for dinner.

"I will skip it. It is already 10.30.pm. It won't be proper to barge in so late," Jeev said.

Seeing Kamath leave, Jeev marvelled what made him work so hard regardless of how contemptuously others treated him. KM derived no support from the Chief or Jeev's predecessors to secure the Agency from its marauding officers. Over the years, he had acquired a reputation of being petulant and Satan's chosen man to hound everyone. No wonder, he failed miserably to enforce punctuality in officers despite his relentless efforts. He produced volumes of surveillance photographs to identify those who habitually clocked in late at work and bunked office regularly but his seniors paid no heed. Most officers derisively joked that if KM had his way, he would turn the Agency into a Guantanamo Bay. Others simply lived in dread of him and kept a safe distance.

KM's alleged madness lay in his insistence to ensure that employees observed what he would define as "security of information, material and premises." Naturally, delinquents begrudged his missionary zeal and thought he was paranoid. Brigadier Vishnu Kant, who joined the Agency on deputation from the Armed Forces, felt that KM's security regime was too suffocating. He found it ridiculous that private taxis would not be permitted to drop him daily inside the building. He was also offended by KM's insistence on obtaining prior permission every time he left on his foreign jaunts to buy fixtures for his newly-built mansion. It was inconceivable for the Brigadier to submerge his starched identity in the Agency's faded ambience in the name of security and frowned when KM denied him permission to display his nameplate outside the door, announcing his name, designations and job description. He found the Agency's dimly lit corridors and drooping shoulders of its officers depressing and the disorderly walk of its employees extremely funny. He actually echoed views of most of his Army mates but unlike him, they preferred to swim with the security ethos of the Agency, hoping for rainy days to cash in. Somehow, loyalty was never Brigadier Vishnu's forte. He fiercely bit the hands that fed him and barked at those who comforted him.

Jeev knew that KM suffered, albeit ironically, from a flawed judgement of his role in the prevailing security environment. KM erroneously believed that his reports were the last words on the conduct of an employee and his evidence did not require a second look for punishing wrongdoers. But what happened was just the opposite of what he expected. His reports invariably found their way to the dustbins in his seniors' rooms. The Agency's penchant for condoning gross misconduct and keeping serious financial irregularities under the carpet used to upset him to no end. He often toyed with the idea of quitting when action was not taken against those who falsely claimed secret allowances, surreptitiously hosted foreigners of dubious background, and amassed wealth out of procurements and source payments. But he ploughed on in the hope of securing the Agency from its saboteurs. What hit him hardest was when his noting against potential spies did not evoke any response from the leadership. No wonder, he found it hard to put his heart and soul in Ravi Mohan's case and waited anxiously for half a nudge from Jeev to call off the investigation.

But Jeev was not ready to allow his protégé to fold up. "You can't let your vigil falter," he would often remind, "regardless of how lonely you may feel in your hot seat." In keeping KM afloat, Jeev wondered whether he was exploiting KM to project his own image as a leader who made a difference.

Jeev returned home to a frosty welcome. Mani was watching the 11 pm news roundup in the living room. They had a quiet dinner, followed by a brief stroll in the lawn. Jeev was surprised that Mani did not accuse him of being insensitive for not informing her in case he had to stay out of the dinner.

"You must be upset with me. I am really sorry," Jeev politely said.

"Not really. I have long ceased to expect any genuine concern from the Agency's sole conscience keeper," she said, as she stepped inside the house.

Day 32

Around noon, KM came to persuade Jeev not to insist on sending CEU watchers to cover the suspect's Patiala visit. He pointed out that except for two junior field officers others were committed on different surveillance duties.

"Alright, then you instruct your boys to follow the suspect up to the New Delhi Railway station, just in case Ravi meets a stranger or someone joins him to travel up to Patiala," Jeev suggested.

A call from the Chief interrupted their conversation. Jeev suddenly left the room, asking KM to wait for him to return.

"How is your suspect doing?" Wasan quipped as soon as Jeev pulled a chair to sit.

"It is worrying," Jeev said.

"Why, what happened?"

"Ravi is seeking inputs on our sources in Europe and copies of Bureau's reports on diplomats' activities from the special cell. He has also obtained a note on the Pakistan-North Korea nuclear/missile programme and details of telephone numbers of our officers in Afghanistan. He has been using an imported shredder in his house for last 18 months and it is so important to him that he is willing to spend any amount on keeping it functional," Jeev informed.

"Why don't you confront him with these evidences and ask him to come out clean. How long can you go on chasing windmills?" Wasan asked in exasperation.

"He may not tell us the whole truth," Jeev said. "Besides, we have no idea why he is asking for source particulars and for whom. In the name of evidence, we have his conversations with our officers that indicate only his inappropriate use of restrictive security."

"Then what's the point in letting the investigation linger," Wasan asked.

"Raj and KM also hold the same view," Jeev remarked. They stopped debating further as the staff officer entered to remind the chief that the visitor had arrived and was waiting to be ushered in.

Back in his room, Jeev informed KM that he might call off the investigation since it was the collective will of everyone involved with the case. KM suspected that something had gone horribly wrong in Jeev's meeting with the Chief, provoking him to say the unthinkable.

"You keep complaining that it is a wasteful drain on your resources, while Raj believes that it is sacrilegious to suspect an officer of Ravi's seniority of being an espionage agent. And now the Chief thinks that I am chasing windmills," Jeev said.

"But, sir, is it not a fact that we are making no headway?" KM asked. "Ravi is actually doing nothing unusual. If we investigate other officers, 80 percent of them will be found guilty of making suspicious inquiries and volunteering unauthorized information to their colleagues," he explained, apparently misreading Jeev's contrived show of despair.

"It is still a mystery to me why we are able to hear calls only from known persons. There has to be someone for whom Ravi is eliciting information with such persistence. I wish we could be a little more patient for the investigation to provide the answer," Jeev expressed.

KM got the message. He left soon thereafter, wondering why Jeev was so relentless in pursuit of the suspect. Was there a background to it? But Jeev was never known to carry animus, he spoke to himself.

Day 33

Jeev paid a surprise visit to the NC to hasten the proceedings. He saw Kamath and Kak listening intently to a repeat of live transmission recorded earlier in the morning while two technicians were busy hearing a pre-recorded tape on the speaker phone. One of them was also simultaneously dictating contents to a PA and the other was making sure that not a word was missed out.

"I wanted to see how the NC works. It's really cool and business like," Jeev said as everyone present in the room scrambled to rise. He pulled a chair and sat down. He suggested to Kak to stay behind when everyone started leaving.

"How do you explain your frequent absence from the desk to Venugopal?" he asked Kak in a lighter vein.

"Sir, he has many more lucrative things to worry about," Kak replied but did not elaborate on his grouse.

"Sir, we were listening to an interesting call intercept," KM interrupted, denying Kak a chance to reel off his litany of grievances. "It is yet to be transcribed. But if you have time, we would like to play it for you," he suggested.

"It's fine with me," Jeev said and put on the ear phones to listen.

> Ravi:"Kamath, this is Ravi Mohan."
> Kamath:"Morning, sir, what can I do for you?"
> Ravi:"It is rather disturbing. Is it possible for you to come over for five minutes?"
> KM:"I am in the midst of preparing a report for Mr Jeev. You know, you can't take chances with him. I can only come in the afternoon."
> Ravi:"Actually, someone called me yesterday twice within a span of 15 minutes. He said I was under watch. When I asked him to identify himself, he put the phone down. Subsequently, I traced the number. It is listed against a public booth in Jorbagh market."

KM: "It could be the mischief of someone whom you may have rubbed the wrong way. But you are such a kind man and so helpful to everyone."

Ravi: "Even Gandhi had Godse."

KM: "You put it so beautifully. Anyway, next time if you get a call like this, let me know."

The call ends.

An eerie silence prevailed in the room. Jeev removed the ear phones and kept thinking for a while. Obviously, the surveillance was not being conducted professionally and if it carried on like this, the investigation was likely to get exposed. Jeev could not let this happen. "You have to tell your boys to be more discreet while watching Ravi's movements," he admonished.

"Sir, the location of the suspect's apartment is such that one can easily spot the extended presence of the same vehicle and the same set of watchers," KM tried to reason. "The Unit has only three vehicles, earmarked for such operations and deploying new faces every day is not feasible due to acute shortage of hands," he explained.

"This is not the time for stock taking of our resources," Jeev rebuffed. "You can hire as many private vehicles as you require. But impress on your watchers to avoid being needlessly aggressive. I don't want to see them burnt out very early in the investigation. It is our sheer luck that Ravi has not been able to detect the watch even after the caller's warning. He is either supremely confident of his modus operandi or he is simply stupid to believe that his activities are too normal to evoke any suspicion," Jeev pointed out.

KM did not respond. Instead, he requested Kak to go out and see if the vendor could serve three cups of coffee. Then he moved on to more juicy stuff. "Sir, Kak mentioned that General Dayal was badmouthing you over your role in the procurement of some secret communication project," he said.

"But I barely know him," Jeev replied.

"General's grouse is that you directed ND Swamy, the Cyber Safety expert, to trash his proposal for procuring hardware for US$ 1.2 million. He also goes around saying that you instigated the Financial Advisor to oppose his pet project on the ground that the concept was technically outdated and procurement procedures were being short circuited at a break-neck pace," said KM.

"What does Kak have to say to this?" Jeev probed.

"He says that all predecessors of Dayal looted the Agency in the name of procurement of equipment so that they could live comfortably thereafter. The General had also come looking for El-Dorado but did not reckon that you would be such a spoilsport," KM said.

"But with the Chief and the Deputy on his side, what was the problem in getting his paying projects through," Jeev replied with half a smile.

"Sir, the problem was you. The General believes that nothing moves in the Agency without your consent," KM said.

"I feel flattered. Someone should go and tell Mani this," Jeev laughed. With Kak and coffee nowhere in sight, he got up, shook hands with KM, and left.

Later that evening KM worked out details of additional deployment of fourteen officers to cover activities of Ravi and his wife on video cameras. It was to ensure that in case watchers missed out something because of fatigue or traffic congestion, the continuous video recording filled in the void. The teams were provided with private vehicles to hide their easy identification and directed to take up positions from next day morning.

Day 35

The reinforcement of surveillance measures brought no respite from mounting disappointment. The elusive running officer or the courier of the suspect's reports were nowhere in sight. However, Ravi's reach to officers, within and outside the

Agency, remained as wide and his interest in subjects as varied as before. Officers continued to volunteer information with abandon. While a few of them up to the rank of Directors were a complete giveaway, those handling critical operational desks showed restraint in discussing their work but did not find anything wrong in having free lunch with the suspect. In view of the repetitive nature of evidences, KM decided to plead with Jeev one more time to close the investigation.

"Sir, we have done whatever we could to crack this case but we are going nowhere," KM said when he went to show the surveillance reports to Jeev.

"You can't really say that," Jeev snapped. "We still have no idea how he disposes of the information and reports that he gathers from his colleagues and takes them out of the building. Perhaps a static video surveillance mounted to cover activities around his room and the entrance to the hallway can throw some light on his visitors and how he conducts himself while arriving and leaving the building. I am not very optimistic about the outcome of this exercise but we must exhaust all our options before we quit."

KM took his time to respond. He sensed that Jeev was in no mood to back off and there was no sign that even if static cameras produced zilch, Jeev would not come up with yet another plan of action. He presumed he had no choice but to play along.

"Sir, I will discuss this issue with the experts and report to you by tomorrow," he finally said.

"I will wait for your call."

"Sir, I have since got some inputs on the shredder," KM mentioned.

"What do they indicate?"

"Nothing much. It's a Xerox Company machine. The suspect paid Rs 2300 in cash for its repairs by the company's Daryaganj service centre," KM informed.

"I see."

"I had also sent a watcher to inspect the daily trash disposed from the suspect's house. It had no trace of shredded pieces of official documents," KM added

"That's a smart piece of work," Jeev complimented. "I may be wrong but sometimes I get a feeling that your heart is not fully in this operation and you are dragging on in deference to my insistence. I hope the results of the static video surveillance will lift up my chief investigator's spirits," he said.

Walking back to the NC, KM involuntarily turned left near the lift and took the staircase to go down to the fifth floor. He gently knocked at the door and pushed it open. Sukumaran, desk officer in the video surveillance unit, was talking to someone on the internal phone. Once Suku was through with the call, KM explained the purpose of his visit. Suku explained that it would be a logistical nightmare to mount static cameras within the office premises. Moreover, since the main entry and exit points were manned round the clock by guards and frequented by hordes of employees, it would be impossible to have a clear view of the suspect's precise movement at the time of alighting or boarding the vehicle at the porch. Similarly, at all times during the day, employees who herded in the corridor were most likely to block the line of sight of cameras, making it difficult to continuously capture the visitors as they went in and came out of the suspect's room.

"So what do I tell Mr Jeev?" KM asked.

"I am not saying I don't want to give it a try but you must be aware of the related hazards. You may also encounter an enormous clerical challenge. Since cameras are going to record indiscriminately, it will be a daunting task for you to edit the video footages," Suku warned.

"I am sure we can handle this," KM said and inquired whether it would be possible to place the cameras during the night.

"It's already 4.30 pm. I doubt if I can assemble technicians, cameras and accessories in the next one hour before the office closes. Why don't we plan it for tomorrow?" Suku proposed.

"The situation is rather serious." KM tried to dramatize the urgency in order to force Suku to get going. "Every minute is critical for the safety of the Agency's secrets. We are virtually sitting on knife's edge and running out of time," he said.

"I will try," said Suku yielding. "Give me an hour to organize."

Later that night, Sukumaran and his boys took five hours to install and test the video cameras. At 2 am, he reported to KM that the assignment was over. Fifteen minutes later, Jeev's RIT rang up. Struggling to keep awake, he reached for the receiver.

"Sir, I am Kamath. I am sorry for waking you up at this odd hour."

"Any mishap?" Jeev inquired.

"Sir, cameras have been placed at pre-designated locations and wired to NC through air ducts. They are working fine. The relief was so overwhelming that I couldn't keep this news to myself." KM sounded apologetic.

"That's okay. I hope it doesn't turn out to be a damp squib," Jeev said.

Day 39

The results of the static video cameras were a dampener. They merely confirmed what the phone tapping had been reporting about officers' identity and the information that they shared with Ravi. However, one particular input caught KM's fancy. The suspect came to the office in the morning and left in the evening holding a dark brown leather bag in his hand, while his peon carried a briefcase, issued by the office and an Adidas sports bag.

Meanwhile, the mobile video surveillance continued to capture disquieting details. Ravi was seen meeting a former Agency Chief, two serving major generals of the Indian Army and a Brigadier, a member of the National Security Council Secretariat and Chairman of the NTRO but what transpired or exchanged was not known. A few inputs brought some cheers initially but dissipated in no time. For example, the surveillance unit reported that a foreigner came out of a white Innova (DL 2CAA 2919) at 9.50 am, went straight inside Ravi's apartment and came out after an hour. Twenty minutes later Ravi left for the office. For the next two days, the same car and the same foreigner visited the suspect's apartment. And, whenever he came, the suspect was always inside the house and left only after the foreigner was gone. The excitement to have at last found a clue to the handler evaporated as reports of the field inquiry poured in.

The vehicle was registered in the name of International Ocean Shipping Pvt Ltd, 75, Sunder Nagar and owned by Captain Vishal Kapoor. The foreigner was visiting India to explore the possibility of expanding his business in partnership with Jeetu Prakash, company's consultant for overseas operations and Vijita's younger brother, who lived in the same building. Ravi who knew the foreigner from his Nairobi days, kept himself available in his apartment to facilitate their discussion and to ensure that his wife also had a share in the business.

Shuffling through the evidence, KM concluded that it was time for Jeev to stop prevaricating but did not know how to persuade his boss to drop the surveillance. Then he hit upon a novel idea.

"Sir, I have prepared an updated note," KM began cagily when he went to brief Jeev in the afternoon. "It brings out the efforts, put in so far in this operation and the evidence that we have collected to prove the suspect's wilful breach of security guidelines. You may like to show it to the Chief to find out his reaction," he said while passing on the note to Jeev along with a folder containing latest photos, video CDs, audio transcripts, and tapes.

"It is premature to submit such reports to Wasan. We still don't know what Ravi is doing inside the Club or his room," Jeev reacted.

But KM was not convinced. "Sir, the chances of getting any feedback on either count are very remote," said KM.

"You don't have to be so despondent. I have already spoken to someone for getting us an access to the club. In the meantime, I suggest you discuss with Sukumaran the feasibility of organizing a video coverage of Ravi's activities inside his room," Jeev said.

KM was piqued at the indifference with which Jeev treated his report. He also felt hurt that Jeev continued to pile up his unreasonable demands when he knew that his health was failing. Lately, KM had developed symptoms of ventricular tachycardia and complained of chest pain, light headedness and shortness of breath. Since he was an acute diabetic, his response to medication was very slow. Being a chain smoker for umpteen years, complications from restrictive lung disease had also begun surfacing, making it difficult for him to breathe normally. On top of it, the stress of conducting the investigation under Jeev's unrelenting scrutiny only made his clinical condition worse.

*

To be fair to Jeevnathan, he had been thinking of giving Kamath a break and entrusting the investigation, in the interim, to Ajay. But Ajay was a time server. Though discreet and reasonably competent, Jeev had doubts if Ajay could lead the team of watchers, surveillance units and technical experts with the same commitment. From day one Ajay wanted to play it safe. Any self-respecting officer in his place would have protested why his deputy was trusted to run the operation. But he was made of malleable stuff and was happy watching developments from the sidelines because he did not believe in being foolishly brave in accepting responsibilities unless they were thrust on him. He seldom offered suggestions on contentious issues and whenever he did, he put across his views politely with lots of 'ifs' and 'buts'. He was intelligent enough to quickly read which way the decision was swaying and came up with arguments to help that decision fructify. Ajay was an ideal subordinate and a quintessential bureaucrat. He consciously displayed a lack of drive to go beyond the script, argued his case with circumspection and made everyone feel important.

In his fragile moments, Jeev would find enormous merit in Ajay's work ethics and wished he had qualities of his deputy and not doggedly pursued what he felt was right. What was the need to make an issue of a subject that did not affect him personally? And, how would it help his career progression if he talked back to his senior colleagues and ran them down for drafting reports badly and fudging information to mislead political leadership into taking wrong decisions, he debated with himself. But he just couldn't be the *tactful* subordinate.

No wonder, Jeev's courtship with troubles began very early in his career. He was barely three weeks in service when he openly called his supervisor corrupt and a moral disgrace. A highly colourful and loud Chief of Police threatened to cut his career short because Jeev would not allow the Chief's astrologer to continue occupying a lucrative piece of land belonging to a poor tribal. Similarly, he did not let a constitutional luminary carry his sweetheart to official functions and thereby bring the exalted office into disrepute. A glamorous politician almost lynched him with her invectives because he refused to commit security forces to capture electoral booths in her favour. Bent upon self-destruction, Jeev once wrote a furious rejoinder to his maverick boss, describing the latter as a hypocrite, a megalomaniac and a hated man, unworthy of loyalty. This was just when Jeev needed a good evaluation to pick up the next higher grade.

Over the years the urge to commit hara-kiri became more pronounced. Jeev trashed a report on the Naxal activities drafted after a great deal of sweat by Krishnan, an officer of the Bureau, who was endowed with a highly inflated ego and streaks of vengeance. Unconcerned of what Krishnan might do to his career, Jeev pointed out that statistics in the report were inadequate and randomly picked, its arguments were completely divorced from ground realities and recommendations were highly impractical. He claimed that since he had moved around in the affected areas for months, he knew exactly why the most committed among the Naxalites, the genuine sympathizers, criminals and the opportunists jelled together to create a heady cocktail that was exploding everywhere. But this whiz kid of the Bureau, who feasted on pampering and supreme reverence by his overawed colleagues, considered it an act of betrayal that someone could find his writing vacuous. Years of reading about Mao had made him imbibe intolerance to dissent and like the "Great Leader" he felled everyone by the wayside in hot pursuit of his personal ambitions.

But Jeev was not a learner. Like a man possessed, he opposed attempts by successive governments and their National Security Advisors to create a bizarre organization by mutilating an institution that had proved its worth both in times of wars and peace. He contested this calamitous move as if the government was acquiring his personal property for pittance. In the process, several colleagues of many years became his sworn enemies and the NSAs, his bête noire. In the end, he was a loser on all counts.

Jeev's DNA was actually his undoing. Successive Chiefs wouldn't let him handle sensitive desks because they considered him 'indiscreet and a loud mouth'. Actually, they feared that he would quickly dismantle the hype around the desk, ground huffy-puffy operators, and expose the so-called critical assets. An Agency chief who was all sugar and honey refused to assign Jeev to a European station, because he was not sure of the safety of the skeletons of sources in the cupboard. Another chief who made the pretence of treating him as a family member, branded him an "operational disaster" once he realized that Jeev would not allow bogus operations to flourish. No wonder, he came to be viewed as impossible to work with and unyielding. The general refrain was that Jeev was unable to see the larger picture and needlessly got enmeshed in petty issues like honest reporting, observance of rules and financial propriety.

Yet he survived the system, because of a few who admired his "idiosyncrasies". A god-fearing chief would cope with Jeev's dissenting notes with a condescending smile and disarm the latter completely with his infectious humility. Karthik Pillai whom Jeev admired for his immense courage of conviction, his imperious standard of personal integrity, and his pathological hatred for sycophancy, was a class apart. He had the rare quality of owing up his omissions and keeping his personal and professional matters in watertight compartments. Another officer who made a huge impact on Jeev was a man in dingy clothes, hanging loosely on his bony shoulders. He was gifted with a capacity to innovate the unthinkable and take aggressive operations beyond accepted frontiers. He was daring and but for the constraints under which he worked, he could pluck the moon and let no one know about it. He would be any intelligence agency's pride but not of his conceited seniors in the Agency. Outside the Agency, Jeev was fascinated by a diminutive, energetic and suave foreign service officer whose intellectual and financial integrity was staggering. He could take quick, out-of-box decisions, once he was convinced of the merits of the case. For him, serving national interest was paramount and he was willing to reach to anyone who served that interest. He was a far cry from hundred others in his own service who were greedy, unreal and vacuous.

Now that his retirement was imminent, the time had come to douse the fire in the belly. Why pursue Ravi's case when evidences were falling far behind his expectations and why not agree with the Chief to close the investigation, Jeev pondered. The Chief, Ajay, KM, the suspect, his collaborating colleagues and his handler would all be happy. The Agency would also be saved of public embarrassment and those who were waiting to pounce on the Agency for its poor housekeeping of secrets would have no claws to scratch. Manini for once, would also have no bite in her remarks.

"Sir, is anything bothering you?" KM asked, interrupting Jeev's reverie.

"Yes, I was trying to self-introspect why I am being so stubborn in pursuing this case and why can't I terminate the surveillance and let everyone live peacefully hereafter," Jeev remarked.

"Sir, you are perhaps upset with my occasional defeatist approach," KM remarked defensively.

"Don't take it personally," Jeev said.

"Sir, I won't let you down," KM assured.

"I know I can always count on you. But lately you have been looking tired and weary. I think you should take rest for a couple of weeks and come back fresh to set up video surveillance inside Ravi's room," Jeev said.

"I am absolutely fine, sir."

"Then let's meet tomorrow again at the same time." However, KM continued to sit.

"What's the matter?" Jeev inquired.

"We intercepted a few telephone calls last week. They indicate that the Chief has approved the suspect's inspection tour to Brunei in the first week of next month. Ravi has since sought permission to go to Bali on a private trip for three days, immediately after inspecting the unit. He has already made bookings for himself and his wife and reserved accommodation in Grand Hyatt, Bali. I suspect he will meet his handler at the resort for a detailed briefing. For all his good work over the years, he is probably being rewarded with a trip to this picturesque island," KM said.

"That's possible," Jeev remarked.

"Sir, covering his activities in Bali would be a tough call. We can't trust our man in Brunei. He comes out in the intercepted calls as extremely obligated to the suspect," KM voiced his concern.

"The tour is still three weeks away from now," Jeev said. "Meanwhile, try to locate a contact at the airport who can enable you to find out the contents in his checked-in baggage. We have to find out whether he is carrying source reports, etc., and gift for his operative. If the cut-out is in Delhi, he will surely meet the suspect before he leaves," Jeev averred.

*

Burdened with another of Jeev's brainwaves, KM went out to meet Sukumaran. When he raised the subject of monitoring suspect's activities inside the room live, Suku was taken aback. He clarified that it was not within his jurisdiction to install surveillance devices inside room of an Agency officer. "You will have to speak to Mr Kutty, director in-charge of video surveillance," he said. "But he may not be helpful unless he receives specific directions from Mr Panda, head of the technical division."

"Is it necessary to get Panda in the picture?" KM inquired.

"I think so. Kutty is a stickler for propriety. He won't agree to undertake any task without involving Mr Panda. Please don't tell him about my association with this operation, although I know that at some stage he is going to ask you how the cables were laid and by whom," Suku mentioned.

"Has Panda not inquired about your frequent absence from the desk?" KM asked.

"No, but he does have an idea of what I am engaged in. I suspect he accepted the situation as a fait accompli out of fear of Mr Jeev. I suggest that you take Mr Panda into confidence lest he leaks the operation and puts the blame on you," Suku said.

KM subsequently discussed the matter with Kutty who agreed to set up the devices but insisted on taking Mr Panda into confidence. "Your project involves committing technical experts for a minimum six to eight weeks and getting specialized devices issued from the stores. I can't do either without his approval," Kutty responded unequivocally.

"Let me consult Mr Jeev," KM said and left. However, he did not act on Kutty's advice for the rest of the day. He thought very poorly of Panda's professional skill and hated him for having progressed steadily in his career by practicing servitude to seniors. He considered Panda a rank sectarian, a weak leader, and a chameleon. Notwithstanding his pathological dislike for the man, KM knew he had no other choice but to keep Panda on board.

*

Jeev reached home around 9 pm, had a quick bite, and left for the airport to catch the last Indian Airlines flight for Calcutta. En route, he called Vivek Modi, North-Western Bureau in-charge, and inquired if he could meet him next day in Delhi.

"I have no problem, sir." The response was typical of the man.

"I won't be in Delhi till 6 in the evening. Come around 8 pm. We can discuss the matter over dinner. Please keep your visit a secret," Jeev advised. He thought of no other officer who could cover the suspect's stay at Patiala.

Over the years, Jeev had come to admire Vivek for his immense courage and operational acumen. As a field operator, he was way ahead of his colleagues and was fanatical about doing something spectacular. For him, means was irrelevant so long as the end was achieved. During the heyday of Sikh militancy in Punjab, he did not hesitate to adopt extra-constitutional measures to wipe out scores of activists who had lost their way. But unlike many of his colleagues, who were subsequently arrested and prosecuted for violating law, he was clever enough to wipe out the blood trail.

Vivek had joined the Agency riding on romanticized notions of using its finances, secrecy, operational freedom and dynamic work culture to eliminate terrorists, insurgents and underworld criminals to make India a safer place to live in. He visualized a distinctive role for himself for taking the fight into enemy's hideouts. However, harsh realities caught up with him sooner than expected. He became somewhat disillusioned with the lack of passion and cautious approach of officers who unfortunately, had a decisive say in defining operational policies. But Vivek refused to relent. He painstakingly built up a huge database on the network of underground criminals and terrorists. But just when he was ready to get physically cracking at the targets, his role was emasculated and he was sent to Jammu. His controlling officer was so mortally afraid of taking failures in his stride that he would instantly get into fits if Vivek talked of "instant action". His Division Head, who seemed to have prematurely attained enlightenment, sniffed blood in every operational proposal that Vivek put up. The Chief hardly helped the matter. He advised Vivek to curb his hyperactive impulses and repeatedly turned down his plea for funds to undertake missions that would have mauled the enemy.

Jeev had watched Vivek's frustration ballooning from a distance. Apprehending that he might also leave the Agency for a more satisfying future in private sector, Jeev taught him a few tricks of surviving among those in the Agency, who were either fit to serve in the Weights and Measure Department or teach in roadside universities. He impressed on Vivek that he was not the only braveheart to despair. There was this officer who used astrology to recruit host of unreachable assets but was felled by the wayside by weak-kneed leadership and overbearing colleagues who could not digest the felicity with which he extracted reports from ministers, their gorgeous wives, and generals in foreign countries. Similarly, an officer who used the enemy's money to destroy their subversive infrastructure, an unparalleled instance of operational innovation, was hounded for eleven years and reduced to a mental wreck by a bunch of empty tin pots.

Vivek learnt his lessons well. Unlike KM who fought his battles hard and was vocal about it, he waited for his chance to go for the kill.

Day 40

For the first time in two years, Kamath walked down to Panda's office. Their meeting was business-like. Neither of them thought it necessary to make the encounter pleasant.

"Mr Jeev wants you to spare your most discreet and hands-on experts for the job. They also have to be willing to work beyond office hours," KM almost dictated after briefly disclosing the purpose of the operation. "They would only report to me and in case they need to make any mid-course correction in the technical aspect of the plan, they would first approach me."

Panda detested KM's manner of speaking. It was better though, than the usually uncouth remarks that KM especially reserved for officers of the technical branches.

"If this is what Mr Jeev desires, I have nothing to say," Panda responded without hiding his bitterness. But he was intrigued why KM made no mention of the Chief's approval. An hour later, he met Jeev to clarify his doubts.

"You heard him right. You have to put your best foot forward this time," said Jeev after he heard from Panda about his discussions with KM.

"Sir, leaving my officers entirely in the hands of a non-technical officer may affect the smooth conduct of the operation," Panda cautioned. "They can take Mr Kamath for a ride because he neither has the experience nor the technical know-how to guide my officers or customize the plan, if needed."

Jeev was aware of Panda's unflattering opinion of Kamath. There had been occasions in the past, when he came up with all kinds of technical excuses to sabotage quite a few of KM's operations.

"I will ask him to seek your advice in case he needs it," Jeev said.

In the evening, KM, along with Kutty, went to discuss the plan of action with Jeev. Kutty was Jeev's favourite in the Technical Division for his expertise in handling operations involving critical use of surveillance devices. But he had one major flaw in his character. Kutty was paranoid of failing and therefore, needed to be constantly encouraged to accept failures as an occupational hazard. Jeev was glad Panda had spared his best man for the job.

"With Kutty by your side, you can sit and relax," Jeev told KM. "I am sure he will make you see and hear what transpires in the room."

Kutty thought Jeev's optimism was a bit premature and promptly interrupted to correct the perception.

"Sir, it will involve laying of wires for a distance of more than eighty metres before they are connected to the ports in the Nerve Centre. This is not going to be an easy task," he said.

"We already have cables running into the NC from the room. You just have to load your devices' output onto the existing wires," Jeev explained.

"Sir, I will check that, but my gut feeling is chat new lines will have to be separately laid. I am also not sure how safe it will be to hide the wires along the ducts. Moreover, since the room is sparsely decorated, it will be quite difficult to hide the cameras at vantage points," Kutty mentioned.

KM frowned at Kutty's pusillanimity.

"But the job has to be done and it is for you to sort the problems out," KM reacted in annoyance.

"Don't worry. Kutty has always been a slow starter." Jeev pacified KM.

After Kutty left, KM decried the casual work attitude of the technical officers. "Sir, there is no one in the Technical Division who has any commitment," he claimed. "They are busy conspiring against each other and quarrelling among themselves for foreign tours. They are just good at pushing files, fabricating scientific claims, and procuring equipment," he complained.

"You are too harsh. Actually, it's we who have failed to harness their enormous talent," Jeev opined.

"Sir, there may be a few exceptions but even they feel discouraged to innovate because of Panda's nepotism," KM claimed.

"We are also at fault. I tried to break new ground along with Panda in the area of punitive operations against hostile targets but was stonewalled by chicken hearts," Jeev said.

"Sir, Panda hardly wields any authority in his unit." KM continued his diatribe. "Officers openly flout his instructions. They think he is professionally ill-equipped to guide those who work especially on evesdropping, hacking, and bugging."

"He has, of course, some limitations but he is really good," Jeev sounded irritated this time. "You may not know how much he helped me track the foreign agents who were trying to hack into our financial database."

KM chose not to interrupt.

"Panda has in fact, spared his best officer and latest devices for your operation and expressed no interest in interfering in your work," Jeev said. "I guess, he would be happy if you do not associate him with this operation. He would love to have deniability should the investigation gets exposed," he added. Jeev's guess was on course. Panda never inquired either about his officers or how the operation was technically proceeding.

Vivek joined Jeevnathan at the family dinner at 8.30 pm. After Mani and his daughters retired to their bedrooms, Jeev confided to Vivek that Ravi Mohan had been placed under surveillance for working for a foreign intelligence service. According to a field report, he would reach Ambala on Thursday by Shatabdi and stay there in a suite at Hotel Narain Continental. He would return to Delhi by the same train on Friday. In order to lend seriousness to the task, Jeev resorted to a bit of exaggeration. He said that during this trip, Ravi was expected to meet his handler and two others. Jeev, however, cautioned Vivek against showing indiscretion or haste during the inquiry.

"I will come back with a detailed report on Friday afternoon," Vivek said, humbled by the gravity of the task.

At 7.45 pm, Kutty and his colleagues entered the building one by one at an interval of every seven to ten minutes. At the outer and inner entry points, the security guards checked their identity cards and authorization slips provided by KM. Once the corridor lights were switched off, Kutty's team started hauling the equipment and accessories up to the designated areas. From 11 pm, they began laying wires through the AC ducts and placing cameras at vantage points in the room. This was followed by several dry runs of the working of all devices.

KM remained present in his room, monitoring the progress on his cellphone.

An accident, however, briefly threatened to blow away the mission. Feeling drowsy and tired at 2 am, a junior technical assistant of Kutty's team, failed to hold a panel firmly while sticking it to the left side of the cavity in the roof. He tried unsuccessfully to grab it as it flipped out of his hand and crashed onto the floor along with the panel and stool on which he was standing. In the stillness of the night, the fall made a piercing sound. The guards came rushing to the scene but before they could arrive, the technician collected the stool hurriedly and hid himself in Ravi's room. The guard commander noticed that a panel was lying on the ground. He cursorily saw the cavity in the roof from where the panel had come off, cursed the maintenance engineers for their shoddy work, picked up the panel and left. He did not think it necessary to move ahead in the corridor and check the rooms or look up closely at the cavity where the wires were dangling.

As soon as the guard commander left, Kutty rushed to report the matter to KM who was fast asleep in his room. KM didn't say a word and kept his anger in check. Both walked down to the accident site in silence. What if the maintenance engineers came looking for the gap in the ceiling in the morning and found new wires protruding, he thought. What if they removed a few more panels and traced the route of the freshly laid cables to the NC. Would it set off an alarm bell for a possible sabotage attempt in the building, forcing the Chief to involve other agencies to conduct a thorough investigation? While KM was weighing the cost of the fallout, Kutty instructed his technicians to remove a panel from the right side of the roof, fix it in the gap on the left, from where the panel had fallen out and keep the cavity on the right open, to confuse the maintenance engineers and mislead them to conduct the repair work at the wrong place.

Kutty completed the mission by 4 am, then went to his room and slept. At 6 am he left the building after informing his colleagues that they could take the day off.

Day 41

Bimal Maira, Director of Security, routinely went through the daily observation register. The comments of the guard commander that a panel had fallen off in corridor 'N' from the roof and needed to be replaced, evoked no particular interest in him. He simply signed the register and instructed his PA to send its extract to the maintenance division for the 'needful'.

Two hours later, a junior engineer accompanied by a mechanic and a helper, inspected the roof and had a cursory look at the cavity on the right side. While the mechanic was on the job of sticking the panel, his helper noticed that the left side panel was not properly slotted in and a wire was protruding from the sides. He brought it to the mechanic's notice but the latter was not interested. He said, it was not listed on the job card and since it seemed like an electrician's work, he wouldn't touch it.

This conversation was instantly reported to KM by a CEU junior officer who was keeping an obtrusive watch of the area since morning. Luckily, no electrician from the maintenance unit turned up during the day to fix the problem. At 8 pm, Kutty and KM arrived along with an electrician, who removed the panel, tucked the wire neatly inside and placed the panel back in the gap.

Day 42

Ravi left for Patiala in the morning. KM reported to Jeev from New Delhi station that the suspect came alone and no one approached him. Later in the afternoon, he informed that during the journey the suspect either slept or read newspapers. At Ambala, he was received by an inspector of police and two others in uniform and escorted to Patiala in a white Baleno.

Day 43

The whole day, KM and Kutty waited in the NC for the suspect to arrive. The purpose was to see the live coverage of his activities inside the room. But he did not turn up. KM had expected that since the train arrived from Patiala around 11 am, the suspect might go to the residence to freshen up and have an early lunch before coming to the office. But he continued to stay away. Finally at 4 pm, KM contacted Mathew, a field surveillance officer, deployed near the suspect's residence. Mathew confirmed that the suspect returned to the residence at 10.40 am but had not come out since then. Fifteen minutes later, NC recorded the suspect telling his PA that he would not attend office.

"So, we have to wait for two more days to test the results of your midnight labour. I don't think Ravi will go to the office during weekends," KM told Kutty as they left NC.

*

At 5.15 pm, Vivek dropped in unannounced to brief Jeev on Ravi's Patiala visit. "You should have avoided coming to the office," Jeev chided mildly. "You know how panicked your boss can get. If he gets to know that you are here to see me without his knowledge, he will go crazy with speculations," he said.

"Sir, that won't happen. It is the Deputy Chief who called me for discussing a Pak operation today where my boss was also present," Vivek informed. Then he took out a report from his briefcase and gave it to Jeev.

The report was silent on Ravi's meeting with any suspicious person. His innocuous activities in Patiala included a private dinner with Khan, a visit to the family priest's ashram, and payment of Rs 8,380 for hotel expenses for coffee, snacks, and overnight stay. In passing, the report made a reference to two ladies, Miss Merylene Nair and Miss Jasmeet Kaur of the US Embassy, who also stayed in Hotel Narain Continental and checked out for Delhi two hours after the suspect checked in. During that period, the suspect spent most of his time in the lobby and the coffee shop. There was no mention in the report whether the suspect met any of the two ladies in the hotel.

"Is it possible that your boys could have missed Ravi at some point of time?" Jeev asked as he finished reading the report.

"It is unlikely. The reception-cum-escort team for the suspect, deputed by Khan included my man. He would have surely reported if something unusual had taken place. Besides, Mr Ravi Mohan would not have accepted a police escort and announced his travel schedule in advance if he had to meet his running officer incognito," Vivek claimed.

"You may be right."

"But what strikes me as odd is his decision to stay in Narain Intercontinental in the Maharaja Suite on a private visit. It's unusual for a serving officer to splurge hard-earned money in this manner," Vivek expressed.

"He has someone else's money to spend," Jeev said with a stony face.

At 7.15 pm, KM went to inform Jeev that the suspect didn't come to the office. "You don't have to be despondent. You can start tracking his activities from Monday when he reports on duty," Jeev said. "Anyway, read this note. It's on Ravi's visit to Patiala."

"Do you see any connection between the two US girls and the suspect?" Jeev asked as KM finished reading the report.

"Sir, there is no reason why the suspect would go to Patiala only two hours before the departure of the two ladies when he could have met them in Delhi at the place and time of his choice by observing simple counter surveillance measures," KM argued.

"We still have to make sure that they are not part of Ravi's baggage," Jeev said. KM was not convinced.

Day 44

Jeev kept agonizing over the presence of Merylene and Jasmeet. The first thing that he did after reaching the office was to call Keshav Nath, a Joint Secretary in the MEA, for a background check on the two women staffers of the US Embassy. Nath who had earlier served under Jeev and built an enduring working relationship, promised to get back to him soon. What always impressed Jeev was Nath's uncanny ability to effectively hide secrets behind the veil of his innocent laughter. The next officer whom he called was Prashant Vaish. He wanted to know whether he could obtain details about Ravi's leave and his assignments. Vaish said that he was on his way to submit the report.

"Was it too difficult to manage Vipul?" Jeev asked light heartedly as Vaish handed over his hand-written note.

"On the contrary, he did not even ask me why I needed this information. Similarly, when I approached Desk Officer, Africa and Europe, they allowed me to scan the data on sources without asking any questions," Vaish mentioned.

"Doesn't it worry you that you can access information from the Agency's officers so easily?" Jeev asked.

"I guess they trust me, sir."

"But trust in you does not mean that they betray the trust that the Agency has reposed in them," Jeev remarked.

"Sir, I have no problem so long as it serves the purpose of your investigation."

"Anything else?" Jeev asked.

"Sir, I had occasions to serve under Mr Ravi Mohan," Vaish recalled. "What you suspect of him can be true. He was, of course, very kind and depended on me blindly but that was more out of his inability to comprehend the complexity of cases. He always seemed to hide something and you could feel that he was not at ease with himself." Jeev listened intently as Vaish vented his feelings.

"Can you be little more specific?" Jeev probed.

"Sir, he was always eager to talk to officers from other operational and analysis branches. He would dispose us off quickly but sit with them for hours," Vaish mentioned.

"Thanks. I will go through the note and call you later if there is anything more that I want to know," Jeev said.

The note added one more straw to his stack of concerns.

The suspect joined the Agency on deputation in 1986 and remained posted at Headquarters till 1994. Thereafter, he was posted to Nairobi on an assignment for three years. The Kenyan climate did not suit him and he fell sick. He was initially treated by local doctors but despite prolonged medication, his recovery was very slow. Then he took leave and went to John Hopkins, Baltimore, USA, for a check-up where his parents lived. After serving for six months in Nairobi, he proceeded on leave again, this time to Vienna. There, he underwent a bypass at the AKH hospital.

The suspect returned to Delhi in 1998 where he worked in different capacities for five years. During this period, he visited his mother in the US twice on leave, once in 1998 and the second time in '99. His next foreign assignment was in Brussels from 2001 to 2004. During this period, he took vacations rather frequently and visited Paris, Amsterdam, Cologne, Geneva, and, of course, Baltimore on three occasions. Four weeks before he left Brussels on transfer to Delhi in January 2005, he intimated Headquarters that he had bought a Toshiba laptop for 1200 US dollars but did not furnish a receipt. In 2006 and 2007 he visited Baltimore, each time for three weeks. In 2007, he went to Washington on 21 days' training to learn interrogation techniques. Two weeks after his Washington tour, he visited Kathmandu on a week's leave with his wife. He had also been deputed to MI6 for three days' training in analysing reports in 2005 and to National Intelligence Agency in Bangkok for two days in November 2007 for consultations.

There were no papers to throw light on how the expenses on his heart surgery in Vienna were met.

The suspect raised seven new contacts at Nairobi. Of these, five were of Indian origin, one was a US Press Attaché Durante and the other one was a lady named Angelien from the Netherland Embassy. Records show that these two were not paid sources but semi-conscious agents who were dropped by Ravi from the roll before he moved to Delhi.

Significantly, the Agency's officer in Vienna had reported to the Europe desk that when he went to inquire about the suspect's welfare in the hospital, there was a white lady present in the room whom the suspect introduced as Angel. Subsequently, when he checked about this girl, he found that an Angelien was listed as an employee of IAEA. He further wrote that since there was a discrepancy in the name, he thought of informing Headquarters to get to the bottom of the matter.

No one ever asked Ravi to explain about Angelien. In the margin, Naik, then Chief Analyst of Europe division, wrote that the Vienna officer should rather concentrate on raising sources rather than sniffing around his seniors' armpits'.

Jeev kept the note aside and asked KM to come over. KM quickly collected the latest surveillance reports, put them in the brief case and briskly walked up to Jeev's office. Before he could take out his papers, Jeev passed on the note by Vaish to him. "What do you make out of Ravi's frequent visits to the US and other places?" he asked, as soon as KM finished reading the note.

"Sir, it is normal for our officers to visit places in Europe during their assignments," KM maintained. "It is also quite natural that the suspect would visit the US to meet his parents who are permanently settled there," he added.

"What about his visit to Washington. It is so close to Langley?" Jeev pressed.

"Sir, the suspect didn't go there on leave. He actually led a team of twelve junior officers from the Agency and the Bureau, duly authorized by the Chief," KM pointed out. "I don't know if you recall what you had commented on the suspect's post-tour report. You had noted that such visits only served the purpose of foreign agencies to recruit our officers for espionage," he said.

"How would you explain his purchase of such an expensive laptop and his refusal to submit its receipt to Headquarters?" Jeev asked.

"This practice is very common with majority of our officers who want to be honest by half," KM clarified.

"And why should he decide to get operated upon in Vienna, when his parents were in the US," Jeev further asked.

"It is weird, but maybe Vienna was cheaper," KM contended.

"On the contrary, it is the most expensive hospital in Europe," Jeev said. He stopped briefly when the PS entered to get his signature on a file.

"And, what do you think of the report of our officer in Vienna?" Jeev resumed questioning KM.

"Sir, honestly the officer is mixing issues," KM claimed. "Angelien cannot be an exclusive name. Angelien of IAEA and Nairobi could be different persons. And, Angel could be anyone; a hospitalist, a nurse, or even a casual acquaintance who would have met and befriended Ravi during his rather long stay at the hospital," he explained.

"I seriously think we should have started this inquiry way back in 1997. Can you find out where Subhendu Roy is posted? He was one of the 12 officers who had gone to Washington for that training," said Jeev.

"Sir."

"I vaguely recall that he did see me on his return and told me something about Ravi. I can't remember exactly what he said, but it was certainly unsavoury. At that time, I did not encourage him to talk loosely about one of his senior officers. Maybe he can defog some of my doubts about the suspect now," Jeev added thoughtfully.

"Do you want me to keep this note in the file?" KM asked.

"You let it stay in my almirah."

"Sir, I know who has written this note," KM said with a bit of mischief.

"I will then take it that you have not seen this note," Jeev said.

As Jeev got up to leave for the day, his PS brought in a sealed envelope. He tore it and was surprised to see an unsigned sheet from Keshav Nath. He did not expect Keshav to provide the information within less than ten hours. He quickly glanced through it and handed the paper to KM.

"Read it at home. We will discuss it tomorrow. The inputs seem interesting," Jeev said.

"By the way, did Ravi come to the office today?" Jeev asked.

"Sir, he did. We were actually struggling the whole day to see the recording live but somehow it was coming all fudged. The tapes were probably unformatted. Kutty is working on it."

"I hope this last gamble pays off," Jeev said.

After dinner KM went upstairs, lay down on the bed and read the note.

> "Merylene is a naturalized Indian and an employee of the US State Department. She has been posted in Delhi since September 2006. Her earlier assignments included a stint in Islamabad as a USAID officer for two and half years, a Desk Officer's job to handle Afghan affairs in the State Department in Washington DC, followed by a two-year tenure each at the US embassy in Colombo and Dhaka. She knows practically everyone who matters in politics in the Indian subcontinent. She is a multilinguist and knows Hindi, Urdu, English, Dari, Pashto, French, Persian, and Spanish.
>
> Jasmeet is a Sinologist. She did her post-graduation in Chinese from Beijing University, followed by a posting in the US embassy in Beijing for five years. Her career profile for the next seven years before she

joined the US Embassy in Delhi in February 2007 remains shrouded in mystery. She knows Chinese, Mandarin, Hindi, Punjabi, English, and Arabic extremely well. She has a fairly large number of friends in Punjab, Delhi, and Mumbai.
None of the two girls is a career diplomat."

Too many puzzles remained unexplained, KM reflected as he tossed around in the bed. The visit of Merylene and Jasmeet to Patiala while the suspect was around, the Angelien connection, the purpose of the shredder, the visit to Nepal soon after his training tour to Washington, the forthcoming Bali trip, goings on in the Zair Club, the purchase of a laptop for his personal use at the residence, etc. The list was growing. KM kept mulling over the till his tired body forced him to sleep.

Day 45

Kutty left very early for office, hoping that he might crack the garbled recordings with no one around to disturb him. On the way, he went to a temple at Mallai to take Lord Urrugan's blessings. Finally at 2.45 pm he identified the glitch. It lay in the encrypting device that was attached to cameras. Normally, the device should have been removed from the cameras before planting them in Ravi's room. Kutty was furious with his technician for not having properly inspected the cameras before commissioning them. The option was either to enter the room again and pluck the encrypting device out or install a compatible recorder in the NC to decode the audio/video signals.

"What is your advice?" KM asked.

"I will go for the second option," Kutty opined.

"Then, install the compatible recorder," KM said.

"That kind of a recorder is available in Sanjay Rao's unit."

"I don't want Rao to be involved in this operation," KM snapped.

"But we don't have a choice," Kutty said and offered to talk to Rao to sort out the problem.

"Let me speak to him. He shouldn't know about your involvement in the operation," KM said and left to meet Rao. Half an hour later, he brought a specialized connector and told Kutty to attach it to the recorder in the NC. Kutty took no time in fixing it. To his immense relief, the tapes began to transmit sharper images and meaningful conversations on the monitor.

At 10 am, the suspect was seen entering the room followed by his peon. He carried a dark brown leather bag and probably kept it on the sideboard behind his chair. Within minutes, his PA came in to inform about the day's appointments. After he left, the suspect started ringing up officers on the intercom but no one answered his call. He finally managed to speak to the China Desk Officer and requested him to brief him on what to ask from a visiting source, an expert in the field of nuclear proliferation in South Asia. He mentioned that the source was camping in Delhi for last two days, interacting with security experts and officials from the Ministry of External Affairs and disclosed that later in the evening, he was also scheduled to meet the source before the latter took a late night flight for Islamabad.

"Sir, my schedule is very tight today. I can at best send you a note on nuclear cooperation among China, North Korea, and Pakistan but the inputs are six months old," the Desk Officer said.

"You know how valuable this asset is. He spoke to me from Bangkok and asked me to keep a list of queries ready so that he can provide specific answers without wasting much time,' Ravi pleaded.

"I suggest you call Somayya, head of the Science Division. He is an expert on the subject and can assist you in resolving technical issues," the Desk officer hung up.

Ravi later called Somayya and repeated the request.

"Sir, I am busy finalizing a report. But if it is convenient, I can come over at 4 pm."

"That's alright." Ravi said. His next call was to an officer of the administration, requesting him to cancel the transfer of his PA to Mizoram. Then he began disposing off pending papers and files. While going through the papers, he picked up documents of his interest at regular intervals and kept these separately in a folder. After that, he sat down on the sofa, stretched his legs on the coffee table, closed his eyes and took a power nap. At 1 pm, Inder woke him up and served sandwiches and an apple for lunch.

At 1.20 pm, Ravi told his PA not to disturb him for an hour. He locked the room from inside, took out a few files from the almirah, placed them on the side table and switched on the photocopier. After that he removed papers from the files one at a time and after photocopying them, placed these back in respective files. Then he photocopied the loose sheets that he had kept earlier in the folder. He counted the copied sheets twice before switching off the photocopier. He collected the photocopied documents and kept them somewhere behind his working chair. After that he put the folder and the files in the outgoing tray, released the door latch and lay down on the sofa.

"So, this is what this rascal has been doing," KM told an equally bewildered Kutty. "How many secret documents, do you think, he would have photocopied?" he asked.

"Why guess? Let's rewind the tape in slow motion and count," Kutty suggested. The repeated viewing of the tape indicated that Ravi photocopied 35 sheets.

"Let's see him live," KM proposed in panic.

"It is better that we first complete viewing of yesterday's recorded tapes," Kutty said and played the tapes, without waiting for KM's reaction.

Ravi was lying down on sofa. At 3 pm, he got up, went to the attached rest room and came out wiping his face with a towel. He sat down on the sofa again. Then he increased the volume of the TV and settled for news on Times Now. At 4 pm, Somayya came carrying an envelope and requested Ravi to go through the note. He said that in addition to the note, he had also given some talking points, highlighting gaps in information.

Ravi asked PA for two cups of coffee. Then he went through the note in a jiffy. "It's an excellent note," he remarked.

"Sir, please do not show this document to the source. It has bits of classified information, provided by highly sensitive sources," Somayya said.

"Don't worry. I will return it to you tomorrow, first thing in the morning. I have to read it again and make my own notes before I meet the source," Ravi lied. "Why don't you join me in the briefing?" he suddenly asked.

"I am not exposed to the source. But if you insist, I can speak to the Deputy Chief for permission," Somayya replied.

"That will not be necessary. I will manage," Ravi quickly made the volte face.

After Somayya left, the suspect locked the door again from inside, took out a pin extractor from the bottom right drawer of the working table and carefully forked out stapled pins. Then he copied six pages and kept them in the same place, which was blocked from the camera's view behind his chair. He spent a few minutes stapling the note at the original place. After he put it back in the envelope, he opened the security latch and rang up Director Pak military operations, Ajeet Bhaduri.

"I was checking if you returned from Srinagar," Ravi said.

"I came back this morning."

"What are you doing right now? If you are free, let's have some coffee," Ravi lured.

"I am about to finalize a draft report on my Srinagar visit. It has to go to the Chief by this evening. I will take another half an hour to complete it."

"That's okay," Ravi said and asked his PA for two cups of coffee. As soon as Ajeet came in, the suspect moved to the sofa and occupied the seat closer to the TV. Ajeet sat next to him. The suspect then increased the volume of TV and inquired routinely whether these review meetings served any useful purpose.

"Not in the least," Ajeet reacted. "It is supposed to review the security situation in J&K and resolve the problems of coordination, bedevilling the security forces and the intelligence agencies, but what you witness is a dogfight," he claimed.

"That's worrying," Ravi said.

"Yes it is. Everyone blames everyone else. The Army complains that it receives vague and generalized intelligence on which no operation can effectively be planned. It claims that it seldom gets actionable intelligence and even these never reach on time. The grouse of the Security Forces, on the other hand, is that the Army commits them invariably against better equipped militants and constantly shoves them into fatal actions, ignoring their stretched out duty hours, poor state of training and weapon holding, and pathetic logistic back up, resulting in heavy body count. They allege that Army commanders deliberately keep softer targets for their troops and operate only when they are sure of success. Intelligence agencies accuse both the Army and security forces of not following up their inputs to their logical end and insist that when they do provide actionable intelligence, the field commanders simply delay the movement of their troops to let the militants disperse in order to escape heavy casualties," Ajeet paused after summarizing his impression of the meeting.

"Didn't the GOC Northern Command shut the intelligence officers up? It's his men who are dying daily and not these sleuths," said Ravi.

"The GOC did protest vociferously and demanded proof to substantiate the allegations. At that stage, the discussion became quite ugly," Ajeet confided. "Anyway, this should give you an idea of why we are unable to crush a handful of militants," he said.

Their conversation was interrupted by a call from Ajeet's PA who said that the report was ready. Ajeet quickly gulped the coffee and left. "I am sorry, I will have to go," he said. "This report has to reach the Chief in the next fifteen minutes."

"Don't forget to show me your final report. I am sure it must be very illustrative of why we are sinking in this quagmire," Ravi warmed up his ego.

"Maybe tomorrow, I will bring over a copy."

The suspect saw off Ajeet at the door, then dialled a number and asked him to come over for coffee. Within ten minutes, the visitor came in. He was Venkatpathy, Desk Officer, Cyber operations. As Venkat took his seat, Ravi further increased the volume of the TV which greatly affected the clarity of their conversation. Amid the humming and screeching noises, Ravi was heard asking questions about hacking. In response, Venkat launched into a discourse on how hacking helped in tracking terrorist network and breaking their codes. It seemed that Ravi did not comprehend what the visitor was trying to explain. After his twenty-minute monologue, Venkat left.

By now it was getting close to 5 pm. The suspect told his PA, that he would leave early to meet a source and asked him to clear the papers and files from the out tray. Then he switched off the TV, checked the photocopier by lifting the top panel to ensure that no paper was inadvertently left inside. Inder went behind the working desk and as he moved away from there he was seen carrying a briefcase and a lunch box. The suspect also visited the same area and came out holding a dark brown leather bag in his hand.

A deafening silence descended in the NC. KM was left numbed while Kutty got busy in switching off the system.

"Let's show an edited version of this shit to Jeev," KM proposed.

"For that I need to use a different video recorder. Let me bring that from my room," Kutty said and went out.

Left alone in the NC, KM tried to contact Jeev on his internal and mobile numbers several times but there was no response. Eventually, he called Jeev's PS who said that Jeev had gone out for a meeting and was not expected to return before 6.30 pm. KM looked at the watch. It was already 5.30 pm.

Meanwhile, Kutty returned with the device and by 6.15 pm, they were ready with an edited version of the tape. Before leaving, KM checked again with the PS who said that Mr Jeevnathan had been held up but he wanted Mr Kamath to wait for him.

"Inform me as soon as he steps in," KM said impatiently.

*

After the meeting, Jeev proceeded towards the office instead of the residence. He guessed something could have gone horribly wrong with the video surveillance because KM was not the one who would send him eleven messages within a span of forty seconds. En-route, he rang up Mani and told her that an unexpected situation had come up in the office but he would try to be on time for the dinner.

"I hope you know that we are the hosts," Mani said and dropped the phone.

When Jeev entered the room, he saw KM and Kutty waiting. "What's the bad news?" he asked even before he sat down.

"Sir, there is nothing that is right," KM reacted. "I was a fool all along. The suspect indeed is an espionage agent," he said.

"That's interesting. What is it that has changed your opinion of Ravi so drastically?" Jeev inquired.

"Sir, I have to show you something," KM said. In the meantime, Kutty placed a mini DVD player on the table, flipped open its screen facing Jeev and played it.

"So, that is why you were so excited," Jeev said after he finished watching photocopying activities of the suspect and his conversation with Ajeet and Somayya. "Let's discuss it tomorrow, first thing in the morning. The night should give us some quiet moments to soberly assess what we have achieved so far and where we go from here," he expressed.

Kutty gathered the tapes and accessories and came out of the room along with KM. "What do you think would be Mr Jeev's next move," Kutty asked as they walked back to their rooms.

"You never know. He may still have several plans up his sleeve that he would like to roll out. For me, it's an open and shut case. Ravi is an espionage agent and the earlier he is arrested the better it is for the safety of the Agency's secrets," KM reacted in disgust.

Day 46

Seeing Jeev in a hurry to leave early, Mani reminded him of his appointment with the doctor at 3 pm for his recurring back pain. "Call me if you are held up in one of your so-called crisis situations. In that case I will go on my own to Safdarjung hospital for my knee therapy," she said.

"I will send the car."

"That won't be necessary," she reacted.

Jeev ignored her bravado, stuffed his briefcase with outstation cables and went past Mani who was reading the morning newspaper in the living room.

"I don't know when you will realize that once you retire in six months' time, most of the medical facilities will be withdrawn and none of these great works that you think you are doing, will rescue you from being incapacitated," she taunted.

"I am sure you will be there to take care of me," Jeev tried to hijack the looming ugliness. Before he got into the car, he said that a crisis had indeed hit the Agency and, this time it was not so-called. He also said that he needed her moral support in tackling it with an uncluttered mind.

"Then send the car with the driver," she responded with a broad grin.

Within minutes of reaching office, Jeev called KM to come in along with Ajay. KM was the first to arrive. He said that Ajay was on the way and would join the discussions shortly.

"So, what's your reaction?" Jeev asked.

"Sir, I could hardly sleep last night. The images of the entire process of his photocopying in such secrecy kept haunting me," KM voiced his concern.

"What do you think he is doing with those papers?"

"Sir, he may be copying the documents digitally at home and storing them in pen drives for subsequently passing them on to his handler. After that, he may be shredding the documents. That's the reason why he was so desperate to get the shredder repaired at any cost. Obviously, he did not want to leave any trace of classified papers at home," KM contended.

"But didn't you tell me the other day that garbage bags from his house carried nothing of shredded documents?" Jeev countered.

"Yes sir, I did. But that's a mystery, I am unable to resolve," KM sounded a bit defensive.

"So, what should be our next move?" Jeev asked as he saw Ajay entering the room.

"The suspect has to be confronted with the recordings and intercepts and coerced to take us to his running officer," KM stressed.

"And, what are your views?" Jeev asked Ajay, assuming that he would have been briefed by KM on the unexpected turn in the investigation.

"Sir, Ravi is definitely doing something devious. We have to ask him to come out clean," Ajay said.

"He is a crook," KM retorted. "You should have seen how he sucked the information out of Ajeet and weaved a fanciful excuse to trap Somayya into leaving the note behind. He doesn't have to be asked. He needs to be thrashed lest we lose more intelligence inputs," KM was all charged up.

However, Jeev viewed the evidence differently and advised both against rushing to conclusions. "For all we know," he maintained, "these documents could be his personal papers. He can also argue that he retained a copy of Somayya's paper for his background information and what Ajeet told him, was public knowledge. I don't think Somayya's note could be more than an intelligent rehash of several downloads because he is not privy to the critical inputs on this subject. Should you detain Ravi now, you can, at most, verbally warn him for making indiscreet enquiries. Regarding taking classified papers to the residence by an officer of his seniority or talking to colleagues about their work, these do not constitute a violation of existing departmental security guidelines," Jeev's captive audience listened in discomfort.

"Sir, this new evidence is mind-blowing but you are right. We still have a few nuts and bolts to tighten up," KM sounded defensive. "In fact, the contents of photocopied sheets are not very readable, because the camera covering the area around the photocopier is transmitting dispersed images of the documents. Similarly, when Ravi keeps the papers on the table and switches on the lamp to sift his end product, the glare of the lamp completely clouds the images. Moreover, we don't know what the suspect is doing with those papers behind his desk," KM explained.

"Has Kutty found an answer to your problems?" Jeev inquired.

"He has. Tonight, he plans to neutralize the switching circuitry of the table lamp, hoping that the room light will make our task of reading the documents easier. He is also going to induct additional camera to cover the area behind the suspect's desk and introduce a more powerful lens to get a sharper look at the photocopier," KM informed.

"Good. I knew Kutty won't let you lose this race," Jeev said.

"Sir, did you notice how Venkatpathy was talking about hacking, decoding, etc. I don't know why we give such critical operational responsibilities to officers who are so junior and inexperienced," he pointed out.

But Jeev had a different perception of Venkat's interactions. "I thought he took Ravi for a joy ride and offered garbage in the name of vital inputs," Jeev remarked.

"Sir, Venkat keeps blustering and is highly pretentious," Ajay, who was sitting quiet, rallied behind his deputy. "We should discourage this officer from meeting Ravi lest he spills information about our cyber operations."

"If you can suggest to him to be discreet without compromising the secrecy of this operation, I have no objection," Jeev said.

*

At 3 pm, Jeev knocked on the door and entered the Chief's room. Wasan was going through a document and simultaneously making notes in his own hand.

"If you are too busy, I can come later," Jeev said.

"Please sit down. Just give me a minute," Wasan requested and continued to jot down notes. After he was finished with it, he kept the document in the briefcase. He said he was reading comments offered by concerned divisions on a document circulated by the National Security Council Secretariat (NSCS), detailing gaps in Intelligence that were allegedly left uncovered by the Agency during last year. NSCS, he disclosed, had graded the overall performance of the Agency as below par.

"What is there to respond?" Jeev asked. "You should tell the NSCS to recommend the Agency's closure to the Government and distribute its responsibilities among the Defence Forces, the Bureau and the Foreign Office. In any case, you and I are retiring, so how does it matter," he reacted light heartedly.

"You can say that in the comfort of this room," Wasan remarked.

"Why don't you take me along to defend the Agency's report card and enjoy the fireworks?" Jeev offered.

Wasan ignored his friend's jibe and instead, briefed Jeev on the deliberations. He said that Sachdeva, Deputy National Security Advisor (NSA) began by enumerating the targets allotted to each of the outfits and then highlighted the shortfalls in their inputs. He singled out the Agency for faring the worst. This was followed by a free-for-all bashing of the Agency's performance by the three Chiefs of the Defence Forces, Director of the Bureau, and the NSA himself. Wasan claimed that he tried to hold the ground as best as he could and finally managed to buy some time so that he could come back with a detailed, factual response.

"What was the general refrain of criticism?" Jeev probed.

"The indictment was typically clerical," Wasan said. "They quoted statistics to claim that we failed miserably in providing precise and timely tactical and strategic intelligence on the build-up and deployment of Chinese and Pak defence forces, developing political changes in our neighbourhood, support to terrorists and insurgents from the establishment in Pakistan and Bangladesh and the current status of nuclear and missile stockpile in the region," he added.

"Did the NSA not defend you against his deputy's supercilious assessment?" Jeev asked.

"No."

"I am surprised. He knows what you are doing but cannot write about. He must also be aware of various covert operations that you are running but cannot explain at a public forum," Jeev said and looked at his friend who chose not to respond. But Jeev had no intention of letting Wasan off the hook. "I suspect, you will defend your case on the basis of facts but it is a trap you should avoid falling into," he cautioned.

"What do you mean?" Wasan asked.

"You know the manner in which these omnibus targets are set by novices. What else can you expect from those who have no intelligence grooming and park themselves in the NSCS for a vehicle and some perks? You are aware of the calibre of the man who drafted this report card and how his sycophancy has catapulted him to the present position. You should simply say that you have no comments to make before an audience of this size and that you will be happy to allay their grievances individually," Jeev contended.

"How can you take such a position when everyone insists for your explanation in the presence of NSA?" Wasan countered.

"In that case, you should take your accusers by their horns. Insist that success and failures are intrinsically built in the

Agency's DNA and since most of its operations take a long gestation period to mature, it would be foolish to use statistics as a stick to make the Agency behave. And, if the stick has to be used, let others also take the beating for their repeated failures," Jeev averred.

"You don't use such language at these gatherings," Wasan pointed out.

"But it is also a sin to take calumny from sinners," Jeev countered. "What does the Bureau say about the Naxalites' relentless march in state after state, insurgents' perennial violence in the north east, mushrooming of indigenous terrorist modules, and the emergence of a powerful parallel Islamic culture riding piggy back on India's secularism? How does the huge Army explain its sleepwalk when Pak armed intruders dig trenches and build defences in Kargil or when armed militants infiltrate daily and keep J&K hostage. What does the Air Force say when Peter Bleach's Latvian AN-26 flies across three-fourths of the country's airspace to drop arms in Purulia or when its fighters disintegrate in air every day at such colossal cost to the national Exchequer? How does the Navy explain its deep slumber when a few suicide bombers sail across the Arabian Sea to the Gateway of India to strike the Taj and Oberoi hotels with guns and detonators? And, how does NSCS account for its existence when not one percent of its reports contribute to influencing political leadership to take major policy decisions on economic, diplomatic, and security issues? Why doesn't the NSCS also issue a report card on its annual performance and that of MEA and economic ministries? They must understand that sporadic failures cannot be cited to deride achievements. It's ironic that the Agency is supposed to be the Prime Minister's exclusive responsibility but everyone else questions its worth except the Prime Minister. A diatribe from you on these lines would have sent your predators scurrying for cover."

"You are taking this matter rather passionately," Wasan observed as Jeev finished his call to the arms. "This is a routine exercise and after a day or two no one will have the time or memory to talk about it till the next annual report is ready for a dogfight," he said.

"That's not the point. In the absence of an aggressive projection of our work, the Agency's image is getting a beating. It will ultimately take away the sheen from the Agency's reputation in the Intelligence community and reduce you to the level of the head of a State Special Branch," Jeev pointed out.

"How many fronts do you want me to open for a fight? The Bureau is breathing down my neck to have its offices in twenty more countries abroad in the name of collecting intelligence on terrorism. The Defence Intelligence Agency is working overtime to have their officers in almost all major countries to collect military intelligence. I am fighting hard to arrest the shrinking space for our operatives. And now this crazy proposal of the NSCS to take away my vital tools for collecting technical intelligence to create an outfit, to provide employment to the unemployables," Wasan expressed in disgust.

"Let history judge you by the efforts that you put in to protect your turf," Jeev replied philosophically.

"I don't care about history. You don't know what I am going through," Wasan said.

"Wasu, you can't blame anybody for that. Your problem is you want to be Jesus without carrying the cross," Jeev remarked.

"I thought you, being a friend, will at least give me no reasons to worry about security issues. But there is hardly a day when you don't come up with cases of cheating, dereliction of duty, moral turpitude, and financial irregularities. It seems as if with my taking over as the Chief, the Agency has suddenly become a cesspool of vices and I have no control over anything," Wasan reacted bitterly.

"I can shove dirt under the carpet for your successor to clean. But that's not the way I have lived my life. I can't shirk responsibility. Maybe you should hire a lazy janitor in my place." Jeev smiled.

"I have no one in mind at the moment. Anyway, did you come to discuss anything in particular?" Wasan inquired.

"I have some bad news," Jeev said.

"Is it about Ravi?" Wasan quipped.

"Yes. The video surveillance shows that he regularly photocopies from files and reports, obtained from various branches and takes them home," Jeev said.

"Why don't we confront him with photographs and give him the option of either resigning or going on voluntary retirement," Wasan suggested.

"The problem is we still don't know whether he is copying from personal or official files. If we search him, we may recover copies of secret documents from his possession but Ravi can always claim that these were meant for his self-study, what most of us routinely do. And, why would Ravi resign or accept voluntary retirement when he has not violated any law or security instructions. If you forcibly retire him, he can go to the court and claim that our case is primarily based on clandestinely obtained evidences, which are not admissible in any court of law," Jeev argued.

"Then do what?" asked Wasan.

"Maybe, we should wait to know the precise nature of documents that he is copying," Jeev contended.

"More importantly we need to stop him from siphoning off information. God knows what he will take away in the next few days," Wasan sounded concerned.

"Ravi has been in Headquarters for the last three years. During this period, he has probably stolen every piece of information that he could lay his hands on. So if he takes away a few more, what difference does it make? The real challenge before us is to collect clinching evidences and expose the intelligence service that is running him," Jeev argued.

"What happened during his Patiala visit?"

"He didn't meet anyone whom we do not know," Jeev said. By now, he could sense that Wasan wanted to be left alone.

*

On his way back, Jeev peeped inside Joshi's room but it was empty. He found it unusual that Joshi would take so much time to arrange for entry of a watcher in the Zair club. He called up Joshi on his cellphone but he was out of reach.

At 6 pm, KM came to report on the suspect's activities of the previous day. He mentioned that Ravi had photocopied nineteen pages during lunch hours and seven before he left for home. The preparatory drill was the same. Five officers dropped in for tea or coffee but they did not discuss anything significant. When KM had nothing more to report, Jeev shared the highlights of his meeting with the Chief.

"How can he allow the traitor to resign or retire? He has to be tortured physically in an interrogation cell and even hanged," KM's reaction was understandably exaggerated.

"Your efforts will not go waste," Jeev assured. "Just keep your intensity intact. I am sure everything will fall into place sooner than later," he added. Their conversation was interrupted by a buzz from the PS. He informed that a Dinesh Mehra was on the line and insisted that he had been asked by Mr Vinod Doshi to speak directly to Mr Jeevnathan.

"Bring him on the line," Jeev said.

"Is that Mr Mehra?" he asked as soon as the PS put him through the caller.

"That's right, sir. Mr Doshi had given me a job. Your man can contact me on my cell phone. I have given the number to your PS. The membership card for the Zair club has been arranged and is with me."

"How much do I have to pay for this?" Jeev enquired.

"Nothing, sir, it's a complimentary membership card for three months. In case you need to extend it, please let me know."

"Thank you," Jeev said. Meanwhile, his PS entered the room and gave Mehra's cell phone number on a piece of paper.

"Take this," Jeev pushed the slip towards KM." "This man will give you a temporary membership card of the Zair club for your watchers," he said. As KM pocketed that slip, Jeev inquired if watchers could come across anything interesting.

"No, sir, except that the suspect takes different routes to get back to his house. I have noticed this pattern of his movement ever since the anonymous caller warned him of being tailed," KM said.

"Are you working on the light and camera adjustments in Ravi's room?" Jeev asked.

"Yes sir. But Kutty wants to take one thing at a time. Tonight, he is only going to neutralize the brightness of the table lamp's light."

"Sounds good," Jeev said.

To Mani's surprise, Jeev returned home at 7.30 pm, an hour before his normal schedule. He had an early dinner and went to bed. When Mani entered the bed room at 11 pm, he was still awake.

"Are you okay?" she asked as she lay down on the bed.

"I am fine," he said.

"Dr Mahajan was inquiring about your back pain. I told him that you had no time for such trivialities of life," she provoked.

"I am seeing him tomorrow," Jeev whispered.

"What happened? Normally you don't show yourself to doctors unless it is life threatening," she asked.

Jeev said nothing.

Day 47

At 9.30 am, Kutty entered the NC, switched on the system and waited for the live action to begin. His effort to disable the table lamp and expose the uncovered areas in the suspect's room was on trial today. KM joined him fifteen minutes later and quietly took a seat in front of another monitor. He was evidently surprised to see everything in the room including the sideboard behind the suspect's chair.

"Did you also relocate the cameras last night?" KM inquired. Kutty nodded in affirmation.

"You must be one of the few in the Technical Division who takes initiative despite having Panda around," KM observed.

"Mr Panda may not be very friendly to you but he is really good at his work," Kutty said.

"Oh! Here he comes," KM exclaimed as he looked at the monitor.

9.55 am: The suspect followed by Inder enters the room. He carries a dark brown leather bag, which he keeps on the sideboard behind the chair. He sits and looks around. He switches the table lamp but it does not work. The peon keeps the briefcase and the sports bag also on the sideboard. Ravi calls his PA on the intercom and asks him to check the lamp.

His PA enters. He brings in papers and keeps them on the table. Then he fiddles with the switch but the lamp does not work.

"Maybe the bulb needs to be changed," Ravi opines.

"I have checked the bulb. The filament is intact," the PA says.

Meanwhile, the peon moves around the table. He points to bits of torn wires lying on the floor near the plug point behind the almirah.

"Sir, the lamp wire seems to have been nibbled by a mouse," he says. The suspect tells his PA to call the maintenance officer to send in an electrician immediately.

The PA calls someone from Ravi's room and talks about fixing the lamp. He informs the suspect that the electrician will be available only in the afternoon. After that he switches on the TV and leaves. The peon gives Ravi a glass of water.

10.30 am: Ravi calls Miss Mukta Sethi. She comes in and confirms that money has been sent to all outstations.

10.34 am: Ravi speaks to Naresh Shukla, Desk Officer for Pakistan and Afghanistan, and asks whether the latter could drop in for five minutes before getting busy with his work.

10.50 am: Miss Sethi enters again with papers and files. Ravi goes through them and returns them. He asks her to give a note on the performance of sources and recommend who among them should be dropped or retained. He inquires about her welfare and tells her not to forget inviting him for her marriage next month. She leaves.

11.02 am: Shukla enters. Ravi calls his PA on the intercom to send in two cups of coffee.

"It's a long time since we talked." Ravi initiates the conversation. "I guess you must be very busy these days, with so many terrorist incidents taking place in the region," he says.

"That's right. With Al-Qaida, Taliban, Lashkar, Kashmiri militants, and foreign forces operating not far away from our borders, the security scenario is grim and unlikely to improve appreciably in the near future," Shukla explains.

He then gives an overview of recent developments in Pakistan and Afghanistan and dwells at length on the fast shrinking space for India to play any meaningful role vis-à-vis the US-Pak-Taliban-Afghan axis in the region. He regrets India's increasing irrelevance to the resolution of Afghan imbroglio and expresses fear that like Republicans who created the Frankenstein in Taliban and ISI, it is the Democrats now who are out to foist a far more deadly cocktail of terrorists in the region by rejuvenating ISI and Pak defence forces with funds and fighting equipment. He claims that prospects of peace in Kashmir and the rest of India are extremely bleak and will become worse once the US and NATO forces withdraw from Afghanistan with no Ombudsman to watch over Pakistan.

Coffee arrives. Shukla takes a few sips and leaves, saying that he has to dictate a note on this subject and submit it to Mr Arun Roy before lunch. Ravi invites Shukla for lunch at the Golf Club. The latter thanks Ravi for the invitation but politely declines. The suspect makes no notes of the discussion.

11.25 am: The suspect reads files cursorily, signs them, and puts them in the out tray. He picks up a few loose sheets from the table, reads them and makes notes separately. He sets aside a few documents and keeps them on the sideboard. He shifts to the sofa and relaxes.

1.15 pm: He leaves.

2.45 pm: He returns, locks the door from inside, lies down on the sofa and dozes off.

3.30 pm: A knock wakes him up. Miss Sethi brings in some papers to show him. He peruses them and then tells her to keep them on the table.

3.45 pm: He calls Ajeet, Director Pak Military Operations, and asks if the latter would offer him a cup of tea.

3.50 pm: He goes out of the room to meet Ajeet.

4.15 pm: The PA enters with files, papers and keeps them on the table.

4.17 pm: The electrician comes. Checks the wire, cuts it, and attaches it to a new pin plug. As he puts the plug in the socket, the line gets short circuited and the wire burns. He tries another socket but the fuse trips again.

4.30 pm: Ravi returns, sits on the chair and watches the electrician try different sockets. The electrician says that because of the problem in the circuitry of the lamp, it will be advisable not to plug it in any electrical point till the concealed wiring of the entire room is checked thoroughly. He says he can try putting the plug of the lamp in the power socket but Ravi prevents him from doing that. "At least the TV and photocopier are working," he says. The electrician leaves.

5.00 pm: Ravi disposes of all papers and files and puts them in the out tray. Then he gets up, closes the door from inside, collects the documents kept on the sideboard and keeps them on the photocopier table. He photocopies eleven sheets and puts them in the brown leather bag. He returns to the photocopier, picks up the original documents, puts them in the outgoing tray, releases the security latch of the door and calls the PA to clear the outbound tray.

5.40 pm: The PA enters, followed by the peon. While he collects papers, the peon switches off the TV and photocopier and keeps the lunch box, water bottle and hand towel in the briefcase.

5.43 pm: Ravi picks up the dark brown leather bag containing the photocopied documents from the rear sideboard and leaves. The peon follows him carrying the briefcase and the sports bag.

While Kutty was busy shutting down the system, KM kept staring at the blank monitor in anguish. "This fellow comes to the office only to steal information," he mumbled. He got up and went to his room, packed his bag and left for home. After six hours of continuously watching the suspect's deceit, he felt exhausted and decided to skip briefing Jeev for a day. However, at 10 pm, he received a call from Jeev. He asked for a note on the suspect's modus operandi. "Give it to me before lunch. I want to show it to the Chief," he said and disconnected the line.

Day 48

KM's note on the suspect's modes operandi was unsettling. He wrote:

(a) The suspect invariably locked the door from inside whenever he photocopied documents and opened it after the job was over.

(b) He diligently went through the files and papers received from other desks in the Agency, selected those of his interest and kept them aside on the table. Then he took out white removable stickers from the drawer of his table and pasted them to cover the classification markings on the original paper. In some cases, he hid the identity of the author and the issuing unit behind those labels. After photocopying, he carefully removed the stickers and put them in the dustbin.

(c) The suspect's visit to the photocopier depended on the number of documents he found useful for copying and the duration for which he could hold the documents in his possession.

(d) He photocopied all the documents himself and invariably inspected the photocopier before opening the door just in case a loose sheet was left behind on the plate.

(e) He counted the photocopied sheets twice before putting them inside the dark brown leather bag, which he kept on the desk behind his chair. He ensured twice that the bag was zipped properly.

(f) He was extremely protective about the bag. At no point of time, he parted with it. After the day's work, he would pick it up from the desk and hold it firmly in his hand while walking along the corridor, standing in the lift, moving towards the foyer and boarding the car. His briefcase containing the lunch box and other papers and the black sports bag were carried by his peon or driver.

(g) He never stapled photocopied documents that he carried daily to the residence.

(h) He was never seen taking out any paper from the bag in the office. [Comments: It is still not possible to read contents of the photocopied documents but with some efforts, the classification and nature of the subjects can be vaguely figured out].

(i) The photocopier was meant to be kept in the PA's room, but Ravi got it installed in his office, arguing in an internal note that "at any other place, the photocopier would be misused for copying personal papers or even office documents with criminal intent". Jeev, on the other hand, suggested to locate all photocopiers at a centralized place where officers, irrespective of the position that they held, should go to copy their documents. Not willing to displease anyone, the debate was deliberately allowed by the Chief to drift, leaving

the option of locating the photocopier to the officers by default.
(j) The suspect had been relentless in ringing up officers working in different operational and analytical branches. He made conscious attempts to cultivate his colleagues and asked searching questions to elicit written reports and oral analysis.
(k) He hosted officers in five star hotels where watchers found it difficult to merge with the background.

Jeev commended KM for putting up an excellent note. "Delete the reference to the debate over placement of photocopier and give me a copy. I will send it to the Chief as it is. Also attach a few photographs showing Ravi's photocopying activities," he said.

An hour later, KM submitted the edited note. Jeev quickly glanced through it and rang up the Chief. "If you are free, I would like to show you something," he said. There was silence for a few minutes.

"I am leaving for IGI in two hours. You are not the one I can dismiss in minutes. Can the show wait for three more days?" Wasan inquired in jest.

"I am not performing. You are unfairly taking the credit away from Ravi," Jeev countered.

"I didn't mean to say that. Your sense of humour seems to have lately taken a nosedive."

"It's intact. I am only averse to factual inaccuracies. Anyway, have a safe journey," Jeev said and hung up. He returned the note to KM and told him to bring an updated version after five days.

Before he left, KM apprised Jeev of the highlights of the previous day's live coverage.

"Has it been possible for you to read the contents precisely," Jeev queried.

"Not so far. Tonight we are going to focus the lens directly on the photocopier, hoping that clarity will improve," KM disclosed.

"Okay."

"Sir, there is something that I want to mention," KM approached the subject guardedly.

"What is it about?" Jeev asked.

KM referred to the enormous increase in the workload and described how much the sifting of field reports, listening and transcribing of calls and watching and editing of 10-hour recordings daily had stretched the physical and mental reserves of the employees of the CEU to the limits. The attrition, he pointed out, was piling up and he was worried that someday it might take a toll on watchers' alertness, causing them to lose sight of critical evidences.

Jeev was unmoved. "It's almost seven weeks and there is no leak in the investigation. It is obvious the pressure of work has not affected the performance of your boys," he said and suggested to KM to persuade Kutty to take charge of the NC for some time. "He has a knack for picking up relevant things. That will save you time and energy for analysing inputs and planning more operations, should they become necessary," he mentioned. KM was not amused. He knew that this was Jeev's way of snubbing him for raising the manpower issue.

"Sir, he is essentially a technician and will not have the necessary skill to manage the NC. He may not be able to assess the inputs and pick up crucial strands in conversations," KM expressed.

"Try him out for a week and then come back to me," Jeev said, brushing aside KM's scepticism.

Day 54

KM arrived at the NC at 8.30 am to obtain the last five days of inputs for updating the note for the Chief. He had not visited the NC ever since Kutty had taken over its charge. He wanted Kutty to work independently. But behind this decision was also a lurking desire to see Kutty fail in his new role.

"I don't know if this will serve the purpose," Kutty remarked while handing over a report on suspect's activities. "I have put down only what is significant. In case you want more details, Avinash has the full transcripts," he said.

KM went through the note minutely:

Day 49

Ravi photocopied fifteen sheets before he left the office. Ajeet gives his assessment of the presence of US troops in Afghanistan and reports on the latest deployment of Pak troops along Pak-Afghan borders and former ISI officers' call to the Pakistan Defence Forces to support Kashmiri militants.

Pratap Mallik, Director of Air Ops, briefs the suspect on his visit to the Paris Air show and brags about how he was instrumental in getting membership of the Air Force Golf Club to the Chief and his Deputy.

Day 50

Ravi photocopied twenty-nine documents, eighteen during lunch and eleven before he left. Explaining his absence from the office on the previous day, Desk Officer, China Military, said he was representing the Agency in a meeting of a visiting PLA delegation from China, hosted by Ministry of Defence. He did not elaborate on what was discussed. Lokesh Kumar, Desk Officer Nepal, talked about Maoist violence and the Royal Nepalese Army's inability to contain armed Maoist volunteers. He also refered to the growing disunity among democratic forces to come to a common understanding to force the Maoists to join the mainstream politics.

Day 51

Ravi photocopied eleven documents. Ashish, Desk Officer Europe, kept his earlier promise and helped Miss

Sethi to fill in the particulars of a source in the format devised by him and admired by the suspect. He also brought along the profiles of a few Agency officers posted in Europe and left that on Ravi's table. Later on, they went out for lunch. Ravi returned alone, copied the document and put the original paper in an envelope and went to Ashish's room to personally hand it over saying that he did not want to retain it in view of its sensitivity.

Mahesh Soni, China analyst, talks about his achievements in raising numerous contacts in South East Asia and CIS countries. He bemoans that his achievements have not been fully recognized by the policemen at the top. Ravi chooses not to respond.

Day 52

Ravi photocopies twenty-four pages, all during lunch hours. The Desk Officer Kashmir updates on the latest security situation in the J&K. Ravi goes out for lunch with him.

The Desk Officer Sri Lanka appears deeply reverential to Ravi. He gives an assessment on the prevailing political scenario and chances of electoral gains by different political parties in the coming elections. Ravi does not show much interest. He invites the visitor for dinner at his residence and said there is a gift waiting for him.

Day 53

Ravi photocopied four documents. Ashish briefed him about US activities in CIS countries and Russian attempts to checkmate them. He also informed him about the views of Ministry of External Affairs on the US support to Pakistan.

The Desk Officer Bangladesh gave an overview of political developments in the country and possibilities of Army's return to active politics.

The Desk Officer Sri Lanka brought a CD and ran it on Ravi's computer. From their subsequent discussions, it appeared that it was the officer's assessment on what political equations might emerge after the elections.

KM put the note in his briefcase. "Now I know why Jeev has so much confidence in you," he said.

"This is the least I can do for him."

"I thought you were working out of fear of him."

"Mr Jeev doesn't scare me. He inspires. Is my probation over?" Kutty asked.

"No, you can't leave this work half way. You may have to video record me today. Ravi has been pestering me to come over. I could meet him at 2.30 pm." KM said.

"That will be interesting."

"Let's see what he has to say," KM said while leaving.

At 2.30 pm, KM entered the suspect's room. After they shook hands, KM took his seat. Ravi mentioned about his forthcoming visit to the US to attend his daughter's engagement ceremony. He talked about the groom and how the marriage was negotiated. KM mostly listened. He was not sure whether the suspect had called him to hear about his daughter's wedding plans. Finding the proceedings boring, KM asked about rumours of his posting to Riyadh.

Ravi: That's right but I won't go. I don't want to land up in a primitive place with my heart problem and can't allow my wife to live behind the veil. It is surprising that the Agency has assigned me to Riyadh even when I have not completed the mandatory three years of posting at the Headquarters.

KM: The Chief obviously thinks highly of you. Your maturity and discreet nature may have gone in your favour.

Ravi: I am not so sure. Anyway, do you know anyone in the Bureau's Surveillance Unit?

KM: Why, is there any problem?

Ravi: Sometimes, I get a feeling that I am being tailed.

KM: I have no idea why anyone should tail you. You don't interact with any foreigner outside the building and whenever you do, it must be with the approval of the Deputy Chief. It is the other officers who deserve to be placed under surveillance because they regularly meet their foreign contacts.

[Silence prevails as fresh lime water is served].

Ravi: The Chief has sanctioned an inspection tour. I am leaving early next week for Brunei. I may take this opportunity to visit Bali on a two days' holiday. Vijita has been planning to go to Bali for a while.

KM: You are lucky. All Chiefs have been indulgent towards you. Mr Wasan finds me uncouth, incompetent, and an embarrassment. That's why he has not sent me on a foreign tour in the past nine years.

Ravi: Have you not taken up this issue with Mr Jeev?"

KM: Less said the better.

KM sensed that Ravi had no more issues to discuss. He decided to leave. Ravi escorted him up to the door, locked it from inside and started photocopying.

KM reached the NC directly from the suspect's room. He saw that Ravi was still busy photocopying. He spent some time there with Kutty, recording his impression of his meeting with the suspect. Before he left, he called Jeev's office but was told that he was out of town.

Day 55

In a major attempt to buy peace, Jeev took his wife on a pilgrimage. His back was still hurting but he considered the risk worth taking. At 6 am, they flew to Kedarnath and Badrinath. The aerial view of snow-clad mountains, lush green valley, and steep gorges was breathtaking. Though the ride was rough throughout, the raw landscape along the route to the deity's abode was awesome. Jeev, an atheist, went through the motion of offering prayers without any feeling. He could never explain to himself why he was not gifted to believe in the concept of God or rituals attached to him. This failing made it perennially difficult for him to relate to Mani, who was deeply religious. The overall cleanliness at both temples left much to be desired. What irked him most was the priest's insistence to know his official position to determine the level of hospitality to be provided for offering prayers. While Jeev fumed and fretted, Mani spoke to the priests sweetly, dropped broad hints of her husband's position in the government and tipped them liberally. In return, they helped her perform the rituals in style, keeping everyone else waiting and seething with anger.

They were back in Delhi by 7 pm. Mani was happy and grateful to the Gods for granting audience despite an inclement weather. Jeev was not so enthused. The back pain had worsened during the journey and he desperately needed rest. He had an early dinner and retired to bed. But sleep eluded him, despite a strong dose of painkiller.

At 9.30 pm, KM rang Jeev, sounding hassled. "There is nothing very urgent, but I need to talk to you, sir. The suspect is running amok," he said.

"Come over. In any case I am not feeling sleepy." Jeev disconnected as he did not want KM to speak more on an open line. Ten minutes later, Mani came upstairs to announce arrival of Kamath.

"Your protégé is sitting in the living room," she said. "You may be badly missing his cloak and dagger tales during the day. I guess it might help you to sleep."

Jeev ignored her barbs and went downstairs. "Did you stumble on any vital evidence?" Jeev asked as KM rose to greet him.

"Sir, yesterday he copied eighty-one sheets, his largest harvest till date and he did it with impunity and a rare confidence. How long are we going to remain mute spectators?" KM said in anguish.

"You know my reaction. I agree that these are not his personal papers but the video has to conclusively show that the suspect is handing over secret documents to someone. Photocopying is only part of our problem. The crucial thing is to know about his running officer. In any case, what Ravi is stealing are just the crumbs of what we produce," Jeev pointed out.

"If we catch the suspect with photocopied documents, raid his house, take him to an interrogation centre and punch him hard, he will surely reveal the identity of the handler," KM argued.

"You can't raid his house without a court warrant. And for that, you need to register a police case. You also don't have the license to physically torture him and make him confess what you want to hear. At best you can question him. His answer would probably be that he photocopied papers and took them home to keep abreast of latest developments. He would explain that he did not permit anyone to handle his brown bag because it contained secret papers and shredded these once he finished assimilating the information," Jeev said.

"Sir, he is definitely stealing classified papers to benefit an intelligence operative," KM insisted.

"Where is the operative? Bring him in and I will terminate the investigation forthwith. For years this pot-bellied fool has been shoplifting the Agency's inputs but it's only now that we have some idea of what he is up to. Let's not lose our cool. It is time to stay focused on exposing his ring master," Jeev spoke persuasively. Realizing the futility of pursuing this topic further, KM raised the issue of suspect's impending inspection tour to Brunei.

"Why are we allowing him to go on the tour when we know what he is engaged in? Are we deliberately facilitating his meeting with the handler in Bali," he asked sarcastically.

"If you stop him now from going, it will unnecessarily ring the alarm bell. He may start fishing for reasons, take elaborate counter surveillance measures or simply lie low. That could make our search for the handler more difficult," Jeev opined. KM did not react.

"Could you get any details about Ravi's personal assets," Jeev enquired.

"Yes, sir. According to his cousin," KM reported, "the suspect's earnings from salary and savings cannot sustain his expensive lifestyle. He has inherited some land but the proceeds are nominal. He is in the habit of borrowing from his relatives and is known in the family for treating his wife shabbily and using her as bait to extract money from his father-in-law, who dotes on his daughter and will do anything to keep her happy. The old man's distrust of Ravi is so intense that he has refused to transfer the ownership of the present flat from his daughter to Ravi and change the ownership of a farm, which is in his daughter's name. I had also asked his cousin whether it ever occurred to the family members how Ravi lived such a lavish lifestyle. He said that Ravi would claim that he held a very senior position in the Agency and as such he received huge sums to entertain sources and cultivate contacts," KM paused.

"That's a clever alibi to hide the disbursing officer," Jeev remarked. "Do the intercepts throw any light on whether anyone is showing undue interest in his tour or offering any logistic support?" Jeev enquired.

"Not yet, but he has been calling the Chief's office daily to find out whether his leave for Bali has been sanctioned. His flight and stay at Bali have been tied up but we have no intimation from the Chief's office," KM said.

Jeev did not know how to respond. Had CEU not been eavesdropping, Ravi's inspection tour to Brunei or his posting to Riyadh would never have come to his notice. The Chief did not consider it necessary to mention that he had approved the suspect's posting or his tour. It was paradoxical that while Ravi would brazenly violate the principles of restrictive security to work for his intelligence operatives, the Chief would rigidly adhere to the same principles to prevent the CEU from tracking the suspect. Jeev tried to convince himself that the Chief's decision could have more to do with his inability to read the two events together than to any malicious design. The problem that he often faced was that the left hand did not know what the right hand was doing in the Agency. Since the visit of officers abroad and their interactions with foreigners in India were kept secret from the CEU, the latter did not know whether officers were meeting sources or their handlers. Jeev did take this matter up, but the Chief felt that if the CEU was kept informed of the nature of all such meetings, the secrecy of high-grade operations would get compromised. Moreover, CEU might be tempted to misuse the information and start digging deep into personal lives of even innocent officers out of vendetta or jealousy. The Chief, however, was willing to keep Jeev on board but was not prepared to institutionalize this practice for posterity. Jeev himself had reservations in this matter. He did not favour sharing of inputs with those who had no stakes in generating them. Precisely for this reason, he had opposed attempts to pool in inputs from all intelligence agencies at the NSCS or at similar nodal points. One just had to buy one officer at these outfits to know everything, produced at other places. The greenhorns in the government justified this move in the name of *coordination* but failed to comprehend that it violated the very foundation of restrictive security.

All of a sudden, in an unprecedented show of indiscipline, KM asked for a glass of water. He said that he was not feeling well. Jeev took out a bottle of water from the fridge and gave it to him to drink. "Go and take rest. It is already 12.30 am," he said.

KM left, looking very sick. Jeev followed him up to the gate and waited till he had driven off.

Day 56

Jeev woke up late. The backache was gone and he was feeling much better. He got ready at a leisurely pace and left for South Block for a meeting at 12 pm. The Chief came separately to join the discussion on resolving the issue of enforcing a sizeable cut in the strength of Agency's field operatives in view of financial constraints. The meeting, piloted by a pretentious Cabinet Secretary, lasted for an hour and half without any decision. He betrayed a complete lack of understanding of the Agency's basic needs of having foot soldiers, however redundant they might appear, and the fact that they could not be substituted by a few antennas and satellite feeds.

As they were coming out of the meeting, Wasan insisted that Jeev join him for lunch at his residence.

Jeev sent his car back to the office and hopped in the Chief's car. En route, Wasan casually mentioned how some of the senior officers were running operations in a whimsical manner and at a staggering cost to the coffer.

"Why don't you suspend funding of their fanciful projects?" Jeev asked.

"I do express my reservations but they won't listen. My problem is that we have worked together for almost four decades and unlike you, it is not in my nature to be rude and dismissive just because I am now the Chief."

"But you do have a responsibility to discharge," Jeev argued. "I have also come across a few files on operations that are simply ridiculous," he said. "For example, why do you approve funding of NGOs, so-called think tanks, journalists, lobbyists, and opinion makers? That's not our job. The Ministry of External Affairs can do it better and with greater transparency. We can surely engage in a bit of disinformation but our maximum initiative, hard work, and skill have to be invested in building assets," he pointed out.

"Which other operational file did you access without my authorization?" Wasan asked in jest.

"The one in which your officers have proposed to equip rebels with weapons and train them in guerrilla warfare. This is insane. It is quite tempting to create a Frankenstein but one always ends up regretting. It has never paid dividends anywhere in the world. Look at the mess that the US and Pakistan have landed themselves in by perpetuating this policy," Jeev argued.

"Why do you get unnecessarily agitated?" Wasan quipped. "We are barely a few months' away from our retirement. Let others face the consequences," he said.

"You are still the Chief. You have to wield the stick," Jeev insisted.

Wasan did not react. Both kept quiet till the car entered the residence.

The lunch was elaborate. Jeev was served his favourite fried spicy potatoes and rotis with clarified butter. One thing, that Jeev never found his friend wanting in, was his infectious hospitality. They left for office around 3 pm. Their conversation en route was polite and evasive. They came out of the lift at the executive floor but instead of branching off for their respective rooms, Jeev followed the Chief.

"You never told me that you were sending Ravi on an inspection tour to Brunei when you knew that he was under surveillance," Jeev fired the first salvo.

"I thought you knew it. If you want, I can cancel it right away," Wasan replied.

"It is not the time to keep him away from our eyes," Jeev said.

"I agree but it was an oversight. Actually I had left this business of selecting officers for inspection tours to the Division Heads. I should have seen the final list more carefully. But I can still amend it," Wasan offered.

"It's too late," Jeev said. "The cancellation will alert him and he may start probing. Anyway, you remember I wanted to show you something prior to your visit abroad?" Jeev asked.

"Yes, I do."

"It was a note on the suspect's modus operandi based on the video surveillance." Jeev took KM's note out from his briefcase and gave it to Wasan who read and re-read it.

"So, what do you want me to do now?" Wasan asked.

"We may be mounting another technical operation in his absence on tour to know for certain what he is copying," Jeev said.

"You must do something urgently to prevent further loss of information. It is almost two months since you started watching him but there is still no lead on his handler," Wasan reminded.

"This case is different in many ways from all known cases of espionage in our country's history. Ravi does not meet or speak to any unauthorized person. He suspects that he is under watch but has stuck to his daily routine. He photocopies papers but we cannot read them legibly. Unfortunately, this is where our evidence ends," Jeev pointed out.

"If you are so helpless, then why don't we sack him under Article 311(2) (c), citing security reasons," Wasan asked.

"You can always do that but if Ravi takes you to court, the present crop of evidences is likely to be thrown out of window because of its inconclusive nature and the manner in which it has been procured," Jeev explained.

"So, we are back to square one," Wasan remarked.

"Are you aware that the suspect has been seeing Vishnoi, one of your predecessors, quite regularly?" Jeev asked, literally sweeping Wasan off his feet.

"Don't tell me that you suspect Vishnoi of being one of Ravi's conscious collaborators too?" Wasan reacted sharply.

"I said nothing of that kind. We still have to find out the exact nature of their relationship. Honestly, I don't want to carry on with this investigation. It is getting murkier with each passing day," Jeev said. Realizing that Wasan was no longer comfortable in enduring his presence, he got up and left.

Back in his room, Jeev tried to contact KM but he was unreachable. Then he spoke to Kutty who said that he was still compiling and evaluating the inputs and it might take some time before the report was ready.

"Could you relocate the cameras as per the plan?" Jeev enquired.

"Sir, we had planned it for tonight but I don't think it will be feasible. In the absence of Mr Kamath, it's not possible to arrange the key of the suspect's room. I did try to contact

Mr Kamath but I don't know where he has gone. We will try to do something with the key tomorrow," Kutty apprised.

"Let me know, in case you encounter any difficulty," Jeev said.

Day 57

KM was incommunicado for the second day in succession. Kutty tried to reach him at his residence and left six messages but there was no response. He called up Ajay who said that he had not seen his deputy lately. Then he contacted the team leader of the mobile video surveillance unit who said that KM spoke to him in the morning but didn't disclose where he was. He merely instructed to file reports daily to Kutty.

At 6 pm, Kutty went to submit the summary of Ravi's last two days of activities. According to the report, the suspect did not photocopy any document on the previous day and spent most of his time in finalizing deal for the commercial use of his property in Gurgaon. Next day, he photocopied nine pages after following his well-rehearsed drill. He had three visitors during the day, one each from administration, accounts, and ticketing sections.

"You are doing a good job, Kutty. I hope you are not very unhappy that we left this tedious work for you to do," Jeev expressed.

"Sir, it shows how much you trust me."

"How is your son? Is he better now?" Jeev asked.

"It's all because of you that he is surviving," Kutty said. His eyes were moist.

"It's God's will although I am hugely sceptic about his existence," Jeev said smiling.

"Sir, I have got some arrears. Can I please repay part of the loan?"

"Keep that for the boy."

"I don't know what to say. You got him a job against all odds," Kutty's voice was cracking.

"Don't spread this rumour. My reputation of being a fair man will get ruined," Jeev said and smiled again.

"Sir, with his handicap, his whole life would have been a misery. And, you never even asked me what this handicap was like," Kutty said.

"I am not a physician. You are an honourable man and that was a good enough reason to help him out." Seeing tears swelling in Kutty's eyes, Jeev decided to change the subject. "Could you contact KM?" he asked.

"No, sir."

"I am worried about him. Day before yesterday, he had come to my residence. He was looking very sick. I wanted to take him off this investigation but the moment I talk of giving him rest, he gets upset," Jeev said.

Later that evening, Jeev finally managed to speak to KM's daughter. She said that her father was admitted in Apollo hospital but she was not aware of the details of the diagnosis. However, she confirmed that the crisis was over.

Day 58

Jeev reached Apollo hospital at 9 am. As he entered the room where KM was recovering, he saw his protégé struggling to rise from the bed.

"Please lie down. How are you feeling today?" Jeev enquired.

"Sir, I am sorry I could not contact you earlier. I will be in the office tomorrow," KM sounded weak. He was looking pale and there was slurring in his speech.

"You are not coming so soon," Jeev said firmly. "What do the doctors say?" he asked.

"They told my wife that I had a mild brush with heart attack. I don't know what that means. I am likely to undergo a few more tests today. You know the way private hospitals make money in these tests." KM frequently struggled for breath while speaking.

"Please don't allow KM to take any unilateral decision on his release from the hospital," Jeev told Mrs Kamath.

"He has never listened to me and there is no reason why he would listen to me in this particular case," KM's wife reacted in a subdued voice.

"Then call me."

"Sir, the suspect is leaving tomorrow on his 4-days tour. I can't afford to be here and do nothing," KM mentioned.

"It's neither the time nor the occasion to discuss such things. I need you to come back strong and healthy," Jeev said before leaving.

On reaching office, Jeev told Kutty that KM was not coming back before a week. He said that during this period it would be Kutty's responsibility to find the key to enter the room, relocate cameras, and manage the collection, collation and analysis work in the NC.

"Sir, I will try not to disappoint you," Kutty assured.

"Thanks."

Jeev then rang up Vinod Doshi and requested him to come to his office. When Doshi entered, he saw Jeev leisurely pacing back and forth in his spacious room.

"Come in. I can't sit for long hours in the same posture without aggravating my back pain. These are early signs of old age," Jeev said.

"Sir, you are still very young. Age is just a number," Doshi remarked.

"That's a cliché. You believe in it when you want to run away from reality," Jeev said and stopped walking. He took out a piece of paper from the drawer and handed it to Doshi. He disclosed that Ravi Mohan was leaving on an inspection tour to Brunei and wanted his check-in baggage to be searched and an inventory made of its stuff before it was delivered to the flight. He said that the flight details were given in that paper. In his typically never-say-die approach Doshi replied that though the task was a bit risky, he was confident of pulling it off.

At 7 pm, Kutty came to brief Jeev. He reported that the suspect remained mostly busy in finalizing his tour programme. Those who visited him were the Director, Pak Military Operations, and the China Desk Officer but they discussed property matters. The suspect photocopied three documents just before he left. Kutty also confirmed that he had made all arrangements to relocate the cameras and was now waiting for the suspect to go abroad.

"That's good. Once you are through with it, I have another task lined up for you. Technically, it will be more challenging," Jeev said.

"What is it like, sir?"

"I want you to bug his apartment to see what he is doing with the shredder and listen to his conversation with his wife," Jeev disclosed.

"We can monitor any area, provided we get an access to the place," Kutty pointed out.

"I will try to arrange for your access," Jeev assured.

Day 59

It was a busy day for Jeev. He left very early in the morning for a secret training location in Arunachal Pradesh. He had expected that his discussions with field commanders would be over before lunch but the debate got intense and occasionally heated. Several commanders wanted to know why they were not being utilized against Naxalites, terrorists, and militants when they were better equipped and better trained and more mobile than any other security force in the country. A few mentioned that ironically, it was their efficiency that was proving to be their biggest drawback. No one wanted to involve them in operations because they invariably outmatched the regular forces in hitting at hostile targets. An officer was bitterly critical about the way they were forced to abandon an operation when they had reached within the striking distance. Another officer wondered whether their gross under-utilization in live operations was not a crime against government resources. Almost everyone claimed that the leadership at all levels was letting them down by not utilizing even five percent of their potential.

"I appreciate your sentiments," Jeev said, wrapping up the debate. "I feel the same way as you do," he added.

"Sir, why don't you do something?" asked an officer.

"That's because I do not occupy a position where a difference can be made. It starts with the Chief and ends with the Prime Minister. The former is too clever to get into this mess and the latter is too ignorant and scared to force the issue," Jeev explained.

"What should we do then, sulk?" shot back another officer.

"Keep training hard without despairing over larger issues of governance," Jeev said, feeling guilty. The discussion carried on during the late lunch session, though less animatedly.

By the time Jeev returned to the office, it was 5.30 pm. During the next one hour, he chaired three meetings without a break. Then, he disposed of administrative files in which sanctions were required most urgently. At 7.45 pm, he told his PS to wind up the office for the day.

"Sir, Mr Kamath is waiting to see you."

"He is incorrigible. Okay, send him in." Jeev was both annoyed and relieved.

"Sir, Mr Kutty also wants to know whether you can see him for five minutes," said his PS.

"Ask him to come quickly." Jeev did not intend to stay for more than fifteen minutes.

"Did you desert the hospital?" Jeev asked as KM pulled out a chair to sit.

"Sir, all the test results were within limits. After that, I saw no point in sticking there. I was feeling suffocated in the hospital. The doctor also told me that if I felt stressed being there, it was better that I left," KM claimed.

"How are you feeling now?"

"I was sitting with Kutty in the NC since 3 pm. The change of place has done wonders. I feel much better now," KM said.

"That's okay. But take it easy."

"Sir, our man has been reporting regularly from inside the Zair club," KM changed the subject.

"Did he face any problem?" Jeev asked.

"No, sir. Mr Mehra took our officer along, made him sign a form and introduced him to the club manager. He was taken around the facilities later. For the last ten days, he has been positioning himself in the club around 5 pm and leaves after the suspect departs," KM informed.

"What has he seen so far?" Jeev asked.

"The suspect does not talk to anyone except for the trainer and concentrates on his work out. He is seen neither carrying the dark brown leather bag inside the club nor handing over any paper to anyone," KM reported.

"Let him watch for a couple of weeks more. We cannot draw a blank for eternity," said Jeev.

Meanwhile, Kutty joined them. He submitted the day's report on the suspect's activities. Jeev cursorily glanced through it. Ravi did not photocopy any paper and was mostly busy in collecting tickets, passports, gifts, and allowances. He had no one visiting him either from the operations or analysis branches. Before he left the office, he called up his son Sankar in the US. Sankar spoke about the strenuous nature of his present work and the belligerence of his boss. Ravi advised his son to take short breaks during work hours, have coffee with colleagues and, if possible, meditate for a few minutes. He also mentioned that he himself followed these practices to cope with the stress of his punishing work schedule in the office.

Jeev gave the report back to KM who quickly went through it. Unable to hold himself, KM reacted that the suspect was highly duplicitous, particularly the manner in which he lied to his son about his work pressure. The pressure that the suspect was referring to, could actually be coming from the handler to deliver.

Jeev did not react. Instead, he enquired from Kutty if he had anything else to mention.

"Sir, we have plans to place another camera to focus on the photocopier later tonight. We will test the results of our efforts tomorrow," he apprised.

"I will leave tomorrow on a reconnaissance mission but should be back by 6 pm. I will contact you as soon as I arrive," Jeev said. He left soon thereafter.

KM and Kutty followed him to the porch and wished him a safe flight.

*

It was 11.30 pm when Kutty returned to the office along with two of his junior colleagues. He waited for an hour for KM but when the latter did not turn up with the duplicate key to open the suspect's room, he stretched out on the sofa in the NC and fell asleep. At 3 am, he woke up and went down to the cafeteria for tea. Half an hour later, he returned to the NC and again dozed off. At 4.45 am, he heard a knock at the door and found KM standing outside. KM apologized profusely for being late. He explained that he overslept and his wife deliberately did not wake him up out of a misplaced sense of concern for his health.

"That was actually a sensible thing for her to do," Kutty observed.

"Can you still do something before the day breaks?" KM enquired.

"We will definitely try," Kutty assured. He immediately set off for the room along with the technicians and the kit. It took them five minutes to unlock the door and enter. In view of the paucity of time, Kutty decided not to position the new camera. Instead, he directed the technicians to replace the lens with new ones and change the focus of their direction to cover the photocopier and the area in its proximity more comprehensively and clearly. He left the other cameras untouched. The work was over by 5.30 am. Ten minutes later, they left the building after deciding to return at 4 pm to test the effectiveness of the lens.

Day 60

The disappointment was writ large on the face of Kutty and KM. The camera focus was right on the copying plate but images were getting diffused in the white light of the tube lights, making it hard to read the contents of the documents. For hours, they analysed the photocopied documents but the problem persisted. The only redeeming feature of the exercise was that they could read captions in bold letter, clearly identify the security classification and the unit, generating the report. Anything from files was still unreadable. By 9 pm, they were exhausted and frustrated.

"Will it make a difference if we change the white light with yellow light?" KM probed.

"We can try."

"Then let's do it," KM reacted impatiently. Kutty asked his junior colleague to loosely hang the bulbs over target areas. The results were marginally encouraging.

"I don't think it's going to work," said Kutty after they returned to the NC and started packing to leave. "You can't have bulbs hanging all over on loose wires. It's not the way you mount a clandestine video bugging," he added.

"I don't know how Jeev is going to react. He was supposed to have contacted us after 6 pm. Maybe he has not returned," KM said while getting into the car. Kutty did not hear as he was at a distance, giving instructions to his technicians about the next day's work.

Day 61

Jeev's first date in the office was with Kamath and Kutty. They briefed him about the bad run of luck and showed video records of a dozen photocopied papers, picked up under the new lighting conditions. Jeev shuffled through the papers a few times and then kept staring outside the window.

"Kutty has done his bit. Let him now go back to his unit," Jeev told KM. "You can ask one of your junior colleagues to man the NC." Both officers kept quiet.

"Any news from the airport," Jeev inquired.

"Sir, the suspect met no one. Our contact managed to have a look at the monitor when the baggage was being screened but he could not figure out anything, except that it contained some documents," KM informed.

"That's alright," Jeev said.

As they came out of the room, KM asked Kutty if he was aware of anything that could have prompted Jeev to relieve him all of a sudden.

"You are reading too much into his decision. I guess, Mr Panda may have requested him to relieve me for another operation. I can find that out once I go back to the unit," Kutty said.

"I thought you would see me through this investigation but I didn't reckon that Panda was lurking around to sabotage my efforts," KM expressed with a tinge of sadness as he turned right to go to his room.

*

Jeev's next visitor was Doshi. He came to show the inventory of Ravi's two pieces of check-in baggage. The documents included Inspection Performa and other related information. There were no photocopies of reports, no floppies, and no pen drives. But there were 4000 US dollars in an envelope, neatly tucked inside his wife's clothes. All items inside the handbags were innocuous and for personal use.

"How could you manage this? It's remarkable," Jeev remarked.

"Sir, it came with a price. I had to shell out two thousand rupees for the job."

"It's peanuts, considering the risk involved," Jeev reacted. He took out Rs 5000 from his locker and gave it to Doshi, explaining that the extra amount was the reward for those who planned and executed this operation.

Later in the afternoon, Jeev shared the inventory of Ravi's checked in baggage with KM. "Sir, we have again drawn a blank," he expressed in despair.

"I don't want you to sound helpless. If you can pull yourself out of your cardiac reverses, I am sure you can also see this investigation through to its logical end," Jeev pepped up KM's spirit.

"Sir."

Jeev then rang up Purnendu Basu, head of the Photo Division, and asked him to come over in case he was free.

KM was aghast that Jeev could even think of involving this pompous individual in such a sensitive operation. He believed that it would be a serious mistake to take Basu into confidence because not only was he indiscreet but also missed no opportunity to proclaim his credentials and brandish operational achievements. However, KM let his reservations rest till he knew exactly what Jeev had in mind.

Jeev had his own reasons for liking Basu. Although Basu was self-opinionated and always compared about not getting his due despite an outstanding operational record, Jeev admired his positive approach and willingness to experiment with new ideas.

"I am beginning to believe that prospects of cracking this case by employing standard surveillance measures are very bleak," Jeev poured out to KM. "But I have some ideas. I want those also to be exhausted before I give up the chase. Maybe Basu can help," he said.

KM kept quiet and waited for the quirky ideas of his boss to be spelled out more explicitly. In his inimitable style, Basu entered brusquely, wished Jeev, and sat down. He completely ignored KM's presence.

"Have you come across a photocopier, which retains in its memory, images of copied documents that one can subsequently retrieve?" Jeev asked without wasting any time.

"No sir. Not so far. But theoretically it is possible," Basu replied.

"I have seen one. Go and look for it in the market," Jeev suggested. "It may be expensive but the cost is not a factor. I will ask Panda to reimburse the amount on priority," he said.

"Sir, it will take Mr Panda a minimum of four weeks to give the money, if he follows the procedure. He will, of course, sanction but won't be able to draw money unless the lady auditor approves. She has no sense of urgency and treats the Agency like any other department of the government. She has no idea why sometimes, non-standardized items have to be bought at a higher price," Basu pointed out.

"The Agency can't afford to dispense with her advice. She is the only check on our reckless procurements," Jeev snubbed Basu mildly. "Give me the bill, I will reimburse it," he said.

Basu left without inquiring why and where the photocopier was needed. Unlike his other colleagues, he never fished for information nor conceded his ground easily. Given proper direction and handled with a bit of kid gloves, Basu was capable of producing wonders. But Panda hated his guts and reduced him to the status of a commercial photographer.

KM kept quiet as Jeev talked about the photocopier with Basu. He was not sure of its availability in the market and how it would help in reading the documents. He also had doubts about the feasibility of making the suspect work on a new, hi-tech copier.

"I operated such a photocopier some time ago." Jeev tried to allay KM's misgivings. "You will be able to retrieve every document that the suspect copies, from its memory. I don't know why it did not strike me earlier to employ this equipment. Anyway it's never too late. My responsibility will be to provide the photocopier to you. How you set it up, is your problem," Jeev said.

"Sir, what we can do is to disable the existing one and when he asks for another photocopier, the technical division can provide the new one," KM sounded upbeat.

"That's a smart idea. I hope the suspect falls for it," Jeev expressed.

Before he left for the day, Jeev called Prashant Vaish to inquire if he had any other input on the suspect.

"Sir, I hear that Mr Ravi has refused to go to Riyadh and even turned down Madrid."

"Where does he want to go then?"

"I asked Mr Ravi before he left on the tour. He said that in view of his heart ailment he would either go to the US where his parents live or stay at the Headquarters."

"That's a clear-headed decision," Jeev said.

Day 62

Basu met Jeev in the afternoon. He informed that he had bought the photocopier of the specifications that Jeev had provided and handed that over to Mr Panda.

"Did you try it out before bringing in?" Jeev asked.

"It's an amazing machine, sir, and capable of retaining thousand pages in its memory. What is remarkable is that it memorizes inputs date-wise. It's going to be a major asset in my unit," Basu spoke excitedly.

"Where is the bill?

"Sir, I have given it to Mr Panda. He didn't know what to do with it or the equipment." Basu said nothing further as he saw Panda entering the room. Jeev nudged Basu to leave.

"Sir, Basu would have informed you about the photocopier," Panda said. "I spoke to Mr Kamath about it. He said he was coming here to seek your instructions and wanted me also to be present." Minutes later, KM entered.

Jeev explained to Panda about the purpose for which the copier had been bought and suggested that he should work out a drill in consultation with KM for installing it in the suspect's room.

"Sir, we had some initial discussion in this matter," KM said. "We still have two more days before Ravi returns. The plan is that we render the existing photocopier dysfunctional. And, then we wait for his return. Our subsequent action will depend on how he reacts to his changed working environment," he explained.

Before Jeev could react, he saw the Chief entering the room. KM and Panda hurriedly got up, wished the Chief and left.

"I hope everything is fine," Jeev said as the Chief occupied the corner seat.

"You were talking about relocating the camera. Can you now read the reports legibly?" Wasan inquired.

"The experiment has come a cropper. The tubelights are not letting the lens do their job. We have now decided to replace his photocopier with a new one, equipped with the facility to retrieve the data from its memory," Jeev mentioned.

"I hope it doesn't turn out to be yet another fiasco?" Wasan poked.

Jeev took it in good spirit. "The entire drill to deploy the photocopier has been worked out," Jeev disclosed. "We are only waiting for the suspect to return from the tour to bite the bait."

Meanwhile the PS entered to serve coffee. After he left, Jeev raised an issue that he knew would upset the Chief. But he couldn't think of a better opportunity to address it.

"Wasu, there is something that I wanted to speak to you. Please don't take it otherwise," Jeev said.

"What is it about?"

"You know these fortnightly meetings in which we review the developments around the world. For the time being, please do not ask questions or encourage officers to speak about operations and the access of their sources. The suspect is mostly present in these meetings. Please try to make the proceedings as insipid as possible. You have always been good at distilling substance from inane stuff," Jeev tried to be as persuasive as possible.

"There could be more pleasant ways of indicting your Chief," Wasan said. It was evident that he did not like the unsolicited advice.

"If possible, kindly instruct your Chief Analysts and Divisional Heads to limit their interactions with the suspect to the minimum," Jeev emphasized.

"I can't promise but I will keep that in mind," said Wasan. "Is Ravi being posted to Riyadh?" Jeev drilled Wasan's discomfort deeper.

"You are right but he is not keen to go. Mr Vishnoi called the other day and requested me to change it for one of the neighbouring countries," Wasan revealed.

"I am told you have now offered him Madrid."

"Not exactly, but yes, the Assignment Board had suggested Madrid as an alternative station. But I have yet to decide," Wasan said.

"Why not one of the countries that Mr Vishnoi suggested to you?" Jeev asked.

"Because, these are places where we operate so extensively and knowing what Ravi is doing, I can't send him there," Wasan clarified.

"I have my doubts if Mr Vishnoi consulted Ravi before suggesting the alternative places," Jeev said.

"What is your information?"

"He will go either to the US or nowhere," Jeev pointed out. "He knows that you will never send him to Washington because of his seniority and perceived mediocrity. And, going anywhere else will not serve the purpose of his handler. Sitting at Headquarters, he can quietly extend his reach, go up in the hierarchy and blossom into our Kim Philby," he explained.

"You could be right," Wasan conceded. "That's the reason I am asking you to put him through a coercive questioning, employ rough tactics and get over with his murky dealings at the earliest," he added.

"I wish we lived in Saudi Arabia, North Korea, or Libya. You cannot lay your hands on him nor bully the courts to convict him on charges framed on the basis of inadmissible evidences. And, how will you handle the activists from a plethora of our civil liberty and human rights groups? You and I are not going to be safe once this man is out of the interrogation centre with bruises to support his alleged horror stories. If I accept what you say, we will be spending our life time's savings and pension on hiring lawyers," Jeev argued dispassionately.

"But, we cannot allow Ravi to parcel out our secrets forever," Wasan retorted. "I think you should have agreed to my earlier suggestion of dismissing him under Article 311(2)(c)," he said.

"In that case, you will end up helping Ravi to stay in Delhi merrily with his circle of friends intact, without our ever knowing about the intelligence outfit which is running him," Jeev countered.

"You are only making my life difficult. I hate the way you refuse to be accommodative but I don't know why I still admire you," Wasan sounded indulgent.

Jeev smiled. "I am sorry the coffee must be cold by now. Should I get another one for you?" he asked.

"Let me gulp it cold and bitter. You don't get anything warmer in this room," Wasan took the coffee and left.

Day 63

All activities related to the investigation froze for next two days. The suspect was away on tour to Brunei. The NC was shut down, surveillance cameras switched off, and watchers and technicians rested at home. Kamath took his wife to Mathura for an audience with Lord Krishna. Jeev mostly stayed at home, catching up with daughters in Cochin and Pune on e-mail, reading an interesting analysis of the impact of Muslim immigration on the European culture, and sleeping. Two incidents briefly threatened to spoil Jeev's holidays. Mani found a Habib Tanveer play that they had gone to watch on Jeev's insistence, too stylized, disjointed, and over-hyped. Jeev enjoyed it immensely and marvelled at the way the director had achieved fusion of a dying folklore with pageants of modern times. The final acerbic words, of course, came from Mani. "It's time," she said, "you grow up and start making your own judgements. You have depended far too long on reviews that are paid for."

In another incident, a head of state, who was already airborne sought permission to land his special aircraft at one of the secret airstrips under the operational jurisdiction of Jeev. He promptly refused. Soon calls poured in from the Chief, Principal Secretary and Cabinet Secretary and the state Chief Secretary. They even threatened to take the matter to the Prime Minister but Jeev refused to budge. "Sir, the pilot has just informed that he is about to land and it is too late for him to divert the aircraft to any other runways," Jeev's Operations Manager was the last to call him. "Block the runway," Jeev instructed. He received no request or threats from any one thereafter. The aircraft landed in the civilian area. Mani thought her husband's handling of the situation was foolhardy. The Chief, however, called to thank him for not bending backwards and saving him from a huge embarrassment.

Day 65

Ravi returned from his overseas tour. On reaching office, he handed over the inspection note to Sharma, his PA, and asked him to put up a draft inspection note based on his comments, recorded in the margin of the performa. He also asked him to take Miss Sethi's help. Then he called Bhan, his supervisory officer, and briefed him about the station's performance.

"Please put down your observations in the report. I will take it up with the Chief," Bhan said and enquired about his trip to Bali.

Ravi said that he didn't find the place very exciting.

At 11.45 am, he took out a bunch of cables from the briefcase and examined them. These had been lying at his residence in his absence. He selected a few cables, took the usual security precautions and tried to photocopy them but none of the keys of the photocopier was functioning. He kept pressing the keys but finally gave up. He called Sharma and Inder and chided them for mishandling the machine in his absence.

"We didn't even touch it, sir," Sharma clarified. But Ravi was not willing to listen. They had never seen him so angry and no amount of explanation could pacify him. After some time, Sharma left the room and went to the Technical Division to bring someone to repair the copier on priority. He came back with an assurance that a technician would come to fix the copier within ten minutes. But no one turned up. By lunch, Ravi's patience ran out. He called Panda and requested him to get his photocopier repaired urgently. He lied that the Chief had instructed him to bring over ten copies of a special report on the rise of Islamic terrorism in the Far East by the evening.

Within half an hour, a technician came. He inspected the machine thoroughly. Then, he used the internal phone in Ravi's room to inform Panda that the internal circuitry of the photocopier had been burnt and it would have to be sent to the company for repairs. He also asked for some help to cart the copier to the store. While he waited for his colleague to arrive, Ravi spoke to Panda again and pleaded to get it fixed as soon as possible.

"The earliest that we can expect the company to return it after repairs is a minimum two weeks," Panda said.

Ravi was devastated.

"Will it be possible for you to provide another photocopier in the interim?" Ravi inquired, trying hard to keep his frustration in check.

"Let me try to locate one," Panda said. "We have recently purchased five new photocopiers in connection with a special operation. I don't know if they have all been issued." Panda hung up and immediately informed Kamath. Half an hour later, an engineer from the Technical Division informed Ravi that he had been instructed to install a photocopier the next day in his room as a stop-gap arrangement.

Ravi did not let this setback affect his desire to scout for information. Ajeet, Director Pak Military Operations, was the first to come in for coffee. He confided that a decision had at last been taken to post Army officers abroad and four of them had already been shortlisted. He said that he was himself being considered for a posting to Jordan. Quoting the Chief Military

Advisor, he recounted that Mr Jeevnathan had so far been able to stall this decision, arguing that Army officers were not fit to operate in covert capacity because of their typical mannerism and oversized demeanour. However, in the last meeting, the Chief and the Deputy Chief managed to push this case through.

The next officer to drop in was Lokesh Kumar. In response to Ravi's pointed query whether the communists in Nepal had any chance of coming into power, Lokesh explained that the elections were not going to throw up any clear winner and what he expected, was a long period of stalemate in the formation of a stable government.

Finally at 4.30 pm, Anuj Nagia, the Desk Officer of Africa Division, visited Ravi at his insistence for *fresh lime water*. Of late, Anuj had been going through an extremely rough patch in his career. He was not only been overlooked for promotion but had also been slapped with an in-house secret enquiry over alleged misuse of secret funds and deserting his post in the thick of activities. For those who knew him, Anuj was an operative's delight. Reckless in taking risks and difficult to be reined in, he was a quintessential field officer and undeniably unfriendly to rules, norms and procedures. He was of no use for time servers who largely populated the Agency. Some of the intelligence missions that he undertook had no parallel in the Agency's history but these were religiously trashed by incompetent and jealous colleagues. Successive chiefs promised to set his records straight, but in the end they all abandoned him. Yet, he survived. He had guts of steel and didn't know how to bend or break.

"Where have you been all these days?" Ravi opened the conversation.

"I wanted to come over but the incessant requirement of reports from seniors kept me tied down. I was also told you had gone out on tour," Anuj said.

"Yes. I came only last night. How is the Agency treating you lately?" Ravi provoked subtly. Thereafter there was no stopping Anuj. He launched into a tirade against almost everyone, talked about operations that he had singlehandedly conducted and lamented how he had been denied his due.

"We have a pack of jokers who call themselves operators but they are totally bereft of initiatives and courage to take the battle right into the heart of the enemy's camp," Anuj claimed. "If I start spilling the beans, the nation will be traumatized. I know first-hand how senior officers and their cronies have built financial empires by running fake sources and falsely justifying ludicrous operations. We are masters in fudging source particulars and removing them from files," he spoke spiritedly.

"What will you do to remedy the situation?" Ravi, who was listening intently, probed.

"Unless you have a man who has grown with the job of running external intelligence and he refuses to soak his hand in the loot, nothing will change," Anuj declared. "This stupid notion of bringing someone from outside as the chief to instill energy, calm, and sanity to the Agency is a complete hogwash. You could be brilliant as a defence strategist, a whiz kid in the Army or MEA, a great operator in the Bureau or a super cop in the Police but here, you will be a fish out of water. Superficial things like foreign visits, glamour of interacting with foreign agencies, and the vast resources under your command will sweep you off your feet. You will be gone at the end of your tenure as a big zero, without understanding even five percent of the reach of the Agency's operations and the frontiers that it can conquer," Anuj paused to sip the lime water.

"If you feel that there is no career progression for you in the current suffocating work environment, I can arrange a job for 200,000 US dollars," Ravi proposed, exploring the possibility of recruiting Anuj for his operative.

"I can only work where there is a scope to innovate and take risks. Besides, it must have to do something with country's security. You know, I don't need money to survive," Anuj remarked.

"I am in no hurry," Ravi said. "You can think over the offer and come back at your own sweet time. You are such a brilliant operator. Any think tank dealing with security matters will grab you with both hands," he added.

"But I am neither good at writing nor at thinking. My forte is planning and executing a task in the field. Moreover, I have not lost hope. There are still officers like Mr Jeevnathan who value an operator's worth. It is unfortunate that today he is handling mundane matters. But I guess, it suits the political leadership," Anuj contended.

"The main purpose of my calling you is to show this source file to you," Ravi said, cleverly changing the course of discussion. "This has been highly appreciated by the Chief. I thought you might like to have a look at it." Having laid the trap, Ravi came to his real agenda. Retrieving a file from the almirah, he took out three sheets of paper containing list of sources and handed those to Anuj. "This format will help you access source particulars quickly, without every time going to the production desk for details," he elaborated.

"There is really no need of this exercise for me. Whenever I need information about a source, I requisition the production desk and it promptly provides the details," Anuj said.

"But my experience has been different. There are times when I need to evaluate a source report on an urgent basis but I can't do that for want of readily available inputs about the access of the source," said Ravi, laying the trap.

"I may not follow your model but I like the way you have devised the performa," Anuj said.

"Actually this format should be adopted by all branches to bring in uniformity in the data of our assets. I also strongly believe that we must engage in limited sharing of source particulars. That will at least help in standardizing payments to sources which currently vary wildly from one desk to the other," Ravi explained laboriously.

"I don't think sharing of source particulars is operationally advisable," Anuj was not the one to be induced easily. "Source payments," he pointed out, "depend on so many factors like his access, his potential to deliver, his personal standing, financial position, and the country where he is from and where he works," he said.

Ravi did not pursue the matter further. Nevertheless, Anuj picked up a copy of the format, folded it, put it in his pocket and left.

KM entered the NC when Anuj was leaving the suspect's room. He rewound the tape and saw the rest of the proceedings in fast forward mode. He noted down the salient points of the recordings and went to apprise Jeev of the suspect's desperation for a new photocopier and the gist of Ravi's conversation with Anuj Nagia.

"Sir, Nagia's ego is too big for his boots. He is extremely irresponsible and had no business to talk like this with the suspect," KM showed his dismay.

"What else would he do if you hound and humiliate him and threaten to take away his job. We are lucky that he does not have a weapon in his hand to wield," Jeev remarked.

KM knew Jeev's fondness for Nagia and therefore decided to change the subject. He told Jeev that Subhendu Roy had arrived and was waiting outside.

"Call him in," Jeev said.

KM went out and brought Roy along. The latter greeted Jeev in reverence and kept standing till Jeev instructed him to sit down.

"Good to see you after a long time. When did you reach Delhi?" Jeev inquired condescendingly. "Sir, I came this morning."

Jeev noticed that Roy had not lost any of his boyish charm. He oozed innocence and astounding sincerity, very rarely found in the officers of his rank.

"The last time, you had mentioned something about Mr Ravi Mohan after you returned from training in the US. Can you go over it again?" Jeev asked.

"Yes, sir. Mr Mohan often missed the outdoor exercises and seldom accompanied us on field trips. He would say that he had gone to visit his friends and relatives. He was very friendly with one instructor called Patrick Burns. On the day of our departure, Mr Ravi did not come with us to the airport and joined us directly from somewhere. We saw Mr Burns arriving along with him at the airport and helping us to pass through the immigration and security," Roy recalled.

"How is Mrs Roy and children?" Jeev did not feel the need for questioning Roy further about the suspect.

"Sir, everyone is fine."

"Is there anything I can do?" Jeev asked.

"Sir, my posting to Siliguri has been a boon. I couldn't have asked for better," Roy said.

"That's okay," Jeev said.

Roy knew it was time to leave.

"Sir, everything fits in place," KM pointed out once Roy was gone. "Ravi must have been picked up and won over by the CIA during this trip."

"I am not so sure if his subversion is that recent," Jeev remarked.

"Sir, Roy's testimony should prove handy whenever we decide to question the suspect about his undue interest in Burns," KM argued.

"Yes, to some extent. Actually, the suspect being the team leader was within his rights to interact more than other officers with the instructor. It is also not unusual for officers of the host service to see you off and extend necessary help at the airport," Jeev pointed out.

With nothing else to discuss, KM collected his papers and left for Basu's room. He spent an hour there, familiarizing himself with the new photocopier but found it too complicated for comfort. He was not sure if the suspect would ever be able to handle it without tampering with its memory.

Day 66

Ravi kept the staff running between his office and the Technical Division to get the new copier installed all morning. But KM was in no hurry.

"Why don't you let me send the new photocopier? Ravi has already called me four times," Panda said.

"I want to gauge the depth of his frustration," Kamath replied.

Finally, at 4.30 pm, he allowed the service engineer to install the new photocopier in the suspect's room. The engineer took ten minutes to make the copier operational and another fifteen minutes to explain its various functions to Ravi. As soon as the engineer left, he closed the door, took out papers and files that were already flagged, used the glue sticks and labels to cover the originator's name, security classification and file numbers and began copying. He photocopied eighteen sheets, kept them in his dark brown leather bag and went home. It was 6.15 pm. An hour later, KM entered the suspect's room to pull out copies from the photocopier. To his horror, what the copier churned out, were blank. The suspect had pressed the wrong button leaving the memory dead.

Day 67

Just before lunch, Ravi took the usual precautions before settling down to photocopy the marked documents. He tried to switch on the copier a few times but it made no movement. He checked the power with a tester. It was there in the line but was not running to the machine. Finally, he put the documents back into the almirah, opened the security latch, and called Panda. Within an hour, a technician from the company came and fixed the problem. Then he explained the functioning of the various digital buttons. Before leaving, he warned that repeated mishandling could lead to a permanent breakdown of the machine.

"When will my photocopier be repaired?" Ravi asked. "This one is very complicated," he said.

"I am not from your office," the visitor explained. "I don't know what repairs you are talking about. I am a service engineer from the Toshiba Company. This photocopier is actually quite easy to handle. Once you get used to it, you will never feel like replacing it."

Ravi, however, learnt his lesson poorly. He photocopied nineteen documents in the afternoon but again pressed the wrong key, disabling the memory. Kamath was understandably irritated. For the second day in succession, he could not retrieve documents. In desperation, he approached the company office and complained about frequent stalling of major functions of the copier. The company promised to send a service engineer soon but he could come to the building only around 9 pm. Avinash escorted him from the outer gate to the suspect's room by a circuitous route. After rectifying the snag, the engineer asked Kamath to photocopy a few documents. Then he made KM draw the data out from its memory. KM was amazed to see the end product.

"It's working fine in your presence but I am not sure what would happen tomorrow. Is there any way that I touch one key and get its major functions like copying and retrieval working right," he asked.

"That may be slightly difficult but let me try," the engineer said. He opened the electronic panel to customize its functions. After he was finished with the job, he invited KM to photocopy a document. "Hopefully you will now be able to pull out copies from its memory, irrespective of how you handle the other touch buttons," he said. In the engineer's presence KM operated the photocopier as clumsily as possible but encountered no problem in retrieving copies of the original text. "After this, I will have nothing else to do," he reassured himself while driving home.

Day 68

Ravi spent the day leisurely. He hardly showed any interest in papers and files that were put up to him. One by one, he called the usual suspects but most of them seemed to be busy. He didn't know what had suddenly happened. In brief spells, he paced up and down in the room and unlike other days, he did not occupy the sofa. He mostly spent his time watching a live cricket match between India and Sri Lanka at Guwahati. His attempts at eliciting information picked up steam only in the afternoon. Among his visitors was the Desk Officer Europe, who informed that several new stations were likely to be opened in the CIS countries and he was tipped to man one of them. Next to come in was Somayya. He revealed that 'Mushroom', Agency's most important source on nuclear proliferation was missing from North Korea. Ajeet was the last to drop in. He disclosed that his tour to Kabul had been approved by the Chief. He also mentioned that he had been sounded to get ready to go on a foreign posting some time later during the year. He hinted that he could join at Prague and not Jordan.

Ravi's mind, however, strayed elsewhere. "Any idea why all the officers seemed to be very busy in the forenoon," he asked.

"I don't know precisely but I was told by General Hari, the Chief Military Advisor, that the US had raised objection to our running of certain operations which they claimed, were promoting terrorism in the region. They want these operations to be discontinued forthwith. The National Security Advisor is coming to the building to discuss those operations with individual officers," Ajeet informed.

"That's interesting. Let me know if you get to hear anything about NSA's reaction," Ravi said.

Ajeet looked at his watch. It was already 6 pm. As soon as he left, Ravi latched the door from inside, took out a paper from his briefcase and photocopied it. Then he buzzed his PA, Sharma and asked him to wind up.

At 7.30 pm, KM entered Ravi's room and switched on the photocopier. What he retrieved, stumped him completely. He could clearly read every letter of the document. Although it was a copy of Ravi's land registration deal, he was thrilled that it was a bull's eye. He rushed to share his joy with Jeev.

"I am glad, it worked," Jeev said nonchalantly. He appeared to be busy in reading a noting on the file. "Any news from your watchers at the Zair club," he asked without raising his head.

"Sir, they have so far taken hundreds of photographs but they tell the same story. Ravi neither meets nor engages in conversation with any foreigner. He does push-ups and at the end of a fairly light exercise, he goes straight to the residence," KM reported. By now, Jeev had signed the file and called his PS to collect it.

"Let's withdraw the surveillance from the club. It has been a waste of effort," he said as he leaned back on his chair.

KM was taken aback. He was not sure if Jeev reacted out of irritation or a sense of helplessness. He wondered whether it was the first step towards winding up the investigation.

Day 69

Ravi came out of a taxi outside the main entrance of the Agency's building and walked up to his room, carrying a dark brown leather bag. He was late by an hour. Soon after settling down, he called Reddy, the Transport Officer, to find out whether he had deputed a mechanic to fix his official car.

"No, sir. There were already eight cars lined up for urgent repairs before your car was brought to the workshop. Anyway, what exactly is the problem?" Reddy queried.

"The self-starter was not working and we had to push the car. It also stalled frequently en route and I was forced to take a cab to come to the office," Ravi said.

"I will look into it," Reddy promised.

At 11.30 am, Ravi received a call from the Chief. "You had sought a personal meeting. What is it for?" he asked tersely.

"Sir, I have been working on the Far East Asia desk ever since I returned from the foreign assignment. If it is possible, kindly shift me to another desk," Ravi pleaded.

"Do you have any particular branch in mind?" The Chief asked.

"Sir, I leave it entirely to you, but I am keen on handling one of the neighbouring countries. You know how successfully I created assets inside the Pakistan Rangers and foiled several of their bids to push across terrorists when I was posted in the north-west Bureau," Ravi said.

"I do not want to disturb the existing working arrangements for the time being. But I will keep your request in mind," the Chief said and hung up.

Ravi was evidently upset. "So, I am stuck here for some more time. I don't know if it would help if I ask Mr Raghvan to speak to the Chief. But why would the Chief act on the request of a retired colleague who never bothered for anyone in his heydays," he mumbled. Meanwhile, his PA brought files and papers and sought instructions on a couple of outstation claims. Ravi did not respond. He also snapped at Miss Sethi on phone and asked her to wait. He regained his composure slowly as visitors started coming in. Commodore Pradeep Nair, Director Naval Operations, dropped in to apprise him of the Navy's intelligence requirements for the next year. The Desk Officer Europe informed him about the Chief's proposed visit to Mauritius. The Desk Officer Nepal gave an overview on the strength of the Nepalese Army and the Marxist cadre. Desk Officer Sri Lanka briefed him on the latest political developments in the island nation.

At 1.30 pm, Ravi had his sandwiches and soup. Then he went through the papers lying on the table, picked up a few of them, lifted the top panel of the photocopier, placed papers inside and pressed the button to operate. But the copier was not working. "What the hell is happening today? First the car broke down, next came the Chief's cockeyed response and now this photocopier is stuck," he spoke to himself. He immediately called Panda who promised to send someone to attend to his problems. Within fifteen minutes, a mechanic turned up. He inspected the machine and told Ravi not to worry about other buttons which were meant for specialized operations by professionals. He copied a few pages and made Ravi rehearse the copying procedure a few times. He also informed him that the old photocopier would be ready for delivery after three days.

"But I would like to retain this one. It generates copies that are clearer and carry no ink marks unlike my previous one," Ravi insisted.

"For that, you will have to speak to Mr Panda," the mechanic said.

Later on, Ravi repeated the request to Panda who agreed to spare it for the time being. At 5 pm, Ravi closed the door and photocopied nineteen documents. He kept them in the dark brown bag and called Negi, his regular driver to bring the car to the porch.

"Sir, mechanics are still working on the car," Negi informed.

"Why didn't you tell me earlier about this?" Ravi was visibly annoyed.

"I tried to meet you twice this afternoon but the door was locked from inside," Negi said.

Ravi disconnected and then called Reddy to find out the status of repairs.

"We are on the job. The car's axel is broken and it can't be replaced today," Reddy reported.

"Then how do I go home? I can't even call a cab inside the building." Reddy took no cognizance of Ravi's umbrage.

"I have made an alternate arrangement," Reddy assured. "A car will report to you in ten minutes. It's the Deputy Chief previous car and is well maintained.

Within minutes of Ravi's departure, KM entered the suspect's room and retrieved all nineteen documents from the copier's memory. These were fortnightlies and daily round up of developments in the neighbourhood.

"So, this is what our suspect has been up to," Jeev remarked contemptuously after he went through the copied documents brought by KM.

"Sir, now that we have these clinching evidences, we should not delay in registering a case of espionage against him," said KM.

"One vital link is still missing. We don't know anything about where these photocopies are headed to yet. Ravi's forced admission and his fairytale about his spying network won't help. Under duress, he may disclose names of his operators but you won't be able to verify them in your lifetime, because no operator ever gives his real name to the source," Jeev explained. KM felt Jeev's reasoning was flawed. "Sir, we have employed every available surveillance tool but we are nowhere near cracking Ravi's delivery mechanism. After being two and half months into this investigation, I also don't see any chance of getting hold of the handler either," KM argued.

"We now know for certain that what Ravi has been ferrying out are not his personal papers. Actually, this is the first direct evidence that we have come across to nail him down as an espionage agent," Jeev countered.

However, KM could not persuade himself to share Jeev's optimism. He wished he could quit but decided to carry on. He was confident that Jeev would soon run out of his ideas or get tired of chasing Ravi's elusive operative.

"Sir, apart from reclaiming copies from the photocopier, is there anything else that you would want me to do?" he asked belatedly.

"I don't know if it ever struck to you that Ravi might be transferring documents to his handler on his way back to the residence. We need to know what he is doing inside the car with the brown bag. Every surveillance device has thrown up some evidence to fill in the dots in our effort to unravel his spying network. Maybe this one will also contribute its share of dots in solving the puzzle," Jeev expressed.

"Sir, it won't be easy to infiltrate his car but I can try."

"I suggest you take Reddy into confidence but keep Samuel, his boss, out of the loop," Jeev advised. "Sam, of course, is very discreet and reliable but he is prone to disclosing information to seniors if it serves his interest. Reddy, on the other hand, is enterprising and resourceful but you will have to rein him in. He has a tendency to go overboard," he explained.

KM looked at the watch. It was 9 pm. He told Jeev that he had a family wedding to attend and left. He rang his wife and told her to get ready. He went to the room, dumped the papers and the briefcase in the almirah and came down to the foyer. While he was walking towards the parking area outside the main gate, he saw lights and random voices coming from the Central Vehicle Workshop. He found it unusual for the workshop to be still open at this late hour. He noticed that Reddy, surrounded by mechanics, was in an animated discussion. He guessed that a sudden requirement of customizing a car for high grade security might have come up. There was no other reason why Reddy, who usually left sharp at 6 pm, would stay back so late.

"Whose car is this"? KM asked.

"Mr Ravi Mohan's, sir," Reddy replied.

KM felt a rush of blood. The chance was right there to bug the vehicle. He asked Reddy if he could have a word with him in private.

"What is wrong with the vehicle," KM enquired.

"It has self-starting problem and the engine is getting heated quickly. These problems have already been rectified. Tomorrow, we will replace the broken axel and by the afternoon we will hopefully deliver it to Mr Mohan," Reddy informed.

"Mr Jeev wants you to detain this vehicle for a few days more," KM said blandly. With Jeev's name thrown in, Reddy decided not to question Kamath.

"But have you told Mr Mohan about this?" Reddy inquired.

"This car is to be used for a special operation," KM decided not to waste time in beating about the bush. "Ravi is passing official documents to an operative of a foreign intelligence service. The exchange of documents probably takes place in the car. We need you to install a camera inside the car to confirm or rule out our suspicion."

Reddy was aghast but he was also excited that Mr Jeevnathan had thought of involving him in such a sensitive operation.

During the last four years, Reddy had become sick and bored of supervising the repair and maintenance work of vehicles. Being enterprising and innovative he wanted to set up the Agency's Central Workshop along the lines of those in Germany and Japan but his boss, Samuel, a firm believer in status quo, pooh-poohed his suggestions for being incongruous with the Agency's management culture. Reddy had actually joined the Agency on deputation, fantasizing that he would one day be asked to customise vehicles to listen to conversations of top foreign visitors and record unsavoury activities of senior officers and politicians while on the move. By vocation, he was a qualified automobile engineer, but he firmly believed that he was gifted not only to manage a fleet of vehicles but also to run sources. No wonder, when KM unveiled the plan of action, Reddy grabbed the offer with both hands. "What do you expect me to do," he promptly asked.

"The car is to be customized," KM said. "I will provide the video camera and you have to conceal it inside the car to record activities and conversation of Ravi Mohan and his companions. Involve only your most trusted mechanics. They will naturally be curious but do not encourage them to discuss the purpose," KM cautioned.

"In that case, it will be better if we customise the car that I assigned to him today. It has more space and fixtures in which the device can be easily concealed," Reddy suggested in a conscious attempt to prove his operational acumen.

"I leave the decision to you," KM said and departed. He picked up his wife from the house and reached the wedding reception around 11.45 pm.

Day 70

As soon as he reached office, Reddy informed the suspect that his car had been repaired and handed over to the driver. But Ravi had other ideas. While thanking Reddy for providing a comfortable car, he wondered whether he could retain it on a permanent basis. Reddy advised him to take it up with his boss Samuel. "I will," Ravi said.

Meanwhile, Kamath dropped in Kutty's office to apprise him of Jeev's latest operational brainwave and sought his help to bug the suspect's car. Kutty noticed that KM was not happy with Jeev for burdening him with more and more operational tasks. "I know, it's not easy to keep pace with Mr Jeevnathan," Kutty said, "but you will end up learning a lot if you can survive the pressure of his demands. As for this task, it is an easy take. We have done it many times before," he claimed.

"Will you go to Panda for approval?" KM asked.

"It's not necessary. Once he approves our involvement in a particular operation, he doesn't expect us to keep running to him for fine tuning," Kutty clarified. Then he called an officer, explained to him about KM's requirement and instructed him to use a particular device that was procured the previous week.

KM took the technical officer along to the service area in the Transport Unit and introduced him to Reddy. He emphasised that in case of any problem, they must call him rather than depend on their instincts.

By 8 pm, the workshop had almost shut down. With no one to snoop around, a mechanic ripped apart the inner lining of the car. The technician fixed the cameras, stuck the wire along the roof and connected it to the console, which was fastened to the floor between the two front seats. After that the mechanic re-laid the lining carefully and called Reddy to test the system. To everyone's relief, it worked flawlessly. The next step was to test the system's operability in driving conditions. Reddy called driver Bisht and taught him how to handle the console. At 11 pm, they both drove the car to a restaurant in Malcha Marg to have dinner. An hour later, they picked up Kamath from his apartment and then went on a test drive that lasted for most part of the night. At 4 am, they reached Reddy's house to play the tape. The visuals were sharp, audio was good, and every detail of activities of KM and Reddy in the rear seat was recorded. Finally at 5.30 am, Bisht dropped KM at his residence and came back to the office to park the car.

Day 71

At 10.30 am, Reddy rang the suspect to inquire if the car was operating smoothly. He said that it was working fine.

"I may have to withdraw your car for a few days," Reddy said cautiously. "Even without your consent, I had indented for a new AC and upholstery for your car. These items have since arrived. I had planned to get them fixed before I go on leave next week."

"That's very thoughtful of you" Ravi replied.

"I will send you the same car as an interim arrangement. Nagarajan will be your driver," Reddy said.

"I do not want him to drive me. He is argumentative and shows his displeasure if he has to stay beyond office hours," said Ravi.

"In that case I will depute Bisht. He is very good at driving, is discreet, and highly disciplined. I am sure you will like him," Reddy laid the trap quietly.

That evening, the suspect was driven home in the customized car by Bisht.

Earlier in the afternoon, KM briefed Jeevnathan on car for clandestine recording of his activities while on the move, relentless customising Ravi's use of photocopier by him, stream of visits by collaborating colleagues to his room and continued absence of any lead to locate the handler. Jeev listened, while disposing of piles of pending files.

"I am not sure if you want me to repeat the same activities of the suspect daily," KM remarked cynically.

"Where do you get such ideas?" Jeev said without looking up at KM. "This is not the time to sit and moan. If I don't react to your daily reports and saddle you with more tasks, it does not mean my focus has shifted," he chided.

"I am sorry for upsetting you. But I do get very frustrated for not being able to deliver the kind of evidence that you are looking for," KM clarified.

"Drop in whenever your adrenaline runs precariously low," Jeev smiled.

Pleased with Jeev's rare expression of indulgence, KM decided to spend the day at NC, watching Ravi's unabashed perfidy.

Day 72

It was like any other day. Ravi reached office on time, made calls to colleagues, and invited them for coffee or lemonade. Lokesh briefed him on the Nepal Marxists' nexus with Naxalites operating in Andhra, Bihar, Jharkhand, Orissa, and Chattisgarh. The Desk Officer Bangladesh discussed the Army's efforts to carve an effective role for itself in the governance of the country. Murali P. Rao, Desk Officer Sri Lanka, gave an overview on the political scenario likely to emerge from the parliamentary elections and how far India would be able to wield its influence in the new political dispensation. After these officers were gone, Ravi rang Shastri, in-charge of high grade operations in Pakistan and Afghanistan, but the later politely declined to come over, saying that he was preoccupied with a visiting Egyptian delegation. Next, he called Naresh Shukla's office but was told that the officer was away on tour. Then he contacted Somayya who came in carrying a paper in his hand. Ravi photocopied it during lunch hour. It was a note that the National Security Advisor had asked for on the latest status of nuclear power plants in Pakistan.

In the afternoon Ajeet, Director Pakistan Military Operations, dropped into Ravi's office. He talked about the recent security situation in the Valley, based on a note that he had submitted earlier to the Chief.

"I wonder if security forces will ever succeed in getting J&K rid of militancy. It's high time Delhi settles for drastic solutions like holding a plebiscite, ceding the Valley to Pakistan or granting outright freedom to Kashmiris," Ravi hurled a loaded question to elicit reportable inputs.

"I don't think Kashmiris will accept anything short of independence," Ajit opined. "The separatists firmly believe that if they can sustain the current intensity of violence for a few more years, our fractured political leadership will readily concede one of these solutions. They have probably assessed that it's just a matter of time when the US withdraws from Afghanistan, leaving the field wide open for Taliban and Al-Qaida to physically and financially assist the LeT and home-grown terrorists to go for the kill. They assume that in the changed security environment, India will have no option but to concede to their demands, with international public opinion mounting pressure against alleged violation of human rights in J&K by our security forces," he said.

"What about giving greater autonomy to J&K?" Ravi prodded.

"It is no longer an option. The Pak Army, the ISI, and a plethora of militant outfits have sensed victory and are not going to allow permanent normalcy to return to the Valley." Ajeet paused to receive a call on his cell phone and then resumed. "The Indian Army is still quite confident of winning this war of attrition. But they worry that the current political and civilian leadership may ditch them and agree to a partial or total surrender of Delhi's sovereign rights over J&K," he said.

They did not discuss the issue further as Ravi got busy with approving draft of the fortnightly report, brought in by Miss Sethi.

After Ajeet left, Ravi photocopied eleven sheets. His last activity of the day was to write a letter to his son Sankar.

Interestingly he photocopied the letter and kept it in a file. Parts of its content reflected the suspect's guilt. Among other things, he wrote that "in the final analysis, it is not the individual's genetic composition but his training, environment and education that define his character. For example, a son from the same parents becomes a saint while his brother turns into a criminal." He concluded by advising his son to draw the right lessons from the holy scriptures and scrupulously avoid falling in bad company.

Later in the evening, KM showed this piece of infinite hypocrisy to Jeev.

Day 73

Ravi spent the day listlessly. He wasn't feeling too well since the night before because of sore throat and a running nose. He wanted to skip office but changed his mind at the last minute. He came to the office mainly to finalise names of officers whom he wanted to invite for a dinner, which was to be held two weeks later. Ravi's dinners were a regular feature and a matter of envy for the Agency's officers. His junior colleagues waited eagerly for their turn to enjoy choicest of food and drinks at his house. His invitees included officers of the Agency, NSCS, Defence Forces and Intelligence outfits. Since his mental capacity to retain inputs emerging out of discussions was abysmally low, he used to cleverly waylay guests either to his study or to the balcony where Kamath suspected, Ravi would have fitted powerful microphones. However, KM was not sure how anyone could record audible words in such noisy surroundings.

After his PA placed the typed list of invitees before him, Ravi rang one by one his colleagues handling international terrorism —Europe, Bangladesh, Sri Lanka, Nepal, Africa, Afghanistan and Chief Transport Officer for dinner at his residence. He said that he would have the invitation cards delivered shortly. Then he disposed of pending papers, had lunch and relaxed. At 4 pm, he photocopied seventeen documents dealing with NSCS's tasking of intelligence requirements for Islamic terrorism in South Asia and updated notes on political developments in the neighbouring countries.

Ravi left early for home in the rigged car. Near the IIT flyover, as Bisht took the left turn, Ravi heard a screeching sound. He told Bisht to drive the car carefully. What had actually happened was that when the driver had switched on the system and it did not respond, he pressed the wrong button in his nervousness, which producing a whizzing sound that kept persisting.

"What is this noise?" Ravi inquired.

Bisht expressed ignorance.

"Get it checked before coming to pick me up tomorrow," Ravi instructed.

Bisht said that he would. A few minutes later, he somehow managed to switch off the system and the noise was gone. After dropping Ravi, he took the vehicle to the Special Service Area and reported the matter to Reddy. The latter contacted the technical expert who came over to check the device, tightened a few loose wires and declared it fully operational.

For Jeev, work began at 7 pm. He had just returned to the office after a ten-hour tour to one of the technical bases in Karnataka. Files requiring his administrative approval and financial sanction had piled up on his table. In addition, there were four drafts proposals for acquisition of expensive communication systems pending for his clearance. By 9.30 pm, he cleared the files but kept the draft proposals in the briefcase for a closer scrutiny at home. As he got ready to leave, Wasan called to check if he was still around. "Where did you pick up this trait of sitting late in the office?" Wasan asked in a lighter vein.

"I inherited this work culture from the Bureau. There, it's a guaranteed recipe for moving rapidly in your senior's esteem as a hard-working, committed, and bright officer. It's not like the Agency where officers are desperate to leave at 6 pm and even earlier, as if their survival depends on chartered buses and car pools," Jeev remarked.

"If you can temporarily leave your files, I can come over to talk shop," Wasan quipped.

"That would be gracious," Jeev's response was officious.

Jeev used the Chief's presence to brief him about the results of various surveillance devices and the customized photocopier. He also showed him the latest photographs, betraying the abandon and confidence with which Ravi copied documents and carried them home.

"What kind of officers do we have, Jeev? Honestly, I never imagined that we were feeding a viper all these years. Look at the gall of this man. Despite knowing what he is up to, he has been trying to use political influence to shift to a productive operational desk. I actually want to see him thrown in the darkest dungeons and hanged as early as possible." Wasan was visibly angry.

"Unfortunately, our evidence is ominously silent on the handler. If only we knew the running officer, we would have struck the suspect long back," Jeev said.

"Is it really so important for us to catch the handler?" Wasan asked.

"In the case of Shetty and Vijay Shekhar, we caught the handler on tape. In this case, there is no trace of the handler in our visuals. As I told you earlier, you can dismiss him under Article 311(2)(c) anytime now. But if you want to file a case against him for espionage, you may have to depend entirely on the unverifiable version of his confession," Jeev contended. Wasan did not appear to be convinced. "Then, let us involve the Bureau to reinforce our surveillance. That could help in locating the handler early," he said.

"You can but before the Bureau presses its surveillance teams into action, it may insist that we permit their officers to look into the technical aids that we have employed to gather evidence against the suspect. Whether you would like these devices to be exposed to the Agency's historical bête noire, will be a call that you have to take. Their next step will be to glean through the reports that the suspect has ferried out so far, and then use this information to tell the government that the Agency cannot be relied upon to ensure the safety of classified documents," Jeev explained.

"To be honest with you, I can't trust the Director of the Bureau. He has inherited pathological enmity of his peers towards our organization, never misses to ridicule our reports, and uses his proximity to the Home Minister to constantly show us in poor light. He has also let his Deputy loose to canvass for an expanded presence of the Bureau abroad at our cost, claiming that we have repeatedly failed in providing terrorism-related intelligence. I can't let this man pry into our operations," Wasan emphasized.

"Even if we agree to involve the Bureau, it has neither the expertise nor the technical resources to improve on our surveillance efforts," said Jeev. "In fact, there is nothing that we do not know about the suspect. I can also make an informed guess about the subverting agency but guesses are not what a professional intelligence outfit should settle for," he said. Wasan nodded his head in agreement.

"Has it occurred to you that for the last two and half months, we have been chasing a senior analyst on the streets of Delhi and keeping a twenty-four hour watch around his house, yet the Bureau has made no inquiry. Either they don't have a whiff of what the suspect has been doing for years or they are simply not doing their job," Jeev pointed out.

Wasan appeared to be mulling over something.

"Notwithstanding our reservations, if something goes wrong with this operation, we will probably be accused of not taking the help of the Bureau to cover up some sinister agenda of ours. They may even question our judgement in not involving the Bureau which is the authorized nodal agency for handling the espionage cases in the country," Wasan pointed out.

"Why do you think our efforts will fail?" Jeev countered. Wasan avoided responding. Instead, he asked whether Jeev would have difficulty in seeking the Bureau's help to monitor Ravi's calls, his e-mails, and text messages to trace the handler.

"You can do that but in order to justify the need for tapping the phone, the Bureau will ask us to furnish all our evidence and not just the suspicion. Their demand for evidence is bound to be intrusive and exhaustive. Instead of assisting, they will become our hangman by taking a moral high ground and debunking our internal security regime," Jeev warned.

"I will go along with your decision. If possible, give me the telephone and mobile numbers of the suspect. I know an officer in the Bureau. He might help in tracing the suspect's calls and his contacts without MHA's sanction," Wasan said as he looked at his watch. It was 9.45 pm. Before he left, Jeev took out a sheet of paper containing the numbers from his table drawer and gave it to the Chief.

Day 74

Ravi began the day in office by inviting the division heads of China and Pan Islamic movement for the dinner at his residence on Monday, 20 June. Around 11.30 am, Commodore Nair dropped in to congratulate Ravi on his posting to Riyadh. Ravi said that it had been cooking for a long time but he had made it clear to the selection board that he would not join at that station.

"Have they offered any alternate station?" Nair asked.

"They have. But I would neither go to Madrid nor to Warsaw," Ravi disclosed.

"I don't know how you can spurn these lucrative offers," Nair said.

"My priorities are different," Ravi clarified. "There is no intelligence work at those places. I am not interested in going as a tourist nor do I have any lust for money. I would rather prefer being at Headquarters," he said.

"Sir, the more I know you, the higher you go in my esteem," Nair said.

Ravi acknowledged the appreciation with a smile.

In the afternoon, Ravi checked with World Wide Travels about the cost and availability of air tickets for the US. He told the agent that he would prefer travelling by British Airways along with his wife on 15 July. When the agent started giving details of fare in different classes, he cut him short and asked for the fare of two persons in First Class.

"Sir, it is Rs 2,69,865."

"Please block the seats in the name of Ravi Mohan and Vijita Mohan. I will send the amount early next week," he instructed.

In the course of the day, he elicited information on the gun and drug trafficking points along Indo-Myanmar border, mentioned to Miss Sethi about the possibility of his visit to Turkey for a liaison meeting and asked his PA to personally collect a note from Ashish on the nature and extent of MEA's lobbying in the US. The Desk Officer Pakistan came to hand over a copy of the report on sectarian violence in Pakistan and dissension in Pak Army over handling of insurgency in the Federally Administered Tribal Agency in the west. The suspect copied thirty-four documents, including the Bureau's report on the open activities of foreigners in India, LTTE's latest procurements, Bhutan-US relations, and Norway's perception of current peace process in Sri Lanka. One of the photocopies was yet another letter to his son, Sankar who appeared to be in some kind of financial trouble. The suspect wrote:

> Money is more important than everything else in life. God rules Heavens but money rules the Earth. No wonder, money is worshipped by Hindus in the form of a deity called Laxmi. It gives freedom to choose hobbies, lifestyle and company you want to keep. Ravi's hypocrisy came alive in his concluding remarks. He cautioned that you can enjoy wealth only if it has been earned in rightful manner.

"Sir, this man is the pits," Kamath claimed as he finished briefing Jeev on the day's developments. "The letter to his son shows his lust for money and his concluding advice lays bare his duplicity," he said.

"Ravi is writing to his son. You can't expect him to share his secrets of earning money from dubious sources with his son. Anyway, do you have any idea why the suspect is going to the US?" Jeev inquired as he finished reading the reports.

"Sir, the ostensible purpose of his visit is to attend his daughter's engagement ceremony. But he is actually going to meet his operatives. He is travelling first class along with his wife. It is obvious, his running officer is paying for their tickets," KM said.

"Are you suggesting that the CIA is operating him?" Jeev probed.

"Sir, that's only my assumption. Given your fetish for clinching evidence, it cannot pass your test."

"Anything else?"

"Sir, the suspect's refusal to go to Saudi Arabia, Spain, or Poland must be entirely the decision of his running officer. They would like him to remain at Headquarters where he has wider reach to information and will have more access to vital inputs as he moves up in the hierarchy," KM contended.

"What next?"

"Sir, he is visiting Patiala again on Friday, 24th June."

"I see."

"Sir, you may have noticed his day's harvest. It's a staggering thirty-four reports," KM said. Jeev did not react and kept looking through the window.

"Sir, is something bothering you?" KM asked.

"The frenetic pace of his copying is quite worrisome. I get a weird feeling that he could be using his laptops to send the inputs to the handler. I don't know if you can win over his servant to have an access to the electronic devices in his apartment," Jeev hinted.

"It won't be easy but I can try," KM said.

Day 75

Jeev was reading the morning newspapers in the car when his mobile vibrated. The Chief was on the line. He asked for a status report on the investigation along with supporting documents by 1 pm. "I am meeting Mr Saran, Principal Secretary to the Prime Minister, in the afternoon. It's about time he is briefed about the case," he said.

"This may not be the right time to brief Mr Saran," Jeev replied coolly. There was a long pause on the other side.

"Princi (a pet name that Agency chiefs often used to address the Principal Secretary in informal discussions to honour his status in the PM's court), is Minister in-charge of the Agency. He is entitled to know about a case that vitally affects our security. It also makes practical sense that we keep him in the loop," the Chief averred.

"Let's not take any hasty decision out of fear or misplaced respect for his position," Jeev reacted politely. "Saran," he said, "has no experience of handling such tricky operational situations. He is bound to get panicky after seeing reports and photographs and will be tempted to give common sense directions that may derail the very purpose of the investigation."

"No, I must bring this case to Princi's notice." The Chief was adamant.

"You will receive the report in time," Jeev said curtly and disconnected. Seconds later, he called KM and instructed him to deliver a factual note, supported by intercepts and photographs personally to the Chief.

"Sir, I will bring the draft within an hour. I want you to see it before I hand it over to him," KM submitted.

"Do as I have said," Jeev instructed.

KM handed over the report to the Chief at 12.30 pm. From there, he went to show the report to Jeev but was told that he had gone to attend a conference and was not likely to return for the day. KM tried to reach him on mobile but it was switched off. Then he left a message, informing that the "suspect did not come to the office the whole day. No one in the office bothered to find out where the suspect was and what he was up to. He also skipped the workout in the Club."

Day 76

It was Sunday. Ravi remained mostly inside his house. At 3 pm, his servant, Jena, came out of the house, moved around in the open area in front of the outer gate of the apartment building and stretched his neck back and forth trying to look for someone. Ten minutes later, he went inside the house. At 4 pm, Ravi and his wife emerged and drove their private car to the Diagnostic Centre in Khan Market. During their hour-long stay in the clinic, Vijita frequently came out looking for someone. At 5.30 pm, they left Khan Market. The suspect dropped Vijita at home and then took a detour via Sarojini Nagar and South Extension to reach the Golf Club at 7 pm. There, he had drinks with a gentleman who was later seen handing over an envelope to him in the parking area. He reached home around 9.25 pm. KM subsequently found out that the gentleman was General Soman of the Northern Command and an old coursemate of the suspect.

At 10.30 pm, watcher Pal went to KM's residence to hand over the day's report. KM was hugely upset. "The suspect has either been alerted or he has noticed you. If I mention this to Jeev, he will lynch all of us. As it is he thinks that the watchers are doing a shoddy job," he burst out.

"That's not true, sir." Pal insisted. "The suspect has noticed none of us so far."

"How are you so confident?" KM asked in annoyance.

"Four of us took turn to watch the suspect's activities right inside the Diagnostic Centre but he kept looking outside. We followed him up to the parking area and stood right behind his car but he had no clue," Pal stressed. KM calmed down. "Anything else?" He asked.

"Sir, you had mentioned about trapping Jena. One of the guards of Ravi's apartment complex is Jena's closest friend and they often drink together. We have taken him into confidence. He has assured that he can take Jena out for a few hours if Mr Ravi Mohan and his wife go out of Delhi," Pal laid out his plan of action.

"How will you get the key to enter the apartment?" KM asked.

"We have also worked that out," Pal sounded upbeat. "Prem Singh the Locksmith, will open the door with the master key, enabling the technical officer to move in quickly for setting up the device. We, of course, need to have the necessary luck," he said.

"That is what has been in short supply throughout this investigation. Your plan is weird but I will take the chance," KM said.

Day 77

On reaching office, Ravi called Mohite, Head of the Administration, to find out if his leave application for the US had been cleared by the Chief.

"I will check and let you know," Mohite said.

"It's rather urgent. I have to make a lot of arrangements before I fly to Baltimore for my daughter's engagement ceremony. I can't plan anything unless I know the status of my leave application," Ravi insisted.

"I don't see any problem in your case. The Chief is very liberal in sanctioning leave for such purposes. But I am told he is very busy these days. He has also not cleared several of my files that I sent to him last week," Mohite said.

"Is it possible for you to remind the Chief?" Ravi prodded.

"I will definitely try," Mohite replied.

Ravi made the next call to Reddy. He said that although the present car was quite comfortable, he would rather prefer to get back his previous car and the driver.

"I am sorry. We have virtually dismantled your car and it may take at least a fortnight to put it back on the road. We are holding back your driver so that he knows what fittings are being installed," Reddy explained. "But is there any particular reason why you want your vehicle back? I thought we had given you a very good car and the best driver out of the present lot," he said.

"Bisht is okay except that he is obsessed with playing the radio. That keeps distracting him from driving properly," Ravi remarked.

"I will ask him to stop playing the music," Reddy assured.

During the course of the day, the suspect told Ajeet that his daughter's marriage had been fixed on Saturday, 8th October in Delhi, followed by a reception the next day. Ajeet offered to get the functions organised in one of the Defence Officers' Mess at a much lower cost but Ravi declined his offer for various reasons. He said that he would rather prefer to hold the ceremonies in hotels because there were too many restrictions in institutional places. Moreover, since Aabha was his only daughter, he would like to do it in style. Ajeet, however, asked him to think it over. He said that it would not be proper for a serving government servant to hire five-star hotels for such ceremonies. "You know the petty mindedness of some of our senior officers. Instead of enjoying the feast, they will start questioning the legitimacy of your resources," he pointed out. Ravi laughed without sounding genuine.

"I can't help it if I am both rich and indulgent," he said. Later on, he called one by one, the Desk Officers of Europe, Sri Lanka and Kashmir, Director Operations Nepal and Director Administration to inform them about the wedding and reception dates.

At 5 pm, Ravi photocopied nine documents, dealing with efforts at government formation in Sri Lanka, heavy fighting between Arakan Liberation Army and government forces in Myanmar, latest round up on Indo-Nepal relations and seizure of arms from ULFA insurgents' dugouts inside Bangladesh. At 6.05 pm, he left office. On his way back, he kept looking behind to see if anyone was tailing him. He skipped the Club and went home. Half an hour later, he emerged with his wife, went to the park in the colony and walked for twenty minutes, stopping frequently to find out whether he was being followed.

At 7 pm KM went to show the day's reports to Jeev and mentioned the counter-surveillance measures being increasingly adopted by the suspect.

"Has he spotted any watcher?" Jeev asked.

"No, sir."

"What could be the reason for his suspicion?" Jeev further asked.

"I guess it is mainly because of his sense of guilt and fear. Or, as a trained agent he may be trying to discover if he is under any kind of surveillance," KM opined.

"Anything else?"

"Sir, when I went to hand over the report to the Chief, he suggested that I update him every two or three days," KM said.

Jeev did not react. Instead, he inquired whether the bugs in the car had produced any evidence of interest.

"Sir, it is also turning out to be a wasted effort. Every evening, the suspect enters the car with the leather bag firmly clutched in his hand and occupies the right corner of the rear seat. He does not stop en-route to meet anyone nor goes anywhere till the bag is taken inside the house. On days when he reaches the Club directly, he removes the bag himself from the car and hands it over to Jena who takes it inside the house. The suspect carries the bag only to the office and back. There has so far been no exchange of documents in the car at any point of time," KM reported.

"I see."

"Sir, Bisht is no longer willing to drive the vehicle. He is mortally afraid of getting caught. Since he had been instructed to play the radio to drown the hissing sound of the tape, he has to keep fiddling with its buttons. But the suspect does not like to listen to music and has been chastising him for fiddling with the system," KM said. Jeev knew what KM was hinting at.

"You can withdraw the car and the driver tomorrow. But make sure that Ravi does not get suspicious. Only this morning Reddy has told the suspect that two more weeks would be required to make his car road worthy. If Reddy changes the plan all of a sudden, Ravi may start fishing for reasons and asking inconvenient questions," Jeev cautioned.

KM visited Reddy in his flat at R.K. Puram to discuss the matter. Reddy argued that it would be too early to wind up the operation but left the final decision to KM. However, he agreed to replace Bisht by Ravi's previous driver, Negi but not before he tucked the console inside the dashboard and connected it to the self-start assembly so that the device got activated as soon as the car started,. He explained that under this arrangement, Negi would have no idea that he was operating a recording device. KM lauded the plan of action and told Reddy to go ahead. He also thanked Mrs Reddy for a nice cup of filter coffee and left.

Day 78

Ravi looked very anxious. Since his arrival in the office he was trying to find out the status of his leave application for the US. The staff officer to the Chief informed that his file had not yet reached the office. But the Director of Administration was insistent that he had sent the leave application to the Chief's office. He, however, clarified that in odd cases the Chief directly marked some files to Jeev for his comments. When Ravi rang up KM in desperation, the latter said that Jeev usually disposed of such routine cases within twenty-four hours of their receipt.

"But why are you so worked up over your leave? The engagement ceremony is still two and half months away," KM asked.

Ravi did not want to answer. He thanked KM hurriedly and disconnected. Kailash Uike, the Head of the Eastern Bureau, was expected to come in any moment. He had called Ravi very early in the morning to say that he had something important to clarify.

"How did you know that I was being tailed and the Chief would not sanction my leave?" Ravi asked even before Uike took his seat.

"That was just a rumour. I overheard it when I visited Headquarters ten days ago and thought of warning you, being a friend," Uike said.

"That's very thoughtful of you. We haven't seen anyone following us."

"I am sure the scare about your leave will also turn out to be false," Uike said.

Ravi's demeanour suddenly changed. He looked more relaxed and ordered for tea. After Uike left, Ravi bolted the door from the inside and photocopied thirty-four sheets concerning deployment of coalition forces in Afghanistan, Chinese supply of arms and communication equipment to Myanmar and factional clashes within LTTE. At 2.30 pm, Ravi went to the Taj Mansingh where he met a tall, well-built man in a grey suit. They hugged each other and went to a room on the eighth floor. Watchers missed out on what transpired inside the room but subsequently discovered that the man was an old NRI friend of Ravi from Vancouver and his name was Baljeet.

Around the time when Ravi was meeting Baljeet, Jeev and Wasan came out of the Executive Lunch Room and started walking back to their rooms. Jeev inquired about the outcome of Wasan's meeting with the Principal Secretary.

"He was quite upset and said that I should not have allowed the investigation to go this far," said Wasan, looking straight down the empty corridor.

"Didn't you ask him at what stage it should have been stopped?" Jeev quipped sarcastically.

"No, I didn't."

"Do you also believe that we are stretching this case unnecessarily, either out of malice or our sheer incompetence?" Jeev pressed for some clarity before he could decide on the future course of the investigation. By now, both had entered the Chief's room.

"Do what you think is best," Wasan remarked in dejection. He was still avoiding an eye contact with Jeev.

"What did he say about involving the Bureau?" Jeev pressed further.

"He didn't want to bring the Bureau in the picture. Basically, he endorsed our views on this issue. He was very worried that if the investigation dragged on, it could adversely impact the emergence of a substantive strategic relationship between India and the US and thus put his years of efforts to naught," Wasan said as he settled down in his chair.

"How did he come to the conclusion that the CIA is running the suspect? Did you coach him on this?" Jeev asked.

"Yes, to some extent," Wasan said.

"I wish you had not speculated. Now I know why his response was so frightened," Jeev said. "Next time if he repeats this fear, please tell him that espionage is a game that intelligence agencies play all the time, irrespective of the course that their political leadership pursues in promoting bilateral interests. Saran must understand that no caveat is ever imposed on an intelligence outfit about whom to recruit as a source and when," he added.

"I won't say anything that is not politically correct," Wasan clarified.

"I am not surprised," Jeev remarked.

*

Ravi returned to the office at 5.30 pm. Before he left for the day, he photocopied three more documents. At 8.30 pm, he reached Maurya Sheraton along with his wife and told Negi to take the car back to the office. Baljeet was waiting for them in Haveli restaurant. After dinner they took a cab, dropped Baljeet at Taj Mansingh and reached home at 11 pm.

*

Earlier at 7 pm, Jeev asked KM to confine briefing to highlight the salient features of the suspect's activities. He said that he would have to leave early to host an official dinner at the Imperial. KM gave a quick rundown on the day's events, drawing Jeev's attention in particular to rumour mongering by Uike, the suspect's desperation to find out the status of his leave application and his meeting with Baljeet.

"Anything else," Jeev asked.

"Sir, it is about the watchers. Everyone is doing eighteen hours of duty. I get a feeling that their responses have dulled and they are beginning to follow the suspect casually. They tell me that they are on a wild goose chase and nothing is ever going to come out their efforts," KM submitted cautiously.

"In that case, I can approach the Bureau to take over the surveillance. It has an army of watchers and can rotate their men easily every two or four hours," Jeev reacted curtly. "After all, we are partners in fighting forces of subversion," he remarked as he got up to lock the vault and drawers.

"Sir, this was not my intention. The Bureau can never be our comrade-in-arms. We all know that they routinely expose our operations and poach on our sources abroad. They run us down in the eyes of High Commissioners and ambassadors, making our life miserable in foreign missions. Every lead that we provide on terrorists, insurgents and underworld criminals, they build on those inputs stories of their success without ever acknowledging our contribution. I would rather let my watchers slog than invite them to trumpet their achievements at our cost," KM stated emphatically.

"But they are better at least in one sense," Jeev said. "They work like a limited company and do not wash their dirty linen in public. They manage their internal dissent extremely well. But look at us. We are always willing to slit each other's throat in the absence of a homogenous culture and revel in bashing our colleagues through media leaks. Ours is a house that is continually on fire with each one of us ready to add more and more fuel. Unlike them, we have no sense of belonging. Yes, we are vibrant in the sense that we can talk, argue, criticize even our seniors to press our points of view but unlike them we lack in discipline to accept what is finally agreed upon. We don't know how to stick together in time of crisis and we certainly do not value the Agency's privacy," he explained.

"Sir, you do have a secret admiration for the Bureau," KM teased.

"Yes I have, but it's nothing compared to what I feel for the Agency," Jeev said, waiting for his PS to take the pending files.

"Sir," said KM hesitantly, "it is rather personal but if I may ask, why did you leave the Bureau?"

"That's because I ran into an officer who acted like a medieval Sultan," Jeev recalled. "You could not disagree with his views. He was vain, arrogant, and unforgivable. He enjoyed tongue lashing and threw back drafts at junior colleagues, finding faults in English as if the Bureau needed a Charles Dickens and not Kim Philby. The pathetic sight of brilliant policemen writing and rewriting drafts was very discouraging. Probably the Sultan had no exposure to reports prepared by intelligence outfits from English speaking countries for whom promptness in despatching information in its raw form was always more important than wasting valuable time on correcting hyphens, spellings, and grammar. The Bureau's informational base was so weak that it required padding up of its inputs with good prose," said Jeev wryly. "The Bureau could never be my natural habitat. My home is here." A whirring in the air conditioner momentarily distracted him bringing to end an unprecedented outburst. Jeev got up and switched off the AC and then called his wife. He told Mani that he had to attend an official dinner and would head straight to the hotel. As he was about to leave, he received a call from the liaison officer. Jeev said that he would wait.

"Why can't the Bureau rise above its pettiness to lend constructive support to the Agency?" KM asked, trying to break the pensive mood that had crept in surreptitiously.

"It is still not reconciled to the creation of the Agency at their expense. There is yet another problem," Jeev said. "Both agencies continuously vie for recognition of their indispensability from the government. They do make a pretence of working together but there is an intense grudge flowing down under. The feeling that the Agency is a glamorous outfit, exercises wider financial powers, has lesser accountability to politicians and media and enjoys a far deeper mystical aura rankles the Bureau. No wonder its officers seldom miss an opportunity to berate the quality of our manpower, which is drawn from unrelated services with no exposure to live operations," he said.

"Sir, their criticism is not entirely unfounded," KM remarked. "Look at whom we have recruited in the past and continue to recruit. Initially relatives, friends and wards of the senior officers joined in hordes. Now it is the UPSC qualifiers and 'deputationists' riding on wrong priorities, who are making the Agency their career," he added.

"The old practice was not without positives," Jeev pointed out. "Initially you picked up relatives from known and tested families, who naturally remained loyal, contended, and discreet. It is only when you started accepting drop-outs and acquaintances on the basis of recommendations that you landed with those who looted your coffers, weakened your operational base and betrayed your trust. An instant case is that of Ravi. But the direct recruits are not a bad crop and have a distinct advantage. They can slide into the cover role of diplomats more smoothly than their counterparts from the Police and security forces because of their demeanour, their raw intellect, and youthfulness," he said.

"But it is the uniformed officers who contribute to the bulk of our substantive output," KM argued.

"There is no denying that they usually bring to the Agency their network of contacts, their investigative skills and their courage to take decision in adverse circumstances. But quite a few of them are also very selfish, dishonest, self-opinionated, and vindictive," Jeev said.

"Sir, maybe we should then involve the Bureau. They won't take long to fix the suspect by planting incriminating objects and book him for committing treason," KM suggested.

"I am not so sure how the Bureau would deal with the case. But if you are seeking my approval to act similarly against Ravi, I will have to disappoint you. A few senior police officers also suggested to me to frame the suspect but as long as I am in charge of this operation, we will not act like a bunch of criminals," Jeev stopped discussing the subject as the liaison officer entered the room.

Day 79

It was a hectic day for Ravi Mohan. After reaching office, he made calls to Hotel Ashok, Claridges, Le Meridian and Taj Palace to find out the availability and rates of hiring halls, flower arrangements, lighting and catering for the wedding and reception on 8 and 9 October respectively. He found the Meridian rates most competitive. The hotel manager, however, told Ravi to close the deal early because there were too many weddings coming up on those dates. Since Ravi did not want to lose time, he reached Le Meridian within an hour. He discussed the arrangements with the manager and paid an advance of Rs 50,000. From there, Ravi drove to Ashoka Hotel and reserved a hall for the ladies sangeet to be held on Friday, 7 October. He returned to the office by 1.20 pm, had his frugal lunch, and rested.

By 2.30 pm Ravi was back on his feet, photocopying documents. His total count for the day was twenty-one papers including branch assessments on Sri Lanka, Pakistan, Bhutan, Myanmar, WTO, Nepal, and China and a list of prospective targets. At 3.15 pm he received a call from a travel agent who confirmed that a seat had been booked for his daughter to travel from New York to Delhi by British Airways on Monday,

3 October and the cost had been debited to his account. The next call was from his PA. He informed him that the Punjab National Bank was refusing to deposit Rs 1,50,000 in cash in his wife's account unless she was present or the deposit slip was submitted along with a copy of her PAN card. Ravi directed him to return to the office. Then he rang up his wife and told her to keep her original PAN card ready and send it through Negi.

"Hold on, Jena wants to speak to you," she said.

"Sahebjee, I met a person outside the Club. He inquired about my well-being and how much I was being paid for the present job. He also offered to pay me a much higher salary if I worked for him," Jena recalled.

"Did he say what work you would have to do?" Ravi asked.

"No, but when I told him that I would report this to you, he said that the choice was mine but I would lose a life time's opportunity to earn big money," Jena said.

"I see."

"Sahebjee, when I went along with Madam to Hauz Khas Market, I saw the same person and two others at the red light on Lodhi road crossing, near Tibet House. But they did not stop at the light and went ahead. I did not see them after that." Jena informed.

"Give the telephone to madam," Ravi directed.

"Did you also see anyone tailing you?" he asked Vijita.

"I don't believe in Jena's ghost stories," she reacted. "We have been trying to look for watchers for the last one month in the park, market places, and on roads but neither of us has noticed anyone snooping around."

"I know," Ravi said and disconnected.

Then he sent Negi to collect the PAN card from home. He spent the rest of the afternoon watching TV and relaxing on the sofa. Before he left for the day, he photocopied seven reports.

At 6.50 pm, Kamath retrieved papers from the photocopier's memory and kept them in the briefcase. On the way to his room, he called Reddy to check whether the device in the car was producing anything worthwhile. Reddy reported that it was working fine but the tapes were mostly empty and carried insipid conversation. Next, he called Kutty but there was no response from his number. His last engagement was to brief Jeev.

"What is your guess? Where does he get this kind of money in cash?" Jeev asked as he finished reading KM's hand-written summary of the day's developments.

"Sir, this must be his remuneration for the services that he has been rendering to his operatives," KM averred.

"It's possible," Jeev said.

"Sir, we have worked out a detailed plan to plant the device in suspect's residence tomorrow," KM informed.

"That's good news but do it carefully," Jeev said. "If Kutty feels jittery at any stage, ask him not to pursue this mission," he cautioned.

"Sir, Kutty is quite confident. His boys would need less than an hour to bug the targeted areas. He has kept them ready to move in as soon as the suspect and his wife leave their apartment for Hotel Ashoka to finalize arrangements for ladies' sangeet," KM explained.

At 9 pm, KM reached the watchers' roving post near the suspect's apartment building. Pal and the watchman were waiting for him. Pal explained the entire drill of how the guard would waylay Jena for an hour and half to pave way for infiltrating the technicians to plant the surveillance device. KM paid rupees two thousand to the guard and left.

Day 80

At 10.30 am, Ravi drove to Le Meridian in his personal car and instructed Negi to follow him. He and his wife spent almost an hour going around the banquet hall and talking to the hotel staff. Vijita approved of the flower and lighting arrangements but suggested a few changes in the menu. From the Meridian, Ravi took his wife to Hotel Ashoka where she went through the arrangements for the ladies musical get together. Then the two went their separate ways. Vijita drove back home around 1.10 pm after an hour's stop over at a friend's flat in Moti Bagh while Ravi went to the office.

Meanwhile, technician Bora from Kutty's Unit, and Prem Singh the locksmith and Pal entered the suspect's apartment at 10.40 am. Closely following the layout of the flat, drawn by KM with the help of the watchman, the locksmith opened the main door, facilitating Bora's entry into the living room. The latter quickly surveyed the target areas and the fixtures in the house. Then, he discussed on the mobile various options with Kutty who was waiting outside in KM's car. While Prem Singh stood near the gate, keeping a watch through the keyhole, Bora planted the devices in the bedroom and balcony and came out at 11.30 am, ten minutes earlier than the time slotted for accomplishing this job. He was perspiring heavily when he got inside KM's car. Once he calmed down, KM patted Bora and offered him a can of coke. Kutty said that only Bora could have pulled it off.

"Sir, it was a touch and go situation," Bora pointed out after regaining his breath. "I don't know how effective these devices will turn out to be. If sitting arrangements are changed or the shredder and laptops are shifted or dust settles down on the lenses, quality of visuals and conversation could be affected," he explained.

"You have done an excellent job. We will leave the rest to luck," KM said.

Kutty suggested "Alice" as the nom-de-plume for this operation, since the devices were meant to explore a wonderland. KM termed the suggestion imaginative but preferred naming it "ALISTER" to give it a professional aura. By then it was 12.20 pm but there was still no trace of the suspect, his wife or Jena.

*

On reaching the office, Ravi rang up four Agency officers and two serving Brigadiers of the Indian Army for dinner on Monday, 20 June at his residence. At 1.30 pm, Venkat dropped in. He apologized for not having answered Ravi's numerous calls because of his preoccupation with an operation in Chennai.

"Do you have any idea if the Chief is going abroad in the next few days?" Ravi inquired.

"He is probably going to London but I don't know the dates," Venkat said.

"How is your other work going on?" Ravi asked.

"It's both very demanding and exciting," Venkat sounded eager to share his work. He then went on to talk about the websites that he claimed to have cracked, tele-communication tools which the Agency planned to exploit for psychological warfare and a proposal for setting up a Code Interpretation Unit at a secret location in the NCR. He also referred to a likely meeting in Dubai of the Deputy Chief with a Non-Resident Pakistani for setting up a financial hub to find out groups and institutions that were channelizing funds to terrorists operating from Pakistan. Then he reeled off names and location of some of those outfits and spilled out the fictitious nom-de-plumes of the Agency's operators who were going to be involved in this operation. Ravi thanked Venkat and enquired he could give some lessons on tracking the websites of extremist Islamic outfits operating in Far East Asian countries. Venkat said that he would do that sometime during the next week.

After Venkat left, Ravi rang up Naresh Shukla, the Desk Officer for Afghanistan and Pakistan. Shukla said that he had just returned from a meeting, convened to discuss phased withdrawal of the US troops from Kabul and its likely impact on our security situation.

"Before you get busy with preparing a summary of discussion for the Chief, why don't we go for a quick lunch to the Oberoi. They serve an excellent buffet," Ravi set the bait.

"I am sorry I won't be able to go."

"That's okay. You remember I had requested you for a profile of all the new Afghan ministers," Ravi reminded him.

"Sir, I am no longer in a position to give that to you," Naresh replied. "Mr Arun Roy has instructed me that unless the requirement of a paper or information from officers of other branches is routed through him, I shall not entertain any verbal request. He has further directed that no junior officer in the Pak/Afghan Division will pass on papers to anyone without consulting him." Ravi was momentarily taken aback. But he hurriedly composed himself.

"That's not a problem but I find his instructions rather quixotic. He has been such a good friend. Did you tell him that I needed this information?" Ravi asked.

"Yes, sir, I did."

Ravi kept the phone down. Then he picked up papers from the incoming tray and photocopied eleven of them dealing with Myanmar-China relations, Pakistan president's visit to Beijing and current developments in Sri Lanka, Nepal, and Fiji. He kept the reports in the dark brown leather bag, had lunch, and stretched on the sofa. He appeared restless, as he reached for a glass of water. He closed his eyes, wondering why Arun, all of a sudden, had decided to instruct his officers not to part with Branch information. He was confused whether he should take it up with Arun Roy or check with KM if similar instructions had been issued by the CEU to all Chief Analysts. He felt worse when Negi, his irrepressible driver, told him about rumours that the CEU caught on their cameras a number of drivers selling petrol/diesel in black market while chasing senior officers for wrong doings. All these drivers had since been placed under surveillance along with suspected officers, he added.

"Where did you pick up this news? Are you also involved in this dirty business?" Ravi asked.

"No, sir," Negi reacted abruptly, being himself a compulsive thief of petrol. Ravi guessed that Uike could have mistaken the watch on drivers to derive wrong conclusions. Feeling a bit relieved, he stretched back and dozed off.

*

Later that evening, KM reported to Jeev about Venkat's operational monologue, the suspect's highs and lows depending on whom he met with, his photocopying activities and arrangements being made for his daughter's wedding.

"What is significant is that despite the fear of being tailed, the suspect continues to photocopy. It is obvious he is under obligation to give out anything or everything that comes his way," Jeev remarked. "He also does not seem to have been recruited as a short term investment. If that were the case, the subverting Service would not have retained him despite consistently producing routine stuff of poor quality," he said.

"Sir, I am not sure about his long term use? He is an absolute nut. Besides, he is neither going to become the Chief nor will the Agency ever assign him to handle critical operational desks," KM argued.

"Don't you see that there is a conscious effort by his operative to discourage him from either aggressively gathering operational inputs or adopting strong counter-surveillance measures?" Jeev countered. "His brief probably is to photocopy every bit of paper that he can lay his hands on in the normal course, strictly avoid physical contact with the handler as long as possible and transfer documents through a complex, unfamiliar mechanism," he opined.

For the first time, Kamath noticed Jeev's grudging acceptance of the difficulty in locating the handler. But he chose not to press his case for suspending the investigation. Instead, he informed Jeev that Operation ALISTER had been successfully commissioned.

"I hope this gambit works," Jeev said.

*

Ravi woke up when the car stopped for the sentry to open the gate of his residence. That evening, in its first transmission, ALISTER saw the suspect sitting in the balcony and shuffling through a magazine. After some time his wife joined him.

"Why are you sitting here alone? Is something bothering you?" she asked as she pulled a chair to sit close to him.

Ravi told her about Roy's latest instructions to his Branch officers on sharing of reports.

"I think you are reading too much in it," Vijita said. "Arun has always been possessive about everything. He may be upset that you don't directly ask for reports."

"Maybe, my interest in reports of other branches is getting adversely noticed," Ravi whispered.

"Then don't ask for it and, please stop brooding. I will get you some tea. Meanwhile, you go and leave the bag in the study, freshen up and come back," Vijita said.

However, Ravi kept sitting in a pensive mood till tea was served.

At 8 pm, Ravi and his wife came out of the building and drove past South Extension, INA, Jorbagh, Nehru stadium, Teen Murti, Dhaula Kuan and Moti Bagh before stopping in Chankyapuri for dinner at Bhan's residence. Throughout the drive, he was quiet. Just to make sure that his fears were misplaced, he got down from the car, hundred meters away from the host's apartment and walked. He did not see any watcher.

Day 81

The refusal of Shukla to part with information continued to torment Ravi. The more he tried to rationalise, the more he lost his nerves. His first caller in the office was an officer from the DRDO who invited him for lunch at Gymkhana but Ravi declined the offer citing an upset stomach as the reason. The next call was from the Chief's staff officer. He informed Ravi that the leave application had just been received from Jeev's office but since the Chief had gone out of the station for a week, the approval would have to wait till he returned.

Ravi sulked. He did not feel like contacting his regular visitors. Files and reports from his branch were yet to start trickling in. Since his PA had taken leave for half-a-day, he grudgingly took out the pending papers and files from the almirah, went through them cursorily and kept aside a few for photocopying. Around 11.30 am, he photocopied nine sheets, deviating for the first time from his normal schedule of photocopying during lunch recess. He kept the photocopies in the dark brown bag, switched on the television and kept channel surfing till he got bored. At 1.45 pm, Inder served him soup and sandwiches.

In the afternoon, Ravi received a call from the Agency's officer posted at Brunei. The conversation was mundane except that Ravi mentioned his absence from Headquarters for two weeks for his daughter's engagement in the US. To an overseas caller, he said that he would be happy in case the former could attend the reception in Delhi. At 4 pm, Ravi rang up Reddy to find out the delivery schedule of his previous car.

"You may have to use the present one for a few more days," Reddy said. "Actually, your car has been fixed but along with a number of other vehicles, it has been held back at the workshop. The security officer has been asked by Mr Jeevnathan to probe into allegations of sale of car parts in the black market particularly in respect of those vehicles that incurred heavy repairs during past six months. But if you insist, I can request him to release it immediately," he suggested.

"No, that's fine," Ravi said.

His last visitor of the day was Hemant Vyas, Head of the North-East Bureau. He came without any prior notice.

"What a surprise!" Ravi said, making an effort to appear enthusiastic. He told Inder to bring a glass of fresh lime water, Vyas's favourite drink, and then casually asked if the government's recent offer of economic and political package had found any takers among the warring Naga factions. Instead of responding to the suspect's pointed query, Vyas gave an overview of the activities of Naga and Manipuri insurgent groups in Myanmar, camps of various Assamese insurgent outfits in Bangladesh and the Chinese intrusions in Arunachal

Pradesh. Ravi's thoughts, however, drifted elsewhere. As soon as Vyas paused for the drink, Ravi asked if he had any idea of how the Bureau's counter espionage unit functioned.

"I don't have any specific knowledge but I guess it is quite effective. It has a huge network of field staff and their success rate in cracking espionage cases is very impressive. Our Counter Espionage Unit, with its paltry resources and half a dozen ill-trained and ill-equipped watchers, is no patch on them. But why are you asking this?" Vyas inquired.

"A friend of mine who is of the rank of a Major General in the Armed Forces, suspects that he is being followed by the Bureau's watchers," Ravi instantly cooked up an alibi. "Since you served in the Bureau for more than a decade, I thought you would know better whether the Bureau accepted such commitments from other departments or mounted surveillance suo moto on the basis of their field reports," he said.

Vyas did not immediately respond.

"Does the Bureau also keep a watch on our officers?" he fished for an answer.

"Yes. This probably is the one area in which the Agency and the Bureau work very closely together," Vyas claimed.

Ravi's face instantly fell and he started looking distraught. He waited for the visitor to finish drinking his fresh lime water and leave.

Day 82

At 9.30 am, Ravi stepped out of his apartment and began to walk. His office car followed him. He briefly stood outside the main gate, surveying the area in front. In between, he spoke to Jena who pointed towards the milk booth and its adjoining stores where the watchers usually parked their cars. The suspect got inside the car and went around the milk booth but found no one. In the office, he routinely disposed of outstation cables and pending papers. He kept a few loose sheets aside for copying. Then he called Munish Das, Desk Officer of the Electronic Unit in the Technical Division and told him that he needed a small favour.

"What is it, sir?" Das enquired.

"A friend of mine has gifted me an imported cellphone but I am unable to operate it. I was wondering if you could make it work," Ravi lied.

Das promised to come within ten minutes.

Das examined the device and offered to get it fixed at a nominal cost. Ravi told him not to worry about the expenses. Das collected the cellphone and got up to leave when Ravi asked him whether he was enjoying his work in the prestigious E-Unit.

"Hardly," Das reacted in apparent disgust. "I had volunteered to join this Unit under a mistaken belief that there would be plenty of operational work and excitement. But I am stuck with merely going through the latest literature and internet downloads on surveillance devices that are available in the market and putting up proposals to Mr Panda for their procurement. I am virtually working as a dealing assistant," he complained.

"Do you have sufficient number of operations on the anvil to justify these purchases?" Ravi prodded.

"That's for Mr Panda and Mr Basu to answer. Much as I would like to, they seldom involve me in operational discussions," Das sounded bitter.

"What kind of surveillance cameras do you have in your unit?" Ravi enquired as tea was served.

"Of every kind," Das promptly claimed. "We can cover any target within a range of 10 feet to 15 kilometres and if required, their monitoring capacity can be extended or reduced."

"What about covering the target from a distance of less than 10 feet in a covered area?" The suspect probed.

"We generally avoid mounting video surveillance for such short ranges. There is a very high risk of exposure because of the close proximity of the target to the cameras," Das explained.

"Do you think Bureau would have the same sophistication to cover their targets as you have?" Ravi further asked.

"I doubt it," Das said. "These devices are frightfully expensive and generally used in overseas operations, where you cannot approach the target from a close range. But I am sure the Bureau must have adequate technical resources to fulfil its counter-espionage responsibilities within India," he added.

"Do you ever lend your equipment to the Bureau?"

"Not since I have joined the Unit," Das said.

"Does your unit also bug rooms?" Ravi pressed.

"There is a separate unit for that, headed by Murthy. Its employees, as you know, keep trotting around the globe in the name of sweeping bugs in our offices abroad. I have been trying to switch over to B-Unit but for that, one has to be a favourite of Mr Panda," Das rued bitterly.

"I don't know Mr Panda well enough to get you posted to B-Unit but I will certainly speak to him," said Ravi.

After Das left, Ravi bolted the door from inside, took out a measuring tape from the middle drawer of the working desk and calculated the height from the table top to the concealed roof lights. Then he measured the distance from the photocopier to the ceiling fan and to the side board on which he kept the dark brown leather bag. He wanted to make sure that his copying activities were well outside the prying eyes of surveillance cameras, in case they were camouflaged in the roof, lights and fans. He repeated this exercise four times. At 12.10 pm, he directed his PA to take out all files from the almirah, marked "PP" and transfer these to his car. Minutes later, his PA came in along with Inder. Together, they removed the files and took them to PA's room.

At 1.20 pm, Ravi latched the door from inside, picked up the loose sheets from the in-tray and photocopied them. He glanced through the copies, put nine of them in the brown bag and shredded the remaining two. Then he kept the original papers back in the tray, opened the security latch and lay down on the sofa.

Meanwhile, his PA stacked the files subject-wise, put them in separate covers and neatly tied them in eighteen bundles.

At 2.30 pm, Inder transferred eight packets to Ravi's car parked in the basement. He collected another five, took the lift and came out on to the main foyer. As he went past the receptionist's desk, two employees of the CE Unit intercepted him. They asked Inder if he had any written authorization from Kamath to carry those files out of the building. Inder panicked and dropped the files on the floor. Before he could run away, Nikhil Batra of the CE Unit caught hold of him and asked him to calm down. Inder insisted that he was merely acting under the instructions of Mr Ravi Mohan's PA. Meanwhile, hangers on in the foyer began to collect and talk in whispers. Before the incident could spin out of control, Batra allowed Inder to leave. Then he collected the files littered on the floor, took them in his custody and sent his colleague to seize files from the suspect's car.

Inder rushed to the PA's room. From there he informed Ravi that two officers of the Counter Espionage Unit had seized thirteen packets of files and refused to allow him to carry any more files without written permission from Mr Kamath. Ravi got nervous. He got up involuntarily, took a glass of water, went to the rest room and returned to his chair. "It's okay," he finally said, struggling to keep his cool since the Desk Officer Myanmar was sitting with him. The officer resumed his assessment on the downturn in Myanmar-India relations over Rangoon's ambiguous support to Indian insurgents and Delhi's ambivalent position on restoration of democracy in Myanmar. Unable to hide his discomfort any longer, Ravi abruptly told the visitor that Bhan had called him to discuss a file. The Desk Officer got the hint and left.

*

At 3 pm, Nikhil Batra walked into Kamath's room with the files seized from Ravi's peon and reported the incident. He was not sure whether he did the right thing by impounding a senior officer's files. KM immediately rang up Jeev, sounding anxious. "Sir, we have confiscated thirteen bundles of suspect's files while they were being shifted by his peon to his car. Should we now raid his room, seize the rest of the documents, and detain him?" He fired his worries rapidly.

"What if these papers turn out to be his personal documents or official papers which he is entitled to carry? You and I will look foolish and vindictive," Jeev pointed out. "Moreover, we can't raid an officer's room of our own volition. It will require Chief's specific approval," he said.

"But there is a fifty-percent chance that we can catch the suspect red-handed for siphoning off secret documents. I don't see any reason why anyone will tape the packets securely unless he has something to hide," KM contended.

"Now that you have detained his files, we are left with only two options. We either return the files or scrutinize them to find out if these are of classified nature. What do you think, we should do?" Jeev asked.

KM said he would go by whatever direction was given.

"Okay, then wait for my call. I will come back to you in a minute," Jeev said and then dialled the Chief. "We have a serious situation at hand. Are you in a meeting?" Jeev sounded concerned.

"Go ahead," the Chief said.

"An hour ago, the CEU intercepted the suspect's peon while he was transferring bundles of files to the suspect's car, obviously under his instructions. Altogether thirteen bundles of files have been seized. We are unaware what these files are about, but we can't let these go without scrutiny," Jeev said.

"I see."

"One option is that we open the packets, see what the files deal with and subsequently detain the suspect for questioning. But the risk is that if files turn out to be personal in nature, we will be hugely embarrassed. The other option is that we check all briefcases and bags and seize unauthorised items at the exit gate before allowing employees to leave the building after office hours. In that case, the suspect might believe that the surprise check was directed not only at him but for everyone. Subsequently, we can legitimately look into his files and find out what he is up to. It may also be a good opportunity to know the wrongdoings of other black sheep of the Agency," Jeev argued.

"Let's go with the second option," the Chief said and hung up.

Jeev then instructed KM to carry out a general search of all employees of the Agency till the last man left the building.

*

As soon as Desk Officer Myanmar left, Ravi angrily protested on the phone to Avinash for detaining his files and demanded their immediate release. "This is ridiculous. How can you treat a senior analyst like this?" he shouted.

"Sir, please speak to Mr Kamath. I am a very junior officer in the CEU to take any decision on such serious matters," Avinash responded politely.

Ravi then called KM and complained bitterly that his junior staff had seized his personal files and would not allow him to take these to his house unless KM gave clearance in writing.

"I don't think the CEU has a right to pry into your personal papers," KM clarified, trying to pacify the suspect. "But now that we are on this subject, let me share a small secret. We are carrying out a security check of bags and briefcases of all employees before they leave the building for the day. Actually, the checking was scheduled to start at 5 pm. Maybe my staff intercepted your files in compliance of that decision and began the exercise a bit early. Please avoid taking any papers out of the building today," he said sheepishly.

"What about my personal files, lying with your officers?" Ravi asked in irritation.

"Now that these have been seized in full view of other employees, it will be proper that we make a show of scrutinizing them. I will release your files as soon as we are through with preparing an inventory of the subjects of your files. I don't want you to be subsequently blamed for removing official documents from the building stealthily. You know the kind of rumour mongering that incessantly goes on in the corridors. In case you still feel aggrieved, you can speak to my senior Ajay Varma," KM said.

"No, that's okay. I will go by your advice," the suspect said but wasted no time in protesting to Ajay about his harassment by junior employees of the Counter Espionage Unit.

Ajay was non-committal. "I am running late for a meeting," he said. "But if you are still in the building around 5 pm, I will try to sort it out before you leave," he pulled a fast one.

Feeling out of sorts, Ravi rang up Col. Paritosh, CMA (China Military Analyst), to check on his four-day trip to Beijing.

"It was a new experience for me because in the Army, you do not get an opportunity to interact with your counterparts from civilian foreign intelligence setups," Paritosh said.

"If you are free, why don't you join me for a cup of coffee?" Ravi suggested.

"I will be there in five minutes," the CMA said.

Ever eager to talk, Paritosh told Ravi about the places where he was taken to and the kind of stifling hospitality that was extended to his delegation. "What struck me as odd was the Chinese insistence on providing round the clock security to each one of us as if terrorists were prowling on the streets of Beijing to shoot us down. It is such a far cry from the way we allow them to move in our country, meet our officers, and visit places of their interest," he remarked.

Ravi smiled weakly. "But this is how their political system has been designed," Ravi explained. "They may be keeping you under constant surveillance to ensure that you do not interact with someone who has not been cleared by their security."

"The head of our delegation kept telling us to rigidly abide by the schedule drawn up by the hosts to avoid unpleasantness. But you know Arvind Munshi and his non-conformist habits. He skipped a sightseeing tour at the last minute. Not only that, he put his Chinese counterpart on the mat by pointedly referring to Islamabad's unabashed complicity in the terrorist violence in J&K. He literally rattled the hosts by warning that they would meet similar fate in Xinjiang unless they pressurized Islamabad to stop trading in terrorism," CMA recalled.

"Arvind has always been irrepressible," Ravi remarked dryly.

"I also noticed that the Chinese officers were consciously circumspect about discussing Pakistan and their own provocative military build-up along our northern borders. But they spitted fire when it came to discussing the alleged separatist activities of Dalai Lama and hinted in no uncertain terms about our culpability," the CMA said.

Paritosh looked eager to share more of his impression of the visit but stopped as soon as the internal telephone rang. It was Lokesh Kumar, Nepal Desk Officer, on the other side. He wanted to meet Ravi urgently to share an important piece of information. Ravi said he would wait for him. Then he lied to the CMA that he had been summoned by the Chief to meet him along with Lokesh Kumar and would have to go. The CMA left soon after that. Ravi waited with suspended breath for Kumar to arrive.

"What is that you wanted to share?" Ravi asked even before Kumar took his seat.

"I heard that one of our officers is under bumper to bumper surveillance. There is a strong buzz in the building that someone, fairly senior, is under investigation by the CEU," Kumar confided.

"Who do you think could their target be?" Ravi inquired with a straight face.

"I don't know but the rumour is that the targeted employee has been compromised by a foreign intelligence service," Kumar said.

There was a hushed silence. Ravi looked at the roof, then opened the drawer of his desk and closed it.

"You never know. It could simply be a kite flying," Ravi said while taking a deep breath.

"That's possible, but something is definitely brewing. I have not seen much of Kamath lately. I hear that he spends most of his time outside the building and comes to the office very late in the evening," Kumar said.

"It is not unusual for an intelligence agency to occasionally watch its officers unobtrusively," Ravi remarked, trying to put up a brave front.

After Kumar left, Ravi looked at the watch. It was 5 pm. He told Sharma that he would be leaving early. While Sharma cleared the desk of papers, closed the almirahs, unplugged the photocopier and TV, Ravi opened the dark brown bag, took out nine sheets that he had photocopied in the morning and shredded them. For the first time, Ravi left the room empty handed, followed by Inder who carried the dark brown bag and his briefcase. As the suspect passed through the main foyer, he saw CEU officers checking bags of employees at three makeshift counters, raised near the exit gate to avoid the queue from increasing. Avinash politely asked Inder to open both the bags and the briefcase in the presence of Ravi, inspected the items cursorily and requested him to move ahead.

*

The hallway was choked with unprecedented anxiety. Since 4.30 pm, two dozen officers from the CEU had positioned themselves near the exit gate. Eighteen of them were busy inspecting bags and briefcases of employees and removing documents and objectionable items. Six others were drawing up a list of the seized items and obtaining the signatures of the concerned officers to ensure that these were returned to the rightful owners after a thorough scrutiny.

It was after two decades that such an exercise had been set in motion. The last time when a search was conducted, the Agency had been turned upside down, with employees organizing protests and physically assaulting the CEU employees on duty. In later years, a few half-hearted attempts were made to frisk the employees for checking pilferage of classified papers and office equipment and to enforce punctuality in the office but these were largely apologetic.

This time around, Kamath was adamant that no one was spared and the search was executed ruthlessly. For a long time, he had a burning desire to teach delinquents a lesson for being careless and indiscreet with their words and documents. He could not let this opportunity go. He, therefore, decided to be physically present in the lobby to make sure that the search was carried out meticulously.

When KM entered the lobby, he saw employees crowding near the exit, unable to decide whether to quickly turn back to deposit bags in their rooms or go ahead to submit their items for inspection. With apprehensions writ large on their faces, a few employees eventually started to move towards the table where bags were being examined. The trickle slowly turned into a long queue with employees jostling with each other to submit their chattels for an early inspection. A number of them had to hurry up to catch the chartered buses and the metro to reach their homes. Those who could not wait walked out of the building after depositing their bags and briefcases with the inspecting staff.

Most employees cooperated but kept making snide remarks about Kamath's inflated insolence under Jeev's direct patronage. A few senior officers raised a hue and cry over the incivility of the checking staff and attempted to barge out of the building forcibly. But once KM moved swiftly to stand by the door and threatened to report the matter to Jeev, they quickly fell in line. A number of junior employees lost their cool when CDs and pen drives were seized, insisting that these contained their personal data, which they would not part with at any cost. But CEU officers stood their ground firmly. These recoveries subsequently turned out to be pornographic material and obscene visuals.

Kamal Mehta, the pot-bellied, slimy busybody of the Agency and a cat's whisker of all chiefs, was furious. He shouted at the top of his voice that he was not a spy or a thief and would not take the humiliation lying down. KM told him blandly that it would be in his interest to submit his briefcase for examination, for there was no way he could be exempted from the search. Mehta then stepped out of the line and spoke to the Deputy Chief on the cell phone, screaming that goons of the CEU were physically preventing him from leaving the building unless he subjected himself to their frisking. What he was advised was not audible. But moments later, he also joined the queue, opened the briefcase and stormed out, swearing at Kamath. Another senior officer had to be manhandled to prevent him from running away with his bag. Even the genial, pleasant, and usually unflappable Neelesh Burman, who headed the Pakistan/Afghanistan Division, cracked when Laxman, a junior CEU employee, demanded that he open his briefcase. In a moment of blinding rage, Burman abused Laxman and before the latter could react, he exited in a hurry with his briefcase, sat down in the car and sped off in a hurry. Kamath, who was watching the fracas from a distance, rushed to block the car. As the car screeched to a halt, he walked up to the backseat and informed Burman that his briefcase would not be opened only if the Chief or Mr Jeevnathan instructed him accordingly. An exception, KM pointed out to the angry officer that his reluctance might send a wrong signal and give currency to rumours that Mr Burman was trying to hide something.

"Don't lecture me," Burman shouted. "These are top secret operational documents that can be seen only by me or the Chief."

KM ignored his protest. "In that case, please call the Chief," he suggested.

"I am not used to taking instructions from a bunch of idiots," Burman reacted angrily.

His many years of experience and discipline helped KM to somehow restrain himself. He pulled out the cellphone and reported to Jeev about Burman's boorish behaviour.

"Stay on course. I am coming down," Jeev said. But before he could reach the lobby, Burman had already subjected his documents for inspection and left in a huff. Anticipating a repeat of similar incidents, Jeev stood there for some time, watching a stream of officers dutifully filing past the inspection counter in an orderly manner. The Chief was the last one to offer his briefcase for scrutiny, adding a dash of seriousness to the proceedings.

The night of the search did not seem to end for employees of the CEU. Over four thousand documents and devices were hauled from the foyer to a hall on the ninth floor and spread out on eleven desks. Almost all staff members were employed to segregate seized items lest their ownership got mixed up. The work of screening and assessing individual officer's culpability was entrusted to four senior officers. Avinash and two of his colleagues were tasked to examine only the suspect's files which ran to 286 pages. By 5 am, everyone was too exhausted to carry on further, despite taking turns to rest. Since the Operation Search was unrehearsed and surprisingly produced a huge volume of paper work, every CEU employee had to be held back for the job at hand. Finally at 5.30 am, KM permitted them to go home and he too retired to his room. He started snoring as soon as he stretched out on the sofa.

Earlier that night around 11.45 pm, Neelesh Burman reflected long and hard on his disgusting behaviour the evening and felt profoundly remorseful. He called up Kamath and apologised profusely. It was unfortunate, he said, that he got swayed by his vanity and small mindedness.

"That's alright, sir. I take it as one of my professional hazards. At least, you appreciate that we were doing a job without malice," KM said on a sombre note.

In another development, ALISTER transmitted the suspect's conversation with his wife in the balcony. He told her about the surprise decision of the CEU to check the bags and briefcases of all employees before they left the building at the end of their day's work and, what Kumar revealed about someone being placed under surveillance. "I don't know if that officer is me," Ravi mumbled.

Vijita did not react.

"They have also seized my personal files," Ravi said a little louder, trying to draw her attention.

"But they have seized documents of other officers as well," she reacted. "I cannot understand why you had this sudden urge to remove so many bundles of files from the building on a single day. Anyone will get suspicious even if these are of innocuous nature," she pointed out.

"It was a mistake," Ravi admitted.

"Stop worrying. No one is watching you. Of late, you have taken to heavy drinking and become paranoid about your security. It's not good for your health," she said.

ALISTER went silent after that.

Day 83

The day after the search, Ravi's mood was in tatters. Negi, his voluble driver, added to his miseries by claiming that the CEU had finally identified their man. He claimed that they suspected their target for a long time of selling secrets of the department. Now it was just a matter of time before he would be detained at a safe house and beaten. Ravi did not react and kept reading the morning newspapers. As he walked into the hallway and went past the visitors' corner, he sensed a deathly silence prevailing in an area that was usually very noisy. In the lift too, no one acknowledged his presence. Officers entered and went out at different floors mechanically. He was not sure whether the search had left everyone too traumatized to react with civility.

Ravi had barely settled down when his PA; Sharma entered the room to narrate his version of what happened during the surprise check. Ravi preferred to listen. Sharma speculated that the search could have been triggered by the sight of so many files being taken out of the building by a peon.

"This cannot be the reason for KM to risk incurring the wrath of the entire building," Ravi retorted. "He had in any case seized my files and could have simply asked me to explain my action," he argued.

Sharma did not dwell on this topic further. Before he left, he wanted to know whether he should check with Kamath's PA about the status of the impounded files. Ravi dissuaded him from taking any hasty action. He said that the CEU might not have even started sifting the documents. In any case, he stressed, he had no particular reason to be worked up. Actually, it was the others who had to explain why they were taking secret documents out of the building, he added. Then he asked Sharma to draw up a list of the remaining files, subject-wise and wait for his decision.

"Sir, it's better to let things cool down a bit," Sharma suggested.

"No, this time I am not taking a chance. I will obtain a written approval from Kamath before I take these files out," Ravi clarified.

Within an hour, Sharma came back with the list of files. The suspect dictated a letter, addressed to KM, detailing the number and subject of files that he proposed to take home. He tried to contact KM both at his office and residence before dispatching the letter but no one answered the phone. Then he called KM's PA who said that KM was working up to 6 am when he complained of chest pain and uneasiness and was rushed to Apollo hospital for a check-up. His PA also mentioned that KM had since returned home and was resting but he was not taking any calls.

"This CEU work will kill him one day. I don't know why he doesn't opt for a lighter desk," Ravi remarked. Minutes later, he called Ajay Varma to find out the status of his seized files. Ajay explained that the CEU had to examine documents and articles of over three thousand employees and each item had to be accounted for. It was a huge task and could take at least two weeks before everything was sorted out.

"But what you have detained in my case, are my personal papers," Ravi pointed out. "I am particularly worried about the original will of my father. I hope it doesn't get misplaced," he said.

"You don't have to lose sleep on that count. KM has separately employed two officers to scrutinize your papers," Ajay informed.

"Will you also have to show the list to Mr Jeevnathan?" Ravi asked.

"No. He has directed the CEU to submit the lists to respective division heads who will suggest the nature and quantum of punishment to be handed to delinquent officers," Ajay clarified.

"It's comforting to hear that. Please ensure that my papers reach Mr Bhan at the earliest," he requested.

Ajay assured to instruct Kamath accordingly.

Ravi brooded for a while, and then moved to the sofa to relax. He called Sharma and asked him to check with the Chief's office about the fate of his leave application. After that he switched on the TV and watched a noisy, frivolous debate on the electoral prospects of the national and regional political parties in the forthcoming parliamentary elections. It was anchored by a man who matched the hypocrisy and banality of panelists with his supercilious eloquence and insufferable interruptions. Ravi went to sleep while the debate, pumped up by contrived gestures, dragged on. Occasionally, he half-opened his eyes. A knock at the door by Inder eventually woke him up at 12.30 pm. Inder wanted to know whether he should send the driver to fetch Ravi's favourite salmon sandwiches and clear vegetable soup from Oberoi for lunch.

"I haven't decided," Ravi said, as he got up slowly, wiped his face with a hand towel and sat in his chair. He took out a bunch of visiting cards from the table's drawer and shredded them. With nothing else to do, he called Pradeep Nair, Desk Officer in charge of Naval Operations, to come over for a cup of coffee. At 1.30 pm, Nair came and sat next to Ravi. Explaining his delay, Nair said that he had been called by the CEU to sign the list of items that were seized from him last evening. "I don't know why they did not question me about the CD," he wondered.

"What was in the CD?" Ravi asked.

"It contains secret data on China's recent acquisitions of hardware for its Navy. I had to work on a paper at home for which I needed this data. I hope Jeev doesn't take an adverse view without giving me a chance to explain," Nair spoke without interruption.

"He will, of course, make pretence of allowing you to clarify your position but he seldom agrees with anyone. He must have already decided on the quantum of punishment. In his scheme of things, views of others hardly matter," Ravi averred.

"What about you? I am told CEU had confiscated over three hundred of your operational files," Nair said.

Ravi laughed deliberately. He clarified that those were his personal files and would not be more than thirty or thirty-five.

"I don't think Jeev is going to spare me," Nair sounded concerned. "I informed Head of the Military Division about my predicament but he was not willing to intervene. He said that Jeev was a difficult person to deal with and was extremely temperamental. He also mentioned that the Chief had a nasty altercation with his Security Head over the necessity and timing of conducting the search and it was only after the latter threatened to resign that the Chief agreed to go along."

"The Chief should have called Jeev's bluff and got rid of his services. You can't afford to have too many power centres to run the Agency effectively," Ravi remarked.

Nair had a more serious issue at hand. "Tell me, will it be possible for you to put in a word to Jeev on my behalf?" he asked.

"I don't think so. Your boss is right. Jeev is highly unpredictable and not easily persuaded. I tried on a couple of occasions to strike a polite conversation with him but it didn't go beyond a few sentences. You always get a feeling that he despises your presence. I invited him once for dinner but he refused point blank," Ravi said.

"But you are friendly to Kamath. Please explain the circumstances in which I had to take the CD out," Nair pressed.

Ravi refused to commit. Nair left, realizing that Ravi was not going to bail him out of this tricky situation.

*

Ravi went home for an unscheduled lunch. After the meal, he went to the bedroom and sat on the armchair. ALISTER saw his wife joining him after a while. He told her to take out Rs 1,00,000 from the almirah and deposit Rs 50,000 each in the Punjab National Bank and the HSBC Bank in Khan Market. At 3 pm, he dropped her at Khan Market. En route, he talked about rumours of someone being detained for questioning by the CEU but Vijita maintained a studied silence. Back in the office, he cleared files and papers without reading them, selected three documents running into fourteen pages, photocopied them but instead of putting them in the brown leather bag, he kept them in the almirah. A few minutes later, he went out of the room, carrying a file.

After he returned, Miss Mukta Sethi came in to brief him on the Indonesian elections and discuss a few operational issues. She enquired whether Harjeet Singh, Head of the East Asia Division, agreed to the proposal for increasing the salary of the subject of "Operation Pearl". Ravi said that despite Bhan's forceful plea, Singh had continued to have serious reservations. He reiterated that Pearl was unreliable and his claims of access to the network that funded and supplied weapons to the Indian insurgent groups, Maoists in Nepal and to the LTTE were seldom matched by the quality of his reports.

"And, what about Pearl's offer of providing economic intelligence and backdoor assistance in clinching projects and contracts for our government agencies?" Mukta asked.

Ravi said that Singh also rejected this idea outright. He was of the view that it was not the Agency's job to stray into unchartered areas of commercial espionage and insisted that this task should best be left to the Ministry of External Affairs and

Ministry of Economic Affairs to handle. "No one," he said, "would relish our involvement in financial deals, irrespective of benefits that it brought to the nation, mainly out of fear that their cut in the loot would get exposed." Before Mukta could ask further, he changed the subject. "How did the search go in your case?" he enquired.

"Sir, I did not carry anything. But almost all the senior officers are upset with Kamath's bravado," Mukta claimed.

"Singh was equally disgusted," Ravi mentioned. "He also felt that the search could have been planned and executed better. He totally disapproved of the way senior officers were grilled in full view of their subordinates. He thought better training and deployment of cultured officers in the CEU could have saved the situation from turning ugly. Anyway, what is your take on the search? Was it for a purpose or just a crazy plan of action carried out in a fit of arrogance?" he probed.

"Sir, the CEU is definitely after a senior officer. You should have seen the way the seniors were being targeted. No one, however, is sure whether the suspected officer is being investigated for espionage or financial irregularities," she mentioned.

Ravi was hit by mixed feelings. The information that a senior officer was under surveillance, was unsettling. But the fact that the identity and the nature of delinquency of the suspect were still shrouded in speculations, made him breathe easy. After Mukta left, Ravi lay down on the sofa, his eyes wide open. Unable to focus on anything, he rang up Viranna Moily, his other Desk Officer, who had a long stint with the CEU before he joined the Far East Asia Division, and asked him to come over.

Ravi was slouching on the sofa when Moily entered along with a draft of the fortnightly report on developments in the Far East. He cursorily went through the draft and returned it without even signing it. Moily collected the draft and got up to leave. Ravi gestured him to sit down while buzzing his PA to send in two cups of coffee. Moily was not sure if it was the right time to discuss the usual corridor grapevine over coffee.

"Did the CEU also check your bag last evening?" Ravi suddenly asked.

"I didn't carry any bag, sir. Actually, one of the junior officers of the CEU who had earlier worked with me, alerted me in advance about the surprise check," Moily said.

"Did you ask him what prompted the CEU to conduct the search?"

"No, I didn't. My gut feeling is it's not a routine exercise. The CEU is definitely after someone whom it suspects of compromising operational information. It is obvious they have not been able to zero in on their target or why else they would take the risk of antagonizing every employee of the Agency and be so ruthless in executing the search," Moily stopped discussing as he noticed that Ravi was gasping for breath. "Sir, are you alright?" he asked anxiously.

"I am fine," Ravi responded with some difficulty. "Actually, I have been suffering from erratic pulse beat since yesterday," he said while vigorously wiping sweat from his face. "It aggravates when I don't get proper sleep," Ravi paused briefly for breath. "I wonder if a general search can really help in apprehending the culprit," he said as he calmed down. "The Agency does not have more than ten, twelve officers holding operational responsibilities. It would have made lot more sense to place only these officers under surveillance," he pointed out.

"For all you know, the search may have been directed against those very senior officers," Moily argued. "I was in the CEU when Shetty's case surfaced," he recalled. "He also held the same rank as you do and was extremely pleasant, bright, and most unsuspecting. I still don't believe that he was unpatriotic but in one weak moment, he ate the proverbial apple and got snared into compromising operational inputs."

"How did you get to know that Shetty was peddling classified information?" asked Ravi.

"Sir, the Kashmir Desk reported that some of their crucial operational inputs on J&K operations were being passed on to the ISI. The suspicion gained currency following decisive assaults by Pak-trained militants against some of our sensitive security targets. What rang the alarm bell was the exposure of a few of our POK-based sources, operated by Shetty. Subsequently, he was placed under intensive surveillance by the Bureau and his movements were video recorded and analysed meticulously. Later on, he was called to Headquarters and detained. Confronted with the video footage of his escapades, he broke down and wrote a long note in which he confessed about his wrongdoings," Moily said.

"So it was a joint operation."

"Yes, sir, but those were different times. The Agency Chief and Director of the Bureau worked in tandem and officers on both sides of the Great Divide could bury their mutual jealousy and years of grievances when it came to serving national security interests," Moily explained.

"Do you notice any similarity in your handling of investigation in Shetty's case and the way the CEU is conducting its investigation now?" Ravi asked, trying to ascertain the exact purpose and target of the search.

"It is difficult to say because one doesn't know who Mr Kamath is after and, why. While investigating Shetty, we had a definite idea of the target and the handler and, therefore, we never felt the need for organizing a mass search. Actually, it doesn't make sense that instead of nailing the suspected officer and his handler outside the building, the CEU should waste its time checking papers from officers' briefcases when it is public knowledge that most officers carry classified documents to their homes routinely. Frankly, I don't know what Mr Kamath is trying to achieve. Maybe, he is faced with a far more serious and complicated situation," Moily indicated.

"Did you ever physically torture Shetty to extract a confession? Do you think the CEU would use third-degree methods like the police against its own officers?" Ravi prodded.

"I don't know what the CEU does now. We subjected Shetty only to intense questioning and repeatedly brought out contradictions in his statements. We selectively used the video images of his activities to nail his lies and when he knew that his game was up, he wrote his confession. What really clinched the case was the footage in which he was seen meeting and passing on documents to the handler," Moily disclosed.

"It must have been an excruciating experience, grilling your own officer with whom you have worked for years," Ravi said.

"I don't want to re-live that experience. Looking at Shetty's vacant and pleading eyes, we often felt that we should forgive him, ignoring the incriminating evidences. But we could not let a crime of that nature go unpunished," Moily mentioned.

Ravi asked him nothing further. Moily did not wait for coffee either, and left. Ravi stretched out on the sofa and closed his eyes to reflect on the day's developments. With his thoughts in complete disarray, he got up after a while and kept looking at the closed almirah in daze. Before leaving, Ravi tried to contact Kamath on the cellphone but there was still no response. As he dropped the receiver, KM returned the call. "I am sorry, I couldn't call you earlier. I saw your missed calls only now," he said.

"Avinash told me that you were not well and had to be rushed to the hospital. I hope there is nothing serious," Ravi enquired.

"It was but I am better now," Kamath sounded weary.

"I was wondering if you could release my papers early. I need them urgently for filing my advance tax returns," Ravi requested.

"Please wait for a day," KM said. "Avinash has started scrutinizing your files. The whole of last night, the poor fellow was busy assisting his colleagues in sifting through to more than a quintal of documents. But don't worry. I had a cursory look at your files. They are quite in order from our point of view."

That evening, Ravi skipped his daily work out at the Club and went home instead. At 7.30 pm, he and his wife walked up to Walia's house, 500 metres away from his residence and stayed there till 11.40 pm. Walia ran a transport business, apart from dabbling in exporting a variety of engineering goods to Central Asian Countries. When they emerged, Ravi appeared to be heavily drunk. He could barely stand straight and was carried to the car by Walia. He kept leaning on the shoulders of Walia and hugging him, much to the embarrassment of Vijita. With some difficulty, Walia managed to push Ravi into the rear seat and drove him up to the apartment building. Jena and the security guard had to physically lift him from the car and take him inside the house.

ALISTER saw Vijita Mohan putting the suspect to bed. A few minutes later, she came out in the balcony, moved an easy chair closer to the railing and slumped in it. Within minutes, she dozed off. Around 1.05 am she woke up and called Aabha, her daughter in the US. She told her that Ravi had been unwell for the last three days and suggested that she call him in the morning to ask about his health. She mentioned that Ravi was probably stressed because his leave for the US had still not been approved. Responding probably to her daughter's enquiry about her own health, Vijita said that she had not suffered from asthmatic attacks after she changed the medicines. She also said that she got four beautiful *lehangas* stitched for the engagement ceremony although she knew that her anglicized daughter would not wear them once the ceremony was over.

Vijita retired to bed around 2 am.

Day 84

Feeling drained after two days' of supervising the scrutiny of seized documents, KM checked in the visitor's lounge, fifteen minutes before his time to brief Jeev. Sitting alone, he went over the transcripts, video recordings, and photographs, and arranged them in separate folders so that Jeev could find it handy to skim through the new evidences. He waited for another half an hour but there was still no word when Jeev would arrive. Finally, he collected his ramshackle briefcase that Jeev had offered to replace many times. His argument was that the bruises on his briefcase kept his greed in check and helped him survive the job despite his idiosyncrasies. While walking back, KM checked the messages on his cellphone and saw one from Jeev who wanted to meet him at 11.45 am.

KM showed up on time. Jeev spent almost an hour going through the papers. In between, he sipped his tea, stretched back on the chair and looked outside the window. "Ravi thinks that his game is probably up. His drunkenness, his reduced visits to the photocopier, and his reluctance to carry photocopies in the brown bag are all evidence in point. He is desperate to know whether you will use third-degree methods to force him to confess his crime and repeatedly convinces himself that he is not the man you are looking for. His confidence appears to have taken a beating," Jeev assessed. "Our effort should now be to tighten the noose around his neck as hard as possible so that he runs to his operator for help," he suggested.

"Sir, there wouldn't be any slackening in surveillance," KM assured. "But officers like Moily and Kumar are going to make the suspect more discreet in his interactions and more restricted in his outdoor movements. Should this happen, the chances of our bumping into his handler will recede further," he pointed out.

"The suspect can't sulk forever, KM," Jeev averred. "Since we are no longer losing secrets, we can afford to continue with the surveillance for a few more weeks. The suspect is still depositing and not withdrawing money. I get a feeling that the mask of his duplicity is about to drop," he said.

For Kamath, to see his boss eternally enthused was no surprise. But his inner strength to carry on with the investigation was drying up rapidly. He often considered taking himself off the case but his pride stalled him from backing away. He also did not want to be labelled a loser nor had the gumption to desert his boss mid-stream.

"Sir, do you think his wife's attempt to explain the suspect's odd behaviour to her daughter is genuine? Is it possible that she is not a partner in his crime?" KM raised the issue that had been troubling him ever since the investigation was launched.

"It seems unlikely but to what extent she is involved, is difficult to say," Jeev kept his reaction as brief as possible.

*

Ravi reached office on time. His face was still flushed as a result of last night's heavy drinking. When his PA brought papers for his perusal, he said that he was having a mild headache due to lack of sleep and might leave early. Then, he asked him to check with the Chief's office about the status of his leave application since all the preparations for his US trip had been finalized. As he was about to leave, Ravi asked routinely whether he had heard anything new about the search. Sharma said that everyone was afraid that the seized material would be selectively used to punish those who tripped at some point of time on Mr Jeevnathan's toes. He also referred to incessant rumours about the imminent arrest of a number of officers. Ravi did not want to hear more. It made him feel worse. He called Kamath but was told that the latter was in a meeting with Jeev. Then he reached for the P&T phone but did not call anyone. He also did not take any incoming calls.

Around noon, KM called back. Ravi picked up the receiver in dread of dark possibilities. "Mr Jeev has cleared your papers," KM said. "I have spoken to Mr Bhan and requested him to send his PS to collect your files from my office, anytime from now."

"I don't know how to thank you," Ravi reacted with a sense of overwhelming relief. "If you are free, please come and have coffee. This is the least that I can offer," he said.

"I will drop in before lunch," KM promised.

Ravi's next call was to Bhan, his boss and chief analyst of the Far East Asia Division. "I haven't seen your files as of now and I am not aware how Mr Jeevnathan wants me to go about your case. Kamath, of course, mentioned that he would send your files over but I can't commit to anything unless I see them," Bhan spoke brusquely.

"Sir, I need those papers urgently. I have a will to execute and a property deal to finalize," Ravi insisted but Bhan was unmoved. He said that he would be busy the whole day in operational meetings. "Maybe tomorrow you can send someone to collect the documents," he said in an effort to cut the conversation short. The line suddenly went dead. Ravi tried to revive it a couple of times but failed. Then he took out a bunch of loose sheets from the table's drawer and shredded them. Meanwhile, the Director Pakistan Military Operations and the Desk Officers of Europe and Naval Operations called him in quick succession to inquire if he was free. Ravi lied that he was busy in a meeting with his branch officers and would revert as soon as he was free. Actually, he was desperate to talk to KM and, since he was not sure when the latter would arrive, he decided not to have any visitor in between. A few minutes later, Sharma reported that the files had reached Mr Bhan's office but there were no instructions to the staff about the mode of their disposal.

It was well past lunch time but KM was nowhere in sight. He deliberately kept sitting in the NC, watching Ravi's fidgety behaviour on the monitor. He grimaced as he saw the suspect pull out an English rendering of Shrimad Bhagvat Gita from his briefcase and turn over its pages, while looking intermittently at the door.

For once, someone desperately longed for Kamath's company. Even in the best of times, he was treated in the Agency like a pariah by the seniors. His colleagues shunned his proximity and considered him untrustworthy and his juniors were in dread of him because of his unpredictable reactions. KM found it ironical that the suspect was more eager to wait for his executioner to arrive rather than confabulate with his usual collaborators who were keen to come and chat with him.

Kamath thought the suspect's fondness for the Gita was quite comical. Here was a man whose entire life and work was an antithesis of the Scripture's core philosophy, defined in terms of vigorous pursuance of truth. The suspect was never known to be a reader of serious books and enjoyed a reputation of going through files and notes casually. But where it mattered, he appeared to be working hard, meticulously sifting value-added inputs and spending hours briefing and debriefing his colleagues without fear or remorse. Maybe in the Gita, KM assumed, the suspect found an escape from his guilt. Convicts usually turned to praying and reading holy scriptures, deriving solace from words of wisdom within the bland, grey and lifeless walls of prison. The suspect was no exception.

It was 2 pm when KM stepped inside Ravi's room. The suspect received him warmly and thanked him for releasing his personal files within forty-eight hours.

"There was never a problem in your case. The delay was due to the time taken in making a list of so many files," KM explained.

"But I was very worried. The files contain details of my property and bank deposits. For unscrupulous officers, it is quite tempting to use such information to prima facie start an investigation for so-called economic offences. The unfortunate part of such an exercise is that even before you are asked to explain, your reputation is already trashed, fuelled by selective leaks," the suspect remarked and made an effort to laugh.

"You are right, but my unit has no vigilance role. We come into the picture only when we suspect an employee of making money in lieu of passing secret information to unauthorized consumers," KM paused and looked closely at the suspect. His face betrayed no emotions. "I am not going to allow anyone to violate the privacy of seized documents or to use any material to coerce, harass, or blackmail officers. I have kept the pornographic videos that we have impounded in huge numbers, in my personal custody so that the holders' name remain a secret. Similarly, I have retained original and photocopies of classified papers and devices dealing with high grade operations with me. These will be quietly dealt with unless our scrutiny reveals that someone is guilty of ferrying secret inputs to foreign agents," KM mentioned, waiting for his host to make some self-incriminating remarks.

The suspect's reaction, however, was strangely bullish. He said that it was high time the CEU conducted the search because officers had become used to taking out classified papers from the building without authorization. Horrified at the suspect's duplicity, KM pointed out that there were no clear cut guidelines about nature of documents that could be taken out and the duration for which they could be retained outside the building. The existing rules, he said, gave a blanket exemption to senior officers. Even junior employees were authorized to carry confidential papers to their residence with their seniors' approval. That was the reason everyone felt free to take away anything that he could lay his hands on. KM further said that even Moily, who had earlier served in the CEU, was caught during the search for carrying secret papers, which he could have easily attended to in the office. KM lamented that the Agency had become a flea market where anyone could trade for any information at their free will.

The suspect rubbed sweat from his forehead with a paper napkin. Noticing him for the first time losing control of himself, KM tightened the noose. "It is a pity, that except for a few officers like you, no one has taken kindly to the surprise check. You should have seen the way the officers reacted. They think we are demons," he said.

"You shouldn't bother about what others say," the suspect counselled, struggling to appear unruffled.

"That's easier said than done," said KM. "During the surprise check, several officers abused our staff. A very senior officer threatened to fix me for my *stupid and foolish behaviour*. One day these officers will become reporting officers and preside over boards to decide foreign and domestic postings and promotions. One of them could even be the Chief. Tell me why anyone would risk his career prospects for the sake of protecting the Agency from espionage agents?" he asked. The suspect was clearly uneasy. He avoided looking into KM's eyes, opened the drawers two, three times without taking out anything and then reminded Sharma to send in coffee quickly. However, KM was not ready to let his prey go off the hook.

"Those who were most vociferous in condemning the search," he went on, "are the ones who carry box-full of papers regularly after office hours to their home. But I don't care. I am not here to please them. I will do what I think is best in the Agency's security interests."

Ravi kept quiet for a long time, sipping water. KM waited for the suspect's nerves to settle down and say something.

"I have always been a stickler in matters of security," the suspect claimed, finally breaking his silence. "I never carry official papers to home. If I have some extra work, I finish it by sitting late in the office. This habit helps me to relax at home and enjoy my evenings with family and friends," he said.

"That is the right thing to do," KM remarked.

"Do you know why I have kept the photocopier in my room?" The suspect suddenly asked. "It is mainly to ensure that no one copies classified documents without my specific approval."

KM chose not to react and was happy that the suspect, of his own volition, raised this issue. Nevertheless, he felt like choking the suspect dead. Deception dripped from every word that he uttered. It became increasingly evident that it would not be easy to crack this iceberg of treachery in the interrogation centre with do's and don't's, prescribed by human rights activists.

"You may not be misusing the photocopier," KM said picking up the issue from where the suspect had left, "but in recent times, we came across several officers, doing all kinds of things with their copiers and computers having Internet access. To stem this rot, Mr Jeevnathan tried to withdraw photocopiers from officers and branches and keep them centrally at a place where one could go with proper authorization to take out copies."

"That, of course, is one way of preventing misuse of a photocopier," the suspect interrupted. "The other is that you give it to officers who will not allow its misuse. I use the photocopier primarily to copy newspaper clippings, which I pass on to the relevant sections for updating their daily reports. Sometimes I receive request from my officers to make copies of their personal papers. I let them do that, but only in my presence. I used to have apprehensions that someone might take out copies when I was not in my room. But that problem has also been taken care of by this new machine. It has a complicated operating procedure which only I know about." The suspect then got up and invited KM to see how the photocopier worked. But KM kept sitting.

"Where do we get officers like you who value secrecy so much?" KM asked. "Over the years, the access to copiers and the Internet and their misuse have become both easy and epidemic. I suspect we will soon be required to deal with a number of officers who abuse these facilities to share information with unauthorized persons," KM warned, feigning anger.

"Why can't you put a stop to this? I thought your boss could steamroll his decisions against all odds," the suspect probed.

"He told me once that when the house was on fire and inmates had run away with hosepipes, the wisest thing was to look at the heavens and pray for rains. Seeing the dismal state of security consciousness among officers, he has also given up and is waiting for divine intervention to remedy the situation," KM said. "But if I have my way," he declared, "I will torture officers to death who try to smuggle secrets out of the building in return for petty monetary gains."

"I couldn't agree more with you," Ravi responded, looking composed.

"A couple of employees," KM further said, "have also come to our notice for procuring documents that deal with subjects concerning areas of others' responsibility. We are looking into these cases to ascertain the motive behind their extra-territorial interests." His questioning got more specific this time.

"This would not have happened if supervisory officers kept in close touch with their subordinates and monitored their activities regularly," Ravi replied calmly.

"Less said the better about the supervision," KM retorted. "No officer of the rank of director and above can identify 20 percent employees working under them. Actually, we practice our restrictive security in funny ways. Over 60 percent employees in the Agency cannot recognize their divisional heads, although they may be fully aware of the scandals surrounding them," KM said.

"This is typical of civilian leadership where everyone fends for himself," Ravi ranted.

"You cannot generalize," KM insisted. "The Bureau, for example, is a far more cohesive entity and works in an environment of collective responsibility. The Agency, on the other hand, is a tin pot. You just have to shake it to hear thousands of defiant voices," he said. Their conversation was cut short when Ravi's PA came in to announce that Mr Jeevnathan was looking for Kamath.

"I didn't realize it was already 3.30 pm." KM made an abrupt exit. It was a call that KM had pre-arranged with his deputy Avinash to escape the nauseating web of deceit woven by Ravi.

*

For those manning the NC, surprises came aplenty. In a clear departure from the past when he played an effusive host, Ravi offered neither coffee nor fresh lime water to KM. He also did not latch the door from the inside as he approached the photocopier and copied a report on the training of Kashmiri terrorists in Lashkar camps in Pakistan. Then, he had his food brought from the canteen, skipping his favourite soup and sandwiches. Surprisingly, as he lay down on the sofa, he started snoring as if his life was at peace with itself. At 4.30 pm, he woke up, washed his face, took out a few pages from a file and photocopied them. It contained points for briefing a Hong Kong-based source who was to visit Delhi next week. Apparently, after his discussions with KM, he felt that he was not the target of the general search. At 4.55 pm, Kailash Uike, Head of Agency's Eastern Bureau, called. He said that he had been summoned by the Chief to discuss the strategy for penetrating the Marxist outfits in Nepal in order to prevent the Marxists from getting uncomfortably close to China and providing logistic and arms support to Naxalites in India. The suspect coaxed Uike to elaborate but the latter was in a hurry. He said he would try to drop in for coffee if the meeting did not spill over the office hours. However, at 5.35 pm he informed Ravi that he would not be able to come because the meeting was yet to start.

"I can wait," the suspect said. He was obviously keen on meeting Uike to find out the outcome of his discussion with the Chief.

"Please don't wait for me. I am not sure when the meeting will be over."

"It's okay," Ravi said and hung up.

A few minutes later, Nidhi Singh, Director in-charge of International Terrorism, called the suspect and requested if he could spare his car for half an hour. She said that she had to deliver a note urgently on operational linkage of Kashmiri militants with radical Islamic outfits in Pakistan, Afghanistan, Egypt, and Iran to the National Security Advisor but there was no staff car readily available. Ravi explained that he had no problem but she must return positively by 6.30 pm. Then he rang up Moily to confirm whether his bag had also been searched by the CEU officers.

"Yes, sir. It was an assessment of Tripod on resident Tamils' future in Malaysia. I wanted to read it at home. I don't know what view the Chief will take," Moily said.

"I cannot understand why you took this paper out when you knew in advance that a search was in the offing," the suspect asked.

"Sir, I completely misread the warning. I didn't believe that something like this could ever happen," Moily sounded worried.

"Anyway, check with your contact in the CEU whether your note has been sent to Mr Bhan. The best I can do is to lie to him that you were taking the note out under my specific directions," he said.

"Sir, I am really grateful," Moily replied in reverence.

The suspect received the next call from someone called Didda. He said that he could meet the Minister now and was calling from his residence. "The Minister has assured that he will call the Chief and request him to assign you to one of the stations in the neighbourhood. He was also annoyed that the Chief was sitting over your leave application," he added.

"Thanks. I will inform you if I hear anything positive from the Chief's office. But do you seriously think that the Minister can make the Chief accept his request?" Ravi asked.

"I am hundred percent sure. He will definitely speak to the Principal Secretary to the Prime Minister, if not the Chief," Didda claimed. With no more calls expected, Ravi lay down on the sofa, waiting for his car to arrive. At 6.40 pm, Nidhi Singh knocked on the door and came in. She profusely apologized for the delay and blamed the NSA for detaining her needlessly while he perused the note.

"That's okay, but what was so important about the note that you had to personally go to hand it over?" the suspect asked quietly.

"The NSA insisted that I must come over in case he had some clarifications to seek before he met diplomats of US, France, UK, and Canada later this evening. He wanted to raise the issue of substantial increase in the supply of funds and weapons to Kashmiri Militants from Arab countries during past six months," she said.

"Do we have any hard inputs to conclusively implicate the ISI or the Pak Army?" he asked.

"We have a surfeit of information. Only one has to start believing in what is obvious. Please have a look at it." She showed the note to the suspect who went through it casually and returned. "It's explosive stuff. Will it be possible for you to spare a copy for my reading?" he asked.

"I am not sure about giving you a copy. But you can read it tonight and return it to me tomorrow morning. As it is, you are late because of me," she said.

After Miss Singh left, the suspect switched on the photocopier and took out copies of the note. He kept the copied sheets along with the original in the almirah and then left.

*

It was 8 pm and there was still no sign that Jeev would wind up early. He had called KM and Ajay to discuss the next course of action in the aftermath of the general search. He told Ajay that he had already heard KM's views on the subject in the morning and it was now his turn to benefit him with his perspective.

"Sir, Ravi has stopped taking photocopies out of the building and drastically reduced soliciting information from his colleagues," Ajay began carefully. "This abstinence is likely to last for a long time. In view of this, we should stop wasting our resources in fishing for fresh evidence and deal with the suspect on the basis of whatever is already available," he argued.

"What would you say to his suggestion?" Jeev asked KM.

"Sir, I am in no hurry to dump the investigation," KM clarified. "The suspect may have stopped taking away classified documents, but he continues to photocopy and retain them in the office. He is only waiting for the panic caused by the search to cool down. If he has reduced his interactions with colleagues, it's mainly because the officers are themselves busy fending for their lapses. Within the four walls of his room, he now looks more confused than ever before and dreads the company of his collaborating colleagues who keep tormenting him with their wildly speculative version of the motives behind the search. He appears to be completely incapable of handling himself. I almost get a feeling that he is about to confess. Till that happens, the operation has to continue," KM insisted.

"But we can't carry on like this forever," Ajay interrupted.

"We have to," KM retorted. "The suspect is precariously holding on to his nerves and contriving to put up a brave front. It's no time to let him break free from our stranglehold. If we cut short the investigation at this stage, we should forget about prosecuting him for espionage," he stressed.

"Sir, KM is actually endorsing my views. We differ only on the timing of closing the investigation, whether it should be now or later," Ajay said. "We are actually stuck in a jam after the search. I can't see any forward movement in tracking his handler in the foreseeable future. The additional evidence can now come only from questioning the suspect and bringing out contradictions in his defence with the help of his recorded activities," he explained.

Jeev finally intervened. "If we fold up now, it will appear that our doggedness in pursuing the handler has been a staggering folly," he told Ajay with a straight face. "We may not have located the handler so far but it is not correct to say that he is inaccessible. The general search has actually brought urgency into our efforts. Despite his bravado, Ravi is now afraid of taking any document out. He is also under increased pressure to deliver, which you can make out from his attempts to elicit information and photocopy documents. It's just a matter of few weeks when he meets his man to find out how to resume his supplies," he stressed.

"Sir, I still believe we should arrest the suspect and break his bones piece by piece, till he throws up details of his network," Ajay insisted.

"Breaking his bones is, of course, out of question," Jeev ruled. "Since he is mortally afraid of the ugliness of third-degree methods, he may not provide you the luxury of his physical questioning. Let's assume for a moment that out of fear of physical torture, he confesses that he works for X, Y, or Z and discloses the name of the outfit that he is working for. How will you verify the genuineness of his claim, for no foreign Intelligence agency will ever own him up? If you flaunt his confession of crime as evidence, you will be ridiculed for levelling baseless allegations not only by the suspected agency but also by the government," Jeev explained.

"Sir, then why don't we remove him from the service on security grounds?" Ajay asked.

"We can but what happens to his involvement in an espionage case?" Jeev shot back.

"Sir, I really hope we don't end up on the losing side of playing this cat and mouse game," KM finally broke his silence.

Jeev saw no point in imposing his directives on tiring minds. "If the suspect does not restart his business and we are still unable to get hold of the handler within two weeks, I will initiate the process to summarily dismiss him under Article 311(2)(c) for being a security risk," he said.

"Sir, it may be too light a punishment for such a heinous crime. The dismissal must be preceded by some public humiliation which is possible only if we arrest him," Ajay insisted.

Jeev was amused. His deputy, for inexplicable reasons, had also started to bay for the suspect's blood.

"We would all like him to be hanged and paraded naked on the streets of Delhi. But we are not cheerleaders," Jeev admonished his deputy mildly. "We have to assess our evidence dispassionately to establish a link between the suspect and his operatives. For me the saddest thing would be to let the suspect go scot free and roam around in the country with a dismissal under Article 311(2)(c) or an acquittal for want of evidence, when we know that he is a traitor," Jeev said.

Ajay discerned for the first time a chink in Jeev's optimism to solve the case on his terms. "Sir, what is the guarantee that even after identifying the handler and the agency that has subverted Ravi Mohan, the courts will sentence him to death or to an extended spell of imprisonment," he asked.

"At least we will know about the perpetrators and their modus operandi and will have enough material to confront the suspected service with embarrassing revelations. It will also throw light on where we failed and which safety valves we have to repair to prevent a recurrence of such incidents," Jeev pointed out.

Ajay, however, was not willing to give up. "Sir, I hope we don't end up courting a catastrophe while waiting for the handler to surface," he averred. "It may still be a safer course to stop gambling further with the investigation and dump the suspect without fussing over legalities," he suggested.

Jeev felt abandoned but kept his cool. Throughout the investigation, he had scrupulously avoided forcing a decision. His idea was to make KM, Ajay, and the CEU learn how to mount and sustain an operation of this nature. No wonder, he gave them full liberty to argue, disagree, and put across their points of view. It was only after he found KM excited about the task, that he allowed the investigation to be set in motion. He knew that if he coerced a team of fifty-two employees to fall in line, someone would surely blow the whistle. While nothing seemed to have gone wrong in keeping the investigation under wraps so far, it was evident that both Ajay and Kamath were now desperate to see the back of the investigation.

"Fine, then both of you put up a self-contained note, suggesting termination of the operation and the reasons for it. I will take the note to the Chief tomorrow after the fortnightly meeting and obtain his approval. Let the handler and the agency he works for, have the last laugh," Jeev said looking outside through the window.

Ajay and KM groped for a response for a long time.

"Sir, what more do you want us to do now?" KM finally asked.

"Nothing really, but if you can, wait as long as it is possible. The time of aggressive surveillance is over. It is now a battle of attrition," Jeev reminded them. "We only have to make sure that the suspect does not return to his normal routine. Anyway, since both of you have run out of patience, just work on the note and give it to me by tomorrow afternoon," he added.

"Sir, where do you think can the suspect go?" KM asked, ignoring Jeev's jibe at their pusillanimity.

But it was Ajay who responded. "The kind of sophistication that is being employed to protect the identity of the handler leaves me in no doubt that Ravi's espionage network is being orchestrated by an intelligence outfit from one of the countries in Europe or Americas," he claimed.

Jeev, however, had no interest in floating trial balloons. Instead, he enquired if he knew the officer in charge of Immigration in the Bureau. Ajay promptly said that he knew Samar Saxena well enough to call him a friend.

"Then request him informally to alert all immigration check posts to prevent Ravi from leaving India without the Agency's clearance," Jeev said.

"Sir, I will talk to him and get back to you by tomorrow morning. But why are we hesitant to officially involve the Bureau in alerting the checkpoints? I guess, Saxena may ask to route our request through his Director," Ajay averred.

"This matter has already been discussed threadbare with the Chief and we are not in favour of officially involving the Bureau in the investigation," Jeev said. There was no further discussion on the subject. Seconds later, Jeev buzzed his PS and told him that he was leaving. As they came out, Ajay went to his room. KM followed Jeev to the porch. Before Jeev boarded the car, KM asked for a lift.

"Of course, is anything bothering you?" Jeev asked.

"Sir, please don't think that I have run out of steam. I am only frustrated for not being able to deliver the handler to you," KM said.

"Don't take it as your personal failing. Frankly, I couldn't have bargained for a more committed foot soldier than you," Jeev reassured him.

"Sir, the sight of the suspect makes me mad. That's the reason I want him to be summarily tried and punished."

"I understand. I also want to punish him, but what's more important is that we do it the right way," Jeev clarified.

"Sir, are you not convinced that Ravi is an espionage agent?"

"Yes, I am."

"Then why can't we fill the gaps to bring him to justice?"

"That will be a travesty of justice. You can't frame him just because you believe that he is working as an espionage agent. If we don't have conclusive evidences, that's our bad luck. Let's not manufacture evidence, which other law enforcement agencies do all the time. Trust me, I am not taking a moralistic stand but somehow I feel that it will be a crime to fix someone for what only *appears* to be his crime," Jeev remarked.

"Sir, it is only a matter of tightening a few loose ends, not even filling the gaps," KM persisted.

"You know, on several occasions I had a compelling urge to withdraw myself from the investigation. I thought someone else, capable of disregarding propriety and legal righteousness, might serve the interest of this case better. But I just couldn't give up. Now it seems I will have to, with no clues coming our way to fill in the jigsaw puzzle," Jeev remarked as the car entered his residence. He got down and instructed the driver to drop KM at his house.

Before Jeev went to sleep, Ajay called. He conveyed that Samar Saxena had agreed to alert the immigration checkpoints on an informal basis. Saxena also asked for photographs of the suspect and his wife which, Ajay said, would be provided the next day.

"What was his initial reaction?" Jeev asked.

"Sir, he does not know the suspect nor showed any interest in the suspect's rank and his work. He did not even ask why we are so concerned about his impending escape. I guess, he thinks that the suspect is a junior employee," Ajay informed.

"Thanks," Jeev said and hung up.

Day 85

The fortnightly meeting was in session for the first time after the general search. Tension crackled in the air as officers took their turns to review developments in their respective regions. The Chief was sitting stiff. Unlike at previous review sessions, he refrained from encouraging first time speakers to freely express their views. He also desisted from providing his inputs to supplement their information and avoided opening up any subject for general discussion. He looked around impassively as if his thoughts wandered elsewhere. To everyone's discomfort, he queried no one but snubbed an officer when he mentioned the nom-de-plume of a source and its access in order to emphasize the importance of a piece of information. The Desk Officer Afghanistan evoked the Chief's instant ire when the former began giving details of the deployment of Allied troops in and around Mazar-e-Sharif. As the turn of Desk Officers of

Sri Lanka and Europe came to speak, the Chief asked them not to waste his time. He also cut short the presentation by an officer who was discussing the ULFA's external links, remarking that the information as stale and largely uncorroborated. Clearly, the Chief was in a foul mood. As the last speaker finished his briefing and the officers started collecting papers to exit hurriedly, the Chief growled.

"There is something that I must speak to you about. All of you are aware that the CEU conducted a surprise check three days ago. They were not chasing windmills but smoke, after their fingers got badly burnt in a fire," he said.

Officers sat up in apprehension.

"It's a shame," he decried, "that hundreds of classified documents were seized from the possession of officers who were attempting to cart them out of the building. I can understand a few senior officers carrying top secret papers to their residence for reading but I can't figure out why mid-level and junior officers would need those papers at home. A huge cache of pornographic videos, pen drives, DVDs, and CDs were also impounded from fleeing officers. Apparently, the employees bring them to the office for viewing and listening during duty hours. A complete breakdown of supervision seems to have taken place at all levels. I am not sure, if anyone has any idea of what is happening in their units with regard to the security of their information, documents, and technical devices. The little that I have seen of the seizures is scary. I won't be surprised if some of them were destined for hostile foreign intelligence agencies. It is obvious that we no longer feel obligated to adhere to the principles of restrictive security because several officers were caught with information, which they had no bloody business possessing." The Chief paused for a few seconds. A deathly silence prevailed in the room.

"I was told that a few senior officers remonstrated wildly and abused the personnel of the CEU who checked their bags and briefcases. This is unforgivable. First, you commit serious security lapses and then you behave like outlaws to browbeat those who want to discipline you. Let me make it loud and clear that from now on, the CEU will conduct searches regularly till the sanity in our security system is restored," the Chief warned. He got up abruptly and left. All the others scampered to their respective rooms, skipping their post-meeting tea session.

KM watched the suspect keenly throughout the Chief's outburst. The suspect sat frozen with his eyes transfixed at the floor. A couple of times, he took out handkerchief and wiped sweat from his forehead. An officer sitting next to him frequently leaned on his right shoulders probably to enquire if he was alright, but the suspect did not respond. For the first time, KM saw the suspect's facade of serenity and laboured poise melting fast under the heat of Chief's tongue lashing.

*

From the meeting, Ravi went to his room and called Bhan. He complained of irregular pulse beat, mild headache and exhaustion, and sought permission to leave the office early. Bhan promptly agreed. Before the line got disconnected, Ravi enquired if Bhan had a chance to look into his personal files, forwarded by the CEU. Bhan said that he had, and that they were lying with him. He also confirmed that he had seen comments of Kamath and Mr Jeevnathan, which were positive, and asked Ravi to get his files collected from his PS.

Ravi later spoke to his physician and explained his symptoms. He was told to come right away for a check-up. He then called his wife. "But you were alright when you left home. Has your leave for the US been refused or has it got something to do with your files that were seized during the general search?" she asked anxiously.

"It's not about leave. It's just that I am feeling a bit uneasy. I am going to see Dr Ghai at Apollo," Ravi said.

"Do you want me to take you to the hospital? You sound low," she asked.

"It's not so alarming."

At 12.15 pm, the suspect reached the emergency counter at the Apollo hospital. He was quickly ushered in by an attendant to Dr Ghai's examination room. The watchers didn't lose him till he emerged from the doctor's room at 1.15 pm. The suspect was later taken for tests to the fourth floor where the watcher's entry was barred. They picked him up again at 2.30 pm, as he came out of the hospital and was driven to his residence.

ALISTER watched Ravi enter the bedroom and slump on a chair with his head on the back rest. Vijita served him a glass of water. The visuals were blurred and partly covered, making it difficult to clearly decipher the suspect's mood and activities around him. However, the audio recording, though too low for KM's liking, was interesting.

"What happened? What did Dr Ghai say?" Vijita asked.

"There is nothing to worry," Ravi said. Then he briefly recounted what transpired at the meeting.

"I am sure, you couldn't be the target. The Chief's ire must have been directed against those who carried classified papers and office equipment out of the building," she tried to reason.

"It's not that. From now on, the search is going to be a regular feature," Ravi said. His wife did not respond. After a few minutes, ALISTER recorded them moving away from its sight. An hour later, Sharma called from the office to enquire about Ravi's health. Vijita said that he was fine and had been advised complete rest for a couple of days.

The suspect did not come out of the residence for the rest of the day.

*

Kamath had never been so proud of his work. For once in his tenure as Director CEU, he felt vindicated for his crusade against the Agency's black sheep. There were times when he felt dejected and thought of quitting the investigation, due to his failing health and his helplessness in neutralizing the potential peddlers of secrets but Jeev's missionary zeal kept him afloat. And now the Chief had openly commended his work. Much to his surprise, the Chief came across in the meeting as a brute enforcer of security norms, a tough leader and an extremely sincere man. Being fairly junior in the hierarchy, KM had never closely interacted with the Chief and thus, formed his opinion of Wasan on the basis of hearsay and latter's cryptic noting on files. The stories that he patronized a few officers and constantly manipulated everyone and everything to serve his career interests were all spurious, KM persuaded himself to belief. Why else, he wondered, would the Chief castigate his favourites in the harshest of words, threaten to punish those who did not fall in line and upbraid those who had resisted search of their bags and abused junior employees. KM came out of the meeting smiling and literally ran to share his thoughts with Jeev.

"Sir, it was a command performance by Mr Wasan. I never expected him to be so supportive of our investigation," KM remarked as he pulled out a chair to sit.

"What was Ravi's reaction?" Jeev asked, ignoring KM's misplaced excitement.

"He was restless, perspiring, and did not look at the Chief even once. If Mr Wasan's diatribe had continued for another fifteen minutes, Ravi might have collapsed. The Chief's reprimand has drilled a big hole into his confidence. If we subject him to a lie detector test right now, followed by a narco-analysis of his brain, he will surely own up his guilt," KM contended with unreserved glee but Jeev was not impressed.

"I am not so sure. Actually, what Wasan has done is irreparable," Jeev said. "Henceforth, the suspect will become more circumspect in his movements and cautious in procuring and photocopying documents. As it is, he was keeping us at bay from having a peep into his modus operandi. It will become much more difficult now to peel off the suspect's real self," he added.

"Sir, the Chief, for a change, batted quite strongly for us. Whether he did it on purpose or not, I don't know but he has injected a much needed urgency to close out the case," KM emphasized. "With his threat of conducting more surprise checks in future, he has actually left no exit path for the suspect," he opined.

"On the contrary, I think, Wasan went overboard," Jeev countered. "I am quite worried about its fall out in the future course of the operation. With his threat looming, I wonder if Ravi will photocopy documents in the immediate future and run the risk of getting caught by the CEU for taking any classified papers to his residence. After our surprise check, I was hoping against hope that Ravi might resume photocopying once the rumours cooled down and seized items were restored to their owners. Regrettably, everything has changed now," Jeev said.

KM did not know what to say.

"I guess Wasan got carried away by his outrage over what Ravi is engaged in," Jeev went on to explain. "It is also possible that Wasan wanted to send a message across to his officers that he is ruthless, unsparing, and nobody's man when it comes to enforcing discipline. He could even be overreacting to a raging canard that it is Jeev and not the Chief who calls the shot on security matters. Whatever the reason, the chances of capturing the handler now appears to be extremely bleak," he said.

"In that case the option that we are left with is to invoke Article 311(2)(c) to dismiss him from the service?" KM promptly reacted.

"I am meeting Wasan at 4 pm today. I will let you know if he is equally impatient to close the investigation," Jeev said. The sarcasm did not bounce off KM who quickly changed the track of discussion. He informed that Ravi went to Apollo hospital for a check-up straight from the fortnightly meeting and was not likely to return to the office for next couple of days.

"I am not surprised," Jeev said. "I guess Ravi will now remain mostly in the house, consulting his wife and children about his next move. He will also avoid any contact with the handler for the time being. It is, therefore, important that we know whom and what he talks to and how he is coping with the Chief's threats. ALISTER's reporting under the circumstances is going to be very crucial," he stressed.

"Unfortunately, ALISTER has been transmitting fudged video images since yesterday," KM reported hesitatingly.

"Did you speak to Kutty?" Jeev asked.

"Yes, sir. He believes that either the lens is covered with dust or something is covering its line of sight. In any case, he does not favour a mid-course correction lest the operation gets exposed," KM said.

Jeev did not react. Instead, he called Kutty on the RIT and switched on the speaker for KM to hear the conversation.

"Are you sure, you cannot fix ALISTER?" Jeev asked.

"I am sorry, sir, but if you insist, I can try to rectify the snags. Mr Kamath will have to arrange for entry of a technician in the suspect's apartment at least for forty five minutes."

"Let me see if it is feasible," Jeev said and disconnected.

*

At 4 pm, Jeevnathan entered the Chief's room.

"Please sit down. I will just take two minutes," Wasan said and resumed his discussion with two outstation officers dealing with Nepal operations. Jeev sat down on a sofa near the window. Right outside was an electric crematorium that was unusually deserted. He kept looking out vacantly till Wasan came and sat on the chair on his right. "Could you make any breakthrough in locating the handler?" he asked.

"No, nor do I expect it to happen in the near future," Jeev said.

"Then let's call off the operation. As it is, Princi thinks that the case has been badly handled and its gravity blown out of proportion. He is of the view that we should have dealt with the case administratively as soon as we knew that Ravi was making conscious efforts to elicit unauthorized information from his colleagues," Wasan said, while pouring tea for Jeev.

"So, he wants to sweep the dirt under the carpet," Jeev said sarcastically. "I don't blame him for these off-the-cuff remarks. Coming from a diplomatic background, he is naturally apprehensive of the adverse impact of the investigation on bilateral relations. He may be wondering why we make such a fuss about the restrictive security when senior officers routinely talk and exchange ideas among themselves. But these are his views. Tell me frankly, what do you make out of our investigation as a professional?" he asked.

"I just want this nightmare to be over," Wasan sighed as he finished drinking tea. "Kindly give me an updated note on the operation by this evening," he suggested after a brief pause. "Princi has called me over to discuss some operational matters tomorrow at 11.30 am. I need this note just in case he raises the issue."

"There is nothing really to update. The suspect is no longer photocopying or eliciting information from his colleagues. And, we still have no leads on the agency that he is working for," said Jeev. Wasan was at a loss for words, finding himself torn between his loyalty to his decades-old friendship with Jeev and his frustration with the latter for landing him in a ham-handed investigation.

"Princi will also like to go through the relevant transcripts," Wasan said, avoiding Jeev's frown. "He feels that you are reading too much into the suspect's conversations and in his activities. He believes that since he is at a distance from the day-to-day investigation, he can be more objective in weighing the evidence and suggesting a more practical course of action."

"I have no problem in making available the transcripts but my fear is, given his lack of exposure to handling espionage cases, he may start giving distorted advice that you will not be in a position to reject or disagree with," Jeev argued.

"But is it not his prerogative to issue instructions?" Wasan asked assertively.

"Not on issues that require expert handling," Jeev was not the one to relent easily. "I am averse to listening to dictates that are not driven by common sense. You must explain to Saran that we are not scripting a spy thriller in which the suspense keeps digging deeper as you turn over the pages. It's a grind that we have to go through. He must know that patience is the key if we want to crack Ravi's espionage module," he pointed out.

"It is easy for you to lecture me," Wasan sounded exasperated.

"You know that it is not a run-of-the-mill police case in which the investigator's job is over once the accused is arrested and the chargesheet is submitted. Delhi Police and the CBI may find the available evidence sufficient to prosecute the suspect but it cannot serve our purpose unless we get a clear insight into the spying network that the accused has built around and have a feel of hands that orchestrate it from outside," Jeev explained.

Wasan found the argument self-serving. "I suggest we let Princi form his opinion after going through the transcripts and watchers' reports," Wasan insisted.

"I will ask KM to send an update along with transcripts," Jeev said as he got up to leave. "I also notice that whenever I discuss this case, you get abrupt and impatient. Why don't you tell me to call off the investigation, setting aside my reservations? After all, you are the Chief and you can always direct me to drop out," he rubbed his views in.

"The suspect's activities are actually getting on my nerves," Wasan confessed. "I don't know why he got us all sucked into this mess. For a retired officer of the Army, I thought the Agency had given him much more than he ever deserved," he said.

"Do you ever regret your decision of entrusting the management of Security Division to me?" Jeev suddenly asked. "I somehow feel that you are not entirely comfortable with the way I have been conducting this case."

By now Wasan got up from his chair. Both were facing each other, literally at an arm's length.

"Not really," Wasan replied, trying hard to hide his disgust with Jeev's infatuation with laws and human rights issues in dealing with a simple crime of treason. "Please don't prolong this agony. If you think it is necessary, book this man for espionage and get a police remand to interrogate him," he pleaded.

"An espionage case at this stage is a non-starter," Jeev reiterated. "There is no evidence to prove that he is working for a foreign intelligence agency or receives payments in lieu of his inputs from unauthorised persons. Moreover, we may have a problem in deciding how much of the evidence procured from clandestine sources can be shared with the trial court and which devices employed for this purpose, can be subjected to the court's scrutiny," he pointed out yet again.

"Ravi's confession will address all doubts of the courts even if we submit a tailored version of the loss of information and the use of surveillance devices. The judges will surely understand our compulsions for not coming clean on complete disclosure of our evidences," Wasan argued.

"On the contrary, the courts will never accept a charge that is supported by unverifiable evidences obtained during the suspect's interrogation. And, if, by any chance, Ravi names the CIA, KGB, MI-6, or MOSSAD as the subverting agency and we don't have clinching proof to seal his accusations, you should be ready to be severely reprimanded by the political leadership for being irresponsible in pointing accusing fingers without any basis," he said.

Wasan was irritated at Jeev's lack of clarity on what he actually wanted. He neither wanted to terminate the operation nor file a case. He was simply dragging the case, Wasan thought.

"You are being over cautious," Wasan said. "I still maintain that we should go ahead and register a case. What happens thereafter is for the CBI or Delhi Police to explain. At least no one will accuse us of shielding the suspect," he argued.

"The courts will certainly accuse you of abdicating your responsibility and failing to critically assess the evidence before filing charges against the suspect," Jeev pointed out. "Surely, you remember what happened in the Samba spy case of late seventies," he reminded.

"Is that relevant?" the Chief asked.

"Both General Malhotra, Chief of Army Staff, and DMI Kunjru had chosen the softer option of confirming the sentence of Court Martial against officers allegedly involved in espionage," Jeev reminded the Chief. "The human cost of their escapist approach turned out to be monumental. Apart from being subjected to merciless physical questioning, a number of brigadiers, lieutenant colonels, majors, JCOs, NCOs, and civilians languished in prison for years on charges of spying for Pakistan. A dozen of them were sentenced to life imprisonment and Rathore and Rana, the two prime suspects, were slapped with fourteen years RI. The Delhi High Court eventually exonerated Rana, a verdict that was later upheld by the Supreme Court. Their ruling was simple. The conclusive link between the suspects and their Pak operatives was missing. This is the exact situation that confronts us in Ravi's case. Neither his handler nor his operating agency have blipped on our surveillance radar," Jeev argued.

"But unlike Rathore and the others, Ravi is a spy, confirmed by overwhelming documentary evidence," Wasan retorted.

"The evidences hold him guilty of only security lapses," Jeev replied.

"The CBI can fill in the gaps from inputs picked up during the interrogation," Wasan reacted tersely. By now he appeared to have reached the dead end of his persuasive skills.

"I have doubts if such evidences will be sustainable," Jeev countered. "My biggest worry is about the story Ravi spins during his interrogation. Apart from the fact that it will mostly be a fairytale, it is also bound to implicate former chiefs, serving and retired officers from the defence forces, politicians, and some of us from the Agency. And, those implicated by him will implicate others. Like in the Samba case, suspects will surface in drove, much to the glee of our all-weather persecutors in various security agencies and the media. Worse, none of the collaborators cited by Ravi, may be ultimately punished but their reputation will continue to be flogged in public forever. I am sure you don't want that to happen," he argued.

"Let's then initiate the process to dismiss him from the service," Wasan suggested impatiently.

"I would rather like the evidence to dictate the course of action. The surveillance is still on and we don't know what other evidence will pop up next. Let the inquiry run its full course lest we regret taking a decision in haste. As you know, even the application of rule 311(2)(c), like Section 18 of the Army Act, can be challenged in courts on the ground of mala fide. So, you are not immune from the court's scrutiny even after you are not in the office," Jeev warned.

"Come on. What mala fide motive can the courts attribute to our action?" Wasan asked. "Unlike the Samba case, we haven't gone into an overdrive to recklessly pursuing speculative and alarmist reports nor have we manipulated circumstantial evidences to lend credence to the suspect's confessions. Our evidence is backed by documents and live footage of Ravi's espionage activities. Instead of going after him blindly, we have opted to mount elaborate surveillance to find out whether he is indeed involved in spying," he explained.

"I am not saying our intent will be questioned by the superior courts. But I still maintain that we should invoke the provisions of 311(2)(c) only after his network and the actors behind his perfidy are exposed," Jeev maintained.

Wasan was still not convinced.

"Actually, we should do what the Director of Military Intelligence did to Samba suspects and register a case against Ravi and wash our hands off," he said. "Let him be interrogated and imprisoned for the crime that he has been committing. Why should we bother about what the courts will say after fifteen or twenty years from now?" he asked.

"That, of course, is one way of looking at it," Jeev said. "The other is, we keep our conscience clear and act responsibly. We shouldn't do a repeat of what happened with poor Nambi Narayanan and Sasikumaran, the two senior ISRO scientists," he reminded.

"In fact, we have been acting far too responsibly and, Ravi certainly does not deserve the tag *poor*. I don't know how you can even compare the two cases," Wasan reacted sharply.

"Both cases have underpinnings of espionage," Jeev countered. "Nambi and Sasi were arrested and interrogated by the Kerala state CID and IB on the basis of a hysterical report from the Bureau in 1994, which claimed that the two scientists brokered ISRO's plans for liquid propulsion engine in lieu of unaccounted millions collected through two Maldivian nationals. Subsequently, they were booked for compromising the safety and sovereignty of India. I hope you don't want Ravi to be similarly booked on the basis of non-conclusive evidences and put us all in a very embarrassing situation," Jeev prodded.

"Why do you say that?" Wasan asked.

"Because, despite the Bureau's and state CID's padding up of the charges and frenzied reporting by media for four years, the Supreme Court termed Sasi and Nambi's case a no show and censured the state government for trying to make political capital out of a non-event," Jeev explained. "Let's not give the court a chance to ridicule us for concocting half-cooked evidences with dubious intent." Wasan thought that his friend was digressing from the main issue.

"My concern is how we are going to be judged now and not after we are gone," he insisted.

"But I want you to live the rest of your life with your head held high. You know that years after the ISRO incident," Jeev went on to clarify his remarks, "President Kalam chose the Bureau's centenary endowment lecture to mention in his inimitably humble style that sometimes in the intelligence game, innocents were unfortunately picked up and framed. He hoped that the Bureau would draw the right lessons from the indignities caused to his friend Sasi and avoid repeating similar tragedies. The sting in those simple words was for everyone present in the auditorium to feel. Would you also like to be publicly snubbed for overstepping the trust reposed in you by the courts and the civil society?" Jeev asked.

"I think you are missing the point," Wasan stressed. "In the ISRO case, evidences were cooked up by inexperienced and politicized officers, while in this case the videos and intercepts are providing live evidence on a daily basis."

"But our evidence does not highlight why Ravi is photocopying documents and for whom," Jeev replied. "I know I am repeating myself but in espionage cases, the link has to be conclusively established between the peddler of intelligence and its receiver. That's the reason the Samba and ISRO espionage cases fell flat on the face of investigators because they could not track the handler from the ISI or Maldivian Intelligence Service respectively. It is good to be patriotic but that does not give any one a license to forge convictions," he asserted.

"We actually have diametrically opposite views on this subject. It's not a happy situation. Frankly, I don't understand you," Wasan reacted in apparent disgust.

Jeev realized their discussion had ended. "I have some good news for you," he said before leaving. "KM and his entire team are thrilled over the fact that you commended their work during the search and pulled up senior officers in the meeting. It was a surprise to them that you could also have kind words about hours of arduous duties that they put in."

Wasan preferred to remain quiet. He was not sure how much of what Jeev said had hidden sting.

Day 86

It was already 12.45 pm but Ravi had still not come to the office. Avinash who was manning the NC ever since Kutty was relieved got fed up of watching the blank monitor for the last three hours. With nothing much to do, he rang KM to find out if he could go to the Branch but was instructed to stay put in the NC till further orders.

From day one, Avinash disliked his work in the NC and requested KM many times to relieve him of the drudgery of gazing at the monitor for hours and listening to inane audio recordings. Ever since the suspect stopped photocopying and eliciting information, the fun of watching him practice deceit was gone. KM also rarely came to the NC and was content perusing daily reports in his room. Avinash assumed that his boss had lost interest in the operation and was probably carrying on under duress from the Security Chief.

With nothing blipping on the monitor and with no calls coming in, Avinash rang Mathew, one of the three watchers on the morning shift, positioned outside the suspect's residence.

"What's happening?" Avinash inquired.

"I was reading a romantic thriller," Mathew said.

"Any news of the suspect?"

"He has been inside the house since morning. It is unlikely that he will go to the office today," Mathew speculated.

"Don't you find your work boring and repetitive?" Avinash asked.

"Yes, sometimes I do," Mathew replied.

"Why don't you tell Mr Kamath to discontinue the surveillance? Look, even after two and half months of watch, we know nothing about the suspect's handler. What's the point in sitting in a vehicle for hours, waiting for him to go to the office and the Club and return to the residence in the evening?" Avinash provoked.

"You are right. This whole exercise of tailing the suspect is turning out to be very frustrating," Mathew concurred.

"One of us should convey to Mr Jeevnathan what we think of this operation. He must have an idea of what the ground realities are," Avinash suggested.

"I am not going to be the one to bell the cat. Why don't you try your luck?" Mathew suggested. Before Avinash could respond, the Phalse telephone operator, sitting next to him, interrupted their conversation. He said that the suspect's wife was on the line. Avinash disconnected and promptly wore the earphones. He heard Vijita informing the PA that Ravi was unwell and still sleeping.

"He won't go to office," she said. "I am sending a self-cheque of rupees one lakh through the driver. Please get it encashed and send the amount home before 3 pm. I have to go to South Extension for some shopping."

Fifteen minutes later, the suspect's official car came out of the residence. Negi was at the wheel. The suspect followed Negi in his private car up to the gate and then drove to Defence Services Officers Institute via Prithvi Raj road, Janpath, and Sardar Patel Marg. He remained inside the Institute for half an hour. From there he drove to the Oberoi. He came out and gave the car key to a valet to park the car, went in, and waited in the lounge. Half an hour later, a smart and handsome man entered the lounge and approached the suspect warmly. Both seemed to know each other well enough to hug and shake hands for an unreasonably long duration. After exchanging greetings, they went for lunch at Three Sixty Degrees. The visitor was doing most of the talking. An hour later, both came out of the hotel. A flag car with defence registration number picked up the officer. While they were waiting in the portico for the car to come, the visitor handed over an envelope to the suspect. A subsequent inquiry identified the officer as Major General Puri, GOC of 16 Infantry Division at Jammu.

The suspect returned to the Club bar and occupied the corner sofa. He ordered a cup of coffee, closed his eyes, and fell asleep. At 3 pm, he woke up, paid for the coffee without drinking it and left. From there, he drove to the residence of Pradeep Nair in Chanakyapuri. His office car was parked outside. He picked up his wife and drove to the residence after instructing Negi to take the car back to the office for the day. For someone who had been driving for more than four hours, strenuously winding his way through Delhi's chaotic traffic at peak time, the suspect appeared to be fairly relaxed and showed no signs of ailment.

At 6.20 pm, ALISTER transmitted a call from Aabha in the US. She enquired about her father's health and the result of his pathology tests. "All the results are within limits. It was just the stress of work that knocked me out briefly," Ravi said.

"I don't know why you take so much strain on you. Can't you ask for a lighter desk?" she sounded concerned.

"I will," Ravi said.

"Papa, I am eagerly looking forward to seeing you. What happened to your leave? Has that been sanctioned?" she asked.

"I have tied up everything," Ravi avoided mentioning the leave. "What is left is to board the flight and reach in time to attend the engagement ceremony of my dearest daughter," he said and handed over the phone to Vijita in the kitchen, beyond ALISTER's recording range.

ALISTER picked up the suspect's conversation again at 8 pm but this time it transmitted fudged images and voices that broke intermittently. When Kamath brought this up with Kutty, the latter opined that ALISTER had virtually gone blind and there was no point in further monitoring its video transmissions. He was, however, confident that he could rectify the snag in the audio signals.

Day 87

The more KM observed Vijita Mohan and listened to her conversations, the more he was confused about her precise role in her husband's espionage network. Was it possible that the suspect kept his wife in dark about the real reason behind hosting his lavish parties, his bloated financial status, regular shredding of official documents at home, and his constant fear of being watched, KM wondered.

"Sir, so far I was giving the suspect's wife benefit of doubt. I thought she was probably not aware that her husband was an espionage agent but I am no longer sure about her innocence," KM opined as soon as Jeev finished reading the surveillance reports of the previous day.

"Any reason for this sudden change in your perception?" Jeev asked.

"It is impossible for any man to carry out such an extensive criminal operation without the active support from his wife. It has to be a collaborative effort," KM pointed out.

"I know. She may have been initially reluctant and even opposed to the arrangement, something which usually happens in such cases," Jeev said, "but at some point of time, she would have acquiesced to make Ravi's plot work."

"Sir, if we go by the surveillance reports, she appears to be clean. She has been telling Ravi that he is paranoid about the surveillance and reading too much in the delay involved in the sanctioning of his leave. So far, we have also not heard her say anything that can even remotely suggest that she either works as a courier or a facilitator, nor have we seen her contacting any stranger. But my gut feeling is she is far more devious than her husband," KM opined.

"You may be right," Jeev said. "If we are not getting any evidence of her complicity that's because she is smarter than us. Women," he explained, "are generally made of stronger stuff and they handle crises better. She may have lots of personal issues with Ravi but since she is financially dependent on him, she must have lined up her support behind her wily husband's misdeeds."

Kamath had nothing more to discuss. He kept the folders in the briefcase and waited for his lemon tea to be served. Jeev was very finicky about the quality of his tea, the colour of brew and quantity of sugar, and lemon drops. He seldom took coffee or spicy variants of tea that he usually served to visitors. While the tea was brewing, KM showed a few intercepts to Jeev, indicating links of politicians from Nepal, Bihar, UP, and Mumbai with underworld criminals who operated as ISI's foot soldiers in India. He said that though these stray inputs could not be the basis for prosecuting the politicians, it was necessary that the Prime Minister was kept posted with such disturbing details.

"If you insist, I can forward the intercepts in original to the Chief," Jeev said. "But I doubt he will show these to the PM. The Chief is a wise man and would not like to put the Prime Minister in an awkward position of knowing about something that he cannot act upon."

"In that case, can the Chief show the intercepts in which officers, personal staff, and family members of politicians are seen amassing wealth from criminal sources," KM asked.

"I did show a couple of such intercepts to the Chief sometime back. He read them with enormous interest but told me that he would not acknowledge their existence. He found the contents too hot to handle and advised that I destroy them," Jeev mentioned.

"But is it not a crime to keep the government in the dark about such wrongdoings?" KM asked.

"The Chief thinks otherwise," Jeev explained. "He believes that people at the top are fully aware of what their siblings, advisors, and favourites are harvesting and from whom. They don't need to be educated by the Agency on this count. But yes, where the ISI is involved, the Chief should share the information with the Prime Minister," he conceded.

"Sir, my hats off to the ISI," KM said. "It has penetrated almost every institution in the country and is giving us a run for our lives everywhere. In response what we do is squirm and shy away from inflicting collateral damages. The ISI must be marvelling at our skill of issuing empty threats and enjoying their luck for dealing with an enemy that has a spine made of rhetoric," he remarked.

Jeev couldn't agree more but he preferred to skip the issue. He was, in fact, waiting for KM to finish his tea and leave. Meanwhile, his PS came in to remind him that he had a meeting scheduled with a source at 1 pm and he was already running late. Jeev wore the jacket and left. KM collected papers and followed him.

"You shouldn't think so poorly of your outfit," Jeev said while walking down to the porch. "It's not that the Agency doesn't have the capability or resources to strike back. The problem lies with the leadership at all levels. Our Chief lacks courage in taking independent operational decisions and the political leadership, seriously inhibited by a myopic vision of what constitutes national interests, won't allow the Agency necessary liberty to operate like, CIA, KGB, Mossad, and ISI," he contended.

"Is there no way we can operate like these agencies?" KM asked.

"I don't see it happening anytime in the future," Jeev said. "Every prime minister desperately wants to carve a niche for himself in history books by improving relations with Pakistan. But he ends up debilitating the Agency's operating infrastructure, built over a long period with enormous sweat and resources, by asking it to suspend its forward operations. What they do not understand is that intelligence operations and diplomacy can run parallel and one need not be sacrificed for the other to succeed." By now, Jeev had reached the porch.

*

Jeev returned to work at 4 pm. As soon as he reactivated the cellphone he saw three missed calls from the Chief. He immediately called Wasan but the latter said that there was nothing very urgent but in case Jeev was free, he would be happy to talk about something of mutual interest.

"I will be there in half an hour," Jeev promised.

"No problem," Wasan sounded unusually upbeat.

Jeev spent the time to chair a meeting that was to recommend cases of officers for promotion to the rank of Senior Managers. Rajamani, the Chief of Maintenance, again failed to make the grade. He had a brilliant mind, was incorruptible, and extremely well-informed about his subject. But he treated his seniors in contempt and openly called them incompetent, crooks, and conniving fools. In turn, his seniors wrote adversely about his quality of leadership and work. Despite Jeev's repeated plea to read beyond the lines of rules and regulations, the career of a bright officer was yet again throttled by stereotypes sitting on the promotion board.

*

Jeev was early by ten minutes when he leisurely walked into Wasan's room. He pulled a chair and sat down. Wasan wasted no time in baring the real intent behind his call. "Last evening," he said, "I showed your latest report to the Principal Secretary. He was furious. He directed that the investigation must be suspended and all forms of surveillance withdrawn with immediate effect. He called me this morning to check if his orders were being complied with."

Jeev looked at Wasan who paused to drink water. His throat, Jeev thought, must have been parched after struggling to choose the right words to stay clear of courting hostility from his long-time friend.

"Please instruct Kamath to hand over all documents and tapes to me by this evening," Wasan said. "I will keep them under lock and key in my safe till Princi decides the next course of action. Also, ask Kamath to shut down the NC and withdraw watchers from all locations," he added. After Wasan had finished, Jeev pushed his chair back, got up and left without any fuss. Surprisingly, he was not angry, neither did he feel like putting up a fight. He returned to his room and rang KM but there was no response. Then he dictated a note to his PS on his deliberations with the subject of Project Rehab held earlier during the day. By now it was 5.30 pm. He called Mani and told her not to get anything cooked for dinner. He offered to take her out for dinner.

"What's the provocation? Got any monetary windfalls?" Mani quizzed.

"When everything crumbles around you, it is better to stand erect among the ruins and enjoy the distorted contours," Jeev said.

"You keep your imageries to yourself. I am sure something has happened in the office which has upset you. Anyway, I will be ready in time to go out for dinner," Mani said.

Meanwhile, Jeev's PS brought the draft of the source meeting and left. As Jeev finished correcting the note, he saw Wasan entering the room, unannounced.

"I know, you are angry but what can I do. These are Princi's orders and whether we like it or not, we have to comply," he said, sitting close to Jeevnathan on the sofa.

"But his orders are palpably wrong and ill conceived," Jeev said.

"Then tell me what should I do?" Wasan asked. "He has the eyes and ears of the Prime Minister and the Chief of the ruling party. As head of the Agency, I am directly accountable to him for all our failings and achievements. If I do not keep him on board, our administrative and operational proposals will suffer," he explained.

"I will check with KM on how quickly he can comply with your instructions. We can't just collect the tapes, videos, transcripts, watchers' spot reports, copied documents, etc., put them in a bag and hand them over to you. These will have to be listed meticulously lest we are accused of selectively passing on evidence to serve some hidden agenda of ours," Jeev remarked sarcastically.

"Princi is not insane, Jeev. His directive has more to do with his lack of exposure to our kind of occupational hazards. As you know, his position has lately become shaky. None of the senior party leaders in the government like him. A sustained campaign is going on, accusing him of corruption, arrogance and wrong political judgement. No one knows how long the Prime Minister can bail him out. He is desperately trying to regain his earlier pre-eminent position by breaking new grounds in building a long term strategic relationship with the US that has remained virtually frozen since the nuclear tests. Therefore, he does not want any ugly issue to surface which may jeopardize his US initiative," Wasan argued persuasively.

"What makes him imagine that Ravi's espionage activities will adversely impact the Indo-US relations?" Jeev asked.

"It could be a guess propelled by panic. He may be worried that being in-charge of the Agency, his detractors will bay for his blood for failing to nip the suspect's mischief in the bud and for allowing laxity to creep in the Agency's security system," Wasan observed.

"I think you have allowed him to assume a much bigger role for himself in the management of the Agency's routine affairs than what he is capable of handling," Jeev remarked.

"That's an unfair charge. What Ravi is doing is not a routine matter," Wasan countered.

"Anyway, when do you think Princi will release the documents and tapes, reopen the NC and send the watchers back to their business?" Jeev asked.

"I have no idea," Wasan said.

"Doesn't it give you a feeling of unease that you are about to put a lid over a case of treason to protect Mr Saran's wobbly vision of forging a strategic relationship with a super power?" Jeev probed.

Wasan did not respond for a while. He knew it was futile to make Jeev toe a pragmatic course of action.

"Please try to be reasonable and take action as I have suggested," Wasan reiterated.

"Do I have an option?" Jeev reacted in anguish.

The two did not speak for a while. Wasan finally left, uncertain of what his incorrigibly righteous and headstrong friend would do. Jeev rang KM and asked him to come over immediately along with Ajay, in case the latter was still around. Then he booked dinner for two at 9 pm in the Delhi O' Delhi restaurant at the India Habitat Centre. Meanwhile, his PS came, cleared the desk of files and papers, and locked the file cabinets and the safe. A little later, Ajay and KM entered the room.

"Anything unusual about the suspect's activities during the last twenty-four hours?" Jeev enquired.

KM reported that the suspect did not attend the office for the second successive day. His branch officers were under the impression that he was sick and resting, whereas the suspect was up on his feet and driving around. He went in the office car an Italian restaurant inside the Santushti complex for lunch where he was joined by a Group Captain of the Indian Air Force and a young scientist from the DRDO. Thereafter, he went to a defence canteen in the cantonment area to draw his quota of liquor. At 4.30 pm he went to meet Vishnoi at the latter's residence in Greater Noida. He came out after an hour carrying a folder in his hand. Before he left, Negi took out a carton of liquor from the car boot and kept it inside Vishnoi's house.

Jeev listened patiently. Later on, he gave a factual account of his two meetings with the Chief, cutting out the friendly jibes and then asked them to suggest the future course of action.

"I don't think we have any choice. If the Principal Secretary does not want the investigation to proceed, so be it," Ajay stated enthusiastically.

"It is hard to digest the Chief's directives but I am ready to hand over all the raw evidence to him right now," KM reacted angrily. "Let him get these analysed by his cronies. They will take years to comprehend these tapes, transcripts and documents," he fumed.

"Sir, KM is missing the point. The Chief simply wants to terminate the operation. So, where is the question of analysing the evidence?" Ajay argued.

"I always dreaded that the Chief won't allow us to take this case to its logical end. When you liberally accept gifts and frequently dine at the suspect's place, how can you punish him? Look at the list of officers who have been feeding information to the suspect. Almost all of them are the Chief's favourites. How can he let his boys be indicted and shamed during trial?" KM shot back.

"You are being extremely rude to the Chief. This is not what Mr Wasan wants. He is merely conveying orders of the Principal Secretary," Ajay pointed out.

"But how can we allow a criminal to walk away in broad day light?" Kamath refused to backtrack.

"Who says Ravi will not be punished? The evidence that the Chief has asked for, is so overwhelming and conclusive that whenever he decides, he can dismiss Ravi. He is just buying time. He is not saying that he is going to dump the case," Ajay argued.

KM repeatedly shook his head in disagreement.

Jeev finally intervened. "My understanding is," he explained "that both the Chief and Principal Secretary Saran find this operation extremely inconvenient, albeit for different reasons. So, we are left with two choices. Either we continue with the investigation until Ravi's espionage network is busted or we follow the Chief's instructions as disciplined officers." Jeev stopped briefly and called Mani to say that he was on the way. "You know, I value discipline dearly," he continued, "but my conscience does not permit me to wind up the case at this stage. We cannot do politics over an act of treason. So, I have decided to ignore the Chief's orders and carry on with the investigation. The Chief can still enforce his orders by divesting me of my current responsibilities as Head of the Security Division. If he does that, I am not going to make it an issue, although he may think that I would," he concluded.

A stunning silence descended. While his deputies continued to sit, Jeev went out of the room. When he returned, his PS followed him. Jeev picked up two files from the stack of files on the table and instructed his PS to send these in sealed covers to the Chief.

"Sir, I can't understand why Mr Saran is against our investigating an espionage agent. I hope he is not indebted to the suspect in some strange ways that we are not aware of," KM quipped as soon as Jeev's PS left the room.

"Let's not impute motives to him," Ajay interrupted. "I hear that his removal is imminent. Already, several names of his replacement are floating around on whisper.com. Maybe, he wants to buy time and avoid giving additional ammunition to his opponents to hack him down. One rumour is that in case he has to eventually go, he will back Krishnan to succeed him, who is equally keen on building a strategic relationship with the US," he contended.

"How can we let him protect a traitor simply to secure his position in the government?" KM replied back.

Jeev was amused to hear his colleagues' opposing arguments. But since it was well past 7.30 pm and he had a date with Mani, he decided to put an end to their discussion. "We need not get unduly agitated over what Mr Saran or the Chief feels. We have taken up an investigation against a senior officer suspected of committing espionage. Our responsibility is to ensure that it runs its full course unless we are laid off the job," he reiterated.

Jeev reached home on time. Mani was waiting in the living room, dressed elegantly as she always did. They reached IHC at 9 pm. Mani ordered for food because Jeev insisted on playing an obedient host.

"What is the matter, Jeev? I have not seen you so relaxed and generous lately," Mani prodded while waiting for the food to be served.

"I was nearly sacked by Wasan today," Jeev said with a smile.

"You must have stretched his patience beyond limits. It's obvious, he can barely wait for you to retire after six months," she gibed.

"You are right. I am a very difficult person to deal with. You have also had a life-long grouse that I am insensitive, headstrong and opinionated. Unfortunately, that's the way my DNA works. Anyway, let's enjoy the food," Jeev said. The conversation during the rest of the dinner was fairly pleasant. Despite Jeev's offer, Mani paid for the bill.

Day 88

Ravi attended the office after two days' of absence. For the first time, he did not carry his dark brown leather bag and avoided the lift to walk up to his room. Once he settled down, Sharma brought in the pending files and papers and enquired whether he would like to take the remaining personal files home. Ravi did not respond. Instead, he asked Miss Sethi and, later, Moily to come over in case they had any paper to show or anything to discuss.

The suspect disposed of Miss Sethi in ten minutes. But Moily was unyielding. His file had still not been released by the CEU and there was a rumour that Jeev was insistent on holding a departmental enquiry against him. He pleaded with Ravi to speak to KM and request him to treat his case as a one-off security lapse. However, Ravi's response was non-committal. He said that he was not sure if one should take up the matter in the current security environment.

At 11.30 am, Ravi asked his PA to check if Paritosh, Analyst Chinese Military Affairs, had returned from his overseas tour. He was told that the visit was called off at the last minute because of some serious developments in Bhutan. Ravi tried to reach Paritosh on his cellphone but it was switched off. Finally, he contacted Mahesh Soni, the China Desk Officer, who was, as usual, unhelpful. Soni said that since he had been kept out of all major operational decisions, he did not think it proper to fish for information. On the suspect's further prodding, Soni mentioned that the development probably had something to do with the seizure of a consignment of Chinese arms destined for ULFA insurgents. When the suspect pressed for more details, Soni disconnected the call.

The suspect then rang Nair, Director Naval Operations, but there was no response. As he kept the receiver in the hold, Ravi received another call. The person confirmed that he would drop in for half an hour for drinks at 8 pm at Ravi's residence later that evening. However, he did not turn up till 11.45 pm. He was later identified as Brigadier Bhagirath of 12 Infantry Division at Dehradun.

The suspect's next visitor was Arvind Munshi, Desk Officer Kashmir Operations. He shook hands with Munshi warmly and invited him to sit with him on the sofa. The suspect complained that Munshi had forgotten him and not bothered to keep in touch for a long time.

"Actually, sir, I had to visit J&K almost twice a week during past four months in connection with an important operation," Munshi explained. Ravi's mood suddenly lifted. "One of my sources has made a major breakthrough in mapping the entire monetary trail from JuD and LeT in Pakistan to Lashkars and local terrorist outfits in the valley via Kathmandu, Dhaka, and Dubai," he claimed.

"That's remarkable. It's seldom that you meet with such success. I am sure the Chief must have patted you," Ravi expressed.

"Not so far. Maybe he would, after the inputs' accuracy is thoroughly verified," Munshi replied.

"If you have time, we can have lunch at the Oberoi." Ravi was not prepared to let the information about the money-trail go untapped. Munshi readily accepted the offer to escape his daily staple lunch of two pieces of sandwiches and an apple, dumped clumsily in his lunch box by his working wife. He left soon with a promise to join Ravi at the hotel between 1.30 and 2 pm.

Ajeet dropped in at 12.10 pm. He talked about the bitterness among officers of the defence forces over the manner in which the CEU targeted them during the search and gave a detailed account of items and documents seized from their possession. Referring to his interaction with officers of the defence forces, he said that the Army in particular was getting increasingly disillusioned with the Agency's repeated failure to provide actionable intelligence on the militants' build-up in the Pak-occupied Kashmir and their ex-filtration schedule. Joining the issue; Ravi explained that the problem actually lay with the acute paucity of ground level sources to cover activities of terrorists and ruled out any qualitative improvement in reporting on this count in the foreseeable future.

Meanwhile, Inder came in to serve coffee. After he left, Ajeet inquired whether his leave for the US had been approved. Ravi said that it was still lying with the Chief.

"Have you booked your tickets?" Ajeet asked.

"I have. Since I am flying first class by British Airways, I will incur heavy losses if we don't make the trip," Ravi said.

"How can the Chief not permit you to go abroad on a purely private visit?" Ajeet queried.

"He is the Chief. I guess he can do anything he likes. At least this is what seems to be in my case," Ravi replied.

"You should not accept this situation lying down. Even in the defence services, you have a right to be heard in such matters," Ajeet provoked.

"It is also my mistake," Ravi conceded. "I thought it was a routine request and the Chief would have no problem in agreeing to it. It seems I will have to seek a personal appointment to sort this out," he said.

"What will you do if he assures you and does not give the approval till the last minute?" asked Ajeet.

"Why do you say that?" Ravi asked.

"You remember Colonel Prabhakar's case. The poor fellow had requested for a week's leave to go to London to attend a seminar and defray all expenses from his saving. When nothing came in writing till the last moment despite his several reminders, he proceeded on leave presuming that Agency had no objection to his visit. On return, he was charged with going to a foreign country without permission and his re-employment was terminated, leaving him jobless," said Ajeet.

Ravi sipped his coffee.

"The Chief is being deliberately mean to you. He is not going to hang you for attending your daughter's engagement," Ajeet insisted.

"Do you suggest that I should go ahead with the US visit with or without the Chief's approval?" Ravi asked.

"Precisely."

"I won't take such extreme measures," Ravi stressed.

"If your meeting with the Chief does not come through, send a note to his office an hour before your departure, detailing the purpose of visit and the circumstances in which you were compelled to leave. I am sure the courts will rule in your favour, should the Agency decide to dispense with your services," said Ajeet.

Ravi did not react. He used the remote to switch on ESPN and increased the volume. Ajeet persisted.

"Colonel Kirath, a colleague of mine, had faced a similar predicament," he said. "The Northern Command sat over his repeated requests to go to the US on eight months' leave for almost a year. Then one day, he left his unit at Rajouri without further waiting for the sanction to arrive. In absentia, he was dismissed from service for unauthorized absence. However, on return from the US, Colonel Kirath moved to the Delhi High Court and was reinstated with full monetary benefits."

"I am not so desperate. If my leave does not come through, I will shift the date of the engagement ceremony," Ravi said.

"I don't know how you can display such equanimity despite grave provocations," Ajeet expressed. Ravi smiled and said that if he reacted fast and furiously as Ajeet suggested, he might not be as lucky as Colonel Kirath to get a reprieve.

*

After lunch, Ravi returned to the office at 3 pm. Munshi followed him in another car. They got down at the porch and went together to the suspect's room. "Let's have coffee before you get busy with your work," Ravi suggested and asked his PA to send in two cups of coffee.

Ravi opened the conversation with an awkward enquiry. "You must be the Chief's biggest favourite or why else would he assign a Kashmiri Pandit and a refugee from the valley to handle the Kashmir Desk," he said. "Look at me. I have been trying to shift to an operationally productive desk for last three years but the Chief won't listen."

Munshi was not amused. In a tongue-in-cheek response, he said that the Chief might have posted him in haste but was yet to regret his decision.

"Please don't misunderstand me," Ravi hastened to clarify. "There is no one in the Agency who knows J&K so exhaustively and reads events so objectively as you do. Tell me, being an insider, how long do you think it will take for this problem to be resolved. Will it happen in our lifetime?" he asked, trying to divert Munshi's attention to a more substantive aspect of the Kashmir issue.

"It's an everlasting quagmire and will last as long as Pakistan's destiny is shaped and guided by its Army and the ISI," Munshi said, still smarting under Ravi's gibe.

"Why do you think so many ideas, proposals, talks, and initiatives including back channel diplomacy have made no headway?" Ravi prodded.

"Because these initiatives are inherently flawed and those who are involved in seeking or suggesting a solution are either intellectually dishonest or mortally afraid of addressing the core issue," Munshi opined. He now appeared passionate about discussing a subject that meant so much to him both as a professional and as a Kashmiri.

"Even our experiment with electoral democracy hasn't cut much ice with people in the Valley. Don't you think Delhi should give independence to Kashmiris or let them cede to Pakistan? The other option is that the LOC be converted into an international border. As it is three-fourths of original J&K is with Pakistan and China," Ravi volleyed a pointed question. Munshi replied that neither of the three options was practical or workable for ensuring permanent peace.

"What is the Agency's position on settling this intractable problem?" Ravi framed his question adroitly to extract the right input for his running officer.

"It is a political issue and has to be addressed to political leadership. Our brief is simply to collect intelligence about militants, carry out little bit of psychological warfare, and occasionally contain fire in the belly of known separatists by stuffing wads of currency notes inside," Munshi pointed out.

"Can the US play any role in making India, Pakistan, and Kashmiris accept a basket of give and take to end the endemic violence in the state?" Ravi asked.

"I don't think so. The US is an irrelevant factor because it has no stake in J&K," Munshi explained. "Washington has historically preferred to be deceived by the Pakistani establishment, its defence forces and the ISI. No wonder, its policy of carrot and stick against Islamabad has been a monumental waste even for its own security interests. I don't know how an average Indian can ever accept Washington as an honest broker when its credentials in the region are so suspect," Munshi remarked. They stopped conversing briefly when coffee was served.

"So, there is no way this bloody conflict will ever end," Ravi prodded.

"Unless you quietly tame the bull by twisting its horns," Munshi interrupted.

"I don't quite understand?" Ravi asked.

"Change the demography of J&K and reduce the separatists to a minority," Munshi suggested forcing Ravi to sit up. "If terrorists can change the Valley's demographic profile by driving out Kashmiri Pandits by use of violence and force Buddhists in Zanskar, Leh, and Ladakh into minority through monetary allurements and inter-faith marriages, why can't you do the same by allowing Indians from different parts of the country to move into J&K by simply dispensing with Article 370 of the Constitution," he asked. "We have a lot to learn from the Chinese in this regard. Look at how slowly but surely they have reduced the Tibetans into abject minority. Unlike us, they do not suffer from delusions of being righteous in national interest," he pointed out.

"Do you think the nation can ever accept substitution of population as a matter of state policy?" Ravi reacted.

"No, because simple solutions are always most difficult to work upon," Munshi clarified. "A mere mention of this idea will evoke calamitous reactions. You will be branded a fool, naive, impractical, irresponsible and, of course, communal. No one will risk his political or official career or lose the state patronage by even whispering about this forbidden option," he said.

"This idea can never have any takers in whichever formulation you try to sell it," Ravi averred.

"The hypocrites who largely populate our government, print media and political parties do not understand that continued retention of Article 370 perpetuates exclusivity, benefiting only Islamabad. I don't know how long we can shy away from even debating the truth," Munshi said. "In the past sixty-six years, the nation has got used to the sight of our leadership juggling with unrealistic options, while J&K burns. Maybe we will have to wait a thousand years more for the fire to cool down," he added.

Ravi did not ask him anything further. He felt that the subject was getting more personal which would not interest his operatives. Both started drinking coffee. Munshi left soon after, promising to send a copy of the note that was being prepared for the Chief, highlighting the role of technical units and his field operatives in tracking down the terrorists' financial network. Ravi stretched out on the sofa and quickly fell asleep. He woke up when Nair came in.

"I had a very hectic morning," Ravi said, as he rubbed the sleep off his eyes.

"I am sorry I woke you up," Nair sounded apologetic, as he pulled a chair to sit down.

"That's okay. I had called you earlier but you were not in your room."

"I had gone to attend a meeting at the NSCS to discuss recent sightings of Chinese naval ships unloading construction equipment and antenna in the Coco Island. Any particular reason why you were calling me," Nair asked.

"I just wanted to chat," Ravi said and buzzed Sharma to send in two cups of coffee. "I am reading a book on Al-Qaida. My son sent it to me from the US. It has been very well researched and gives an idea of how and why Qaida succeeds in operating at will in spite of all odds and why intelligence agencies have failed to make a dent in its support system even after committing enormous muscle power and funds," he explained.

"That's interesting. Maybe, I will borrow it one day," Nair said. "I see there is also a copy of Srimad Bhagwat Gita on your table. It shows your remarkable spread of reading interest, from Al-Qaida to the Gita."

"I always keep a copy of the Gita with me. It teaches you to draw the right lessons in life," Ravi said. Then he rang the staff officer of the Chief to find out the status of his leave application. The latter conveyed that his file was still with the Chief and would hopefully be cleared by the evening.

"If it does not come through, please let me know. Also please tell the Chief that since I am running short of time, I would like to meet him to explain my problem," Ravi said.

Nair who was listening to Ravi's conversation was itching to interrupt. "It is scandalous the way your request for leave is being handled by the Chief," he reacted. Ravi ignored his friend's show of outrage. They spent another ten minutes sipping coffee together and sharing gossip about a lady officer who perpetually complained about everything to everyone.

After Nair left, Ravi called KM to find out whether a departmental inquiry was being contemplated against Moily and whether there was any chance of his being let off with a letter of displeasure. KM said that he had no idea what they had decided in Moily's case.

"He is very nervous," Ravi said.

"It may be difficult for me to get him exonerated but I will try. Jeev is furious that having worked in the CEU earlier, Moily should have appreciated the limits of disregard for security provisions," KM said.

"I know. How was my case viewed by the Chief?" Ravi asked.

"Actually, I explained that these were your personal files and you were in any case authorized to carry them home without prior approval of the CEU. The Chief agreed," KM said.

"What was Mr Jeevnathan's reaction?" Ravi asked.

"He suggested that your motive in shifting the files should be investigated in more details," KM said.

As Ravi did not react for long, KM disconnected.

Ravi's next visitor was Kamal Mehta who still fretted and fumed over the surprise check. He claimed that he met the Chief and complained that not once in his thirty-two years of service, he had been subjected to such indignity in presence of so many junior officers. The Chief felt sorry for the incident and assured that in future, the CEU would be instructed to show greater restraint in dealing with senior officers' sensitivities. Ravi knew that Mehta was narrating a half-truth.

"But that's not the impression I got from the way he pulled up officers in the meeting. Actually he endorsed the action of the CEU very strongly and patted its employees on their back," Ravi pointed out.

Mehta laughed unconvincingly. "You don't know the Chief. His fuming was for public consumption and his threat to continue with similar searches was hurled in a moment of frenzy. He is not going to allow the CEU to repeat its hooliganism," he claimed.

Ravi felt relieved and started to clear pending files. But Mehta was unyielding. "I still can't get over the way senior officers capitulated and stood in queue like impounded cattle, surrendering their briefcases to junior employees for inspection," he remarked.

"What else could they do? I can understand their predicament because I was one of them," Ravi said in a rare display of disagreement. By now he had signed the files and kept them in the out tray. Then he inquired about Mehta's availability for dinner. "I plan to host a dinner for the Chief and his close aides sometime next month but I am not sure if Mr Jeevnathan would come," he said.

"Forget about him," Mehta reacted contemptuously.

Lokesh Kumar was the last to visit Ravi for his customary evening coffee. Though coming from different professional background, he trusted Ravi and shared Agency's petty politics and juicy gossips with the latter regularly. Since the current topic of interest was the Chief's admonition of officers in the meeting, Kumar went on to describe the reaction of individual officers in his inimitable story-telling style. Ravi listened vacantly. Kumar realized that something was amiss with his friend. "Is your leave for the US through?" he enquired.

"Yes," Ravi lied. "I will mostly be in Baltimore but may go to Washington DC for a few days. I will give you my mobile number so that you can keep me updated about what is happening here," he said.

After Kumar left, Ravi gave Rs 10,000 to Sharma to buy train tickets for him and his wife for Jammu by the Rajdhani Express. He said he would leave New Delhi on Friday, 24th June and return two days later. He instructed Sharma to buy two tickets in the Tatkal quota in case seats were not available in the normal course and book a suite in Hotel Jammu Ashok or Hari Niwas Palace through Emerald Travels.

"Shall I inform the office at Jammu about your programme?" Sharma asked.

"No. It's a private visit to Vaishno Devi before we leave for the US. I don't want anyone to be bothered," Ravi said.

Ravi left the office at 5.30 pm. He spent nearly 45 minutes in the Club. At 9 pm, ALISTER recorded his conversation with his son Sankar. Ravi informed that his leave had finally come through.

"That's great, Daddy. How is mom coping with her asthma in Delhi's sultry weather? Where is she?" Sankar asked.

"Wait for a second. I will hand over the phone to her," Ravi said. As he moved away from the balcony, ALISTER stopped transmitting.

*

The Chief did not call Jeevnathan the whole day. By 7.30 pm, Jeev finished the day's work and moved over to the side sofa to relax. He rested his neck on the back seat, closed his eyes, and reflected over his meeting with the Chief on the previous day. Was his decision to defy the handing over of evidences to the Chief legitimate? Jeev was not so sure since all efforts to find out the handler's identity had failed miserably. Principal Secretary Saran and the Chief were probably right to initiate a departmental inquiry against the suspect and get over with this muddle. It would at least spare the Agency relentless needling not only by the media but also by the government, he thought. What if the handler was fortuitously caught because of Jeev's insistence to carry on with the investigation? How would he counter the mayhem that would emerge, with angry calls coming from Raisina Hills, opposition political parties, and security experts to punish the subverting the Agency, and the latter making outright denials? Did he have a plan to deal with their demands of expelling the running officer and the threats of the suspected agency and its government to retaliate? Will the Prime Minister's office be able to absorb a few expulsions and a spate of textbook reactions from both sides? How would he cope with the indictment of the Foreign Office for ruining an emerging strategic partnership? And what was the guarantee that if he was allowed to investigate as long as he considered it necessary, the suspect would be hanged or sentenced to life imprisonment for committing espionage, he wondered. Would it, therefore, not be prudent to wash his hands off the case and deposit evidences in the Chief's coffers? What was he really trying to prove by becoming so stubborn, Jeevnathan asked himself. Was he working for a public recognition of his ceaseless search for truth? Was he not setting a bad precedence for colleagues by refusing to carry out orders of the Chief? Jeev had no clear answer to any of these questions. He stopped debating with himself as soon as he sensed KM's presence in the room.

"I was a bit tired and dozed off. I hope you have prepared the list of documents, tapes etc. to be handed over to the Chief," Jeev said. He was surprised that he had opted for this course of action.

"But you said yesterday that the investigation would carry on," KM reacted in disbelief.

"That's right. But I have since changed my mind," Jeev clarified.

"Sir, you could have done that before. I told you on several occasions to close the case but you were adamant on finding the handler," KM said.

"I know I am being dishonest with myself but it's better for all of us to terminate the operation," Jeev remarked as he shifted to make room for KM to sit.

"Sir, has anything happened since yesterday?" KM asked.

"Not exactly, but yes, there was something I didn't mention to you earlier. When the Chief came to my room, he went straight to the side desk on which telephones are kept. He turned the instruments upside down twice to check if these had bugging devices. He repeated it when he came to sit next to me on the sofa. It was apparent, I had lost his trust. I quickly decided that having lost a friend, there was no point in losing sleep too," Jeev spoke in a matter of fact way.

"Can I brief you on the day's developments?" KM asked, ignoring Jeev's wishlist. Not waiting for an answer, KM said, "I suspect Ravi will go to the US with or without leave," he said.

"What makes you think so?" Jeev inquired.

"He has bought air tickets and tied up all the travel formalities. He seems to have bought the idea floated by Colonel Ajeet that he can go to the US without the Chief's approval and nothing will happen to him. He has given his itinerary to Kumar and his son, Sankar. He lied to both that his leave had been sanctioned. He has also decided to make a quick trip to Jammu along with his wife to seek blessings from Vaishno Devi, eighteen days before he leaves for his daughter's engagement ceremony. What is, however, perplexing is that he has invited his colleagues for dinner at his residence followed by another dinner for the Chief in the next few days when everyone is so tense and afraid to open up," KM pointed out.

"It's too much of a risk for the suspect to go to the US without leave and hope to return to his desk honourably. He is too timid to bite this kind of bullet. Either he goes forever or doesn't," Jeev opined.

"Sir, the handler appears to be applying pressure on him to resume work. The suspect has started eliciting vital inputs although he remains apprehensive of taking anything out," KM pointed out.

"Ravi is their long-term investment. I don't see why they will push him hard when threat of a personal search is looming," Jeev remarked.

"Sir, another search has been discounted by Kamal Mehta and the suspect seems to have bought his views," KM indicated.

"I don't think he will take out photocopies in the immediate future. He will surely be advised to wait till the dust of uncertainty fully settles. I guess he has to meet his handler somewhere to discuss his precarious position. Jammu could be an ideal rendezvous for this purpose," Jeev contended.

On the way back to his room, KM could not help smiling. For once, he had prevented Jeev to walk away from what he believed, was right. Pleased with himself, he decided to go home early. He dumped papers lying on the table inside the safe, picked up his briefcase, locked the room and went down to the basement. As he was entering the car, his cellphone beeped. It was Jeev on the line. "KM, I am glad you are no longer a reluctant support. I am sure that we can make it together," he said and hung up.

Day 89

Throughout the night, it had been raining in spurts after several days of oppressive heat, inducing humidity to rise steeply. Soon after dinner, Vijita began to suffer from breathing problems. Around 11.45 pm, her asthma relapsed with a vengeance, obstructing her normal breathing. When medicines brought her no relief, she came out of the bedroom and sat in the balcony for fresh air. ALISTER transmitted her laboured efforts to breathe and Ravi's half-hearted offer to take her to the Trauma Centre. "Don't worry. I will survive the night," she said with some difficulty.

In the morning, Ravi took her to a doctor in Jorbagh, dropped her back at home and reached office around 1 pm. He rang his colleagues one by one, but they were busy either preparing reports or attending meetings. He also made half a dozen calls outside, but none of them could be reached. Later on, he gave a cheque of Rs 30,000 to his PA and asked him to get it encashed at HSBC, Khan Market. With nothing much to do, he retired to the sofa and rang KM to find out whether it would be advisable to take the rest of his personal files home. KM said he would come over and explain.

Fifteen minutes later, KM walked in. "I will advise you to wait for a couple of days more," he said. "The impounded items of other officers are still lying with the respective division heads who have been instructed by Mr Jeevnathan not to release them till further orders."

"What could be the reason?" The suspect asked apprehensively.

"I understand he is working on a paper, delineating guidelines on the type of documents that officers of different ranks could carry home with or without authorization," KM said. "Perhaps a copy of these guidelines would be sent to the erring officers along with their seized items for future guidance," he added.

"I hope he does not make the guidelines far too rigid and comprehensive. If he does that, officers will find ways to circumvent them," the suspect pointed out.

"I don't know how he is going to strike a balance between permitting officers to take out classified papers and his heightened concerns for security of information. There could be hundreds of genuine reasons for officers to read secret papers at home. For example, how can he stop officers from accepting outstation cables at home? Besides, what would he do with classified papers that we receive after office hours from various government departments?" said KM.

"Can I ask you something as a friend? Please don't answer if you don't want to," Ravi said.

KM was a bit surprised. "What is it about?" he asked without appearing ruffled.

"You remember," the suspect quizzed, "the Chief mentioned in the meeting about smoke and fire. Was he referring to any black sheep of the Agency for having come to his adverse notice for passing information to our enemies?"

"You know that all employees are not patriots," KM took a few minutes to explain. "I don't know which black sheep he was referring to, but to be honest with you we do have several black sheep of different breed among us and they are thriving because we are notoriously shy in punishing them," he said. "I have forwarded to the Chief over a dozen cases of officers who routinely share intelligence with unauthorized persons, run business abroad by using their sources, claim payment for sources that never existed and pass on edited downloads from the internet as source reports. I have also sent to him case of an officer who siphoned off gifts meant for high level contacts and ran fictitious operations because she soaked in patronages from her Division Head."

"I thought Mr Jeevnathan and the Chief were very strict in enforcing discipline," the suspect taunted.

"Unfortunately, there is a feeling that we can't punish the erring officers on the basis of evidence collected from clandestine means and surveillance reports due to their inadmissible nature in courts," Kamath said. There was still no change in the suspect's level of comfort.

"But you can always dismiss them for security reasons," the suspect argued.

"Even this course of action can be challenged in the courts. It's a price that an intelligence agency has to pay for operating in an open society," KM lamented.

"I can now appreciate why the Chief sounded so frustrated in the meeting," the suspect remarked.

KM looked at his watch. It was past 2.15 pm. He excused himself and departed. On the way he collected the tape of his conversation with the suspect from the NC, invited Ajay to join him and together they went to brief Jeev. They waited in the ante-chamber for Jeev to get free from his meeting with a visitor from Beijing.

"What is in the tape that makes you sit up so excited?" Ajay asked.

KM played the tape. But Ajay was not impressed. "Ravi is saying nothing new. It only reinforces our view that he is deliberately duplicitous and has been trained well to craftily deflect whatever is thrown at him," he said.

"You should read between the lines, particularly his anxiety to know if we are looking for an espionage agent and the kind of rules that are being framed to regulate flow of documents from the building. Obviously, his handler wants to have an access to these critical inputs before a decision is taken on how to employ him for siphoning off secret papers in future," KM argued.

Ajay found his deputy's arguments largely spurious. He also knew that KM was simply repeating what Jeev had been saying all along. "I still feel that the Chief had offered us an excellent opportunity to get us out of this mess but Jeev spurned it for no valid reasons. We should have handed over the evidence," Ajay reminded him.

At this point, Jeev's PS informed that Mr Jeevnathan had gone out of the building along with the visitor and was not likely to return before 6 pm. After that, they both got up and left.

*

The suspect sat frozen in his chair long after Kamath left. In between, his telephone rang intermittently but he did not take the calls. PA Sharma buzzed him repeatedly but he refused to respond. He tried to call someone from his cell phone but disconnected before the call could materialize. Then he took out a paper from his briefcase and started dialling officers one by one to cancel dinner at his residence, scheduled for Saturday, 25 June. He explained that because of a sudden commitment, he would have to go out of town but promised to make up for the cancellation, a few weeks later. After that he told Sharma that he would leave at 5 pm to see an asthma specialist in connection with his wife's ailment.

*

Jeev returned to the office at 5.50 pm. It was more than forty-eight hours but there was still no word from the Chief querying why the surveillance had not been withdrawn and tapes and documents handed over to him. He asked KM whether he had received any message from the Chief on the subject.

"No, sir, but I want to play a tape to you," KM proposed.

"Anything earth shattering?"

"No, sir."

"Then drop in around 9 pm. We can review the day's developments on our way back home. I am a bit tied up right now," Jeev said. Then he rang the Chief to inform that Ravi was going to Jammu on Monday, 27th June and that he had asked Kamath to cover the visit just in case the suspect tried to meet his running officer. The Chief thanked him officiously and kept the receiver down.

An hour later, as Jeev got ready to leave, the RIT rang. It was Wasan calling. "I am sorry for having sounded abrupt when you'd called me earlier. I was briefing the incumbent Indian Ambassador to Yemen. I informed Princi now about Ravi's visit to Jammu. He wants the trip to be covered fully. He also said that he would take a final call in the matter after seeing your report on the visit," Wasan said all of this in one breath, fearing that his mercurial friend might drop the line.

"That's okay with me," Jeev said. Minutes later, he went out of the building to meet Octopus in Green Park Extension who was visiting Delhi after a decade and half under depressing circumstances. For a person who was so garrulous and excited about everything, Octopus sounded weak and withdrawn when he had spoken to Jeev earlier in the morning. He was Jeev's lifeline during the struggle for restoration of democracy in Nepal and the first one to ignite the spark for people to rise in revolt against King Birendra, a quintessential medieval monarch. Since then, democracy in the Himalayan kingdom had been suffering due to petty squabbles among mainstream political parties and distorted revolutionary visions of Marxists. In this melee, Octopus was left stranded by the wayside, rejected not only by his own people but also by his operatives in the Agency. Despite Jeev's persistent inquiries, no desk officer could unearth particulars of Octopus in files. And, when he came to know, it was too late. Octopus was in the last stage of dying of undifferentiated carcinoma.

*

KM wound up his work by 6.30 pm. His meeting with Jeev was still two and half hours away. He decided to spend that time with the watchers. As he was walking down to the porch, his cellphone vibrated. Reddy, Transport Officer, was trying to reach him. "Where are you now? I have to show you something," Reddy spoke in excitement.

"What is it about?" KM asked.

"After a long gap, the device in Mr Ravi's car has recorded something interesting. It's his conversation with a foreigner. Would you like to hear the tape now or tomorrow"? Reddy enquired.

"I will wait for you in my room," KM said and walked back to his room.

The recording began with Ravi asking Negi to take leave for five days. Negi wanted to know where they would go this time. Ravi told him that the place was still to be finalized but it would be one of the cooler places. After a few seconds Negi said that he had already exhausted his casual leave and Ravi might have to speak to Reddy to permit him to take earned leave. Ravi asked him not to worry. He said that these days security was very tight and it would be advisable to obtain leave prior to leaving the headquarters.

The rest of the conversation was inaudible. But KM kept listening. Soon, even the humming went dead. He was about to stop playing the tape, when he suddenly heard the suspect talking to someone on his mobile.

"Where are you speaking from? How come you are back so soon?" Ravi sounded surprised.

"I am in Delhi. I came from Toronto two days ago and went straight to Chandigarh. You remember I had told you the last time about finalizing a deal for a plot of land there. My visit to Chandigarh was in connection with talking to builders for constructing a house on that plot," said the caller.

Ravi: "How long will you be in Delhi?"

Caller: "Another ten days. The sooner I get out of this muggy weather, the better for children."

Ravi: "I know. Why don't you plan to go to Shimla or Manali?"

Caller: "That's not a bad idea. It will be great fun if all of us could go together. You decide the place, date, and time and I will bear the expenses."

Ravi: "Let me speak to Viji."

Caller: "Viji will never say no. She has always been a great sport."

Ravi: "If I decide to go, it will have to be within next few days. Getting leave during weekdays is a big problem in our department. Fortunately, the coming weekend is four days long. We can leave early morning on Saturday, 25th June and return on Tuesday, 28th June."

Caller: "That's fine with me."

Ravi: "Why don't you come and join us for dinner tonight?"

Caller: "I am already committed for dinner but we can come over for drinks. Will 7.30 pm be alright?"

Ravi: "Perfect. I will wait for you."

Caller: "When are you reaching Baltimore? You didn't tell me what we have to bring along for Aabha's engagement ceremony."

"We would be happy if you could just attend the ceremony." The call got disconnected. Seconds later, Ravi was calling his wife.

Ravi: "Baljeet is in town, Viji. He and his wife are coming over for drinks."

Viji: "Why didn't you invite them for dinner? They had done so much for us when we last visited Toronto."

Ravi: "I did offer, but he was committed elsewhere. Balli has a plan. I will discuss that when I reach home."

There was no further transmission. KM took out the tape from the recorder and kept it in his briefcase. He locked the door and left.

*

It was still an hour and ten minutes before KM was scheduled to meet Jeev. Instead of going to meet the field surveillance officers, he visited the Special Unit (SU) where the recording and processing of ALISTER's transmissions took place. His purpose was to see and hear live transmission of Balli's visit to the suspect's residence for drinks. He stayed in the SU till 8.45 pm but ALISTER remained tight-lipped. Finally, he picked up the tapes, recorded earlier and returned to his room. As he randomly picked up a tape and played, he heard the suspect's wife talking.

Vijita: "What plans Balli could possibly have?"

Ravi: "He wants to go to one of the hill stations for a few days and requested us to join him."

Viji: "It's not a bad idea. You also need a break from your work."

The rest of the tape was empty. As KM put another tape in the recorder to play, Jeev called. "It's already late. We will talk in the car," he said. KM quickly stacked papers and tapes in the briefcase and walked briskly towards the porch. Jeev was waiting for him. They got in the car and drove off.

KM began by saying that the suspect's activities were quite puzzling. He told his children that he was all set to go to the US, whereas his leave was yet to be sanctioned. Then he cancelled dinner for no plausible reasons within two days of fixing it. He asked Negi to apply for leave to drive him to a cooler place outside Delhi but where he would go and when, he was not prepared to reveal. He bought railway tickets to visit Jammu on Monday, 27th June but subsequently offered to join Baljeet on a trip to one of the hill stations during this period. Obviously the suspect would have to cancel one of the two trips. What, however, intrigued KM most was the tenor of Vijita Mohan's conversation. She knew what her husband was up to, yet she remained guarded in whatever she said. He wished the Agency had been half as discreet. By now, the car had reached Jeev's residence.

"Keep me posted with developments. I get a sense that the suspect is bewildered and is about to approach his handler," Jeev said as he came out of the car.

KM could not trust his ears. How could anyone be so unrealistic, he failed to understand.

After dinner, Jeev called Ajay to find out whether the Head of the Bureau's Immigration cell had instructed his outlying posts to be on the lookout of the suspect. Ajay said that he would check and come back.

"You should. Let's not be casual," Jeev reprimanded.

Day 90

Ravi reached office on time. En route, he told Negi that he had dropped the idea to go out of Delhi for the time being. As he settled down, Sharma came in with pending papers and files and tried to initiate a conversation but Ravi paid no heed. Instead, he instructed Sharma to get the rail tickets and hotel reservations in Jammu cancelled. Ravi told Sharma, on his own, that his friends, who were visiting him from Canada, were not keen on going to Jammu in this heat and he might take them now to a hill station during the weekend.

"Sir, in that case, can I go to Lucknow to see my parents during your absence?" Sharma promptly filed his request.

"I have no problem with that," Ravi said.

Miss Sethi came next with a file. Ravi signed it before she could even sit down. She found the behaviour of her boss strange, because he was generally very polite and indulgent towards her. She left in a huff, missing the customary chat. Minutes later, Ravi received a call from Ajay who wanted to know whether his leave for the US had been cleared.

"Not yet," Ravi replied.

"I find it really inexplicable," Ajay opined. "I did raise this issue with Mr Jeevnathan yesterday but he looked the other way," he lied. "Since he is a stickler for working on a need-to-know basis, why don't you meet him in person and see what he has to say?" he suggested.

"I have sought an appointment. Let's see when I get it," Ravi said without meaning it.

*

From the NC, Kamath reported to Jeev that the suspect had been grouchy since morning and acting very rude to his personal staff and officers of his Branch. He had also cancelled his visit to Jammu.

"Any particular reason," Jeev asked.

"He told his PA that he cancelled the plan because Baljeet was not willing to travel in this heat, whereas the fact is that it was Ravi who suggested to his Canadian friend to go to a hill station," KM pointed out.

"What else?"

"ALISTER has stopped transmitting. The tapes are running empty. I discussed the problem with Kutty. He is of the view that the device has either become defective or someone has accidently tripped over it," KM said.

"Is there anything that we can do to make this device operational?" Jeev asked in anguish.

"Sir, we had planned to enter the suspect's apartment during his visit to Jammu but since he has cancelled that trip, we will now have to wait till he goes out during the weekend," KM said.

"I will call you back in a minute," Jeev disconnected and picked up a call on the RIT.

Ajay was on the line. He confirmed that his Bureau contact was regularly in touch with all the immigration posts and no one matching with the suspect's particulars had come to their notice. Jeev then called the Chief and apprised him that Ravi had cancelled the Jammu trip.

"Some relief," Wasan expressed. "I will inform Princi and let you know of his reaction." There was no further talk. After that, Jeev rang up KM to find out if he had anything new to say. KM indicated that the suspect was likely to take his remaining personal files to the residence before the weekend and sought Jeev's specific direction whether the CEU should insist on seeing his files before he took them out of the building.

"Yes," Jeev was emphatic.

"Sir, sometime back you had told an officer in Delhi police to monitor the suspect's calls? Has he provided any details?" KM inquired.

"He has submitted a huge list of calls that Ravi has been making but these numbers are known. He has also been using different SIM cards purchased from different locations in Delhi, Chennai and Mumbai but their usage is restricted to 1 to 3 seconds. The problem is that the carriers won't reveal the text of his calls or messages unless the Ministry of Home Affairs gives its approval," Jeev said.

"Sir, we had also passed on the suspect's numbers to the Chief. Did you hear anything from him?" KM reminded.

"His list is a mini version of the list provided by the Delhi police. It means nothing unless you monitor the numbers and that is possible only if the Home Secretary gives the approval. It's a Catch-22 situation," Jeev explained.

Their discussion was interrupted by a call from the Chief.

"I informed Princi that Ravi's Jammu trip is off," Wasan said. "His instructions are that we should lower down the scale and intensity of surveillance to ensure that the situation does not spin out of control during the next few days," he added.

"His suggestion is comical," Jeev reacted. "You can't have a half-hearted surveillance. Anyway, did your Princi ask you why the operation had not been wound up so far?" he asked.

"No."

"Why is he asking for a few days' of reprieve?" Jeev probed.

"Next week, the Cabinet Committee on Foreign Policy Affairs is meeting to hear a presentation from the Principal Secretary on various initiatives that he has undertaken to forge a strategic relationship between India and the US," Wasan disclosed.

"And, he does not want any hiccups to upset his game plan during this period?" Jeev interrupted.

"That's right. Once he is fully secure in his hot seat, he will take a final call on Ravi's case. In the meantime, let's not do anything overly provocative," Wasan suggested.

"Anything less than aggressive surveillance is no surveillance," Jeev remarked. Wasan had nothing more to say.

Jeev then called KM and apprised him of what had transpired between him and the Chief. "These are his instructions. You can brief your watchers accordingly. Tell them to avoid uncomfortable proximity to the suspect but they must not lose him at any point of time. I know these are clever guidelines and is likely to leave gaps in the surveillance but as the Chief says, it is only a matter of few days," Jeev explained.

"Sir, if I tell watchers now to relax even one bit, they will simply fold up," KM warned.

"I see your point. Please do what you consider is best under the circumstances. Don't assume that I am passing the buck. If anything goes wrong, you can count on my support," Jeev stressed.

*

For the rest of the forenoon, Ravi slouched on the sofa. In response to his calls, Desk Officers handling Nepal, Bangladesh, China and Afghanistan dropped in quick succession. The discussions mainly centred round the rumours floating in the building about the type and quantum of punishment that were to be meted out to the erring employees. Each visitor also provided his insightful information on what actions were being contemplated to tighten the security measures. Ravi was throughout circumspect in offering his views. The last to come in was Colonel Paritosh, the China Military Analyst. He informed that his leave for Singapore had been cleared. "What about yours?" he asked.

"Enjoy your vacation." Ravi avoided talking about his leave. Paritosh sat for a while, abusing Jeev and Kamath for their arrogance and for terrorizing everyone into submitting to their whims and caprices. Ravi nodded his head in agreement but his thoughts strayed elsewhere. As soon as Paritosh departed, Ravi spoke to Baljeet to find out the approximate time of his arrival for dinner. Next, he called the Chief's staff officer and mildly protested against inordinate delay in sanctioning his leave for the USA. The staff officer assured him that the Chief would see him in a day or two. After that Ravi went home for an unscheduled lunch.

Ravi returned to the office around 4 pm. Inder handed over the cancelled railway tickets and the balance amount. Just before he left for the day, he took out three files from the almirah, photocopied all pages one by one and kept them in his briefcase. These were copies of his private, official and diplomatic passports that had been issued to him from time to time. He reached home around 7 pm. Baljeet and his wife came for dinner at 9 pm and left around midnight for Hotel Ambassador.

Day 91

It was the last working day before the long weekend. The first thing the suspect did after reaching the office was to shred papers, lying in the drawers of his working desk. Meanwhile, Sharma brought in pending papers and files which he signed and returned without going through their content. He appeared to be in a hurry to be left alone. As he got up and started pulling out files from the almirah, a call came on the external line.

"I tried to reach you earlier but you were not in your room," the caller said.

"I had gone for a meeting," the suspect instinctively lied.

"They are quoting an unrealistic price for the Noida property. May be we should wait," the caller suggested.

"The delay will actually suit me. I may be leaving for the US after three weeks for almost a month. Please keep me posted with developments," the suspect said.

A few minutes later, Anuj Nagia, Desk Officer Africa, dropped in unannounced. He shook hands with the suspect vigorously, pulled a chair and sat down. In his inimitable style, he asked for coffee and blueberry pastries from Hotel Oberoi. Always abrupt in his manners, Anuj seldom allowed anyone to take the centre stage once the discussion started. He was also gifted with dramatizing even the most bizarre incidents and making every word of his appear incredulously important. He revelled in exaggeration and the passion with which he argued his case, converted temporarily even his worst critics.

The suspect restored the files to the almirah, asked his PA to arrange for coffee and pastries and invited Anuj to sit with him on the sofa. The latter promptly took charge of the conversation. He said he had an urgent message to deliver but typically went on building tense atmospherics before coming to the point. Describing the general search as a whimsical exercise, he explained in details the extent to which it had hurt and humiliated officers. He called KM a raging bull in a china shop and accused him of unleashing unbearable uncertainty in the Agency. He repeatedly faulted Jeev for allowing Kamath a free run to discredit everyone in the organization.

"But what was it that you wanted to share with me so urgently?" Ravi interrupted Anuj's blabbering.

"My sources have informed that you have been placed under surveillance by the CEU for last one and a half months. It is entirely Kamath's mischief. I am not sure if Mr Jeevnathan is even aware of it," Anuj claimed. The suspect increased the volume of the TV.

"It can't be me," the suspect muttered. "I have never carried any classified papers out of the building. Unlike in the case of others, the CEU has returned all my files. It has neither questioned me nor sought any written explanation from me," he insisted.

"I don't know but you should better be on your guard," Anuj suggested. A prolonged silence ensued, both being uncertain of what to say next.

After Anuj left, the suspect took out seven files from the almirah, removed papers from inside and shredded them. Then he tried to contact Baljeet but was told by the receptionist at the hotel that no one was answering the number. After lunch, he called Prabhakar, one of the Desk Officers in Technical Division, to check if he had returned from his long leave. Prabhakar said that he returned only last night from Munich and would soon come over to hand over a gift.

Prabhakar was one of the many beneficiaries of Ravi's generosity in the Agency. The latter had not only arranged admission for his son in Khalsa College, Delhi but also helped his wife find a decent job in a private firm. In return, Prabhakar took care of the maintenance and repairs of the suspect's electronic equipments including computers, shredder and audio systems. The suspect missed him badly in the past few months. "Did anyone tell you what happened in the building in your absence?" he asked as soon as Prabhakar sat down.

"Yes sir."

"Has the Technical Division mounted any surveillance against any officer?" The suspect asked pointedly.

"I met Mr Panda, Kutty and Das this morning but no one mentioned anything of this nature," Prabhakar replied. Before he left, he wanted to know whether he could bring his wife along during the coming weekend to hand over a gift to Mrs Mohan.

"We are not going anywhere. Just give me a call before you leave for my house," the suspect said. All of a sudden, he asked whether Prabhakar could organize sweeping of his room just to make sure that it was bug-free. Prabhakar was stunned. "Why would anyone bug your room?" he asked.

"It's one of those wild apprehensions that you sometimes run into, while working in an intelligence setup," the suspect said calmly.

"I can request my colleague to send a sweeping team," Prabhakar suggested but the suspect did not want anyone else to get a whiff of his predicament.

Immediately after Prabhakar left, Sharma came in with a note for permission to leave the Headquarters. The suspect signed the note without even looking up at Sharma. At 3.30 pm, he locked the room from inside and approached the photocopier, peering at it from all sides. Here was Ravi's favourite machine, ensconced in a corner deserted by its master, who didn't know whether to plug it in or leave it to mock at his helplessness. In that confused state of mind, he approached a huge Board hanging on the wall, on which maps of India's neighbouring countries were affixed. He stood there for some time, then turned around and climbed on the working desk after two failed attempts, to check if any surveillance device had been concealed in the roof light and the overhead ceiling fan. After that he dragged a chair up to the door and windows to comb the pelmets and almirah. He also went behind the almirah and closely inspected the TV and air conditioner to locate the bugs. Then he lifted the table lamp and telephone sets, turned them around to examine their bottom for any suspicious device. His exhausting efforts, however, brought him no rewards. Breathing heavily and perspiring, he sat down on the sofa, then stretched his legs and kept gazing at the false ceiling till his neck became stiff and sleep set in his weary eyes. He was woken up by a call from Sharma who said that Mr Lokesh Kumar was standing outside and wanted to know whether he should go back in case Ravi was busy. The suspect looked at the wall clock. It was 5 pm. He rubbed his face with a towel, got up and opened the door. Lokesh entered, pulled a chair and sat down. He wanted to know whether Ravi would be interested in watching a play on Gandhi during the weekend. The play, he said, had been reviewed very generously by critics.

"I would have loved to but I am not feeling very well. I will prefer to rest at home. I may, however, go to Rishikesh for a day or two just for a change," he said.

"I can also give you company if you don't have a problem," Lokesh proposed.

"I will let you know if I decide to go," the suspect replied.

The last visitor to meet him was Kamal Mehta. He wanted to know if Ravi would be available for lunch next day at the Gymkhana. The suspect expressed his inability saying that he had invited Viji's cousin and his wife for lunch at the Delhi Golf club. Before Kamal could react, his mobile rang up. He left hurriedly thereafter, wishing Ravi a pleasant weekend.

At 6 pm, Sharma and Inder entered the room. Sharma collected papers and files and deposited them in almirahs, while Inder switched off the TV, unplugged the photocopier, picked up the briefcase and left. However, the suspect kept sitting, possibly to avoid the stampede that was caused daily by employees, desperate to leave the building for the day. At 6.40 pm, he switched off the room light and came out of the room. Walking past the cleaning and security staff and acknowledging their greetings, he took the officers' lift, came down to the foyer which was still crowded and moved at a slow pace towards the porch. He took out Rs 5000 from the purse and gave it to Sharma to bring a sari from Lucknow for his wife. As he waited at the porch for his car, another car pulled in and Panda and Burman came out. They briefly exchanged smiles with him, shook hands and went inside the building. At the main exit, he noticed Kamath herded with five of his junior colleagues. En route, neither Negi nor he spoke a word. On reaching his residence, he asked Negi to bring the car next day at 4 pm. Jena took the briefcase and escorted the suspect inside the house. Negi turned the vehicle around and drove off. At 7.40 pm, Baljeet visited Ravi in a taxi and after staying for forty minutes, returned to Hotel Ambassador.

Day 92

Since morning, the air had been warming up rapidly and by 10 am it turned into a heat wave. When KM left the house, the temperature had touched 49 degrees Celsius. To add to his misery, the car air conditioner stalled within minutes of hitting the main road. But like his more fortunate colleagues, he could not afford to sit at home, host lunch or visit hill stations when an espionage agent was working overtime.

KM first went to check with watchers, deployed in the proximity of the suspect's residence. Pal, who relieved Mathew at 8 am, gave a hand written night observation report to KM, left behind by Mathew. It mentioned that though the thick curtains were drawn, one could make out that the suspect probably slept only around 2.40 am. Till then, lights in his bedroom were switched on and shadows of varying sizes were occasionally moving up and down. Earlier at 2.10 am, Jena was spotted talking to the night guard outside the main gate. The guard confided to a watcher in the morning that Mr Ravi Mohan was feeling very restless after dinner and when his condition deteriorated, Jena came out looking for a taxi to take his master to a doctor. However, by the time taxi arrived, Mr Mohan's condition stabilized and he went off to sleep.

"And, what have you observed," KM asked Pal after he finished reading the report.

"I have noticed nothing unusual," Pal said. "I could not speak to the watchman because he was changed before I came on duty. I have also not seen the suspect since morning," he added.

"Why did the guard volunteer the information?" KM asked.

"Sir, he is the one who had facilitated our earlier break-in for setting up ALISTER. I had asked him to also keep my colleagues informed of all developments that he came to know in my absence. I will find out more details when he reports back on duty at 2 pm," Pal mentioned.

"I am going to the office. Give me a call as and when Ravi leaves. I have kept two teams ready at the Headquarters for moving at short notice. It is possible Ravi and Baljeet may leave separately and meet at a pre-designated location for resuming their onward journey to one of the hill stations," KM explained as he got inside the car. On his way, he called Reddy to enquire if the device in the suspect's car had picked up any conversation on the previous day. Reddy said that he would call back within half an hour. KM then contacted Avinash and instructed him to rush to the office and wait for him in the Nerve Centre. At 11.30 am, he reached the main entrance, got down and walked up to Reddy's office. Since he was running against time, he declined Reddy's offer to serve a hot cup of coffee, collected the tapes and left for NC. He played the tapes but they were virtually blank. After that, he rang up Bhadra who was to relieve Pal at 2 pm. He informed that Negi had been asked to bring the car to the suspect's residence at 4 pm. In case, the suspect went out, Bhadra must follow him and if necessary, ask for extra manpower by calling Avinash. He barely finished instructing Bhadra, when Pal called him on the other line.

"Sir, I spoke to the guard just now. He is confident that in case the suspect goes to see a doctor along with his wife, he can take Jena out of the building during that period. That's the time our technician can enter the house to repair ALISTER," he submitted.

"Can you trust him?" KM asked.

"Sir, I have committed Rs 5000 for the job. Fifty per cent will be paid as advance and the rest after he facilitates entry of our men. I don't think he would risk this kind of remuneration by making false claims," Pal argued.

"Please stay there. I will, meanwhile, request Kutty to keep his technicians ready," KM said. Then he began recording his impression of events, based on reports and intercepts received within last twenty four hours. At 2.40 pm, Jeev called him to enquire about the suspect's activities on a holiday. KM said that he could come over to brief him within fifteen minutes. But Jeev preferred to meet around 4.30 pm unless there was a crisis.

At 3 pm, Pal complained to Kamath that Bhadra had still not reported for duty although it was well past 2 pm. He said that he was feeling hungry but could not desert the post for obvious reasons. KM reproached Pal for raising frivolous issues at a critical time. "I have also not had lunch. If you can wait, I can have pizzas delivered to you," he said. This is how KM usually quelled dissensions in ranks. Before he went out to pick up food, he rang up Kutty on the cell phone to tie up the entry of the technicians in the suspect's residence. He was mildly surprised to find Kutty in the office. "What are you doing here on a holiday?" he asked.

"A new operational task came up last evening," Kutty disclosed. "Mr Panda is also here in that connection. But don't worry. Pal told me about your requirement. I have already made arrangements. You just have to sound me fifteen minutes before the house is empty," he said.

"That's not what I had called you for. If you are free for ten minutes, I want to visit the suspect's room along with you," KM confided.

"What for?"

"I will explain to you when you come," KM said. Twenty minutes later, KM opened the suspect's room and requested Kutty to check if all devices were in place. Kutty confirmed that nothing had been disturbed.

"Ravi Mohan is really a duffer." He literally ransacked the room yesterday in an attempt to locate your devices but tumbled on none," KM said.

"It's not fair. You are taking away credit from our technical experts," Kutty countered in a lighter vein. A call from Panda interrupted their conversation. Kutty left soon thereafter. KM locked the suspect's room, walked up to the parking area briskly and drove off to meet Jeev.

Jeev appeared worried as he read KM's note on the suspect's activities. "Ravi is saying different things to different officers about his plans to spend his weekend. He is probably waylaying everyone," Jeev averred. "I am also amazed at the stupidity of the officers who are scaring him to flee. Ravi is definitely smarter than these jokers who are billed as our best operatives. Look at how he is taking them for a joy ride and they think that they are his conscience keepers," he remarked. His exasperation was cut short by a call to KM from one of the watchers. Suddenly, Kamath appeared tense.

"What was he saying?" Jeev inquired impatiently.

"Sir, Negi took the car to Ravi's residence at 4 pm, but came out alone within five minutes. I must intercept him to find out whether the suspect is really too sick to remain confined to his apartment the whole day," KM explained in a hurry and left.

Meanwhile, Negi drove from the suspect's residence to a petrol pump near Khan Market where he sold ten litres of fuel from his car. After that, he went to the office, parked the car in the basement, signed off at the Transport Control Centre and walked out. KM intercepted him near the outer gate and instructed him to follow. Negi panicked, fearing that the CEU had probably caught him on their video for selling petrol in the black market. As soon as they stopped near the fire hydrant, KM asked tersely whether he had seen Ravi Mohan lying in his sickbed. Negi informed nervously that while he was waiting downstairs, Jena came and told him that sahib was indisposed and would not go out anywhere. He felt relieved that his thieving was not the issue. KM further asked whether it was possible that Ravi and his wife had gone out to see a doctor in their personal car. Negi said that he had seen their car parked in the garage. Moreover, Jena repeatedly told him that sahib wanted the car to be brought next day at 11 am. Since Kamath had nothing more to ask, he allowed Negi to leave.

KM entered the building and took the stairs on the left to barge in the Agency's Control Room, unannounced. Once the commotion over his surprise visit subsided, he inquired from the officer on duty, if anyone had gone to Mr Ravi Mohan's residence to deliver cables received from the outstations. The officer confirmed that cables and other papers were being regularly received at Ravi's residence and showed the receipt book in support of his assertion. KM noted that Viji was actually receiving papers on behalf of Ravi but her signature was unsteady and not very legible.

"Sir, is there any problem?" The officer inquired anxiously.

"No. Actually, Mr Ravi has been complaining for some time that your Dak carriers often deliver cables of other officers to him and his cables land up elsewhere. I was only trying to verify it," KM explained.

"Sir, our Dak riders are usually very responsible but I agree, they do mess up occasionally," the officer conceded. KM then rang up suspect's mobile number but there was no response. Next, he dialled the residence number. Jena answered the call.

"I am speaking from the Control Room," KM spoke abruptly. "Give the telephone to Mr Ravi Mohan," he said.

"Sir, he is not well and is sleeping. He has instructed me not to disturb him," Jena responded politely.

"Where is Mrs Mohan? Tell her that Kamath wants to talk to her," KM thundered.

"Sir, she has gone to meet her father," Jena said.

"What is her mobile number?"

"Sir, she is not carrying her mobile. It's lying in the bedroom and it is locked."

KM put down the receiver, shook hands with the officer and left. While driving home, he called Jeev and apprised him of the gist of his conversation with Negi and Jena.

"So, Jena is the source of all information about the suspect. I suggest that if you don't see him by tomorrow, then send one of your officers to their house with a bunch of sealed envelopes and make sure that he delivers them only to Ravi or to his wife, Jeev said.

*

KM had barely finished his dinner when Mathew, who took over the surveillance duties from Bhadra at 8 pm, called. He said that the target and his wife had left for Hyderabad at 7 pm by air.

"How did you come to know?" KM reacted in haste.

"Sir, Jena gave this information to the guard a few minutes ago," Mathew reported. KM dropped the phone and immediately contacted Bhadra who flatly denied having seen the target leave. Then he called the Agency's officer located at the domestic airport. He informed that Ravi Mohan and his wife

Vijita Mohan had left for Hyderabad at 6 pm but he did not know the flight that they had taken. He wondered whether their flight could be identified for a follow-up action.

"Sir, I am not sure if private airlines will permit me to see their manifest," the officer replied.

"I am running short of time. I trust you can do this. But keep it a secret," KM said.

The Airport officer returned the call sooner than later. He reported that names of Mr and Mrs Mohan were missing in all manifests. However, the manifest of 6E307 carried the names of Mr R. Mohan and Mrs. V Mohan. He was not sure whether this information would suffice.

"That's a great piece of information," KM was quick to acknowledge. Subsequently, he spoke to Hegde, the CEU officer posted at Agency's office in Hyderabad and directed him to rush to the airport.

"Sir, is any big fish coming from down south?" Hegde enquired.

"Just listen to me," KM snapped. "Ravi Mohan and his wife Vijita are fleeing the country. They are travelling to your location by 6E307, leaving Delhi at 8.50 pm under the names of Mr R. Mohan and Mrs V. Mohan. They may take a connecting flight from Hyderabad to go abroad. I want you to identify these passengers. If they happen to be Ravi and his wife, find out where they are staying and whether they are booked on a connecting international flight. If they attempt to exit, detain and bring them to the safe house and if they create a furore, use force to subdue them but do not let them escape. I will wait for your call," KM fired his instructions rapidly.

At 11.40 pm, Hegde reported back. He said that Mr and Mrs. V. Mohan were actually Ramdas and Vaijayanti Mohan. They lived in Chennai and ran their own business of manufacturing bearing for Ford and Tata Motors. They were visiting Hyderabad to attend the wedding of the daughter of their friend.

"Thanks," KM said and went to sleep. He was not sure whether he felt disappointed or relieved.

Day 93

KM was woken up at 5 am by a call from Jeev. He wanted to know whether the suspect's presence in the house could be confirmed.

"No sir," KM struggled to sound coherent.

"Get on to your feet fast. You have to tighten too many loose ends today. Try also to meet Baljeet at the hotel. His presence or absence can explain lot of things. But be careful. You are not a police officer and you don't have any immunity from trespassing into anyone's house or from questioning a Non-Resident Indian roughly," Jeev advised. KM thought that Jeev was too impractical to be in the business of running intelligence operations. He could not quite appreciate the fixation of his boss for clean investigation and his fetish for correctness in dealing with an espionage agent. "You can't use the same yardstick in dealing with a murderer and an offender of traffic rules. If someone stabs you from behind, how can you subdue him without your hands getting dirty with blood stains? Jeev is definitely in the wrong job and should have been a mascot for a human rights organization," he muttered as he got up from the bed.

"Whom are you talking to?" his wife asked.

"Don't worry. There is still some time before I become insane," KM assured.

*

KM reached Hotel Ambassador at 9.30 am. Manjeet, who was keeping a vigil at the hotel, guided KM to Room 304 where Baljeet was staying. KM knocked at the door but there was no response. He thought of forcing open the door but abandoned the idea in view of Jeev's pointed advice not to take law into his hands. He also briefly toyed with the idea of approaching the hotel manager to find out where Baljeet could have gone but gave it up for fear of prematurely exposing the operation. He came out of the hotel and left after instructing Manjeet to be on the lookout for Baljeet. On the way, he asked Avinash to meet him in the office within fifteen minutes.

The hallway was deserted, when KM entered the building. Only a few guards on essential security duties loitered around. Walking past the corridors he reached his room, wondering if it was worthwhile wasting holidays for something that, except for Jeev and himself, had no takers. Before he could flirt more with cynicism, Avinash entered the room.

"It's time now to be proactive," KM stressed. "I will generate a few fake documents. You carry them to Ravi's apartment and tell Jena firmly that these are to be handed over only to Mr Mohan," he said. "Show your identity card if he creates ruckus and if the sentry tries to be difficult, take Pal's help to neutralize him," he added. Then he took out blank sheets from the drawer of his desk, put them inside four separate envelopes, sealed them and passed on to Avinash.

Seconds after Avinash left, KM went to the canteen to have a cup of tea. From there, he drove to Defence Colony, just in case Avinash was refused an entry in the suspect's building or assaulted for trespassing. As KM was getting inside the car, Pal rang up. He reported that Negi brought the office car at 11 am but was asked to take the car back to the office by the guard. Pal also informed that he had put a watcher on Negi's trail and gave a mobile number in case KM wanted to speak to the watcher.

KM came out of the car and walked back to his room. He called Avinash and told him not to deliver the envelopes and wait for further instructions. Then he rang up Jeev for his advice on how to react if Jena or suspect's relatives physically obstructed him from entering the building. He wanted to be sure that he did not overstep the forbidden line drawn by Jeev in the interest of preserving the *sanctity* of rules and norms.

"If you are reasonably certain that Ravi is not inside the house, you can force your entry and question the housekeepers. The servant or anyone else has no legal authority to receive classified papers in his absence," Jeev clarified.

KM felt a sudden surge of comfort in Jeev's belligerence. He was relieved that he could now go for the kill. As soon as Jeev disconnected, KM contacted the watcher who was tailing Negi. The watcher reported that the driver had just parked the car and was going towards the main gate. KM rushed out and intercepted Negi some 20 meters away from the prying eyes of the sentries and took him aside in the lawn for questioning.

"Did Ravi himself ask you to bring the car today at 11 am," KM asked with a straight face.

"No sir," Negi said, literally quivering.

"Why did the guard return you from the gate itself?"

"Sir, it was not the guard but Jena who told me that sahib and memsahib were not at home and would probably be back after three-four days," Negi clarified.

"Did you ask him where Ravi had gone?"

"No sir. But sahib was planning to go somewhere and in fact, he had asked me to remain ready to move out at a short notice. Later on he cancelled the visit and decided to stay back. I don't know what happened after that," Negi said. KM did not question the driver further. A few minutes later, he left for the suspect's residence. While driving, he instructed Avinash to commence 'Mission Delivery'.

*

Avinash parked the motor cycle close to the entrance gate of the suspect's apartment building. He switched off the ignition, took off his helmet, collected envelopes from the boot and approached the guard. He said that he had come from Ravi's office to deliver official letters. The guard requested Avinash to wait, then went inside and brought Jena along. Jena said that sahib was not at home but he offered to accept the papers on sahib's behalf.

"You are lying. Mr Ravi Mohan is very much inside the house. He hasn't taken any permission from the office to go out of Delhi," Avinash reacted strongly.

"I am telling you he is not at home," Jena insisted.

"I have to verify this fact," Avinash deliberately raised the pitch of his voice to cow the servant down and tried to physically force open the gate. Hearing the commotion, a few inmates of the building came out to inquire what the fuss was all about. As soon as Avinash showed his identity card and explained the purpose of his visit, most of the onlookers quietly disappeared, while Jena ran back to the apartment. A building inmate, who introduced himself as Bhatia and a cousin of Vijita Mohan, however stayed on. He told Avinash that Ravi and Viji were actually not at home but he had no idea where they had gone.

"That's precisely the reason why I am here. Jena is receiving classified papers which are meant only for Mr Ravi Mohan. I have to retrieve those documents," Avinash insisted. Bhatia said nothing and went back to his apartment. Meanwhile, KM and Pal who were watching the unfolding events from a distance joined Avinash and all of them proceeded towards the suspect's apartment. Pal pressed the calling bell two to three times, followed by some persistent knocking at the door. Jena opened the door but kept firmly standing in the passage. Before he could open his mouth, Avinash held his neck in his grip and forced him to sit on the floor. With no one around and the gravity of the situation rapidly sinking in, Jena began pleading that he was innocent.

"That, I will find out soon. First, you take us inside and return the papers that you received in Ravi's absence," KM was curt. Jena led them to the living room. KM asked Jena for a glass of water and used his absence to post Jeev about the latest developments. Jeev advised KM not to go around in the house inspecting and removing suspicious items on his own. He asked him to request Mr Bhatia or Ravi's father-in-law who stayed next door, to be present while he looked around for incriminating evidence. "I don't want them or Ravi to accuse you later of stealing," Jeev cautioned.

KM made the next call to Kutty and asked him to rush his man to remove the devices from the apartment. He said that he was sending Avinash to the gate to escort Bora inside.

Meanwhile Jena came with a glass of water. KM thanked him and asked him to sit down on the floor.

"Now tell me truthfully where has Ravi gone?" KM questioned.

"Sir, he has gone to Rishikesh."

"If you knew that he was going to Rishikesh, why did you tell the guard that he left for Hyderabad in the evening by Air?" KM pressed.

"Sir, it was sahib's instruction to mention like that to the guard."

"Why did he go to Rishikesh?"

'Sir, he told me that he would join a health camp there for three days and asked me to receive all his papers and sealed envelopes in his absence and put them safely in the drawer of his bed side table," Jena sounded very nervous.

"When did he leave?"

"Sir, I don't know the exact time but it was before 2 am yesterday."

"Why did he have to leave at this odd hour?"

"Sir, I don't know."

"Did Baljeet come to pick him up?" KM further grilled.

"No, sir. But he came in the evening. Both had drinks together and he left after an hour."

"How did Ravi go? I saw his car parked in the porch."

"Sir, he left along with memsahib by a taxi. He said he was too tired of work and was escaping to the mountains simply to unwind himself. He did not want Negi to drive the car because the latter was in the habit of talking too much and would have spoiled sahib's peace of mind during the journey," Jena said.

"What did they carry?"

"Two hand bags, sir."

"Did he call you today?"

"No, sir."

While KM kept Jena busy in the balcony, Avinash quietly smuggled the technician in, who plucked out ALISTER, stacked it in the bag and left. His operation lasted for fifteen minutes. With technician gone, KM asked Jena to take him to Mr Krishna Prakash, suspect's father-in-law. The old man received him with enormous hesitation and frowned at having been disturbed. KM pulled out a chair to sit, completely ignoring the old man's grumpy look and explained the seriousness of the situation in a very polite manner. He stressed that it was necessary that Mr Prakash remained present when official papers were retrieved from the suspect's bed room.

"Cant' you wait for three days?" The old man asked in a feeble voice.

"Sir, these are top secret papers which cannot be left in the hands of a servant who has been forging the signature of Ravi and Vijita to receive them. If you think I am being unreasonable, I can ask my boss to clarify the position either in person or on phone," KM submitted. Mr Prakash found it futile to reason further. He got up reluctantly, went inside and came out immaculately dressed. He announced that he was ready to go. He walked straight but at a leisurely pace, followed by Pal and Jena. KM was walking alongside.

"You know, the last time I visited their apartment was almost two years ago," the old man confided.

"I can understand. It is difficult at your age to negotiate even a couple of steps," Kamath tried to show his concern.

"It's not that. There are many things that I don't like about Ravi. He does not treat my daughter well, is greedy and extremely conniving," the old man said. KM avoided probing, although the temptation was overwhelming. Once inside the apartment, he made Mr Prakash sit comfortably in a chair in the bedroom and went around minutely observing every item. He noticed that the shredder was in the right end corner near the window and two laptops were lying in the study on a table. KM whispered to Avinash to remove the laptops and keep them in the car while he covered Jena. As soon as Jena bent down to clear the sealed envelopes from the drawers of the table, Avinash put the laptops in his bag and rushed out. Meanwhile, KM took the envelopes in his custody, counted their numbers and wrote down the details on two separate sheets. He made the old man sign two sheets, gave one to him and retained the other after endorsing his signature on both. After that he helped Mr Prakash to rise from the chair and escorted him back to his house. He pleaded forgiveness for causing inconvenience and promised not to bother Mr Prakash again.

"That's alright. After all you had a job to do," the old man said and offered a drink but KM excused himself.

By now, it was 4.10 pm. KM dropped Avinash and the technician at the office. Before he left to meet Jeev at the latter's residence, he told the technician to find out if ALISTER's back-up disc contained anything worthwhile. He said that he was not very optimistic about the outcome, but under the circumstances, one had to clutch on to every piece of straw to survive, particularly when odds were so heavy. Around 5.30 pm, Kamath reached Jeev's residence and gave a blow by blow account of what happened at the suspect's apartment. "I am relieved the whole exercise went off smoothly," Jeev remarked. He was, however, positive that Jena was still not coming out with truth and he definitely knew where Ravi had gone.

"Sir, that's also my feeling. I wanted to isolate him and tackle him hard but the situation was a bit tense. I will visit him again in the evening to extract more juice out of him," KM said. Jeev advised him to be careful. Before leaving, KM took out the suspect's laptops from his car and kept them in Jeev's study.

Later on, Jeev posted the Chief with the day's events. The Chief enquired if all the immigration checkposts had been alerted. Jeev confirmed, saying that Ajay had sounded Bureau's immigration officer on an informal basis.

"How can you sound so cold and detached?" the Chief expressed annoyance. "I can't believe that an espionage agent is missing and your deputy is merely engaged in informally consulting immigration officers," he reacted in panic.

"We are doing whatever is possible." The line got disconnected.

*

KM reached home, walked past his wife who opened the door and slouched on the easy chair in the living room. His body promptly caved in. He had no idea when he fell into sleep. At 9 pm, his wife finally mustered courage to wake him up. She said that Avinash had been calling frantically and even Mr Jeevnathan wanted to speak to him urgently.

"You should have woken me up," KM reacted in irritation. He tried to reach both Avinash and Jeev but their numbers were constantly engaged. Finally he decided to leave.

"You haven't eaten since morning. I will get the food ready in five minutes," his wife said.

KM, for a change was not dismissive of her suggestion. He followed her to the kitchen. While she was warming food, the telephone rang. Jeev was on the line.

"I am sorry sir, I fell asleep," KM said.

"It's alright. Avinash was actually trying to reach you. ALISTER seems to have recorded some useful inputs which he thinks, are explosive. He first tried to contact you and then called me. He wanted to share the information but I did not encourage him to speak on an open line. I have asked him to listen to the tapes once again and come over as soon as the transcripts are ready," Jeev said.

"Sir, I will be in the office within next fifteen minutes," KM said. He quickly had his food while his wife brought the car keys. As he reversed the car in haste, he hit the flower pot hard but drove off without examining the extent of damage.

*

Avinash and the technical officer were busy checking the accuracy of the hand written transcripts when KM entered the Nerve Centre. "What is that you wanted to show me so desperately?" he asked.

"Sir, these transcripts are hot stuff," Avinash said and passed on the legible copies to KM to read.

Day 88: (After the suspect returned from the Club)

Vijita: Did you hear anything about your leave?

Ravi: The PS to the Chief assured me that it would be cleared on the first working day after the coming weekend.

V: Are you sure, you are telling the truth? (Tape runs blank for a few seconds).

R: I don't know if my leave will ever be approved. Maybe I should seriously consider rescheduling the engagement date.

V: Do you suspect that Mr Jeevnathan and the Chief have caught whiff of your dealings?

R: It is possible. Aren't we being watched?

V: We have not seen anyone tailing us so far. I know you have been apprehensive for quite some time and more so after the general search. You never know, the CEU may be targeting someone else.

R: Life is no longer the same in the Agency, Viji. Everyone is suspicious of the other. But I am the one who is talked about most.

V: Take it easy, Ravi.

R: I can't take it any longer.

V: I still think you are overreacting. Just settle down. Everything will be okay.

R: Don't tell Balli about my leave problems.

Day 88: (After ALISTER had transmitted the suspect's conversation with his son in the US)

V: Why did you lie to Sankar about your leave? What will you tell him if your leave is not sanctioned and you are not able to go?

R: I will find out some excuse.

Day 89: (During Mr and Mrs. Baljeet's visit to the suspect's residence for drinks)

(Too many voices, none of them recognizable, are heard most of the time. Then suddenly a conversation ensues which is somewhat audible).

Baljeet: Are you really serious about our visit to Manali?

Ravi: Yes, of course but I have yet to plan out the details.

B: If you are busy, I can ask the hotel to fix up everything including our transport and accommodation in Manali.

V: We still have time. I will tie up everything by tomorrow.

Day 90: (During Mr and Mrs Baljeet's visit to the suspect's residence for dinner)

Ravi: There is a slight change in the programme. We may be going to Nepal.

Baljeet: I don't think it's a good idea. Travelling alone will take three and half days.

R: We can extend the trip by another two to three days.

Baljeet's wife: That's fine with me. But why did you drop the idea of going to Manali?

R: We can visit Manali even during the week or on any Saturday/Sunday. But this weekend is long, so I thought why not visit Kathmandu and Pokhra.

B: I am game if Pokhra is included in the trip. I hope we don't encounter any problem from Maoists while travelling by road.

R: I don't think so. They don't harm Indian tourists.

B: Have you booked hotel accommodation?

R: No, I first wanted to make sure that you agreed to my suggestion. I have my friends and contacts in Nepal. They can book rooms in the best hotels at both places within no time.

B: Do you want me to hire one or two cars?

(At this stage Vijita requests everyone to come inside for dinner).

Day 90 (After the Baljeets were gone)

Vijita: Are you really serious about your Nepal visit?

Ravi: Yes. I have already obtained permission from Mr Bhan to leave the station. I told him that we had friends visiting us from Canada and I had promised to take them to Nepal during the weekend. First, he was hesitant but subsequently on my insistence, he agreed. He, however, cautioned that I must not mention this to anyone since Nepal is a foreign country and for that, Chief's permission was mandatory.

V: I think you are taking too much of a risk unless you are hiding something from me.

The tape runs blank thereafter.

Day 91

Vijita: What's the matter? You are looking pale. Do you want me to call a doctor?

Ravi: No, I am fine.

V: Are you sure you can travel this distance in your current physical state?

R: I am not driving. Balli and his wife will.

ALISTER went silent thereafter.

Day 92: (From somewhere outside Delhi)

Ravi: Has anyone enquired about me?
Jena: No sir.
R: Has the dak been delivered from the control room in the morning?
J: Yes sir. I have received envelopes and kept them in the bedroom.
(A long pause ensues)
J: How is Memsahib?
R: She is fine. If Negi enquires, tell him that I will come after four days.
(The tape runs blank.)

*

Kamath kept the transcripts in the briefcase, told Avinash to lock the NC and meet him in the parking area. He went to his room at a brisk pace to pick up a recorder and from there he literally doubled up to the basement, where Avinash was waiting. They quickly got inside the car and drove off. By the time they reached the main gate of the suspect's apartment building, it was 11.30 pm. The guard opened the gate as soon as he noticed KM but the latter did not enter the building. Instead, he asked the guard and Avinash to go inside and bring Jena along. When Jena arrived, he was still rubbing his eyes to remain awake.

"I will ask a few questions. Answer them and don't lie. You see this recorder. It has details of all your conversation with Ravi," KM said in a low voice. He did not want other inmates to wake up.

"Ravi never told you about his Rishikesh visit," KM said. "Why did you then manufacture this information?" he asked. Jena realized that his bluff had been called.

"I am sorry, sir. Actually he told me that he was going to Manali," Jena said.

"You are again lying. I will have to ask Avinash to take you to our torture chamber for a special treatment," KM threatened. Jena started sobbing. He said that he was actually guessing about the places and didn't know where they had exactly gone.

"You did receive a call from Ravi this morning. Where was the call from?"

"I don't know but you can check the number from the telephone," Jena said, wiping his tears with bare hands.

"Take Avinash to the apartment and let him note down the number," KM said.

Avinash returned soon with the requisite information. It was an outstation number, received at 8.20 am. KM liberally tipped the guard and asked him to keep the watchers informed of Jena's activities. From there, both KM and Avinash went to the Telephone Exchange in Safdarjung Enclave. While KM waited in the car, Avinash went inside to check the details of the call from his contact. He was told that the call originated from a public booth in Gorakhpur. Armed with these details, KM drove to the residence of Jeev. Standing outside the gate, he called Jeev on the mobile and found him awake.

"Where are you? I was waiting for your call. Is there anything worthwhile in the tapes?" Jeev inquired.

"Sir, I am standing outside?" KM surprised Jeev.

"That's like KM. Wait, I am coming down," Jeev switched on the passage lights, opened the door and led KM to the living room. He occupied his easy chair and went through the transcripts. As he kept mulling over their implications, KM mentioned about the origin of the suspect's calling number.

"If Ravi has called from Gorakhpur and has plans to visit Kathmandu, it is obvious that he would have crossed over into Nepal at Bhairahwa. Please speak to Ajay in the morning and ask him to find out from his contact in the Bureau's immigration office whether Ravi was spotted by his officers at any of the checkposts along the Nepal border. Meanwhile, I will sound my Nepalese sources on the suspect's whereabouts," Jeev said.

"Sir, did you notice that Vijita, for the first time, lowered her guard and referred to Ravi's *dealings*."

"I did."

"I had all along suspected that she was actively colluding with her husband. She has now confirmed our fears," KM said.

"I agree. You have mostly been on the course on most of the issues," Jeev flattered his terrible enfant. With nothing more to discuss, KM left.

Jeev pulled out *The Adventures of Amir Hamza* from the bookshelf, stretched fully on the easy chair and spent the rest of the night reading it. That was his way of weathering the storm.

Day 94

At 6 am, Jeev gave an update on events of the last twenty-four hours to Wasan.

"And where do you think this idiot would have vanished?" Wasan asked dreading dark possibilities.

"I am not so sure but since he called last from Gorakhpur, it is possible he would have entered Nepal at Bhairahwa," Jeev said.

"Have you alerted anyone in Nepal just in case the suspect chose to fly out from Kathmandu to his eventual destination?" Wasan pressed for a helpful answer.

"Not yet."

"You should have sounded Bhandari earlier and sent to him the passport particulars of the suspect and his wife," Wasan reproached.

"We received information about his presence in Gorakhpur only at midnight. I was also not confident if Bhandari could be trusted with vague and raw inputs at such an early stage. My fear was that he might start making blind inquiries, alerting the suspect's operatives to camouflage their modus operandi and trail. My prime concern, as you know, has always been to expose the handlers and the subverting outfit. I didn't want Bhandari to blow up our months of efforts in seconds," Jeev pointed out. Wasan was not impressed with his friend's argument and insisted that passport particulars be sent immediately to Bhandari.

"You know how his tendency to brag about his access and ability to deliver, led you in the past to make commitments to the government that could not be fulfilled. Knowing him, he will readily agree to take up the task to impress you again of his operational reach but I am afraid, he may botch up just when we are so close to exposing Ravi's spying network," Jeev quipped. There was no response for a few seconds. Suddenly, Wasan changed the track of discussion. "I think your night watcher should have followed the taxi," he said. His tone was accusatory.

"I don't want to hold a brief for Mathew but he insists that he saw no one in the taxi when it was turned back from the gate by Jena," Jeev said.

"But did Jena not tell you that they left by taxi carrying two bags?" Wasan countered.

"He did but I know Mathew. He won't cover up for his lapses," Jeev claimed.

"I wish the watchers had been more alert and deployed in more numbers," Wasan pointed out.

Wasan, "it's no time for nitpicking. We can settle that later," Jeev tried to calm his nerves.

"Whether you agree or not, I still feel Mathew has let us down," Wasan sounded very low in spirits.

"How can you expect him to have a closer look at the inside of a car from a distance of 120 meters on a dark night? You can at best blame him for paying a price for our ill-conceived decision to drastically reduce the intensity of surveillance," Jeev hit back sarcastically. Wasan did not wish to extend the skirmish further.

Jeev stretched fully in the easy chair. When Mani came down to the living room at 7.30 am, she found him fast asleep. She switched off the light and went outside for a stroll in the lawn. By the time she returned, Jeev had woken up and was waiting for her to lay out the usually elaborate morning tea. Mani avoided probing him for reasons to spend the night in the living room. While tea was being served, Jeev rang up Venkat and asked him to come to his residence between 3 and 3.30 pm. Next, he called KM and told him to hand over the passport details of the suspect and his wife urgently to the Chief. Mani watched her husband give snappy directions to officers but chose not to make her presence felt. She didn't want Jeev to lie through his teeth so early in the day.

*

KM got ready and left for the office. The receptionist was surprised to see him enter the lobby so early in the morning. It was only 7.30 am and because of the holiday, even the floor cleaners had not turned up. Since all lifts were temporarily out of service, waiting for engineers to come for carrying out the mandatory weekly maintenance, KM took the staircase to reach the seventh floor. He felt acute breathlessness as he walked toward the NC. He rested for a while, then took out photocopies of the official and private passports of Ravi and his wife, put them inside an envelope and came down to the basement. He got into the car and left for the Chief's residence. The Chief opened the envelope, shuffled through the papers and dismissed KM summarily, making his annoyance with the latter abundantly clear. In any case, the Chief was never fond of Kamath.

KM reached Hotel Ambassador around 9.45 am. On the way, he called Jeev and apprised him of his frosty reception at the Chief's residence. Jeev counselled him to take it easy and explained that the Chief was equally or possibly more stressed out because of the unexpected turn in the events. On reaching the hotel, KM went over the reports submitted by Manjeet but they had no helpful inputs. In a spot decision, KM took Manjeet along and walked up to the third floor. He gently tapped the door of Room no. 304 but there was no response. The housekeeper in-charge of the floor, who watched KM and Manjeet fiddle with the door knob, said that the guests were not occupying the room since day before yesterday. "They have also not left the room keys at the reception desk. We have been cleaning and making beds in their absence by opening the door with our master key," he informed.

"Is it not weird that they have vanished with the keys of the hotel room?" KM asked.

"It's not very unusual. But if you suspect anything foul, I can inform the Assistant Manager," the housekeeper suggested.

"That's okay," KM said promptly. He did not want to precipitate the matter without first checking up with Jeev. He came out of the hotel and informed Jeev that Balli was also missing since the morning of Saturday, 25th June.

"So both the families are in Nepal," Jeev said. "Ask Manjeet not to move from the hotel and contact you as soon as Baljeet checks in. Meanwhile I will go and tap my only surviving Nepalese asset," Jeev said.

KM passed on the instructions and left for Sagar restaurant in Defence Colony. Since he had left home very early and missed out on breakfast, he was feeling hungry. He took a corner seat in the restaurant and ordered for rasam and a plain dosa. While he waited for eats to be served, his mobile vibrated. The Chief was on the line.

"Where is Ajay and why is he not picking up mobile?" he asked harshly.

"I don't know," KM responded.

"And, where are you?"

"Sir, I am on my way to the office," KM lied.

"Come to my residence immediately," the Chief commanded in one breath and put down the receiver. However, KM was defiant. He took his own time to finish breakfast and pay the bill. He left the car outside the gate of the Chief's residence and leisurely walked up to the porch where the Chief was waiting.

"I have been trying to fax the passport particulars of Ravi Mohan and his wife to a contact of mine in Nepal but he is unable to receive them legibly. Do you have a secure fax machine in the CEU?" the Chief asked brusquely.

"Yes, sir."

"Then fax these details. Here is his name and number." The Chief passed on a piece of paper and dismissed him.

KM reached the office for the second time in a span of less than two hours. He opened the room, switched on the secra-fax and tried to fax the passport particulars but failed despite repeated attempts. Finally he dialled the number. Someone who introduced himself as Bhandari came on the line.

"The Chief has instructed me to fax some details to you but the number that he has given is not responding," KM said.

"Please note down another number. Maybe, that will work," Bhandari said.

KM tried the alternate number and this time there was no hitch. Bhandari confirmed that he had received the documents and would revert soon. KM thought of conveying his accomplishment to the Chief but didn't feel like interacting with him. Instead, he called Jeev but the latter had switched off the mobile. Next, he rang up Ajay and complained to him about the Chief's rude behaviour. He felt that the Chief probably hated him because he was investigating Ravi Mohan.

"Don't worry. You are not alone in facing his ire. He was also very upset with me," Ajay poured his heart out. "He wanted to know why I was not keeping him posted with developments and why I had surrendered the entire responsibility of conducting the operation to you. His problem is that he can't pull up Jeevnathan, so he finds it easier to shoot at us." KM avoided commenting. He was not sure how much of Ajay's hurt was genuine.

*

At 11 am, Jeevnathan drove down to the Rajiv Gandhi Cancer Institute. Octopus, his Nepalese source, had been admitted there soon after his last meeting and was struggling to survive. Jeev carried a bouquet of flowers and a basket of fruits.

"It wasn't necessary," Octopus said with a wry smile.

"It was. You were always very special to me," Jeev said. He pulled a chair closer to the bed and sat down holding the unsteady hands of Octopus. They talked about their numerous midnight rendezvous on both sides of the border to draw up plans for restoring democracy in Nepal. Jeev recalled how much Octopus had laughed in their first encounter at the idea of channelizing the resentment of people into a powerful protest movement. Octopus admitted that but for Jeev he would have never realized his own potential to play such a decisive role. Jeev said that he had come to tap the potential of his friend one more time. He disclosed the purpose of his visit and sought his help in tracking down the fugitives, suspected to be hiding in Bhairahwa, Pokhra, or Kathmandu. He passed on with lot of hesitation, particulars of the suspect and his wife on a piece of paper and profusely apologised for being selfish at a time when his friend was so unwell. Octopus looked at the details for a while. "Don't feel bad," he said in his feeble voice and reached for a small notebook, tucked below his pillow. He opened it, pointed a number to Jeev with some difficulty and asked him to connect. Jeev called that number and as soon as a man with gruffly voice came on the line, he handed over the cellphone to Octopus. After talking to his contact in Nepalese, Octopus told Jeev that his man would make necessary inquiries and report to him directly, introducing himself as Shrestha. "He is an important office bearer of the Unified Communist Party of Nepal (Maoist). If you need to draft him, let me know," Octopus spoke feebly.

"Thanks. I would have paid any price to cultivate him especially when you are recommending. But I no longer handle Nepal and I won't like to pass him over to officers whose experience in planning and executing long term operations is woefully limited and their approach to deal with Marxists is blinkered and ill-conceived," Jeev pointed out.

"I understand. What you feel about your officers, I feel the same way about our present crop of politicians," Octopus remarked. Jeev decided to terminate the conversation as he saw his friend tiring. He held the asset's hands in silence for a while, staring at his vacant looks and when it became impossible to hold his emotions from melting, he made a quick exit. He reached home around 2.30 pm. Mani was waiting for him to join her at lunch. Jeev did not speak a word while eating, unable to brush aside images of Octopus in his dissolving state.

*

Jeev barely finished his food when Wasan called. "Bhandari's initial feedback is not very helpful," he said. "He checked with the airport immigration, travel bureaus and hotels but no one with the passport details of the suspect and his wife, has either exited out of Kathmandu or staying in any local hotel," he conveyed.

"It is possible the suspect may not have shown his papers to the Nepalese immigration and simply walked over. For all you know, he may be sulking in a nondescript hotel or a safe house, waiting for the handler to charter his next move," Jeev explained.

"Do we have any inputs on the probable date of arrival of the fugitives in Kathmandu and the point of their entry so that Bhandari could inquire more meaningfully?" Wasan asked.

Jeev said that KM was trying to figure that out and would communicate as soon anything worthwhile came to his notice.

Venkat arrived at the appointed hour. Jeev asked him to collect the two laptops from the study which had been seized from Ravi's house. He wanted Venkat to dig deep into the hard disc for any data that threw light on how the suspect communicated with his operatives. Venkat assured that he would do his best but was not too excited about the results since the suspect's operating knowledge of computers has been abysmally poor. However, the seizure of the Nikon camera was very significant, he pointed out. Jeev ignored his tentative views and asked him to submit the report within a day or two.

"Sir, have we already caught and detained Ravi Mohan?" Venkat suddenly asked.

"Not yet. But your suspicion about Ravi's involvement in espionage was bang on target," Jeev said. Venkat felt vindicated for the courage that he showed as a whistle blower.

*

Jeev continued sitting in the study, going through outstation cables received since morning. Unable to overcome intermittent bouts of sleep, he went to the living room, lay down on the sofa and instantly dozed off. At 5.30 pm, Mani woke him up for the evening tea. As the first cup of tea was being served Wasan called, asking frantically whether Ravi could be traced.

"Not so far," Jeev responded mechanically.

"I informed Princi that the suspect and his wife were missing from the residence. He was furious that watchers had let us down by lowering their guard," Wasan said.

"Can we please stop talking about Princi for a few days?" Jeev asked. "Was he not the one who instructed you to suspend the investigation and withdraw all forms of surveillance?" he reminded in exasperation. Wasan did not react and disconnected. Jeev was still fuming when his cell phone rang. "It's me, Shrestha," the caller said.

"I was waiting to hear from you," Jeev responded politely.

"Do you have pen and paper readily available? Please note this down."

"Yes I have. Please go ahead," Jeev said.

"A Baljeet Singh, a Canadian citizen and his wife Pamella Singh, crossed Bhairhawa checkpost in a Toyota Innova at 3.40 pm, day before yesterday, along with two other passengers. The registration number of their car is DLZ 426690. The Nepalese Immigration has no details of other passengers. I searched every local hotel. There is no booking in the name of Baljeet Singh in any hotel. Baljeet and his wife have since returned to India. They crossed over yesterday sometime in the afternoon," Shrestha informed

"Are you sure Baljeet has left for India?" Jeev asked.

"That's what the Nepalese Immigration told me," Shrestha clarified.

"Thanks. You mind if I call you again?" Jeev asked.

"Not at all. My leader has spoken very highly of you," Shrestha said and ended the call. Jeev came down to the living room, rang up KM and briefed him about what Shreshtha told him. Next, he called the Chief and shared the inputs.

"The suspect is now in Nepal. How are you going to unmask his handlers now?" Wasan taunted.

"Was that ever a priority for you?" Jeev did not let the Chief's acerbic remarks go uncontested.

"Whether you accept it or not, I can foresee difficult times looming ahead. If he has fled, both of us are going to be the butt of everyone's ridicule," Wasan remarked.

"Who is this 'everyone' that you are referring to?" asked Jeev.

"The Committee of Secretaries that I will have to go to for obtaining approval for dismissing the suspect under Article 311(c) of the Constitution for security reasons. All of them will question me why we did not arrest and interrogate the suspect or slap a case of treason and sent him to prison. The Bureau Director will want to know why his outfit, equipped with far better resources, was not involved in covering the suspect's movements. The media, the security analysts, the PM and his security advisors will accuse us of handling the case ineptly and even impute motives for Ravi's vanishing act," Wasan pointed out.

"You live with your nightmares," Jeev reacted sharply. "I have no patience for distorted perceptions. I dare any agency to replicate this kind of investigation. I am not going to arrest and release persons depending on how that serves the interests of political expediency, personal ambition or mob hysteria. That is not the way civilized societies are run. And, I am certainly not in the business of answering catcalls," he emphasized.

"I guess you will never understand my predicament," the Chief rued. "You have to convince only me, whereas I have to convince a disparate group of ill-informed individuals who occupy important positions in the government," he said.

"If you feel that way, take me to the so-called wolves. I won't let you have a single scratch," Jeev assured. Wasan hung up. Mani who was listening to their conversation could no longer hold her curiosity back.

"Whom were you lecturing? Was it Wasan?" she asked as she poured the second cup of tea.

"Yes. Somehow, he is neither sure of my allegiance nor of my ability to be reasonable," Jeev remarked.

"I sympathize with him. Don't you always disagree with everyone and everything?" Mani pulled the punch.

Jeev let his wife's sneer pass and instead called Ajay. "Any news from the Bureau?" he inquired.

"Sir, Samar still maintains that the suspect has not been sighted at any immigration posts," Ajay said.

"The suspect is already in Nepal. Only Baljeet entered his passport particulars at Bhairahwa checkpost. Immigration probably did not feel the necessity of noting down details of the suspects because they were Indian nationals," Jeev remarked.

For the rest of the evening, Jeev attended to the pending files. At 9 pm, KM called him from the Ambassador hotel. He said that neither Baljeet nor Ravi had returned and wanted to know whether he could go home since there was nothing else to do. Jeev asked him to post someone at the hotel and the suspect's residence during the night, just in case the suspect or Baljeet returned in the meantime.

Day 95

Jeev was still in bed when Wasan called. He wanted to know if any breakthrough had been achieved in locating the suspect. Jeev said he had no more inputs to share and queried back whether Bhandari passed on anything new.

"He was asking for some definite clues," Wasan reiterated and then got back to playing the blame game. "I wish you had listened to me and arrested this bastard," he let his restraint slip.

"Arresting him was never an issue," Jeev retorted. "The objective had always been to obtain clinching evidences for unmasking his espionage module and the beneficiaries," he said.

"But we are neither here nor there," Wasan asserted. "He has disappeared and so have the chances of knowing about the subverting agency, the handler, and mechanics of his operation," he insisted.

"I am still hopeful," Jeev replied and disconnected.

*

Exhausted of sitting and waiting at the hotel for Baljeet to appear since the previous evening, Manjeet came out of his surveillance car at 11.30 am and went inside the lounge to escape from the scorching heat. He occupied the sofa facing the porch and the reception desk and ordered for a cup of coffee lest his prolonged, solitary presence aroused unwanted curiosity from the hotel staff. A few minutes later, he saw one of the watchers rushing in. He whispered in Manjeet's ears that DLZ 426690 was parked outside the hotel. Manjeet rushed out to verify the information. The car was indeed there. Intuitively, he ran to third floor and knocked at Room No.304. Balli came out, looking tired and sleepy. Manjeet apologized for disturbing him. He said that he was actually looking for a friend who stayed on the same floor but in a hurry, appeared to have given the room number incorrectly. The alibi worked perfectly. Balli said it was alright and closed the door. Manjeet came out of the hotel in a flash and reported to Kamath about Balli's arrival. "Don't let him slip away from your sight. I will be there in twenty minutes," Kamath said.

KM first drove to Defence Colony to check if the suspect had also arrived. The watchers denied having seen anyone enter the building. Then, he spoke separately to the guard and Jena. Both insisted that Sahib had not returned. From there, KM went to the hotel, parked his car outside on the main road and walked towards the surveillance vehicle where Manjeet was waiting anxiously.

"Where is Balli? KM asked.

"Sir, he is in the room," Manjeet said and repeated details of his encounter with Baljeet.

KM did not react. His mind was working overtime on how to approach the target. What if Balli was also an accomplice and refused to open up or threatened to involve the Canadian High Commission, alleging that one of their citizens was being harassed by Indian intelligence agencies, KM wondered. But Balli was his last hope. He alone could lead him to the suspect.

KM came to the lounge and took a corner seat. He was still looking for some clarity about his next move, when Manjeet spotted Baljeet emerging in the lobby and identified him to KM. They saw him going to the parking area, opening his car and retrieving some papers from the rear seat. After that, he returned to the lobby and took the lift for his room.

Minutes later, KM decided to gamble with courage. He gently knocked at the door. Baljeet came out, looking surprised to see an unknown visitor standing in front of him.

"Do I know you?" he asked.

"No. I am a senior officer from the Agency and a colleague of Mr Ravi Mohan. This is my identity card," KM spoke without beating about the bush and displayed his ID.

Balli had a close look at the ID and then handed it back.

"What's the matter?" he asked.

"If you could please come to the lounge for ten minutes, I shall be grateful. I don't want to disturb the lady inside," KM was effusive in his politeness.

"I am very tired. I suggest you come tomorrow to talk to me," Balli requested.

"It's a rather serious matter. I am afraid it can't wait," KM insisted.

"Okay. Then give me five minutes," Balli closed the door. However, he took more than fifteen minutes to come out. KM guessed that he might be talking to the suspect. They took the lift to come down and sat down in the lounge without exchanging a word. KM came straight to the point.

"We have documented evidence to prove that Ravi Mohan is an espionage agent. We have also recorded all your conversation with him. They indicate that he used you to escape to Nepal. My fear is that if this information becomes public, the police will come looking for you for being a collaborator. The fact that you returned alone after delivering an espionage agent to his running officer will only reinforce their suspicion about your complicity in the crime," KM stopped briefly to watch his subject's reaction.

"What do you want me to say?" Balli interrupted. He was looking tense.

"All four of you were supposed to spend holidays together at Kathmandu and Pokhra. What suddenly made you to leave Ravi and his wife at Bhairahwa and proceed no further?" KM asked.

"After we checked in Hotel Yeti, Ravi told me that he and Viji would have to fly next morning to Kathmandu for an urgent official work. I offered to fly with him or join him later during the day by road but he was adamant that we returned to Delhi. He mentioned that the road journey was extremely unsafe as there were daily occurrence of murder, loot, kidnapping and road blocks, organized by Maoists. That left me with no choice but to come back. It was apparent that he had planned everything in advance. Although I felt cheated, I did not raise hell because he was an old friend," Balli explained lucidly.

"I have a copy of the room reservation chart of the hotel with me. Your name does not figure anywhere. How would you explain this?" KM pulled a fast one. Shrestha had only mentioned that no hotel at Bhairahwa had bookings in Baljeet's names.

"You are right. Mr Gilbert, a white man, had done the booking of our rooms in his name," Balli disclosed. "He received us, gave us the room keys and subsequently paid for our rooms and food."

"Did you know that Gilbert was going to make arrangements for your stay before you left Delhi?" KM asked.

"No."

"Why did you not insist on paying?"

"I did but Ravi wouldn't let me pay. He said that Gilbert was an old friend of his and would get upset if we declined his hospitality."

"Can you please recount the sequence of events at the hotel in more detail? That will help me prepare the case in a manner that absolves you of charges for abetting Ravi's crime," KM threw the bait.

Balli's face fell. He kept looking through the window. KM preferred to be patient.

"I can now see it more clearly why you suspect Ravi of being a spy," Baljeet said, finally breaking his silence. "After dinner, when we went to Ravi's room to finalize the next day's programme, he mentioned that he might have to leave for Kathmandu by an early morning flight to attend an urgent official work. I suggested that Pammi and I could also fly or go by road to join him at Kathmandu and sought the name and address of the hotel where he would be staying. He did not react to my suggestion. Instead, he talked about the arrangements made for his daughter's engagement ceremony in Baltimore. Meanwhile, Gilbert joined us and ordered for coffee and liquor. Ravi and Gilbert discussed the situation in Pakistan, Afghanistan, Kashmir, Bangladesh and Nepal. We mostly listened. Gilbert painted a very grim picture of the law and order situation in Nepal and advised us not to travel further by car. Around 1 am, we retired to our rooms, with a clear understanding that we would meet downstairs for breakfast at 9 am to finalize the next day's programme. However, at 6.30 am a call from Ravi woke me up. He said that he and Viji were leaving by air for Kathmandu by an early morning flight. He also said that we could have our breakfast at leisure which had already been paid for and return to Delhi as early as possible to escape the Maoist disturbances en-route. He apologized for putting us in this impasse. We left the hotel around 11 am and reached Agra very late at night. We checked into Oberoi Amarvilas. Since we were extremely tired of travelling, we spent an extra day at Agra to recuperate and do some sightseeing. We got back only a couple of hours back."

"Do you have any idea of the flight that they took?" KM asked.

"No. I don't. Actually I felt very bad the way he behaved. Once he told me in the morning that he was also taking his wife along, I knew that he was not coming clean on the purpose of the trip. But since I wanted to avoid unpleasantness, I didn't pick up a fight," Balli said, appearing relaxed.

"Did you see Gilbert in the morning?" KM further probed.
"No."
"What do you think is Gilbert's nationality?" KM pressed.
"He introduced himself as a US national," Balli said.
"Why did only you and your wife submit your passports at Bhairahwa check post for scrutiny by the immigration?" KM asked.

"Ravi told me that Nepalese immigration did not need to record entry details of Indian passport holders. And he was right. When I informed the Immigration that two Indian nationals were also travelling with me, they asked nothing nor went to the car to verify the facts," Baljeet mentioned.

"Did you pick up Ravi and Vijita from Defence Colony for your onward journey to Nepal?" KM asked.

"They came by taxi to the hotel around 11.30 pm. They had earlier given me two bags to carry in my taxi to the hotel."

"Did they tell you why they couldn't carry the bags themselves?"

"They said they were going to a friend's place for dinner and from there they would directly come to the hotel in a taxi," Balli replied.

"One last question. Did you speak to Ravi while I was standing outside your room?"

"I tried a couple of times but the operator said that it was not a valid number."

"I am sorry for questioning you like this. Please go and get some rest. You must be exhausted after a gruelling journey," KM said, as he stood up.

However Baljeet kept sitting. "Do you think that Gilbert is not his friend but his handler?" Balli asked.

"I don't have the slightest doubt," KM claimed.

"It's all very scary. This idiot has unnecessarily sucked me into this mess," Balli expressed nervously.

"Don't be scared. You have my word," KM promised. "You can plan your departure as per the original schedule. But don't discuss this with anyone including your wife while you are in India," KM cautioned.

"I won't."

"I also have a secret to share. Our conversation has been recorded by Manjeet to ensure the accuracy of what we spoke to each other. This will never be used as evidence but if you have difficulty in trusting my words, I can destroy it in your presence," KM pointed out.

"You seem to be an honourable man," Balli said. He warmly shook hands with KM and parted.

*

KM drove from Hotel Ambassador to Jeev's residence to post him with the dramatic turn in the investigation. Jeev, an avid soccer fan, was watching a live match between Real Madrid and AC Milan in the living room. He lowered the volume when Mani came in to inform that KM was waiting for him in the study. Jeev got up reluctantly, lowered the volume of TV and went to meet KM. "Anything serious?" he asked.

"Yes, sir. I want you to listen to this tape," KM said hurriedly and played the tape.

"You have done a wonderful job. I never knew you could be so polite and restrained in such adverse situations," Jeev commended.

"What are the instructions for me?" KM asked.

"Please pass on the relevant information to Bhandari. You can use my secra-phone," Jeev said and returned to witness the rest of the match.

Due to frequent disruptions in the link, KM took almost forty minutes to convey the inputs. Bhandari found the details extremely useful. KM collected the tape and went to the living room to inform Jeev that the details had been passed on.

"What was Bhandari's reaction?" Jeev asked.

"Sir, he was hugely satisfied with the inputs."

"Where are you going now?"

"Sir, I may go to the Defence Colony to question Jena one more time."

"What for?" Jeev enquired.

"Sir, what is yet to be conclusively established is how and when did the suspect leave his house for the hotel?" KM explained.

By now it was 6 pm. KM was feeling very hungry. The day's events had moved at a frenetic pace, leaving no time for him to take lunch. He went to Khan Market, bought sandwiches, and ate them on way to Ravi's residence. To his mild surprise, he saw Jena talking animatedly to a watcher near the gate. They stopped conversing when they saw KM alighting from the car. KM walked a few steps towards the gate and asked Jena and the watcher to follow him.

"I have called the police to arrest you and take you to Tihar jail," KM said as Jena came closer to him. Jena tried to run away but KM held his collar firmly and the watcher grabbed his waist from behind.

"Don't raise your voice. Just listen. If you behave, I will set you free but if you continue to lie and create a nuisance, we will hand you over to the police and they will break your bones into pieces," KM threatened.

Jena, who was shaking and sobbing, fell in line and promised to reply truthfully.

"That's better. Now tell me, did Ravi and his wife leave at 1 am?" KM asked.

"No, sir."

"What time did they leave the building?"

"Sir, I didn't see the time but they left soon after his friend from Canada left."

"So, he didn't go by taxi."

"No, sir. Mr Bhatia took them in his car to his daughter's apartment in South Extension for dinner."

"Did they carry the two bags?"

"No, sir."

"Then who carried them?"

"His Canadian friend, sir."

"Did Ravi tell you that he won't come back after dinner?"

"Yes, sir."

"Did you ask him where he was headed to?"

"Sir, I asked memsahib. She said, she didn't know."

"Did you ask him why he was not carrying his clothes when he was going out on a vacation?"

"No, sir."

"What excuse did Ravi give for not taking his car out for attending the dinner?"

"Memsahib told Mr Bhatia that they would have to skip his daughter's birthday party because Ravi was not feeling too well to drive the car. Mr Bhatia then offered to take them in his car and bring them back early," Jena said.

"Did Bhatia ask about Ravi the next day?"

"Yes, sir. After he returned from his daily morning walk, he came to the flat to enquire about his health. I told him that he had gone out of Delhi on a vacation."

"What was his reaction?"

"He was surprised. He said that sahib left the party last night complaining of chest pain. He was under the impression that his wife would have taken sahib to a hospital," Jena said.

KM asked the watcher to loosen his grip of Jena and told the latter that he was at liberty to go.

"Sir, I forgot to mention one thing. Before they went for the party, sahib and memsahib had a big fight. I couldn't follow much of what they argued about. But I heard memsahib mumble that sahib had ruined her life," Jena said.

"If you recall anything more, call me on my mobile," KM said. Before he left, slipped Jena a 1000 rupee note and told him that it was a reward for speaking truthfully for the first time. Then he rang up Jeev and posted him with the gist of Jena's interrogation.

"Please remove the devices from Ravi's official car, his room and the foyer tonight itself. You are likely to get busy tomorrow in fire fighting and answering meddlesome employees when office reopens after the long weekend," Jeev suggested.

KM told him that it would not be easy to get hold of officers from the technical division to do the job at such a short notice. Jeev disconnected without reacting.

KM's initial impulse was to ignore Jeev's advice and go home. However, on second thoughts, he saw some merit in pulling out the surveillance devices that night itself. As he was waiting for the traffic light to turn green at the Moti Bagh crossing, he asked the driver to turn left and go to the office. Enroute, he called Kutty who, as usual, responded positively. The latter promised to come over along with his two officers within half hour. Then, he spoke to Kak and Reddy and conveyed Jeev's instructions. They were curious to know if Ravi had been caught but KM snubbed them for talking loosely on an open line. They also contested the urgency and timing for undoing the mischief but he was adanant. It was 10.15 pm when he reached the office. He lay down on the sofa and waited for the technical experts to arrive.

Around 10.30 pm, Kutty came along with his technical officers. While they plucked out the bugs and removed cameras and wires from all over the place, KM went down to the workshop where Reddy and a mechanic were busy getting the recording system detached from Ravi's car. By 12.30 am, Kutty and his officers finished their work and left. Ten minutes later, Reddy reported in his inimitable operational style that *his mission was over*. Kak turned up around 2 am. He took an hour to fix the leaks in the lines and departed without informing KM. He had still not got over the fact that he had to come to the office at such an odd hour. KM reached home around 4 am. To his surprise, his daughter came to open the door. She said that mummy was running high temperature and was down with viral.

Day 96

It was the first working day in the office after the long weekend. Since morning, Jeev was busy going through a draft proposal to set up a forward Radar Monitoring Unit in the north-western sector. He was briefly interrupted by a call from Venkat. He wanted to know whether he could come over to submit the analysis of the laptops' data. Jeev said that he would eagerly wait for his whistleblower. Venkat dropped in a few minutes later and handed over the report. It provided startling details:

Over 23,100 files had their imprints on the hard disc. None of the files had any images and they are all blank. A few documents that could be read were either draft of letters that he wrote to his son and daughter or disjointed summary of Ravi's discussions with his colleagues.

However, two documents were of relevance. In one of these, suspect was seen adjusting a camera on a document placed on the table, while someone, whose face was partially visible in the frame, was holding the suspect's right hand from behind. In another photo image, the suspect was looking at the monitor while a lady (face not seen but the gender is recognizable from a golden band tied around her thin wrist and shapely hands) stood at his right side holding the camera in her hand. (The suspect was probably receiving training from operatives to use the web cam for transferring documents).

It was evident that the suspect was not proficient in typing because whatever he wrote was replete with spelling mistakes and the texts were incoherently arranged. (To overcome this deficiency, the handlers may have trained him in making extensive use of digital cameras to transfer the data).

The suspect could have been taking pictures of documents using the camera and storing them in its external flash memory. Later these pictures could have been transmitted after porting the flash memory on to the laptop using it as a docking station. The images of documents seem to have been transmitted using a secure file transfer internet protocol.

The suspect's password for Internet communication was 'friends for ever'.

Of the two laptops, one was a Dell, purchased from a store in Frankfurt, Germany. The second laptop was a Toshiba Satellite, bought from a store called COMP USA in Washington DC. The second laptop was used more frequently and extensively.

All files were regularly deleted.

Jeev read the note. He realized why the handler was not being revealed. He commended Venkat for doing a great job and admitted that initially he had misgivings about his ability to crack the hard disc. "I am glad you proved me wrong for the second time," Jeev said. "First time when you tipped me off about the suspect, I thought you were seeing phantoms where they did not exist. And, now this breakthrough in finding how Ravi was filling his cup of sins," he added.

"That's okay, sir."

After Venkat left, Jeev called KM to his room and gave him Venkat's note to read. KM went through the note carefully. He said that he had also examined the acquisition of the two laptops based on Ravi's personal files and recorded a note. He opened the briefcase, took out a paper and showed it to Jeev. It said:

> The Dell laptop was purchased from Europe when the suspect was posted in Brussels. It was meant to be sold in the European market and its shelf life roughly coincided with the suspect's European tenure. The suspect might have visited Frankfurt to pick up the laptop. As usual, he chose not to keep the office informed either of this acquisition or his visit to Frankfurt.
>
> The second laptop was in all likelihood, handed over to the suspect when he went to Washington DC in connection with a training course. Interestingly he went to Nepal on five days' leave, one week prior to his departure for the US.
>
> Nepal was the suspect's favoured destination. He visited Nepal at least once every six months without, of course, informing the office. These visits were undertaken mostly during the weekends or extended holidays.

Jeev placed a copy of Venkat's note and KM's comments in an envelope and asked him to personally hand it over to the Chief. KM collected the envelope and left. Jeev then went to have lunch with the Chief where Director Bureau and his Deputy were also present. The post-lunch discussion on operational issues of mutual concern carried on till 4 pm.

When Jeev returned to his room, he saw an encrypted fax lying on the floor near his chair. He picked it up. It was addressed to the Chief and its copy was marked to him only for information. Since he was not the original recipient, he kept it aside and began disposing of pending files. An hour later he had a relook at the faxed sheet and noticed a familiar number printed on the top. He became curious and guessed that it could be from Bhandari. He instructed his PS to close the door from the outside and not to disturb him for some time. After that he took out the crypto keys from the safe and began to superimpose them on the coded words. As he progressed, meaningful sentences began to pop up slowly but surely. After he finished deciphering the text, he could not help smile, albeit wryly. He had finally got his man and a conclusive peep into Ravi's espionage network. For once, Bhandari had been meticulous in his investigation. He reported that:

> Gilbert, a tall, moustached, burly looking US national is the CIA Station Chief at Kathmandu. His name figures in the US Embassy's list of diplomats as Counsellor (Economic Affairs).
>
> On Day 92, Gilbert flew to Bhairahwa by YT 161 and checked into Hotel Yeti. He received Ravi and his party in the evening and took them to Room nos. 205 and 206. He himself was staying in Room no. 211. All three rooms were booked on Day 91 in the name of Gilbert by Abheek Pokharel of Himalaya Travels located in Kathmandu. On the same day, air tickets were purchased care of US embassy vide bill no. 1953 that included Gilbert's one-way ticket to

Bhairahwa and three tickets for return journey for Gilbert and Mr and Mrs Ravi Mohan.

On Day 93 Gilbert, Ravi and his wife checked out at 8 am from Hotel Yeti. Gilbert paid for their rooms and food expenses. Later on, he escorted Ravi and his wife to the airport and flew together to Kathmandu by YT 162, leaving Bhairahwa at 0950 hrs. Their seat numbers were 8, 9, and 10.

Ravi and his wife were not lodged in any hotel in Kathmandu. They were probably kept at a place to which only CIA officers had access.

On Day 95, Ravi and Vijita boarded BA-292 at 21.10 hrs at Tribhuvan International Airport for Dulles, Washington. They travelled on the strength of US passports issued by the "Authority", as Prasoon Virdi and Usha Virdi. Their US passports bore their real photographs but their signatures were for assumed names. Their passport numbers were SA-2374509 and SA-2374508 respectively. The dates of birth of Ravi and his wife entered in the passports were 21.6.1972 and 4.11.1974 respectively, which were different from the dates appearing in their original Indian passports. There was no entry in the column of the date of issue of their US passports.

Angelien, who flew down from the US the previous day, accompanied Ravi and his wife to the Dulles International Airport. Her US passport had also been issued by the "Authority". In the flight manifest of BA-292, the names of Angelien, Prasoon Virdi, and Usha Virdi figure serially at 43267, 43268, and 43269.

The British Airways tickets for the Virdis and Angelien were bought on Day 95 through Himalaya Travels and bills for these were raised against Mr Gilbert of the US Embassy.

Jeevnathan buzzed the PS and asked him to unlock the door. He shredded the encrypted fax and deposited its decoded version along with the crypto keys in the safe. Then he called Kamath. "Terminate the operation. There is nothing more to investigate," he said and disconnected.

*

Epilogue

Ravi Mohan and Vijita landed at Dulles International Airport at 3.40 am. They were accompanied by Angelien. As they came out of the aircraft, they were received by a man who introduced himself as Patrick Burns. He whisked them away, bypassing Immigration and Customs and took them to a secluded house in the heart of Maryland Woods. Angelien left for her home in Washington DC.

The fugitives stayed incognito, while documents were being arranged to permanently wipe out their real identity. Three weeks later, Ravi and Vijita were set free to live their American dream as fake individuals, burdened to carry the sin of betraying their nation for the rest of their lives.

Back home, Ravi Mohan was dismissed from service under Article 311(2)(c) of the Indian Constitution, following the Government's decision not to retain him further in the Agency for security reasons.

The Chief summoned Douglas Walters, the CIA station Head in Delhi, to the office and conveyed his anguish over the role played by Gilbert in Ravi's defection to the US. He also demanded to be briefed about whether the decision to subvert Ravi had been authorized by the Director CIA or planned and executed by a rogue operative as part of his general brief to recruit officers of the Intelligence Services in the region. Walters routinely pleaded ignorance. He claimed that he was not even aware of the presence of any CIA officer the name Gilbert at the US Embassy in Kathmandu. However, he promised to get back after checking with his officers at the Headquarters in Langley.

A week later, Walters reported that the CIA had absolutely no knowledge of the incident nor had it any employee carrying names of Gilbert or Angelien on its roll. He mentioned that Langley had separately checked with US immigration which confirmed that no one in the name of Ravi Mohan and Vijita Mohan or in their allegedly assumed names of Prasoon Virdi and Usha Virdi had passed through their immigration during the past eight weeks.

Fearful of the fall out of demanding apology from the CIA and the US Administration and immediate extradition of Ravi Mohan on the Indo-US strategic relationship, the Chief wrote a mild protest note to his counterpart, enclosing documents to prove his charges. In a deftly worded response, the DCIA pointed out that the passports in question were clearly forged and could have been procured by miscreants to enter the US illegally. This, he maintained, was evident from the fact that the US passports were never issued by any "*Authority*". He argued that there was no reason why the CIA would plan to subvert an officer of the Agency or organize his defection, when the two services were regularly sharing intelligence on matters of their mutual security concerns. He, however, assured that he would make further inquiries and come back if anything worthwhile came to his notice. It was the last time that the DCIA wrote on the subject.

Meanwhile, Principal Secretary Saran manipulated the government to draft the services of Krishnan, a former Bureau veteran and a congenital baiter of the Agency, to inquire into the circumstances of Ravi's escape and recommend measures to prevent recurrence of similar security lapses in future. For Krishnan, it was an opportunity of a life time to run down the Agency. He grabbed the offer with both hands. With the zeal of a possessed man, he interrogated the Chief for hours, burning gallons of midnight oil but miserably failed to pull the dead rat out of the chestnut of evidences. Essentially trained as an analyst, Krishnan was unable to comprehend the enormity and complexity of this operation. In the end, he produced a report, replete with impressions and claims, acquired in the comforts of hindsight. He debunked the investigation as ill-conceived and unprofessionally executed and placed the blame for Ravi Mohan's escape on in-fighting among officers, existence of parallel centres of power, and collapse of restrictive security at all levels. Ever a prisoner of words, he used the expression, "systemic failure" to sum up his warped opinion of what led to the escape.

The Chief emerged from the inquiry, physically weak, thoroughly humiliated, and defenceless. Since he was not involved in day to day investigation, his deposition was almost always factually incorrect. Worse, he made it appear throughout the inquiry that he was hiding a lot to cover his tracks. Krishnan frequently pounced on these weaknesses to tear him apart.

Kamath had a harrowing time defending the investigation. Caught between Krishnan's relentless questioning and the Chief's vengeful gaze, he bravely tried to put across the investigation in proper perspective. Throughout, he stuck to the truth like a blind man, oblivious of the irretrievable harm it could bring upon his career. At one stage, he was so exhausted that he had to be rushed to the Apollo Hospital for treatment of a serious neurological disorder.

Armed with his inquiry report, Krishnan made his next decisive move. He arm-twisted Saran to get his man brought in to replace the Chief, claiming that the Agency badly needed a leader who could weed out the suspects and moles, stamp out widespread corruption, bring warring factions into submission, and restore the Agency's earlier reputation of being the best in the business of managing external intelligence. With the new man by his side, Krishnan cleverly exploited the deafening demands from zealots to get a case registered against Ravi Mohan under sections 3(1)(c) 5(10)(c) and (d) and 5(2) of the official Secrets Act in a Delhi court.

The case, however, was doomed from day one. For obvious reasons, evidences collected through clandestine means could not be adduced nor the identity of collaborators revealed. The Agency managed to secure a non-bailable arrest warrant against Ravi Mohan from the court and approached the CBI to secure a Red Corner Notice from Interpol.

Krishnan enacted this farcical drama to impress the gullible in the government of his no-nonsense approach to hunting the fugitive out. The bluff was quickly called when Interpol asked for intelligence that was allegedly shared by Ravi with the CIA and sought details on how these were procured, thereby laying a minefield, which the Agency could not afford to step on. The Agency could also not reveal its working framework or its secrets that the accused passed on in operational interests. Interpol naturally refused to oblige.

Not willing to give up, Krishnan forced the government to resort to yet another gimmick to acquire Ravi. The US Administration was approached to arrest Ravi Mohan and his wife as per the provisions of the Indo-US Extradition Treaty and return them to Delhi. But where would the State Department find the renegades? There was no legal document in which their names figured. Referring to the Indian media's brouhaha over the case, a US senator sought to know before the Senate Ethics Committee whether the CIA had organized the defection and whether it was aware that in doing so, it had put the emerging friendly relations between the two countries in jeopardy. The counsel appearing on behalf of the State Department responded that all talks of the CIA's involvement in the incident were hogwash and assured that no amount of allegation and insinuation could affect the growth of a productive relationship between the two great nations.

Six weeks later, in a bizarre twist to the case, a Roben Singh applied for asylum in the US. In his petition, Roben claimed that he was recruited by the Agency and that over a period of thirteen years, he submitted hundreds of source reports on the activities of insurgents operating in the North-East. One day when he was ordered to assassinate his cousin, a top ranking ULFA leader, Roben decided to quit and escape to the US. He also testified that he would be killed by the Agency if he returned to India. The US Immigration Judge, however, denied him asylum and refused to give him relief under the Convention Against Torture (CAT). A month later, the Board of Immigration of Appeals (BIA) affirmed the decision of the Immigration Judge. Subsequently, Roben went in for an appeal for a review of the ruling to the US Court of Appeals, New York. The Judge reversed the ruling of the BIA and asked them to evaluate the facts more "realistically". Since then, the case has remained frozen at that stage.

Roben was none other than Ravi Mohan. The tale of his so-called misfortune is what is on record. Also, on record are scratchy details of his lost Indian passport in the name of Roben Singh, which cannot be verified by Delhi, because it was never issued. The US passport issued to him in the name of Virdi at Kathmandu does not exist anywhere. Roben currently stays as a refugee in Florida. So where would the US State Department and Interpol look for Ravi Mohan and Vijita Mohan?

For months, the media ran stories expressing horror at the incompetence of the Agency to let a traitor run away to glory. A columnist dubbed the CEU of the Agency as totally ill-equipped to manage an operation of such complexity and wondered why it did not seek the Bureau's help. Another columnist claimed that the accused escaped because the case was mishandled by a quarrelling team of the Chief and his Deputy. Yet another correspondent wrote that the case was goofed up because the Agency was split vertically. He emphasized that while one set of officers called for immediate action against Ravi Mohan, others refused to give the green light. The time lost provided an ideal opportunity to the espionage agent to make a quiet get-away. Extending this line of argument further, a stringer stressed that the escape was the result of a cold war among officers in the Agency. A naive editor-in-chief, taking Agency bashing to a new height, pointed out that there was little evidence to show that policemen who manned most of the senior positions, had the sophistication to understand the intricacies of such operations. Not to be outdone, a columnist opined that the accused could outwit the watchers because the government directed the Agency to deliberately look the other way in order to prevent the Indo-US relations from derailing.

Reactions sometimes went berserk. A reporter speculated that had Ravi been arrested, he would have spilled the beans about the involvement of several retired and service officers, serving in the sensitive departments of the government and the defence forces in espionage activities. No wonder, he argued, that Ravi Mohan was neither arrested for siphoning off top secret documents nor for possessing disproportionate income running in hundreds of crores. Joining the issue, another reporter averred that the decision on when to allow the suspect to defect had been taken by the Chief and his investigators much before the investigation got messier. The choice had narrowed down to either allowing Ravi Mohan to leave quietly for the US or eliminating him. The first option was preferred since the latter would have been far more difficult to handle. A special correspondent, known for his proximity to spooks of various intelligence outfits, went a step further. He disclosed that Ravi would have remained unexposed forever but for a slip up on the part of a US official who inadvertently mentioned his closeness to Ravi Mohan and the latter's admirable grasp of the security situation in South East Asia.

It is easy to understand why the media's response was fast and furious. Unfortunately, the journalists were not trained to sift facts from fiction when it came to writing about covert operations. Since they were unable to cultivate right assets, they had to take recourse to *leaks* coming from gossips. They wrote their indictments based on briefings from *informed*, *top level*, and *inside* sources of the Agency, whose words they accepted as gospel truth. So when Ravi escaped, they quickly sounded these assets, who served plates-full of delectable inputs. What readers, however, got in the process were speculative stories and agitated opinions.

Investigative journalism is actually akin to running an intelligence operation. In both cases, building assets is a tortuous process, fraught with prospects of frequent failures. It also demands enormous investment and painstaking efforts over a long period of time. But who has the time and patience to pick the chaff from the grain?

The blame for waylaying the media lay squarely with the Agency, which remained a natural habitat for conspirators. With lots of fanfare, the Agency had been built as a town hall with doors wide open from all sides, so that entrants could bring along fresh and bright ideas and their distinctive scholarship. Somehow, it could not be appreciated that these visitors would actually come to extract their pound of flesh, depending on the intensity of their hunger. For reasons that could satisfy only the daydreamers, the pioneers went about building a "vibrant and multi-disciplinary edifice to generate cutting edge intelligence", but made the fatal mistake of using bricks and mortars, procured from disparate backgrounds with opposing working ethos. This made the principle of working in a collective bond be given a hasty burial. As a result, tribal loyalties emerged, with each group and service standing firm with its own tribe. They saw colleagues not as partners in trade but as enemies, promoting bitter turf wars, factional fight and motivated propaganda. There was no longer a collective pride in standing by the achievements and failures of fellow colleagues in the Agency. Their passionate tribal commitment did not allow them to look beyond their own tribe and learn lessons from other organizations that refused to wash their dirty linen in public and instead, addressed their frustrations and grievances within their own system. Attempts at subduing the Agency's tribalism remained ineffective, paving way for the media to have abundance of *inputs* from *inside sources*.

Ironically, Ravi Mohan left behind misfortune for his operatives and reprieve for his collaborators. Gilbert, the CIA station head at Kathmandu, was recalled from Nepal and retired compulsorily for badly handling Ravi's escape and exposing the CIA's involvement. He was charged for travelling to and fro in his original name on Kathmandu-Bhairahwa sector which figured in the passenger manifest, bought tickets in serial of 475286, 87 and 88 for himself, Ravi and his wife, authorised Himalaya Travels to bill him in his real name and designation, which had details of his one way ticket from Kathmandu to

Bhairahwa and three tickets for return journey. Gilbert was also accused of indiscretion for introducing himself in his actual name to Baljeet and later on, signing in his real name on the receipts for payments at Hotel Yeti for the rooms and food. He was also indicted for taking no measures to destroy the records of the passports, issued by the "Authority", Washington DC and details of tickets in the office of the Nepalese Immigration.

Timothy Glenn, Director, Operations for South East Asia at Langley, was reprimanded for failing to ensure that the *Agent* was evacuated covertly, without leaving any tell-tale marks behind. He was pulled up for using Angelien as an escort when she had long ceased to be involved in running the *Agent* and for putting the CIA in a fix for a source, whose performance throughout was low on benefits and very high on the cost. Glenn left the CIA within weeks of receiving his indictment. He now teaches at Stanford. Angelien was returned to the Homeland Security and is now posted at Chicago.

Fifty-seven employees, who shared information regularly with Ravi Mohan, continue to serve in the Agency. Twenty-six of them, viewed in an internal assessment as unconscious provider of intelligence, were never asked to explain their conduct. Thirty-one others, who actively colluded with Ravi and shared extensive operational details, were quietly posted abroad to Asian, European, and American stations. The remaining two retired on completion of their tenure.

Comically, the bonanza was reserved for those who had nothing to do with the investigation. An officer who was brought in from outside to file a police case against Ravi Mohan in a Court of Law, was rewarded with the membership of the Human Rights Commission. Krishnan was nominated to the Rajya Sabha in recognition of his deft handling of the post-defection issues that threatened to fatally embarrass the government and the Agency. Principal Secretary Saran carried on in his job till he delivered to the nation a contentious Indo-US deal. Later on, he was inducted into the cabinet.

Ravi's persecutors received the rawest deal. The Chief retired quietly and has since been spending his time in praying, playing with grandchildren, and attending to his huge social obligations. But he is not at peace with himself. He frequently gets upset over the government's handling of security issues and constantly rues the fact that there are no takers at Raisina Hills for his informed views, based on decades of first-hand experience.

Ajay Verma was under clouds for years. He was first despatched to languish at an operationally inclement station and then slapped with successive average annual reports. His perennial regret is that he was barely involved in the investigation against Ravi Mohan and yet, he had to pay a very high price for just being at a wrong place at the wrong time.

Kamath was pilloried, ostracized, and promptly removed from the CEU. His office was snatched and his PA was withdrawn. He was briefly rehabilitated and then consigned to a clerical job. After a few months, he was promoted but not allotted a desk for a year. For months, he came to the office on time, walked from one corridor to the other and returned home, dejected. He bore his blisters bravely for a couple of years and then, his health started giving up, reducing him to a skeleton. He has since retired and settled down in his hometown. But he has absolutely no regrets for investigating Ravi and is ready to do it again, should Jeev give him another opportunity. Though physically weak, the fire in his belly still burns.

Jeevnathan retired to his farm where he grows organic fruits and vegetables. In his spare time, he plays Wi, writes stories for children, and watches soccer. Whenever he suffers from bouts of intense hatred for hypocrisy that pervades politics, bureaucracy and individual relationships, he goes out and talks to poor villagers in the neighbourhood. For a couple of years, he tried to float an NGO to help them become financially self-reliant but couldn't go far because he wouldn't pay "commission" to officials and politicians or fudge reports to obtain funds. Since he loathed publicity and sycophancy and insisted on propriety, donors of every denomination shunned him.

His friends found it weird that Jeev should waste his wealth of experience by retreating to a remote village and questioned his wisdom in spending the last few years of his life at a place that did not have even rudimentary medical facilities. But he has remained unmoved. He strongly believes that his initiative for poor would work someday despite the pervasive cynicism and rampant corruption. The city-bred Manini continues to stay by his side despite her unfailing reservations.

ABOUT THE AUTHOR

Amar Bhushan served as Special Secretary in the Cabinet Secretariat before he retired in 2005. There was never a dull moment in his career that spanned nearly four decades and engaged him in various shades of policing, investigation and intelligence. However, due to his compulsive habit of dissenting, his passion to experiment with new and bold ideas, his penchant for rallying behind lost causes and his intense dislike for stereotypes, he always remained an outsider in his profession. He now lives in Jasidih, a sleepy village in the state of Jharkhand.